Samuel Taylor Coleridge

Poetical Works of S. T. Coleridge

Vol. I

Samuel Taylor Coleridge

Poetical Works of S. T. Coleridge
Vol. I

ISBN/EAN: 9783337094065

Printed in Europe, USA, Canada, Australia, Japan

Cover: Foto ©Andreas Hilbeck / pixelio.de

More available books at **www.hansebooks.com**

THE

POETICAL WORKS

OF

S. T. COLERIDGE.

WITH A MEMOIR.

VOL. I.

BOSTON:
JAMES R. OSGOOD AND COMPANY,
LATE TICKNOR & FIELDS, AND FIELDS, OSGOOD, & CO.
1871.

ADVERTISEMENT TO THIS EDITION.

The present edition of the Poetical and Dramatic Works of Coleridge is a reprint of the latest London edition of 1852, published under the supervision of the poet's son and daughter. The poems were prepared for the press by the late Mrs. H. N. Coleridge, a person eminently fitted for the duty, because in her the zeal of the daughter was tempered by the discretion of the accomplished critic. The preface and the greater part of the illustrative notes were written by her; and the selection and arrangement have been determined almost wholly by her judgment, or by records in her possession. The rest of the notes were added by the Rev. Derwent Coleridge, who also prepared the preface to the Dramatic Works.

A proper biography of Coleridge is still wanting, but there is prefixed to this edition a sketch of his life in which the more characteristic facts have been gathered from every accessible source of information, and given with as much fulness as was consistent with the plan of this series.

ADVERTISEMENT.

THIS volume was prepared for the press by my lamented sister, Mrs. H. N. Coleridge, and will have an additional interest to many readers as the last monument of her highly-gifted mind. At her earnest request, my name appears with hers on the title-page, but the assistance rendered by me has been, in fact little more than mechanical. The preface, and the greater part of the notes, are her composition ; — the selection and arrangement have been determined almost exclusively by her critical judgment, or from records in her possession. A few slight corrections and unimportant additions are all that have been found necessary, the first and last sheets not having had the benefit of her own revision.

DERWENT COLERIDGE.

ST MARK'S COLLEGE, CHELSEA,
May, 1852.

CONTENTS.

VOL. I.

CONTENTS.

CONTENTS.

POEMS WRITTEN IN EARLY MANHOOD, AND MIDDLE LIFE.

SIBYLLINE LEAVES.

I.—POEMS OCCASIONED BY POLITICAL EVENTS OR FEELINGS CONNECTED WITH THEM.

II.—LOVE POEMS.

CONTENTS.

III.—MEDITATIVE POEMS.

PREFACE TO THE POEMS.*

As a chronological arrangement of Poetry in completed collections is now beginning to find general favour, pains have been taken to follow this method in the present Edition of S. T. Coleridge's Poetical and Dramatic Works, as far as circumstances permitted — that is to say, as far as the date of composition of each poem was ascertainable, and as far as the plan could be carried out without effacing the classes into which the Author had himself distributed his most important poetical publication, the "Sibylline Leaves," namely, POEMS OCCASIONED BY POLITICAL EVENTS, OR FEELINGS CONNECTED WITH THEM; LOVE POEMS; MEDITATIVE POEMS IN BLANK VERSE; ODES AND MISCELLANEOUS POEMS. On account of these impediments, together with the fact, that many a poem, such as it appears in its ultimate form, is the growth of different periods, the agreement with chronology in this Edition is approximative rather than perfect; yet in the majority of instances the date of each piece has been made out, and its place fixed accordingly.

* By Mrs. H. N. Coleridge. It is dated March, 1852.

In another point of view, also, the Poems have been distributed with relation to time : they are thrown into three broad groups, representing first the Youth, — secondly, the Early Manhood and Middle Life, — thirdly, the Declining Age of the Poet ; * and it will be readily perceived that each division has its own distinct tone and colour, corresponding to the period of life in which it was composed. It has been suggested, indeed,† that Coleridge had four poetical epochs, more or less diversely characterized, — that there is a discernible difference betwixt the productions of his Early Manhood and of his Middle Age, the latter being distinguished from those of his Stowey life, which may be considered as his poetic prime, by a less buoyant spirit. Fire they have ; but it is not the clear, bright, mounting fire of his earlier poetry, conceived and executed when " he and youth were housemates still." In the course of a very few years after three-and-twenty all his very finest poems were produced ; his twenty-fifth year has been called his *annus mirabilis*. To be a " Prodigal's favourite — then, worse truth ! a Miser's pensioner," ‡ is the lot of Man. In re-

---

* S. T. Coleridge was born Oct. 21, 1772, and died July 25, 1834.

† See Supplement to the Second Edition of the *Biographia Literaria*, vol. ii. p. 417.

‡ Wordsworth's Poetical Works, vol. v. p. 294. *The Small Celandine.* See motto to the last section.

spect of poetry, Coleridge was a "Prodigal's favourite," more, perhaps, than ever Poet was before.

1. The Juvenile Poems (now called Poems written in Youth,) so named by the Author himself when he had long ceased to be juvenile, were first published in 1796. The second edition, which appeared in May, 1797, omitted nineteen pieces of the previous publication, and added eleven new. The volume, says Mr. H. N. Coleridge, in a note to the *Biographia Literaria*, comprised poems by Lamb and Lloyd, and on the title-page was printed the prophetic aspiration :—"*Duplex nobis vinculum, et amicitiæ junctarumque Camœnarum, — quod utinam neque mors solvat, neque temporis longinquitas.*" *

In the London edition of 1803, fifty-two of the pieces, contained in the first and second, were again presented to the public, but what is now difficult to account for, unaccompanied by many fine poems which were undoubtedly written by that time, but saw not the light till, in 1817, they formed a part of the "Sibylline Leaves," beside the "Ancient Mariner," "The Foster-Mother's Tale" (an off-shoot from "Remorse," then entitled "Osorio,") and "The Nightingale: a Conversation Poem," which entered the world along with the afterwards celebrated and ever immor-

---

* *Biographia Literaria*, 2d edit. vol. i. p. 4.

tal "Lyrical Ballads" of William Wordsworth. Only thirty-six of the Juvenile Poems were included in the collection of Coleridge's "Poetical and Dramatic Works," published by Mr. Pickering in 1828. These all produced before the Author's twenty-fourth year, devoted as he was to the "soft strains" of Bowles, have more in common with the passionate lyrics of Collins and the picturesque wildness of the pretended Ossian, than with the well-tuned sentimentality of that Muse which the over-grateful poet has represented as his earliest inspirer. For the young they will ever retain a peculiar charm, because so fraught with the joyous spirit of youth; and in the minds of all readers that feeling which disposes men "to set the bud above the rose full-blown" would secure them an interest, even if their intrinsic beauty and sweetness were less adequate to obtain it.

2. Poems of Early Manhood are "The Ancient Mariner," "The Wanderings of Cain," "Kubla Khan," "Christabel," Part I. The "Sibylline Leaves" of 1817 comprises many minor poems of the same date as those just mentioned, and likewise another set, which must be referred to Middle Life, that collection extending from 1796 to the time of publication. The second part of "Christabel" we know, on the Poet's own authority, to have been composed in 1800; it therefore occupies an intermediate station between the two eras.

" Remorse " was first cast at Stowey, in 1797
or 8. Alvar's Soliloquy (Act v. Scene 1,) was
published with the " Lyrical Ballads," in 1798,
under the title of " The Dungeon." The translation of " Wallenstein " was made in the winter
of 1800. " Zapolya," published in 1817, must
have been composed somewhere between 1814
and 1816.*

3. Poems written in Later Life. The second
edition of the " Sibylline Leaves " contained a
certain number of short poems, quaintly desig-
nated " Prose in Rhyme, Moralities, Epigrams,
and Poems without a Name." The whole of
these as late productions, are placed in the last
section, and to them are added many other pieces,
serious and sportive, which are known to have
been the harvest of the latest season accorded to
the Poet in this state of existence.

The present Editors have been guided in the
general arrangement of this edition by those of
1817 and 1828, which may be held to represent
the author's matured judgment upon the larger
and more important part of his poetical productions. They have reason, indeed, to believe, that
the edition of 1828 was the last upon which he
was able to bestow personal care and attention.
That of 1834, the last year of his earthly sojourning, a period when his thoughts were wholly en-

---

* See Dramatic Works.

grossed, so far as the decays of his frail outward part left them free for intellectual pursuits and speculations, by a grand scheme of Christian Philosophy, to the enunciation of which in a long projected work his chief thoughts and aspirations had for many years been directed, was arranged mainly, if not entirely, at the discretion of his earliest Editor, H. N. Coleridge, who, not to mention the boon he has conferred on the public in preserving so valuable a record of his Uncle's conversation as is contained in the Table Talk of S. T. Coleridge, performed his task in editing *The Friend, The Literary Remains, The Church and State* and *Lay Sermons,* and *The Confessions of an Inquiring Spirit,* in a manner which must ever procure him sentiments of gratitude from all who prize the writings of Coleridge. Such alterations only have been made in this final arrangement of the Poetical and Dramatic Works of S. T. Coleridge, by those into whose charge they have devolved, as they feel assured, both the Author himself and his earliest Editor would at this time find to be either necessary or desirable. The observations and experience of eighteen years, a period long enough to bring about many changes in literary opinion, have satisfied them that the immature essays of boyhood and adolescence, not marked with any such prophetic note of genius as certainly does belong to the four school-boy poems they have retained, tend to injure the general effect of a body of poetry. That a writer, especially a writer of verse, should keep out of sight his third-rate performances, is now become a maxim with critics; for they are not, at the worst, effectless: they have an effect, that of diluting and weakening, to the reader's feelings, the general power of the collection. Mr. Coleridge himself constantly, after 1796, rejected a certain portion of his earliest published *Juvenilia:* never printed any attempts of his boyhood, except those four with which the present publication commences; and there can be no doubt that his Editor of 1834 would ere now have come to the conclusion, that only such of the Author's early performances as were sealed by his own approval ought to form a permanent part of the body of his poetical works.

The "Allegoric Vision," as it cannot be considered poetry in the full sense of the word, and may be read with much more advantage in its proper place — the Introduction to the Author's second Lay Sermon, — the Editors have thought fit to withdraw from this collection. And a piece of extravagant humour, printed for the first time among the Author's works in 1834, rather it would appear with his acquiescence, than by his desire, has been excluded for the reasons assigned by the Author himself in the Apologetic Preface. The "Devil's Walk," having been reproduced with his full authority in the Edition of 1828, has

B

been retained,— restored, however, as in the Edition of 1834, to its original form and completeness. To this extent a discretionary privilege has been exercised, for which, it is believed, that little apology will be required by the public.*

It must be added, that time has robbed of their charm certain sportive effusions of Mr. C.'s later years, which were given to the public, in the first gloss and glow of novelty in 1834, and has proved that, though not devoid of the quality of genius, they possess, upon the whole, not more than an ephemeral interest. These the Editors have not scrupled to omit on the same grounds and in the same confidence that has been already explained.

Four short pieces only have been added, the third and ninth Sonnets [pages 49 and 55] from the edition of 1796, the " Day-Dream " [page 266] from the Appendix to Coleridge's " Essays on his own Times," and the " Hymn " [vol. ii. page 70] which is now printed for the first time.

* This humorous piece first appeared in the *Morning Post*, when, according to the Editor of that Journal, it made so great a sensation that several hundred sheets extra were sold by them, as the paper was in request for days and weeks afterwards.

PREFACE.

COMPOSITIONS resembling those of the present volume are not unfrequently condemned for their querulous egotism. But egotism is to be condemned then only when it offends against time and place, as in a history or an epic poem. To censure it in a monody or sonnet is almost as absurd as to dislike a circle for being round. Why then write Sonnets or Monodies? Because they give me pleasure when perhaps nothing else could. After the more violent emotions of sorrow, the mind demands amusement, and can find it in employment alone : but full of its late sufferings, it can endure no employment not in some measure connected with them. Forcibly to turn away our attention to general subjects is a painful and most often an unavailing effort.

> " But O! how grateful to a wounded heart
> The tale of misery to impart —
> From others' eyes bid artless sorrows flow,
> And raise esteem upon the base of woe! "
>
> SHAW.

The communicativeness of our nature leads us to

describe our own sorrows; in the endeavour to describe them, intellectual activity is exerted; and from intellectual activity there results a pleasure, which is gradually associated, and mingles as a corrective, with the painful subject of the description. "True!" (it may be answered) "but how is the Public interested in your sorrows or your description?" We are for ever attributing personal unities to imaginary aggregates. What is the Public, but a term for a number of scattered individuals? Of whom as many will be interested in these sorrows, as have experienced the same or similar.

> " Holy be the lay
> Which mourning soothes the mourner on his way."

If I could judge of others by myself, I should not hesitate to affirm, that the most interesting passages in all writings are those in which the author develops his own feelings? The sweet voice of Cona* never sounds so sweetly, as when it speaks of itself; and I should almost suspect that man of an unkindly heart, who could read the opening of the third book of the Paradise Lost without peculiar emotion. By a law of our nature, he who labours under a strong feeling is impelled to seek for sympathy; but a poet's feelings are all strong. *Quicquid amet valde amat.* Akenside therefore speaks with philosophical accuracy

---

* Ossian.

when he classes Love and Poetry, as producing the same effects:

    " Love and the wish of Poets when their tongue
      Would teach to others' bosoms, what so charms
      Their own.   **PLEASURES OF IMAGINATION.**

There is one species of egotism which is truly disgusting; not that which leads us to communicate our feelings to others, but that which would reduce the feelings of others to an identity with our own. The atheist, who exclaims " pshaw ! " when he glances his eye on the praises of Deity, is an egotist; an old man, when he speaks contemptuously of Love-verses, is an egotist; and the sleek favourites of fortune are egotists, when they condemn all " melancholy, discontented " verses. Surely, it would be candid not merely to ask whether the poem pleases ourselves, but to consider whether or no there may not be others, to whom it is well calculated to give an innocent pleasure.

I shall only add, that each of my readers will, I hope, remember, that these poems on various subjects, which he reads at one time and under the influence of one set of feelings, were written at different times and prompted by very different feelings; and therefore that the supposed inferiority of one poem to another may sometimes be owing to the temper of mind in which he happens to peruse it.

My poems have been rightly charged with a profusion of double-epithets, and a general turgidness. I have pruned the double-epithets with no sparing hand; and used my best efforts to tame the swell and glitter both of thought and diction.* This latter fault, however, had insinuated itself into my " Religious Musings " with such intricacy of union, that sometimes I have omitted to disentangle the weed from the fear of snapping the flower. A third and heavier accusation has been brought against me, that of obscurity; but not, I think, with equal justice. An author is obscure, when his conceptions are dim and imperfect, and his language incorrect, or inappropriate, or involved. A poem that abounds in allusions, like the Bard of Gray, or one that impersonates high and abstract truths, like Collins's Ode on the poetical character, claims not to be popular—but should be acquitted of obscurity. The deficiency

* Without any feeling of anger, I may yet be allowed to express some degree of surprise, that after having run the critical gauntlet for a certain class of faults, which I had, viz., a too ornate, and elaborately poetic diction, and nothing having come before the judgment-seat of the Reviewers during the long interval, I should for at least seventeen years, quarter after quarter, have been placed by them in the foremost rank of the proscribed, and made to abide the brunt of abuse and ridicule for faults directly opposite, viz., bald and prosaic language, and an affected simplicity both of matter and manner—faults which assuredly did not enter into the character of my compositions.—*Literary Life*, i. 51; *published* 1817.

is in the reader. But this is a charge which every poet, whose imagination is warm and rapid, must expect from his contemporaries. Milton did not escape it; and it was adduced with virulence against Gray and Collins. We now hear no more of it: not that their poems are better understood at present, than they were at their first publication; but their fame is established; and a critic would accuse himself of frigidity or inattention, who should profess not to understand them. But a living writer is yet *sub judice;* and if we cannot follow his conceptions or enter into his feelings, it is more consoling to our pride to consider him as lost beneath, than as soaring above us. If any man expect from my poems the same easiness of style which he admires in a drinking-song, for him I have not written. *Intelligibilia, non intellectum adfero.*

I expect neither profit nor general fame by my writings; and I consider myself as having been amply repaid without either. Poetry has been to me its own " exceeding great reward; " it has soothed my afflictions; it has multiplied and refined my enjoyments; it has endeared solitude; and it has given me the habit of wishing to discover the Good and the Beautiful in all that meets and surrounds me.*

S. T. C.

* The above preface was prefixed by the author to the third edition of the Juvenile Poems, in 1803, and transferred by him,

without alteration, to the collected edition of his poetical works in 1828. It is made up from the Prefaces to the first two editions of his Poems, and referred, in the first instance, to the earlier productions of his Muse. In the Preface to the Sibylline Leaves, which he did not reprint, he states that that collection was " presented to the reader as perfect as the author's skill and powers could render them; " adding, that " henceforward he must be occupied by studies of a very different kind." The motto which appears on a subsequent page is taken from the same place and points to a similar conclusion.

D. C.

MEMOIR OF THE AUTHOR.

SAMUEL TAYLOR COLERIDGE was born on the 21st of October, 1772, at Ottery St. Mary, Devonshire.* He was the youngest of ten children, and, as his father, the vicar of the parish of Ottery, and master of the grammar school, had but a small salary, the means of the family were much straitened. Of his mother but little has been handed down, beside the fact that she made her youngest child her spoiled favorite.

There are some stories respecting the eccentricities of the vicar which are interesting only as one can trace in them the origin of some of the peculiarities of his more distinguished son. Coleridge in a letter to his friend Thomas Poole, says of his father, "The truth is, my father was not a first-rate genius; he was, however, a first-rate Christian, which is much better. I need not detain you with his character. In learning, good heartedness, absentness of mind, and excessive ignorance of the world, he was a perfect Parson Adams."

* "St. Mary Ottery, my native village,
　In the sweet vale of Devon."
　　Lamb's *John Woodvil*, Act V, last Scene.

The early years of the future poet were unhappy enough. He described them as follows:

" So I became fretful, timorous, and a tell-tale; and the schoolboys drove me from play and were always tormenting me. And hence I took no pleasure in boyish sports, but read incessantly. I read through all gilt-covered little books that could be had at that time, and likewise all the uncovered tales of Tom Hickathrift, Jack the Giant Killer, and the like. And I used to lie by the wall and mope; and my spirits used to come upon me suddenly, and in a flood; — and then I was accustomed to run up and down the churchyard, and act over again all I had been reading on the docks, the nettles, and the rank grass. At six years of age I remember to have read Belisarius, Robinson Crusoe, and Philip Quarles [Quarll]; and then I found the Arabian Nights' Entertainments, one tale of which (the tale of a man who was compelled to seek for a pure virgin) made so deep an impression on me, (I had read it in the evening while my mother was at her needle,) that I was haunted by spectres, whenever I was in the dark: and I distinctly recollect the anxious and fearful eagerness with which I used to watch the window where the book lay; and when the sun came upon it, I would seize it, carry it by the wall and bask and read. My father found out the effect which these books had produced and burned them.

" So I became a dreamer, and acquired an indisposition to all bodily activity; I was fretful,
and inordinately passionate; and as I could not
play at any thing, and was slothful, I was despised
and hated by the boys; and because I could read
and spell, and had, I may truly say, a memory
and understanding forced into almost unnatural
ripeness, I was flattered and wondered at by all
the old women.   And so I became very vain, and
despised most of the boys that were at all near
my own age, and before I was eight years old I
was a *character*.   Sensibility, imagination, vanity,
sloth, and feelings of deep and bitter contempt for
almost all who traversed the orbit of my understanding, were even then prominent and mani-
fest." *

It appears that his father, simple-minded as he
was, recognized the peculiar gifts of the child of
his age, "for," says Coleridge, "he had resolved
that I should be a parson."

In 1781, before Coleridge was nine years old,
his father died.   He continued to live with his
mother at Ottery till the spring of 1782, when
he was sent to London to remain with his uncle

---

* This passage is taken from one of a series of autobiogra-
phical letters addressed by Coleridge to Mr. Poole in the year
1797.   These letters relate only to his early life.   They appeared for the first time in a Biographical Supplement to Mrs.
H. N. Coleridge's edition of the *Biographia Literaria*, London, 1847.

for a few weeks previous to entering Christ's
Hospital.

"My uncle was very proud of me, and used to
carry me from coffee-house to coffee-house, and
tavern to tavern, where I drank, and talked, and
disputed as if I had been a man. Nothing was
more common than for a large party to exclaim
in my hearing, that I was a prodigy, &c.; so
that while I remained at my uncle's, I was most
completely spoilt and pampered, both mind and
body." *

In July, he was admitted to Christ's Hospital,
and there underwent that trying experience in a
boy's life, when, for the first time separated from
home, he is thrown upon his own resources and
compelled to make a place and friends for himself.
Coleridge remained at Christ's Hospital for eight
years.

Here it was that his friendship with Charles
Lamb, which death alone was permanently to in-
terrupt, commenced; and long afterward Lamb
embodied his recollections of the school-boy life
of his friend in the beautiful essay, "Christ's
Hospital five-and-thirty years ago." Who that
has read his glowing description of Coleridge at
this time, so sad from the contrast with his later
life, can forget it, and who that has read it once
but will be glad to read it again?

---

* Letter to Mr. Poole. *Biographia Literaria*, ii. 326.

" Come back into memory, like as thou wert in the dayspring of thy fancies, with hope like a fiery column before thee, — the dark pillar not yet turned, — Samuel Taylor Coleridge, — Logician, Metaphysician, Bard ! — How have I seen the casual passer through the Cloisters stand still, entranced with admiration, (while he weighed the disproportion between the *speech* and the *garb* of the young Mirandula,) to hear thee unfold, in thy deep and sweet intonations, the mysteries of Jamblicus, or Plotinus, (for even in those years thou waxedst not pale at such philosophic draughts,) or reciting Homer in his Greek, or Pindar, — while the walls of the old Grey Friars reëchoed to the accents of the *inspired charity boy !* "

The Reverend James Bowyer was at this period head master of Christ's Hospital. He was a stern master ; " J. B. was a rabid pedant," says Lamb, but he knew how to teach his boys, and Coleridge was accustomed to speak in warm terms of the obligations which they were under to him, not only for his discipline of their intellects, but also for his cultivation of their taste. Nothing was done for their religious or moral education ; though Coleridge long afterward declared that he had received one just flogging at school, on his taking occasion to declare himself an infidel. " My talents and superiority made me," he says, " forever at the head in my routine of study, though utterly without the desire to be so ; without a

spark of ambition ; and as to emulation, it had no
meaning for me ; but the difference between me
and my form-fellows, in our lessons and exercises,
bore no proportion to the measureless difference
between me and them in the wide, wild, wilderness of useless, unarranged book knowledge and
book thoughts." *   Such was his standing, indeed,
that in 1790 he was elected to College, and bade
farewell to school in the sonnet, beginning, —

> " Farewell, parental scenes ! a sad farewell !
>   To you my grateful heart still fondly clings,
>   Though fluttering round on Fancy's burnished wings
>   Her tale of future joy Hope loves to tell."

On the 5th of February, 1791, Coleridge entered
at Jesus College, Cambridge. He was not yet
nineteen years old.

His natural taste and fortuitous circumstances
had led him to read all sorts of books, whether
" he understood them or did not understand them ; "
and he had spent much time over metaphysical
and theological writers, whose abstruse speculations had bewildered and unsettled a mind originally not well balanced. He had neglected mathematics and the other branches of exact science,
and late in life he thus expressed his sense of the
great disadvantage which this had been to him : —
" In a long brief dream-life of regretted regrets,
I still find a noticeable space marked out by

* Biographical Supplement, *Biographia Literaria,* ii. 330.

the regret of having neglected the mathematical sciences. No weeks, few days, pass unhaunted by a fresh conviction of the truth in the Platonic superscription over the portal of Philosophy,—

Μηδεὶς ἀγεωμέτρητος εἰσίτω."

The want of that strict discipline of the reasoning powers which is gained by the study of mathematics was a loss of more than usual importance to Coleridge. His memory was very retentive, but deficient in method and arrangement. Highly endowed with imagination by nature, his education had tended to develop this faculty still further, until it had assumed a disproportionate influence over his life. " History and particular facts lost all interest in my mind," he says. He was always forming plans and laying out great projects, which were rarely brought to the point of execution. His moral perceptions were strong and acute in regard to matters of theory, but his conscience was silent and inoperative in the affairs of every-day occurrence. He had no fixed principles, and, keeping no object to live for steadily in view, he was continually shifting from one aim to another.

The summer after he entered college, he gained Sir William Brown's gold medal for the Greek ode. It was on the Slave-trade. Once or twice afterward he was an unsuccessful candidate for

college honors, though there can be no doubt that
at this time he was a very considerable proficient
in classical studies.

An old school and college friend,* who shortly after Coleridge's death published some reminiscences of these days, said of him, — " Coleridge was very studious, but his reading was
desultory and capricious ; he was ready at any
time to unbend his mind in conversation, and for
the sake of this, his room was a constant rendez-
vous of conversation-loving friends." Two years
were spent at Cambridge, the only fruits of which
now remaining are a few short pieces in verse
published among his " Juvenile Poems." They
were unsatisfactory years to himself.

> " Prodigal and reckless of his priceless wealth,
>   Time, talents, energies, occasion, health,"

he gave himself up to indolence and accomplished
little but the increase of an already immense heap
of undigested miscellaneous learning. In lines
written about this time he says,—

> " To me hath Heaven with bounteous hand assigned
>   Energic reason and a shaping mind,
>   The daring ken of Truth, the Patriot's part,
>   And Pity's sigh that breathes the gentle heart.
>   Sloth-jaundiced all ! "

---

* C. V. Le Grice. " College Reminiscences." *Gentleman's
Magazine*, December, 1834. " Many were the ' wit combats '
between him and C. V. Le G——," says Elia of their school
days.

It is difficult from the want of dates to most of his early poems, to assign them to any particular years; but the few that we are able to attribute to the period of his residence in Cambridge are characterized rather by facility of expression and metrical harmony, than by vigor of thought or power of imagination.

The summer of 1793 he spent at Ottery, and returned to Cambridge in October. He had not been there a month when suddenly he left his college and went to London. The motives which led to this hasty step can only be conjectured. Mr. Henry Nelson Coleridge, who is perhaps the best authority, says that he left Cambridge in a moment of despondency and vexation of spirit, occasioned principally by some debts, not amounting to one hundred pounds. Mr. Gillman thinks that his despondency was increased by his friend Middleton's leaving the University. Mr. Cottle says that Coleridge had told him that it was produced by the rejection of his addresses by a Miss Mary Evans, to whom he had written one or two poems, and whom he a year afterward mentions in a letter to his college friend Masters as "Mary Evans, *quam afflictim et perdite amabam.*"

Not long after reaching London "he was reduced to want, and, observing a recruiting advertisement, resolved to get bread and overcome a prejudice at the same time, by becoming a soldier." He accordingly enlisted in the 15th (Elliot's)

Light Dragoons, and, in order to keep his initials, gave his name as Silas Titus, or Silas Tompkins, Comberbach. His adventures as a soldier, as he afterwards related them, were uncomfortable and amusing enough. His friends meanwhile were at a loss to account for his sudden disappearance, when fortunately, after a military career of four months, his situation became known, and his family, with some difficulty, effected his discharge.

In April, 1794, Coleridge returned to Cambridge, where he remained till the beginning of the summer vacation. But the adventures of the preceding six months had broken the continuity of his college life, and given birth to many new plans for the future. He had now no chance of obtaining a fellowship at the University, and had moreover become a professed Unitarian, a change which, of course, would shut him out from all those advantages that might have lain open to him had he remained a member of the Established Church.

In June, leaving Cambridge he went to Oxford to visit an old school-fellow, and here for the first time met Southey, who was then an undergraduate at Baliol College. They were interested in each other at once; Southey wrote to his friend Bedford, " Coleridge is of most uncommon merit, — of the strongest genius, the clearest judgment, the best heart ; " — and this

chance visit laid the foundation of a friendship of
the utmost value to Coleridge through the whole
of life.   He did not long remain at Oxford, but
soon, in company with two or three friends, set
off on a pedestrian tour through a portion of
Wales.   On his return from this journey, Coleridge went by appointment to meet Southey at
Bristol.   Here they were to make arrangements
for putting into execution a plan, formed probably
at Oxford, for emigrating to America, accompanied
by a few college friends, visionaries like themselves, and, settling

    " Where Susquehanna pours his untamed stream,"

" form a social colony, in which there was to be a
community of property, and all that was selfish
was to be proscribed."   This scheme, " as harmless as it was extravagant,"* under the title of
Pantisocracy, had filled the minds of the young
men with the most brilliant anticipations, and they
determined to set earnestly to work to accomplish
them.   They proposed to emigrate in the spring ;
and in the course of the winter intended " to learn
the theory and practice of agriculture or car-
pentry."

    After a short stay at Bristol, where he was in-
troduced to his future wife, and to Mr. Joseph
Cottle, then a publisher in that city, and a writer

---

* *The Friend*, ii. 29. See also Southey's *Life*, chapter ii.

of verse himself, Coleridge returned for the last
time to Cambridge. Here he published " The
Fall of Robespierre," a drama written jointly by
himself and Southey. It was little better than
a versified newspaper, and did not possess merit
enough to supply the want of dramatic interest
common to it with most plays founded on contem-
poraneous events. He then went to London, and
renewed his friendship with Lamb. They used to
meet in the evenings at the Salutation and Cat
Inn, and here, " drinking egg-hot, and smoking
Orinooko," (" associated circumstances," as Lamb
said, " which ever forcibly recall to my mind our
evenings and nights at the Salutation,") they sat
together through the winter nights, building up
golden plans, unsuspicious of impending sorrows.

Early in 1795, still full of Pantisocracy, he
returned to Bristol and Southey, intending to
set sail for America in March. But a serious
question arose : how they were to obtain the
means necessary to carry out their scheme. Both
the young men, moreover, had fallen in love, and
with sisters, Sarah and Edith Fricker, and they
wanted something to enable them to make provi-
sion for their marriage. They therefore determined to give public lectures at Bristol, and the
winter and spring were occupied in this way.
Coleridge lectured on political, religious, and moral
subjects, Southey on historical. Two of his lectures Coleridge published under the title of " Con-

ciones ad Populum," and a third called " The Plot
Discovered; " but they did not attract much attention, or add much to his income.*

About this time, at Cottle's solicitation, Coleridge was preparing a volume of poems, for which
he was to receive thirty guineas.   His indolence
and frequent neglect to furnish copy at the time
promised are curiously illustrated by the notes
which Cottle has preserved.   Sometimes one en-
gagement interfered, sometimes another; now "a
devil, a very devil had got possession of his left
temple, eye, jaw, throat, and shoulder," and he
could not write; now, he was "over the mouth and
nose doing something of importance at Lovell's;"
and so on, until Cottle at last grew tired of urging.

The volume was still further delayed by Coleridge's marriage, which took place on the 4th of
October, 1795.   He went immediately with his
wife to a cottage at Clevedon, near Bristol, which
must have been fitted up rather to gratify the
taste than to satisfy the wants of its occupants, as
two days after his marriage we find Coleridge
writing to Cottle to ask him to send down "a
riddle slice; a candle-box; two ventilators; two
glasses for the wash-hand stand; one tin dust-
pan; one small tin teakettle; one pair of candle-
sticks; one carpet-brush; one flour-dredge; three

---

* " Your *Conciones ad Populum*," writes Lamb, in the earliest
letter of his that has been preserved, " are the most eloquent
politics that ever came in my way."

tin extinguishers; two mats; a pair of slippers; a cheese-toaster; two large tin spoons; a Bible; a keg of porter; coffee; raisins; currants; catsup; nutmegs; allspice; cinnamon; rice; ginger and mace." * The next day, probably after the receipt of these articles, Coleridge writes to Poole, calling it "our comfortable cot." In the same letter, he says, — "In the course of half a year I mean to return to Cambridge, having previously taken my name off from the University's control, and, hiring lodgings there for myself and wife, finish my great work of Imitations in two volumes. My former works may, I hope, prove somewhat of genius and of erudition; this will be better; it will show great industry and manly consistency." † But before the end of the year he had moved from Clevedon to Bristol, then, to Stewey, to visit Mr. Poole, and then back again to Bristol. Here once more he set about preparing his poems for publication; but delay on delay occurred as before, and the volume made but slow progress. In February, he wrote, during a fit of despondency occasioned by the clouds hanging over the future, and by the sense of his own remissness, —

"It is my duty and business to thank God for all his dispensations, and to believe them the best possible; but, indeed, I think I should have been

---

* Cottle's *Reminiscences*, p. 30.
† Biographical Supplement, *Biographia Literaria*, ii. 348.

more thankful, if he had made me a journeyman shoemaker instead of an author by trade.   I have left friends; I have left. plenty; I have left that ease which would have secured a literary immortality, and have enabled me to give to the public works conceived in moments of inspiration, and polished with leisurely solicitude; and, alas! for what have I left them?   For ——, who deserted me in the hour of distress, and for a scheme of virtue impracticable and romantic."

It is not plain what prospects of plenty or ease Coleridge can refer to in this letter, as having been left by him, or of whose desertion he complains, unless it be that of Southey, with whom he had had a quarrel some months before, on occasion of the abandonment of the Susquehanna scheme, which Southey's good sense and improved prospects had led him to renounce, before Coleridge was convinced of its extravagance.

At last, in April, 1796, his volume of poems appeared, containing most of those pieces which have since been published under the title of Juvenile Poems.   Among them were his well-known sonnet to Schiller, and the long poem called Religious Musings, which contains passages of much beauty.   Meanwhile, Coleridge, who had "given up" in October "all thoughts of a Magazine for various reasons," had issued proposals in December for "a Miscellany to be called The Watchman, to be published on every eighth day from the first of March, to supply at once the places of a Review, Newspaper, and Annual Register." He spent a month on a tour to solicit subscriptions, and visited Worcester, Birmingham, Liverpool, and other places, preaching as a Unitarian wherever he could get an invitation to do so. He returned to Bristol in February, 1796, having succeeded in obtaining a large number of subscribers. The first number of The Watchman was issued on the 1st of March, the tenth and last on the 13th of May. The causes of its sudden failure were numerous. Coleridge himself wrote not more than a third of it, and even his portion had little striking merit. The prospectus had promised too much; the subscribers, becoming dissatisfied, fell off faster than they had been obtained, till at length the work did not pay its expenses.* Whatever in it was valuable and of a permanent nature was included in his later publications.

Plan after plan now succeeded, with such rapidity as to prevent any one of them from being carried into execution. First, Poole proposed to

---

* In a letter to Poole, Coleridge says: — "I have received two or three letters from different *Anonymi*, requesting me to give more poetry. One of them writes thus: —

'Sir, I detest your principles; your prose I think very so so; but your poetry is so beautiful that I take in your *Watch man* solely on account of it. In justice therefore to me, and some others of my stamp, I entreat you to give us more verse and less democratic scurrility.

'Your Admirer, — not Esteemer.' "

purchase an annuity for his friend, of which Coleridge writes, — " Concerning the scheme itself I
am undetermined. Not that I am ashamed to
receive; God forbid! I will make every possible exertion ; my industry shall be at least commensurate with my learning and talents; if these
do not procure for me and mine the necessary
comforts of life, I can receive as I would bestow,
and in either case, — receiving or bestowing, —
be equally grateful to my Almighty Benefactor." *
From this time Coleridge seems to have been
contented for the most part, to be dependent on
his friends for the means of support. During the
last year or two, Cottle had made him frequent
presents. He had given him the paper on which
The Watchman was printed, had borne a large
share of the burden of the loss on it, and seems,
through the whole course of his acquaintance with
Coleridge, to have been a generous and unexact-
ing friend.

The plan for the annuity failed, and Coleridge
thought of taking charge of a school, which was
offered to him on very advantageous terms. At
the same time, Mr. Perry, the editor of the London
Morning Chronicle, proposed to him to write for
his paper, with the promise of liberal compensation ;
but Coleridge hesitated, and nothing was done.
Not long after, Mr. Charles Lloyd, the son of a

* Biographical Supplement, *Biographia Literaria,* ii. 367.

banker at Birmingham, where he had become
acquainted with Mr. Coleridge, proposed to be
received as an inmate in his family, "and made
him such a pecuniary offer that Mr. Coleridge
immediately acceded to the proposal." Lloyd
was a young man of amiable disposition, and of
considerable literary taste. Suffering from a de-
ranged state of the nervous system, he imagined
that a residence with Coleridge would at once
enable him to cultivate his mind and improve his
health. Coleridge consequently took a house at
Stowey, near Mr. Poole. Here his eldest son
was born, inheriting in equal measure the genius
and the infirmities of his father. He was named
after the metaphysician David Hartley, of whom
Coleridge was then an admiring disciple. Wordsworth was living near Stowey, and with him
Coleridge had already contracted a close inti-
macy. And now, with a home of his own, and with
friends around him, there seemed nothing to prevent him from accomplishing some of those literary projects of which he had so often dreamed.
Two years before, he had read to Cottle " a list of
eighteen different works, which he had resolved
to write, several of them in quarto." Now was
the time for him to prepare at least some one of
them. But " men of genius," it is said, " are
rarely either prompt in action or consistent in
general conduct. Their early habits have been
those of contemplative indolence, and the day-

dreams with which they have been accustomed to amuse their solitude adapt them for splendid speculation, not temperate and practicable counsels." *

So Coleridge wrote this very year, and such is the record of his literary life. His poems, however, were now to be published in a second edition, and with them were to be connected poems by his two friends, Lamb and Lloyd. The volume advanced but slowly, and we must leave the story of its completion to take notice of a letter which is of the highest importance, as connected with the history of Coleridge's life. On the 5th of November, 1796, Coleridge writes to Poole as follows : —

"I wanted such a letter as yours, for I am very unwell. On Wednesday night, I was seized with an intolerable pain from my right temple to the tip of my right shoulder, including my right eye, cheek, jaw, and that side of the throat. I was nearly frantic, and ran about the house almost naked, endeavouring by every means to excite sensation in different parts of my body, and so to weaken the enemy by creating a division. It continued from one in the morning till half-past five, and left me pale and fainty. It came on fitfully, but not so violently, several times on Thursday, and began severer threats towards night; but I took between sixty and seventy drops of laudanum,

* *The Friend*, ii. 188.

and sopped the Cerberus just as his mouth began
to open. On Friday it only niggled, as if the
chief had departed, as from a conquered place,
and merely left a small garrison behind, or as if
he had evacuated the Corrica [*sic*], and a few
straggling pains only remained. But this morning he returned in full force, and his name is
Legion. Giant-Fiend of a hundred hands, with
a shower of arrowy death-pangs he transpierced
me, and then he became a wolf and lay gnawing
my bones!—I am not mad, most noble Festus!
but in sober sadness I have suffered this day more
bodily pain than I had before a conception of.
My right cheek has certainly been placed with
admirable exactness under the focus of some invisible burning-glass, which concentrated all the
rays of a Tartarean sun. My medical attendant
decides it to be altogether nervous, and that it
originates either in severe application or excessive anxiety. My beloved Poole, in excessive
anxiety I believe it might originate. I have a
blister under my right ear, and I take 25 drops
of laudanum every five hours, the ease and spirits
gained by which have enabled me to write to you
this flighty, but not exaggerating, account. With
a gloomy wantonness of imagination I had been
coquetting with the hideous possibles of disappointment. I drank fears like wormwood,—
yea,—made myself drunken with bitterness; for
my ever-shaping and distrustful mind still mingled

gall-drops, till out of the cup of Hope I almost poisoned myself with Despair." *

This strange letter, apparently written under the excitement consequent upon excessive use of laudanum, "records," his daughter says, " Coleridge's first experience of opium." In after years, Coleridge himself repeatedly affirmed that bodily pain first led him to make use of this drug, which became the terrible curse of his life; but he was accustomed to give an account altogether different from that in this letter of his first experience of it. Writing in 1826, he said, — " I had been ignorantly deluded by the seeming magic effects of opium in the sudden removal of a supposed rheumatic affection, attended with swellings in my knees and palpitations in my heart and pains all over me, by which I had been bed-ridden for nearly six months." † But there is no notice, among the numerous letters and memoranda, belonging to his early life, of this illness, and there can be little doubt that he deceived himself in this statement with regard to the origin of the evil habit which became fixed upon him.

On the 8th of November, 1796, in the midst of his own bitter sorrows, Lamb writes to him with the utmost tenderness as follows : —

" My brother, my friend, — I am distressed for

* Biographical Supplement, *Biographia Literaria*, ii. 380, 381.

† Gillman's *Life of Coleridge*, i. 246. See also Cottle's *Reminiscences*, p. 272.

you, believe me I am; not so much for your painful, troublesome complaint, which, I trust, is only
for a time, as for those anxieties which brought it
on, and perhaps even now may be nursing its
malignity. Tell me, dearest of my friends, is your
mind at peace, or has any thing, yet unknown to
me, happened to give you fresh disquiet, and steal
from you all the pleasant dreams of future rest?
Are you still (I fear you are) far from being
comfortably settled? Would to God it were in
my power to contribute towards the bringing you
into the haven where you would be! But you
are too well skilled in the philosophy of consola-
tion to need my humble tribute of advice; in pain,
and in sickness, and in all manner of disappoint-
ments, I trust you have that within you which
shall speak peace to your mind." *

That peace of mind which Lamb trusted was in
his friend's possession was never again permanently his. Shortly after the letter just quoted
comes another full of feeling from Lamb, beginning;—

" My dearest friend,— I grieve from my very
soul to observe you in your plans of life, veering
about from this hope to the other, and settling
nowhere. Is it an untoward fatality (speaking
humanly) that does this for you — a stubborn,
irresistible concurrence of events — or lies the

---

* Talfourd's *Life of Lamb*, p. 12.

fault, as I fear it does, in your own mind? You seem to be taking up splendid schemes of fortune only to lay them down again; and your fortunes are an *ignis fatuus* that has been conducting you in thought, from Lancaster court, Strand, to somewhere near Matlock; then jumping across to Dr. Somebody's, whose son's tutor you were likely to be; and would to God, the dancing demon may conduct you at last, in peace and comfort, to the ' life and labours of a cottager.' " *

In May, 1797, appeared " Poems by S. T. Coleridge. Second Edition. To which are added Poems by Charles Lamb and Charles Lloyd."

The motto on the title-page was as follows :—
" *Duplex nobis vinculum, et amicitiæ et similium junctarumque Camœnarum ; quod utinam neque mors solvat, neque temporis longinquitas.*" To this was subjoined a fictitious reference, *Groscoll. Epist. ad Cav. Utenhof. et Ptol. Lux. Tast. ;*—the professed quotation and the reference being equally the fabrication of Coleridge.

This year has been called the *annus mirabilis* of Coleridge's life ; his poetical powers had reached their culminating point. That wonderful poem, The Ancient Mariner ; the first and more beautiful part of Christabel ; the finest of his tragedies, Remorse, were all composed in its course, as well as the beautiful little poem entitled

* *Final Memorials of Charles Lamb*, i. 62.

Love, and those lines, whose exquisite melody is equalled by their weird fancy:

> "In Xanadu did Kubla Khan
> A stately pleasure-dome decree;
> Where Alph, the sacred river, ran,
> Through caverns measureless to man,
> Down to a sunless sea."

This was enough for one year, a year of which we have no other memorials.

The next begins, somewhat sadly, with a quarrel between the three friends. Their joint volume had not met with success, and in March, 1798, Coleridge wrote to Cottle, — " Times change and people change; but let us keep our souls in quietness! I have no objection to any disposal of Lloyd's poems except that of their being republished with mine. The motto which I had prefixed,—'*Duplex*,' &c., from Groscollius, has placed me in a ridiculous situation, but it was a foolish and presumptuous start of affectionateness, and I am not unwilling to incur the punishment due to my folly." * And in June, Lloyd, who was no longer an inmate of Coleridge's house, writes to Cottle,—" I thank you many times for your pleasing intelligence respecting Coleridge. I cannot think I have acted with or from passion towards him." † The state of Lamb's feelings during this transient interruption of a life-long friendship appears in a very amusing letter which he wrote to

* Cottle's *Reminiscences*, p. 124.   † *Ibid.* p. 129.

Coleridge about this time, and of which he trans-mitted a copy to Southey, saying : —

"Samuel Taylor Coleridge, to the eternal re-gret of his native Devonshire, emigrates to West-phalia, — 'Poor Lamb (these were his last words) if he wants any *knowledge*, he may apply to me ;'— in ordinary cases, I thanked him, I have an 'En-cyclopedia' at hand; but on such an occasion as going over to a German University, I could not refrain from sending him the following proposi-tions, to be by him defended or oppugned (or both) at Leipsic or Gottingen.

"*Theses quædam Theologicæ.*

I.

"Whether God loves a lying angel better than a true man ?

II.

"Whether the archangel Uriel *could* knowingly affirm an untruth, and whether, if he *could*, he *would ?*

III.

"Whether honesty be an angelic virtue, or not rather belonging to that class of qualities which the Schoolmen term 'virtutes minus splendidæ, et hominis et terræ nimis participes ? '

IV.

"Whether the seraphim ardentes do not mani-fest their goodness by the way of vision and theory? and whether practice be not a sub-celestial and merely human virtue ?

D

V.

. " Whether the higher order of seraphim illumi-
nati ever *sneer* ?

VI.

" Whether pure intelligences can *love*, or whether they can love any thing besides pure intellect?

VII.

" Whether the beatific vision be any thing more
or less than a perpetual representment to each
individual angel of his own present attainments
and future capabilities, something in the manner
of mortal looking-glasses ?

VIII.

" Whether an ' immortal and amenable soul'
may not come *to be damned at last, and the man
never suspect it beforehand* ?

" Samuel Taylor hath not deigned an answer;
was it-impertinent in me to avail myself of that
offered source of knowledge ? "

Two years later the quarrel was forgotten.

In February, 1798, the Unitarian clergyman of
Shrewsbury came to settle at Bristol, and Coleridge determined to offer himself as his successor
at Shrewsbury. His preaching was liked, and he
received an invitation from the parish ; but meanwhile the Messrs. Wedgwood, the distinguished
manufacturers, who had become acquainted with
Coleridge at Birmingham some years before and
had formed a high idea of his talents, determined
to prevent him, if possible, from becoming a Uni-

tarian clergyman. Their own religious views were much opposed to those which Coleridge professed, and they regretted that his talents should be employed in promulgating what they held to be false opinions. Accordingly, Mr. Josiah Wedgwood offered £100 to Coleridge if he would reject the Shrewsbury invitation. This offer was declined, and Coleridge accepted the invitation to Shrewsbury. The Messrs. Wedgwood now offered him an annuity of £150 a-year for an indefinite series of years, if he would then, at that late hour, give up the idea of becoming a clergyman. Coleridge says, — " The moment I received Mr. J. Wedgwood's letter, I accepted his offer." *

His principles were worth more to him than one hundred pounds, but one hundred and fifty pounds a-year weighed down the scale !

This arrangement having been concluded, Coleridge seems to have given himself up again to forming plans for the future. Wordsworth's first work, the " Lyrical Ballads," was published in the course of the summer, anonymously, and in the volume appeared The Ancient Mariner. During the autumn, Wordsworth and Coleridge determined to carry out an intention, long held, of visiting Germany together. In September, they left England accompanied by Miss Wordsworth, Mrs. Cole-

---

* Cottle's *Reminiscences*, p. 131.

ridge remaining at home.   After landing at Ham-
burg, Coleridge went almost immediately to the
pretty town of Ratzeburg, where he remained for
four months domesticated in the house of the village pastor.   From here he went to Göttingen,
and passed five months in reading and loitering at
the University.*

His residence in Germany seems to have been
uneventful and agreeable.   He said of it himself,—
"I made the best use of my time and means, and
there is therefore no period of my life upon which
I can look back with such unmingled satisfaction."†   In a letter to Mr. Josiah Wedgwood,

---

* See " *Satyrane's Letters.*"   *Biographia Literaria*, ii.
187–251.

† *Biographia Literaria*, i. 211.   One of Coleridge's companions at Göttingen, and in some excursions which were
made from there, was a student of medicine, named Car-
lyon.   In 1843, this person published a book called " Early
Years and Late Reflections," which is in great part the
merest trash, but which contains some few amusing anecdotes
of his residence in Germany and acquaintance with Coleridge.
One of them presents the future seer of Highgate in a
light different from that in which he is usually shown, and
illustrates Coleridge's humour and love of fun, — traits which
became dim in later years.   It describes a scene on a journey
to the Hartz Mountains.

" Coleridge, I need not say, was always a very noticeable
personage among us, and having moreover no objection to be
noticed, whoever the noticers might happen to be, he conceived the ludicrous idea of making a plenary sacrifice of common sense to the experiment of filling the natives, at fitting

dated Göttingen, May 21, 1799, he says,—" I have read and made collections for a history of Belles Lettres in Germany before the time of

times and places, with the utmost possible astonishment. Accordingly, after conning over the respective merits of several nonsensical stories which he had in some corner of his brain—such as the tragical ballad of ' Titty mouse brim,' ' where the youngest (sister) pushed the eldest in ; ' the story of Dr. Daniel Dodds, and his horse Knobs — who drank the wine-dregs at the Dapple Dog, in Doncaster, &c. &c., he concluded by giving the preference to a narrative connected with the traditions of his own native parish.

By mutual arrangement, therefore, and after some preparatory rehearsals, when sitting at the end of a table in the long and perhaps only room of a village hotel,—a room appropriated to all purposes, and common to all travellers, and not without a proper halo of tobacco-smoke to increase the effect,—huddled together, apparently in earnest conversation, so that the eyes of the assembled rustics were fixed upon us, there ensued a momentary pause. Taking advantage of this, and assuming a phiz of more than usual importance, whilst we all were looking at him with mute attention, Coleridge would begin to relate how that ' Once upon a time there lived an old maiden lady of the name of Mary Row—Mrs. Mary Row. The place of her residence was Ottery St. Mary, which is situated in the county of Devon, about twelve miles from Exeter and four from Tiverton. To get at it, you must leave the great road from Bath to Exeter at an inn near the late seat of Sir G. S. Sir George got into parliament, ruined his fortune, and sold his beautiful estate to an East-Indian Nabob; in short there are many anecdotes that might be related of Sir G. S. But to return to Mrs. Mary Row. This Mrs. Mary Row had the reputation of being a witch. She had always near her an old black cat. This old black cat was thought to be her familiar—and, on the death of Mrs. Mary Row, the opinion of her having been a witch was confirmed in the following extraordinary manner. The

Lessing, and very large collections for a life of Lessing." In November of the same year, he returned to England, and went immediately to London with the purpose of gaining a living by writing daily for the Morning Post. In January, 1800, he writes to Mr. Thomas Wedgwood,—

"Thank God, I have my health perfectly, and am working hard, yet the present state of human affairs presses on me for days together, so as to deprive me of all my cheerfulness. It is probable that a man's private and personal connections and interests ought to be uppermost in his daily and hourly thoughts, and that the dedication of too much fear and hope to subjects which are perhaps disproportionate to our faculties and powers is a disease. But I have had this disease so long, and

old black cat got on the top of the house of its late old maiden mistress, and audibly thrice exclaimed, as numbers were ready to testify,

        Moll Ro—o—ow — Moll Ro—o—ow
        Moll Ro—o—ow is dead!'

Here we all joined in chorus—imitating the cat-call like a well trained band of tom-cats—to the amazement of all present.

That we fully succeeded in making tom-fools of ourselves no one can doubt; yet I can never recall the scene to my recollection without a smile, for nothing could surpass the ludicrous effect of this farce upon the faces of our auditory, which was not a little increased by the serious contour into which our own instantly subsided, leaving ample room for conjecture as to the meaning of the singular performance enacted by us."—*Early Years and Late Reflections*, i. 132.

my early education was so domestic, that I know not how to get rid of it, or even to wish to get rid of it. Life were so flat a thing without enthusiasm, that if for a moment it leaves me, I have a sort of stomach sensation attached to all my thoughts, like those which succeed to the pleasurable operations of a dose of opium." *

He goes on to speak of his literary occupations, says he is about to write essays on the drama for the Morning Post, and then says,— "Two mornings and one whole day I dedicate to essays on the possible progressiveness of man, and on the principles of population. In April, I retire to my greater work,—The Life of Lessing."

In February, he seems to have been reporting for the Morning Post, and to have written various essays on general subjects for its columns. But Mr. Stuart, who was then its editor, says, writing in 1838 in the Gentleman's Magazine,—" Coleridge totally failed in the plan he proposed of writing daily on the daily occurrences." From this time, however, until 1802, he continued to write at intervals for the paper, his essays frequently exciting attention from their point and ability.

Toward the end of July, 1800, Coleridge wrote to Mr. Josiah Wedgwood,—" Have you seen my

---

* Cottle's *Reminiscences*, p. 318.

translation of Wallenstein ? It is a dull heavy play. I am now working at my Introduction to the Life of Lessing, which I trust will be in the press before Christmas ; that is, the Introduction will be published first." *

The translation of Wallenstein had just appeared. The opinion that Coleridge expressed at this time concerning its merits is very different from that which he afterwards held. In 1821, writing to Mr. Alsop, he says :—

" I am glad you are now to see the Wallenstein for the first time, as you will then see a specimen of my happiest attempts, during the prime manhood of my intellect, before I had been buffeted by adversity, or crossed by fatality." †

The translation is, indeed, one of the best of

* In another letter, written in November, he says:—" Immediately on my arrival in this country, I undertook to finish a poem which I had begun, entitled Christabel, for a second volume of the Lyrical Ballads. I tried to perform my promise, but the deep, unutterable disgust which I had suffered in the translation of the accursed Wallenstein seemed to have stricken me with barrenness,—till one day I dined out at the house of a neighbouring clergyman, and some how or other drank so much wine, that I found some effort and dexterity requisite to balance myself on the hither edge of sobriety. The next day my verse-making faculties returned to me and I proceeded successfully."—Cottle's *Reminiscences,* p. 325.

† *Letters, Conversations, and Recollections of S. T. Coleridge,* p. 65.

Coleridge's works, and one of the finest translations that our language possesses. It has all the vigour and freshness of an original work, and in fact it has a claim to be regarded as such, for some passages added by Coleridge are among the most powerful in the play. It is not the version of a mere translator, but it is the rendering of one poet by another.

Before 1800 was over, Coleridge, driven by unconquerable restlessness, had left London and was living at Keswick, where he had taken a small house. His son Derwent was just born, and here in quiet he intended to finish some one or more of his literary undertakings. He writes to Wedgwood,—" You will in three weeks see the letters on the ' Rise and Condition of the German Boors;' they are in the printer's hands." But many a three weeks passed, and Mr. Wedgwood never saw them.* For the next two years, from November, 1800, to August, 1802, there are few records of Coleridge's life. His fine Ode to Dejection, addressed probably to Miss Wordsworth, and that beautiful poem, the Complaint and Reply,† are almost the only compositions of this period. He had

---

* " Must Lessing wait for the Resurrection before he receives a new life," writes Southey in March, 1801.

† In the Literary Remains, this little poem is assigned to the year 1809; but Mrs. H. N. Coleridge says it was written in 1802.

a plan of going to the West Indies, and another of going to Italy, and formed such numerous schemes of literary work that Southey wrote, " You spawn plans like a herring." In August, 1802, Charles and Mary Lamb made a three weeks' visit to Coleridge, which Charles Lamb has commemorated in pleasant letters. About this time Coleridge wrote some further essays for the Morning Post, and in October he says to Mr. Thomas Wedgwood :—

" I shall in a few weeks go to press with a volume on the prose writings of Hale, Milton, and Taylor, and shall immediately follow it up with an essay on the writings of Dr. Johnson and Gibbon, and in these two volumes I flatter myself I shall present a fair history of English prose. If my life and health remain, and I do but write half as much and as regularly as I have done during the last six weeks, this will be finished by January next; and I shall then put together my memorandum-book on the subject of poetry. . . . I have, since my twentieth year, meditated an heroic poem on the siege of Jerusalem by Titus. This is the pride and the stronghold of my hope ; but I never think of it except in my best moods. The work to which I dedicate the ensuing year of my life is one which highly pleased Leslie,* in prospective."

* The eminent Edinburgh Professor.

In 1803 he visited London, and on his return to the Lakes, left in charge to Lamb the superintendence of a new edition of his poems.* In the course of the summer Southey proposed to him to take part in the preparation of a great work on English Literature which it was then in contemplation to execute. Coleridge replied, proposing in turn a splendid scheme for a work of this kind to be embraced in nine quarto volumes. It was a design too vast for any genius but his own, and Southey's letter in return is marked with equal good sense and tenderness. " Your plan " he says, " is too good, too gigantic, quite beyond my powers. If you had my tolerable state of health, and that love of steady and productive employment which is now grown into a necessary habit with me,— if you were to execute and would execute it, it would be, beyond all doubt, the most valuable work of any age or any country ; but I cannot fill up such an outline. No man can better feel where he fails than I do ;—and to rely upon you for whole quartos ! Dear Coleridge, the smile that comes with that thought is a very melancholy one ; and if Edith saw me now, she would think my eyes were weak again, when, in truth, the humour that covers them springs from another

* " Bless you, old sophist," writes Lamb to him after his departure, " who, next to human nature, taught me all the corruption I was capable of knowing."—*Final Memorials of Charles Lamb*, i. 136.

cause." The original plan was soon after given up.

The few remaining memorials of this year of Coleridge's life are mostly sad ones. In a letter dated in September, he says :—" I will not trouble you with the gloomy tale of my health. When I am awake, by patience, employment of mind, and walking, I can keep the fiend at arm's length; but the night is my hell! sleep my tormenting angel. Three nights out of four I fall asleep, struggling to lie awake, and my frequent night-screams have almost made me a nuisance in my own house." * Again, in January, 1804, he says,—" I have been ill, very ill," † and refers to similar sufferings. He then speaks of going to Madeira to restore his health, and says,—" Wordsworth had, as I may truly say, forced on me one hundred pounds in the event of my going to Madeira, and Stuart had kindly offered to befriend me." But no southern island had balm to restore his wasted health, and no friend could assist with aid such as he needed. In the same letter he says,—" I am eager to hope all good things of my health. That gained, I have a cheering, and I trust prideless, confidence that I shall make an active and perseverant use of the faculties and acquirements that have been intrusted to my keep-

---

* Cottle's *Reminiscences*, p. 345.
† *Ibid.*

ing, and a fair trial of their height, depth, and width."

The sufferings detailed in the foregoing extracts were the natural result of his continued excessive use of opium. In the Confessions of an English Opium Eater, sufferings of the same nature are depicted with a terrible vividness. Nothing can be more mournful than the warnings which Coleridge himself has left us. In his Friend, he says :—

" Restlessness can drive us to vices that promise no enjoyment, not even the cessation of that restlessness. This is, indeed, the dread punishment attached by nature to habitual vice, that its impulses wax, as its motives wane. No object, not even the light of a solitary taper in the far distance, tempts the benighted mind from before ; but its own restlessness dogs it from behind as with the iron goad of destiny." *

And again, in the poem called The Visionary Hope :—

" Sad lot to have no hope!   Though, lowly kneeling,
   He fain would frame a prayer within his breast;
   Would fain entreat for some sweet breath of healing,
   That his sick body might have ease and rest;
   He strove in vain! the dull sighs from his chest
   Against his will the stifling load revealing,
   Though Nature forced; though like some captive guest,
   Some royal prisoner at his conqueror's feast,
   An alien's restless mood but half concealing,

---

* Vol. i. p. 137.

> The sternness on his gentle brow confessed
> Sickness within and miserable feeling:
> Though obscure pangs made curses of his dreams,
> And dreaded sleep each night repelled in vain,
> Each night was scattered by its own loud screams:
> Yet never could his heart command, though fain,
> One deep full wish to be no more in pain."

In the spring of 1804, his state of health both bodily and mental becoming more and more miserable, he determined to go to Malta.* He could hardly have adopted a worse plan. Removed from his friends, exposed to the enervating effects of a southern climate, he fell more completely under the bondage of opium. For some time he performed the duties of public secretary of the island; but his habits were too irregular for such a post, and before long he was superseded. During his residence in Malta, he saw much of Sir Alexander Ball, then civil commissioner of the island, and he speaks in his Friend " of that daily and familiar intercourse with him which made the fifteen months from May, 1804, to October, 1805, in many respects the most memorable and instructive period of my life." There are very few other records of this period.†

---

* Mrs. H. N. Coleridge states that he lectured in London in 1804, before going to Malta.

† Decatur was at this time stationed in the Mediterranean, and was frequently at Malta. He met Coleridge at Sir A. Ball's table; they felt a mutual interest, and in after life both referred to their intercourse at this time with pleasure. See Mackenzie's *Life of Decatur*, p. 123.

From Malta, Coleridge went to Italy, and remained in Rome for some months. Here he
became acquainted with Mr. Allston, and this
acquaintance ripened into a friendship of many
years, which Allston commemorated in a sonnet
written after Coleridge's death.

After some months' residence, Coleridge was
hurried away from Italy, as a suspicious person,
he having written for the Morning Post, three
years before, invectives against Napoleon.*

In December, 1806, Charles Lamb writes—
" Coleridge has come home, and is going to turn
lecturer on taste at the Royal Institution." It
does not appear, whether any lectures were delivered.

De Quincey, who saw Coleridge in 1807,
says of him,—" Never had I beheld so profound
an expression of cheerless despondency ; and the
restless activity of Coleridge's mind in chasing
abstract truths, and burying himself in the dark
places of human speculation, seemed to me in
great measure an attempt to escape out of his

---

* After this time the materials for a sketch of Coleridge's
life become less complete than for the earlier years. The
Biographia Literaria contains nothing of autobiography after
this date, and the Biographical Supplement to it has little
narrative referring to a period later than 1800; Cottle, except
as regards one point, deserts us at the time of the Malta voyage; Gillman's beggarly volume is worth almost nothing with
respect to the biography of Coleridge, while from the miscellaneous sketches of his life but few facts can be gleaned.

own personal wretchedness." And wretched he must have been, now at London, now at Keswick and Grassmere, now at Stowey and Bridgewater, finding no relief from the miserable sufferings which goaded him to a continual restlessness. It was at this time that he wrote to his friend Mr. Wade the following strange and melancholy words :—

"It is not of comparative utility I speak; for as to what has been actually done, and in relation to useful effects produced, whether on the minds of individuals or of the public, I dare boldly stand forward, and (let every man have his own, and that be counted mine which but for and through me would not have existed,) will challenge the proudest of my literary contemporaries to compare proofs with me, of usefulness in the excitement of reflection, and the diffusion of original and forgotten, yet necessary and important, truths and knowledge; and this is not the less true, because I have suffered others to reap all the advantages. But, O dear friend, this consciousness, raised by insult of enemies and alienated friends, stands me in little stead to my own soul,—in how little, then, before the all-righteous Judge ! who, requiring back the talents he had intrusted, will, if the mercies of Christ do not intervene, not demand of me what I have done, but why I did not do more; why, with powers above so many, I had sunk in many things below most !

But this is too painful, and in remorse we often waste the energy which should be better employed in reformation,—that essential part, and only possible proof, of sincere repentance." *

In the course of this year, Mr. De Quincey, who was a young man of fortune, presented to Mr. Coleridge, anonymously, through Cottle, a gift of three hundred pounds. He had become deeply interested in him through sympathy with his sufferings as an opium-eater, and had an excessive admiration for his powers of mind.† This sum of money for a time rendered Coleridge easy in his circumstances ; but before long a large portion of it had been spent in procuring opium. At length, in 1808 or 1809, leaving his wife and children to be taken care of and provided for by Southey, at Keswick, he went to live with Wordsworth at Grassmere.

Here The Friend was projected, and in good part written, and here its publication, in numbers, commenced on the 8th of June, 1809. In the prospectus of it, extracted from a letter to a correspondent, he says : —

" It is not unknown to you, that I have employed almost the whole of my life in acquiring, or endeavouring to acquire, useful knowledge by

* *Cottle*, p. 257.

† Writing in 1834, De Quincey speaks of him with characteristic extravagance as having " the largest and most spacious intellect, the subtlest and the most comprehensive, in my judgment, that has yet existed amongst men,"

E

study, reflection, observation, and by cultivating the society of my superiors in intellect, both at home and in foreign countries. You know, too, that at different periods of my life I have not only planned, but collected the materials for, many works on various and important subjects ; so many, indeed, that the number of my unrealized schemes and the mass of my miscellaneous fragments have often furnished my friends with a subject of raillery and sometimes of regret and reproof.* Waiving the mention of all private and accidental hinderances, I am inclined to believe that this want of perseverance has been produced in the main by an over-activity of thought, modi fied by a constitutional indolence, which made it more pleasant to me to continue acquiring, than to reduce what I had acquired to a regular form. Add, too, that, almost daily throwing off my notices or reflections in desultory fragments, I was still tempted onward by an increasing sense of the imperfection of my knowledge, and by the conviction, that, in order fully to comprehend and deve-

* Lamb, in a most humorous letter to Manning, dated December 25th, 1815, says,—" Coleridge is just dead, having lived just long enough to close the eyes of Wordsworth, who paid the debt of nature but a week or two before. Poor Col! but two days before he died, he wrote to a bookseller proposing an epic poem on the ' Wanderings of Cain,' in twenty-four books. It is said he has left behind him more than forty thousand treatises in criticism, metaphysics, and divinity, but few of them in a state of completion."—Talfourd's *Life of Lamb*, i. 174.

lop any one subject, it was necessary that I should make myself master of some other, which again as regularly involved a third, and so on with an ever-widening horizon."

These sentences, which very truly depict one portion of Coleridge's intellect, give the secret of the want of success attending the first publication of The Friend. He had proposed to himself too much in stating,—" The object of The Friend is to uphold those truths and those merits which are founded in the nobler and permanent parts of our nature against the caprices of fashion, and such pleasures as either depend on transitory and accidental causes, or are pursued from less worthy impulses." The design was too vast and vague to admit of satisfactory execution. Neither author nor readers were satisfied with desultory disquisitions, which, however excellent in themselves, had little or no relation to each other, and which, while showing great powers of mind, and a most unusual variety of acquisition, showed at the same time the irregularity of the one and the ill assortment of the other. It is somewhat difficult, however, to judge of the merits of The Friend, as first published, from the later editions. For the edition of 1818, which succeeding ones have followed, " was rather a *rifucimento*," as the author said, " than a new edition, the additions forming so large a portion of the whole work and the arrangement being altogether new."

The 27th and last number of the Lake edition was issued March 15th, 1810. It had proved a disastrous speculation in a pecuniary point of view, but, as affording Coleridge a regular employment for so long a period, it had been of essential service in restoring a somewhat more healthy tone to his mind. But again left without employment, his old habits returned and increased upon him, so that the next year is a blank in his life, and we know nothing more of him till we find him, in 1810, accompanying Mr. Basil Montagu to London, having left Keswick and Grassmere forever. Before many months had passed, however, he went from Mr. Montagu to live at Hammersmith, with a Mr. Morgan, a gentleman whom he had known when at Bristol. Whilst here, he delivered a course of lectures before the London Philosophical Society. The prospectus was in part as follows : — " Mr. Coleridge will commence on Monday, November 18th, 1811, a course of lectures on Shakespear and Milton, in illustration of the principles of poetry, and their application, as grounds of criticism, to the most popular works of later English poets, those of the living included." Of these lectures a report has been preserved, in notes taken at their delivery by Mr. J. Payne Collier, and published by him in 1856, under the title " Seven Lectures on Shakespeare and Milton. By the late S. T. Coleridge." In the same year, Coleridge wrote frequently for the Courier, a paper which Mr. Stuart, the former editor of the Morning-Post, now conducted. His communications were highly valued and well paid for. For some time he wrote with regularity, and it is not clear on what grounds he ceased to write for that paper.

In Mr. Morgan's family Coleridge remained for a year or two, and during this period his health again improved. "The Morgans," says Southey, in a letter writen in 1815, "with great effort, succeeded in making him leave off opium for a time, and he recovered in consequence health and spirits;" and Coleridge himself refers to the fact, in a letter written in April, 1814. But the victory was not complete, and the drug quickly re-established its awful dominion over him.

In the winter of 1813, his tragedy, Remorse, was performed with the most flattering and merited success at Drury Lane. It was brought upon the stage through the influence of Lord Byron, who was at that time associated with Mr. Whitbread in the management of the theatre. Coleridge writes to his friend Mr. Poole, on the 13th of February:—"I have never seen the play since the first night. It has been a good thing for the Theatre, ... and I shall get more by it than all my literary labours put together; nay, thrice as much, subtracting my heavy losses in the Watchman and the Friend, including the copyright." *

* Biographical Supplement to *Biog. Lit.* ii. p. 413. When the play was first written, Sheridan, who had urged Coleridge to write for the stage, refused to bring it forward, as unsuited to theatrical representation. After this, and before it was brought out, the last three acts were recast.

In 1814, he delivered a course of lectures on Shakespeare at the Royal Institution, and when he had completed this course in London, he went down to Bristol to repeat it. But now, as when delivering a former course in London, as described by De Quincey, "never did a man treat his audience with less respect, or his task with less careful attention." Sometimes he would keep his audience waiting for an hour or more, and sometimes he would not appear at all. Meanwhile, his manner was strange, and he complained much of illness. At length, his old friend, Mr. Cottle, addressed a long and earnest letter to him, beseeching him to renounce the use of opium and spirits. Coleridge replied in the following painfully degraded words :—

"You have poured oil in the raw and festering wound of an old friend's conscience, Cottle! but it is *oil of vitriol!* I but barely glanced at the middle of the first page of your letter, and have seen no more of it,—not from resentment, God forbid! but from the state of my bodily and mental sufferings, that scarcely permitted human fortitude to let in a new visitor of affliction.

"The object of my present reply is to state the case just as it is,—first, that for ten years the anguish of my spirit has been indescribable, the sense of my danger staring, but the consciousness of my GUILT worse,—far worse than all! I have prayed, with drops of agony on my brow; trembling, not only before the justice of my Maker, but even before the mercy of my Redeemer. 'I gave thee so many talents, what hast thou done with them?' Secondly, overwhelmed as I am with a sense of my direful infirmity, I have never attempted to disguise or conceal the cause. On the contrary, not only to friends have I stated the whole case with tears and the very bitterness of shame, but in two instances I have warned young men, mere acquaintances, who had spoken of having taken laudanum, of the direful consequences, by an awful exposition of its tremendous effects on myself. . . . . . Had I but a few hundred pounds, but £200,—half to send to Mrs. Coleridge and half to place myself in a private madhouse, where I could procure nothing but what the physician thought proper, and where a medical attendant could be constantly with me for two or three months (in less than that time, life or death would be determined,) then there might be hope. Now there is none!! O God! how willingly would I place myself under Dr. Fox, in his establishment; for my case is a species of madness, only it is a derangement, an utter impotence of the volition, and not of the intellectual faculties. *

His plan of going to an asylum for the insane Coleridge proposed again, and wrote to Cottle to ask him to get up a subscription among his, Col-

* Cottle's *Reminiscences*, pp. 272, 278.

ridge's, friends, to defray the expenses attendant
on its execution.   To this, however, Cottle was
averse, and wrote to consult Southey, with whom
Coleridge's wife and children had been living for
several years, as to what was best to be done.
Southey's reply was as follows :—

" *Keswick, April,* 1814.

"My dear Cottle,—You may imagine with
what feelings I have read your correspondence
with Coleridge.   Shocking as his letters are, perhaps the most mournful thing they discover is,
that, while acknowledging the guilt of the habit, he
imputes it still to morbid bodily causes ; whereas,
after every possible allowance is made for these,
every person who has witnessed his habits knows
that for the greater, infinitely the greater part,
inclination and indulgence are its motives.

" It seems dreadful to say this, with his expressions before me ; but it is so, and I know it
to be so, from my own observation, and that
of all with whom he has lived.   The Morgans,
with great difficulty and perseverance, *did* break
him of the habit, at a time when his ordinary
consumption of laudanum was from *two quarts
a week* to *a pint a day!*   He suffered dread-
fully during the first abstinence, so much so as
to say it was better for him to die than to endure
his present feelings.   Mrs. Morgan resolutely replied, it was indeed better that he should die than
that he should continue to live as he had been

living. It angered him at the time, but the effort
was persevered in.

"To what, then, was the relapse owing? I
believe to this cause,—that no use was made of
renewed health and spirits; that time passed on
in idleness, till the lapse of time brought with it a
sense of neglected duties, and then relief was again
sought for *a self-accusing mind ;*—in bodily feelings, which, when the stimulus ceased to act, added
only to the load of self-accusation. This, Cottle,
is an insanity which none but the soul's physician
can cure. Unquestionably, restraint would do as
much for him as it did when the Morgans tried
it; but I do not see the slightest reason for believing it would be more permanent. This, too, I
ought to say, that all the medical men to whom
Coleridge has made his confession, have uniformly
ascribed the evil, not to bodily disease, but indulgence. The restraint which alone could effect-
ually cure is that which no person can impose
upon him. Could he be compelled to a certain quantity of labour every day, *for his family*, the pleasure
of having done it would make his heart glad, and
the sane mind would make the body whole.

" I see nothing so advisable for him, as that he
should come here to Greta Hall. My advice is,
that he should visit T. Poole for two or three
weeks, to freshen himself and recover spirits,
which new scenes never fail to give him. When
there, he may consult his friends at Birmingham

and Liverpool on the fitness of lecturing at those
two places, at each of which he has friends, and
would, I should think beyond all doubt, be successful. He must be very unfortunate, if he did
not raise from fifty to one hundred pounds at the
two places. But whether he can do this or not,
here it is that he ought to be. He knows in
what manner he would be received; by his children with joy; by his wife, not with tears, if she
can control them,—certainly not with reproaches;
by myself only with encouragement.

" He has sources of direct emolument open to
him in the Courier, and in the Eclectic Review.
These for his immediate wants, and for every thing
else, his pen is more rapid than mine, and would
be paid as well. If you agree with me, you had
better write to Poole that he may press him to
make a visit, which I know he has promised. His
great object should be, to get out a play, and appropriate the whole produce to the support of his
son Hartley, at college. Three months' pleasurable exertion would effect this. Of some such fit
of industry I by no means despair; of any thing
more than fits, I am afraid I do. But this, of
course, I shall never say to him. From me he
shall never hear aught but cheerful encouragement, and the language of hope. . . . . . I hope
you next will tell me that he is going to Mr. T.
Poole's. I have communicated some of your letters to Mrs. Coleridge, who you know resides

with us.   Her spirits and health are beginning to
sink under it.   God bless you!

" Yours affectionately,

" ROBERT SOUTHEY."

Cottle now proposed to raise an annuity of £150,
to be held in trust for Coleridge, and Southey again
writes to him :—

" Of sorrow and humiliation I will say nothing.
Let me come at once to the point.   On what
grounds can such a subscription as you propose
raising for Coleridge be solicited?   The annuity
to which your intended letter refers (£150) *was*
given him by the Wedgwoods.   Thomas, by his
will, settled his portion on Coleridge, for his life.
Josiah withdrew his about three years ago.   The
half still remaining amounts, when the income tax
is deducted, to £67 10s.   That sum Mrs. C. receives at present, and it is all which she receives
for supporting herself, her daughter, and the two
boys at school ;—the boys' expenses amounting to
the whole.   No part of Coleridge's embarrassment
arises from his wife and children,—except that he
has insured his life for a thousand pounds, and
pays the annual premium.   He never writes to
them, and never opens a letter from them !

" In truth, Cottle, his embarrassments, and his
miseries, of body and mind, all arise from one
accursed cause,—excess in *opium*, of which he
habitually takes more than ever was known to be

taken by any person before him. . . . . . Perhaps you are not aware of the costliness of this drug. In the quantity which C. takes, it would consume *more* than the whole which you propose to raise. A frightful consumption of *spirits* is added. In this way bodily ailments are produced, and tho wonder is that he is still alive.

"There are but two grounds on which a subscription of this nature can proceed,—either when the object is disabled from exerting himself, or when his exertions are unproductive. Coleridge is in neither of these predicaments. Proposals after proposals have been made to him by the booksellers, and he repeatedly closed with them. He is at this moment as capable of exertion as I am, and would be paid as well for whatever he might be pleased to do. There are two Reviews, the Quarterly and the Eclectic, in both of which he might have employment at ten guineas a sheet. As to the former, I could obtain it for him; in the latter, they are urgently desirous of his assistance. *He promises, and does nothing.* . . . . . . Nothing is wanting to make him easy in circumstances, and happy in himself, but to leave off opium, and to direct a certain portion of his time to the discharge of *his duties.* Four hours a day would suffice." *

But to every plan that Southey proposed Coleridge was irreconcilably averse, and he sank still lower in the depths of that misery into which with

* Cottle's *Reminiscences*, pp. 279, 280.

eyes open he had plunged. For a time he placed himself in the hands of a physician, and while under his care he wrote,—"I cannot be too grateful for the skill with which the surgeon treats me;" and again,—"It is true I am restored as much beyond my expectations almost, as my deserts." But

> "What boots it at one gate to make defence
> And at another to let in the foe?"

At this very period he employed himself in obtaining laudanum, without the knowledge of his physician, by actual deceit.*

About this time he wrote the following letter to Mr. Wade.

"*Bristol, June 26th*, 1814.

"Dear Sir,—For I am unworthy to call any good man friend,—much less you, whose hospitality and love I have abused; accept, however, my entreaties for your forgiveness, and for your prayers.

"Conceive a poor miserable wretch, who for many years has been attempting to beat off pain by a constant recurrence to the vice which reproduces it. Conceive a spirit in hell, employed in tracing out for others the road to that heaven from which his crimes exclude him! In short, conceive whatever is most wretched, helpless, and hopeless and you will form as tolerable a notion of my state as it is possible for a good man to have.

* Cottle's *Reminiscences*, p. 285.

"I used to think the text in St. James, that 'he who offended in one point offends in all,' very harsh; but I now feel the awful, the tremendous truth of it. In the one crime of OPIUM, what crime have I not made myself guilty of!—Ingratitude to my Maker! and to my benefactors—injustice! *and unnatural cruelty to my poor children!*—self-contempt for my repeated promise-breach, nay, too often, actual falsehood!

"After my death, I earnestly entreat that a full and unqualified narration of my wretchedness, and of its guilty cause, may be made public, that at least some little good may be effected by the direful example.

"May God Almighty bless you, and have mercy on your still affectionate, and in his heart grateful

"S. T. COLERIDGE." *

There is hardly in the whole gallery of biography a more mournful picture than this. The splendid promise of youth was broken; the powers of mature genius were running all to waste; and, in the very prime of life, an insane infirmity of will was making the present and the future alike terrible.

> —— He flung away
> Those keys that might have open set
> The golden sluices of the day,
> But clutched the keys of darkness yet.

---

* *Vide* Cottle's *Reminiscences*, p. 292.

There is now another blank in Coleridge's life. His friends could do no more for him. Southey had heard nothing directly from him for more than a year, during which period Mrs. Coleridge and her children had continued to reside with, and to be supported by him. Hartley was to be sent to college, and Southey wrote to his father concerning him, but no notice was taken of the letter. We hear at length of Coleridge residing at Calne, again with Mr. Morgan. A year passes, and he writes to Cottle, begging for money as an advance on poems which he promised to send him then comes a second letter still more urgent, the last that Cottle ever received from him. From April, 1815, to April, 1816, is another unrecorded year.

On the 9th of April, 1816, a physician, Dr. Adams, wrote to Mr. Gillman of Highgate, likewise a physician by profession, telling him that a gentleman, who had for some years been in the habit of taking large quantities of opium, was desirous " to fix himself in the house of some medical gentleman, who will have courage to refuse him any laudanum, and under whose assistance, should he be the worse for it, he may be relieved," and ended by requesting Mr. Gillman to receive him into his family. Gillman was not averse to the proposition. He met Coleridge on the 12th, they were mutually pleased with each other, and on the next day Coleridge addressed to Mr. Gillman the following pitiable letter.

'42 *Norfolk Street, Strand, Saturday Noon.*
April 13, 1816.

"MY DEAR SIR :—The first half hour I was
with you, convinced me that I should owe my
reception into your family, exclusively to motives
not less flattering to me, than honourable to yourself. I trust we shall ever, in matters of intellect,
be reciprocally serviceable to each other. Men
of sense generally come to the same conclusions ;
but they are likely to contribute to each other's
enlargement of view in proportion to the distance,
or even opposition of the point from which they
set out. Travel, and the strange variety of situa-
tions and employments, on which chance has
thrown me in the course of my life, might have
made me a mere man of *observation,* if pain and
sorrow, and self-miscomplacence, had not forced
my mind in on itself, and so formed habits of
meditation. It is now as much in my nature to
evolve the fact from the law, as that of a practical man to deduce the law from the fact.

"With respect to pecuniary remuneration, allow
me to say, I must not at least be suffered to make
any addition to your family expenses, though I
cannot offer anything that would be in any way
adequate to my sense of the service ; for that
indeed there could not be a compensation, as it
must be returned in kind, by esteem and grateful
affection.

"And now of myself. My ever wakeful reason,

and the keenness of my moral feelings, will secure you from all unpleasant circumstances connected with me, save only one, viz. the evasion of a specific madness. You will never *hear* any thing but truth from me :—prior habits render it out of my power to tell an untruth, but unless carefully observed, I dare not promise that I should not, with regard to this detested poison, be capable of acting one. No sixty hours have yet passed without my having taken laudanum, though for the last week, comparatively trifling doses. I have full belief that your anxiety need not be extended beyond the first week ; and for the first week, I shall not, I must not be permitted to leave your house, unless with you. Delicately or indelicately, this must be done, and both the servants and the assistant must receive absolute commands from you. The stimulus of conversation suspends the terror that haunts my mind ; but when I am alone, the horrors I have suffered from laudanum, the degradation, the blighted utility, almost overwhelm me. If (as I feel for the *first time* a soothing confidence it will prove) I should leave you restored to my moral and bodily health, it is not myself only that will love and honour you; every friend I have, (and thank God! in spite of this wretched vice, I have many and warm ones, who were friends of my youth, and have never deserted me,) will thank you with reverence. I have taken no notice of your kind

F

apologies. If I could not be comfortable in your house, and with your family, I should deserve to be miserable. If you could make it convenient, I should wish to be with you by Monday evening, as it would prevent the necessity of taking fresh lodgings in town.

"With respectful compliments to Mrs. Gillman and her sister, I remain, dear Sir,

"Your much obliged

"S. T. COLERIDGE."

On the 15th of April, Coleridge went to Mr. Gillman's to reside. There for eighteen years he lived, and there he died.

Mr. Gillman seems to have been an amiable, weak-minded man. He was flattered at the notoriety which he acquired by having so distinguished an inmate in his house, and pleased himself by setting the highest importance on all that concerned Mr. Coleridge. He became his professed admirer, and Mrs. Gillman, who was a kind-hearted woman, moved by the forlornness of his story, and won by his quick perceptive sympathy, and sweetness of manner, soon shared in her husband's veneration for their guest. Coleridge's morbid vanity was gratified, his wounded self-love was soothed, and he bestowed in return, frequent and warm expressions of personal attachment and regard. He had not of late been accustomed to be the object of such attention and respect, and he was stimulated to make exertions to support a character answering to the peculiar circumstances in which he found himself. In the society of this worthy couple, who watched over him with solicitous partiality, he obtained what he had never possessed before, a home congenial to his disposition, and unattended by any domestic responsibility.*

The direct influence that Mr. Gillman attempted to exercise over Coleridge's habits seems never to have been very great; but within a short time of his becoming domesticated at Highgate, the quantity of opium in which he indulged was much diminished, and his mind began to assume a more healthy tone. It does not seem probable, however, that, at any subsequent period of his life, he altogether abstained from the use of laudanum. His later letters contain not infrequent references to sufferings occasioned by its recent use.† The habit had become fixed too deeply to be uprooted, and during the few years preceding 1815 his mind

* After Coleridge's death, Mr. Gillman published the first volume of a memoir of him. It was very poorly done; wretched equally in style and in arrangement, meagre in facts, and full of specious glossings. It is not strange that a second volume never appeared.

† See *Letters, Conversations, and Recollections of S. T. Coleridge*, p. 57. This book was got up by Mr. Alsop, a friend of Coleridge's later years. It contains some curious biographical matter, but in other respects is even worse than Mr. Gillman's volume. The author appears to be deficient in common sense.

had sustained a shock from which it never afterwards fully recovered. At some periods, indeed, he himself believed that his faculties were restored to their original vigour, and he felt confident that he might yet repair the waste of years. But these were temporary periods of satisfaction, arising from what might be called his own *mis-self-com-placence,* and from the foolish flattery of excited friends. At times he was contrite with sincere repentance, while at others he bewildered himself in a maze of vain excuses for the past, or indulged in the cheap cant of self-condemnation. His mental and moral condition continued as irregular and variable as ever. Good dispositions and weak resolutions, elation and melancholy, splendid projects and magnificent self-deceptions, vague speculations and glowing fancies followed each other in quick succession. Days of comparative cheerfulness were succeeded by nights of gloom. His mind was like the ruin of some great Eastern palace, that in its days of prime was full of contrasts of splendid spacious halls and dark narrow chambers, of real glories and of tawdry imitations, and which now, with its walls cracked, its ornaments defaced, its entrances choked, still retained bright relics of its ancient beauty, and was invested with the glow of famous memories.

But there was little peace to be found even in the shelter of Highgate. And perhaps the saddest experience of many sad years, and the sharpest of the sharp stings of conscience came to Coleridge here, as he saw from his retreat the result and effect of his own life and character exhibited in the life and character of his dear first-born son, Hartley.

> The sad forms of scenes and deeds long past
> Blend into spectral shapes, and death-like life,
> And pass in silent, stern procession.—
> The storm is past;—but, in the pause and hush,
> Nor calm, nor tranquil joy, nor peace are mine.

After having spent a year with the Gillmans, Coleridge published what he called a Lay Sermon. It was entitled, "The Statesman's Manual, or the Bible the best Guide to Political Knowledge and Foresight." This was followed, in the next year, by a second sermon, "addressed to the higher and middle classes on the existing distresses and discontents;" and he proposed to write another addressed to the lower classes. In the latter editions these Lay Sermons are associated with a little book, first published in 1830, on the Constitution of the Church and State. Neither Coleridge's experience nor his habit of mind fitted him to be a safe guide in matters of religion or politics, and these tracts are of little value to the statesman or to the man in private life. They will hardly be remembered by another generation.

In the course of 1816 and 1817, the two parts of Christabel (the second part for the first time) were published in a small volume, with Kubla

Khan and the Pains of Sleep. This was shortly followed by the volume of poems entitled " Sibylline Leaves," " in allusion to the fragmentary and widely scattered state in which they had been long suffered to remain." In this volume were many of his finest poems, and his reputation as a poet was greatly increased by their publication together.

The Biographia Literaria was published in the same year. It had been in great part composed some years before. He intended it in the main as a statement of his principles in politics, religion, and philosophy, and an application of the rules deduced from philosophical principles, to poetry and criticism. Again, as was so often the case, he fell far short of his mark. His principles of politics and religion were but slightly touched upon, and his principles of philosophy were borrowed from Schelling, Maasz, and Fichte, without sufficient acknowledgment of the sources whence they came. Coleridge's plagiarisms in this book, and others of his works, were somewhat harshly pointed out by De Quincey and by a writer in Blackwood's Magazine, which led Mrs. Henry N. Coleridge, in a long and rambling Introduction to the last edition of the Biographia Literaria, to enter into a defence of her father. One sentence from it seems to cover the whole ground.

" If he was not always sufficiently considerate

of other men's property, he was profuse of his own; and in truth, such was his temper in regard to all property, of what kind soever; he did not enough regard or value it, whether for himself or his neighbour." *

By far the most valuable portion of this desultory book is the analytical criticism and estimate of Wordsworth's poetry, which occupies almost the whole of the second volume. It is a fine appreciation of the peculiar characteristics of Wordsworth's style, and a warm assertion of the beauty and power of his poetry. The judgment of the world has slowly confirmed the truth and justice of Coleridge's opinion, but there has never been a more able statement, than in this early essay, of the grounds upon which this judgment now rests.

In the autumn of 1817, Zapolya, a Christmas Tale, was composed and published. It contains passages of much beauty, but as a whole is deficient in dramatic interest; and though popular for a time with the reading public, was not brought upon the stage. During the winters of 1817 and 1818, Coleridge lectured for the last time in public. He very seldom wrote out any lectures previously to delivery, except when he was lecturing at Bristol before his marriage, and nothing

* *Biographia Literaria*, vol. i., Introduction, p. xviii.

but fragments of his different courses are left. In the volumes of his Literary Remains "we have extracts from lectures of all dates from 1802, partly in the words of the critic's own manuscripts, partly the mere notes of his hearers; we have isolated memoranda, of which most are the writer's own, but some are only quotations; we have changes of opinion stated without being accounted for, and hints of other opinions insufficiently explained." And yet these fragments contain much that is valuable. His criticisms on Shakespeare, which were first delivered in one of these courses, and which have since been collected and published by themselves, are among the best in the language, and though of very unequal value, are distinguished by their keenness, subtlety, and discrimination.

But few letters which were written during the years of his residence at Highgate have since been published. The most of them are to be found in the work already referred to, entitled, . "Letters, Conversations, and Recollections of Samuel Taylor Coleridge." Worthless as Mr. Alsop's portion of this book is, the volume is nevertheless of much importance in furnishing the means for forming an estimate of Coleridge's character during the period to which it refers. It was no work of friendship to publish it. It presents a sad picture of intellectual vagaries and conceit.

In a letter, written in January, 1821, very remarkable for the view it gives of his state of mind and plans during this period, Coleridge says,—

"My health, I have reason to believe, is so intimately connected with the state of my spirits, and these again are so dependent on my thoughts, prospective and retrospective, that I should not doubt the being favoured with a sufficiency for my noblest undertaking, had I the ease of heart requisite for the necessary abstraction of the thoughts, and such a reprieve from the goading of the immediate exigencies as might make tranquillity possible. But, alas! I know by experience (and the knowledge is not the less because the regret is not unmixed with self-blame, and the consciousness of want of exertion and fortitude) that my health will continue to decline as long as the pain from reviewing the barrenness of the past is great in an inverse proportion to any rational anticipations of the future."

He goes on to give a very extraordinary account of the interruptions to which he was exposed,—letters from lords and ladies urging him to write reviews, letters from actors, entreaties for money, or for recommendations to publishers, &c.; he then states that he had the written materials and contents, requiring only to be put together, of a work on Shakespeare and the English Drama, which with every art of compression would amount to three volumes of five hundred pages each. In the same state with this was a Philosophical Analysis of the Genius and Works of Dante, Spenser, Milton, and other poets, in one large volume. "These two works will, I flatter myself, form a complete code of the principles of judgment and feeling applied to works of taste; and not of *poetry* only, but of poesy in all its forms, painting, statuary, music, &c." But besides these, he had, thirdly, in a state of preparation,

"The History of Philosophy considered as a Tendency of the Human Mind to exhibit the Powers of the Human Reason, to discover by its own Strength the Origin and Laws of Man and the World, from Pythagoras to Locke and Condillac. Two volumes. — IV. Letters on the Old and New Testaments, and on the Doctrine and Principles held in common by the Fathers and Founders of the Reformation, addressed to a Candidate for Holy Orders; including Advice on the Plan and Subjects of Preaching, proper to a Minister of the Established Church."

For the completion of these four works, he says he had literally nothing more to do than to transcribe; but from so many scraps, from the margins of books, from blank pages, that unfortunately he must be his own scribe, or they would be all but lost.

"In addition to these—of my *great work*, to the preparation of which more than twenty years of my life have been devoted, and on which my hopes of extensive and permanent utility, of fame, in the noblest sense of the word, mainly rest— ...... of this work, to which all my other writings (unless I except my poems, and these I can exclude in part only) are introductory and preparative; and the result of which, (if the premises be—as I, with the most tranquil assurance, am convinced they are—insubvertible, the deductions legitimate, and the conclusions commensurate, and only commensurate, with both,) must finally be a revolution of all that has been called *Philosophy* or Metaphysics in England and France, since the era of the commencing predominance of the mechanical system, at the restoration of our second Charles, and with this the present fashionable views, not only of religion, morals, and politics, but even of the modern physics and physiology— (you will not blame the earnestness of my expressions, nor the high importance which I attach to this work; for how, with less noble objects, and less faith in their attainment, could I stand acquitted of folly, and abuse of time, talents, and learning, in a labor of three fourths of my *intellectual life?*)—of this work something more than a volume has been dictated by me, so as to exist fit for the press, to my friend and enlightened pupil, Mr. Green. . . . . . And here comes, my dear friend, here comes my sorrow and my weakness, my grievance and my confession.   Anxious to perform the duties of the day arising out of the wants of the day, these wants, too, presenting themselves in the most painful of all forms,—that of a debt owing to those who will not exact it, and yet need its payment, and the delay, the long (not live-long, but *death*-long,) behindhand of my accounts to friends, whose utmost care and frugality on the one side, and industry on the other, the wife's management and the husband's assiduity, are put in requisition to make both ends meet,— I am at once forbidden to attempt, and too perplexed earnestly to pursue, the *accomplishment* of the works worthy of me, those, I mean, above enumerated. . . . . . Now I see but one possible plan of rescuing my permanent utility.   It is briefly this, and plainly—for what we struggle with inwardly, we find at least easiest to *bolt out*,— namely,—that of engaging from the circle of those who think respectfully and hope highly of my powers and attainments a yearly sum, for three or four years, adequate to my actual support, with such comforts and decencies of appearance as my health and habits have made necessaries, so that my mind may be unanxious as far as the present time is concerned; that thus I should stand both enabled and pledged to begin some one work of those above mentioned, and for two thirds of my whole time to devote myself to this exclusively till finished, to take the chance of its success by the best mode of publication that would involve me in no risk, then to proceed with the next, and so on till the works above mentioned, as already in full material existence, should be reduced into formal and actual being; while in the remaining third of my time I might go on maturing and completing my great work, (for if but easy in mind, I have no doubt either of the reawakening power or of the kindling inclination.) and my Christabel, and what else the happier hour might inspire.

.... Now Mr. Green has offered to contribute from thirty to forty pounds yearly, for three or four years; my young friend and pupil, the son of one of my dearest old friends, fifty pounds, and I think that from ten to twenty pounds I could rely upon for another.   The sum required would be about two hundred pounds, to be repaid, of course, should the disposal and sale of my writings produce the means."

The character which is shown, and the facts which appear in these extracts, might be still further illustrated by passages from other letters and writings belonging to this period. But let us rather draw a veil over a picture so melancholy.

The first edition of the Aids to Reflection was published in 1825; a work which from its desultory plan was suited to Coleridge's genius, and in which consequently the characteristics of his style of thought and composition are displayed to advantage.

But the principal intellectual occupation of Coleridge's later years consisted in conversation. From the time of his college life he had been distinguished for the power and beauty of his oral discourse. To his friends he would talk for hour after hour, allowing them small chances to reply. He one day said to Lamb, " Charles, did you ever hear me preach?" " I never heard you do any thing else," replied Lamb. But another saying of this true, genial, friend was, " Only now listen to his talk : it's as fine as an angel's." Many visitors used to go to Highgate to listen to it. On Thursday evenings there was often a gathering of disciples and friends to hear the genius of the place discourse. A certain peculiar *prestige* soon attached itself to these meetings. Coleridge was the high-priest of mysteries from which the vulgar world was excluded. The Gillmans were the acolytes of the temple, and there were always to be found enough burners of incense. At this time a certain hazy grandeur of reputation invested the retreat of the so esteemed sage, the outlines and foundation of which no one of his disciples undertook to define or exhibit. Nor was it strange that it should be so. The versatility of his mind, its very irregularity with deeps and shallows, the variety of his attainments, and the unusual nature of some of them, the occasional displays of extraordinary brilliancy produced by unnatural stimulants, the peculiarity of his position, the known sadness and strangeness of his past experiences, his exhibition of strong religious feeling, his assumption of intellectual superiority not only over those with whom he was brought into association, but also over the leading men of the time, the very obscurity in which he often bewildered his hearers, the sweetness of his disposition and the benignity of his manner,—all united to give a false value in the eyes of his admirers to the philosophy which he delivered to them in oracular monologues. His talk was not of a kind to be well retained even by the firmest and most practised memory, and few reports of it have been preserved. After his uncle's death Mr. Henry Nelson Coleridge, the husband of his only daughter, published, under the title of Table Talk, such scraps of it as he had been able to note down. In these fragments there are the greatest inequalities. Now and then occur fine thoughts finely expressed, and now passages equally striking for their ignorance and arrogance. But such passages can give no idea of the style of his conversation, as it continued, in an unbroken strain, for hour after hour. In the Gentleman's Magazine for December, 1846, is a curious report somewhat in full, of an evening's talk. It begins as follows:—

"G—— took me to see and hear Coleridge. I was sadly disappointed in his appearance. I looked for the light of genius which had exercised such influence on his age, but I could not find it. G—— attacked him on his having said that the interview of Hector and Andromache, in the 6th Iliad, was a modern interpolation, and supported his argument for its authenticity very well. . . . . . But Coleridge never listened in the least to more than the first words, and seemed restless till G—— had done, and he could speak himself, to tell us that we did not understand him, that in fact nobody ever did understand him, but that he would some time or other publish something which would explain every thing. 'The chief difficulty of understanding what I said about Hector and Andromache arises from the want of training in the rising generation, a want as well bodily, I may say, as mental.'"

In the Life of John Sterling, by Archdeacon Hare, are preserved the notes that Sterling took of his first interview with Coleridge. They are interesting. not only as showing the commencement of an intercourse which was to colour much of Sterling's unsettled life, but as exhibiting very clearly some of the marked characteristics of Coleridge's style of talk. "Mr. Coleridge," says

Sterling, "happened to lay his hand on a little old engraving of Luther with four German verses above it;" and from this the talk took its beginning. From the portraits of Luther Coleridge turned to speak of Luther himself, and then of Calvin, and then of landscape-gardening, "and then he went into a long exposition of the evils of commerce and manufactures." From this he took up over-population and the division of labor, then spoke of the want of churches, the influence of Christianity, the harm done by Captain Cook's voyages, the religious ideas of savages and of the ancient world. Then he talked of Dr. Chalmers's preaching, and of Irving's notions about the second coming of our Lord. "I was in his company," says Sterling, "about three hours; and of that time he spoke during two and three quarters. It would have been delightful to listen as attentively, and certainly easy for him to speak just as well, for the next forty-eight hours. On the whole his conversation, or rather monologue, is by far the most interesting I ever heard or heard of." . . . . . . "He speaks rather slowly, but never stops, and seldom even hesitates."

After this first interview Sterling had many others with Coleridge, but of none of them has he left an account. The best description of Coleridge during the later years of his life, is that by Carlyle, in his biography of Sterling. Its humor is too bitter for perfect fairness, but it affords a vivid representation of him during this period, and with some passages of it the sketch of these Highgate years may well close.

" Coleridge sat on the brow of Highgate Hill, in those years, looking down on London and its smoke-tumult, like a sage escaped from the inanity of life's battle; attracting towards him the thoughts of innumerable brave souls still engaged there. His express contributions to poetry, philosophy, or any specific province of human literature or enlightenment, had been small and sadly intermittent; but he had, especially among young inquiring men, a higher than literary, a kind of prophetic or magician character. He was thought to hold, he alone in England, the key of German and other Transcendentalisms; knew the sublime secret of believing by 'the reason' what 'the understanding' had been obliged to fling out as incredible; and could still, after Hume and Voltaire had done their best and worst with him, profess himself an orthodox Christian, and say and print to the Church of England, with its singular old rubrics and surplices at Allhallowtide, *Esto perpetua*. A sublime man; who, alóne in those dark days, had saved his crown of spiritual manhood; escaping from the black materialisms, and revolutionary deluges, with ' God, Freedom, Immortality' still his: a king of men. **The**

practical intellects of the world did not much heed
him, or carelessly reckoned him a metaphysical
dreamer: but to the rising spirits of the young
generation he had this dusky sublime character;
and sat there as a kind of *Magus,* girt in mystery
and enigma; his Dodona oak-grove (Mr. Gillman's
house at Highgate) whispering strange things,
uncertain whether oracles or jargon.

"The Gillmans did not encourage much company, or excitation of any sort, round their sage;
nevertheless access to him, if a youth did reve-
rently wish it, was not difficult. He would stroll
about the pleasant garden with you, sit in the
pleasant rooms of the place,—perhaps take you
to his own peculiar room, high up, with a rear-
ward view, which was the chief view of all. A
really charming outlook, in fine weather. Close
at hand, wide sweep of flowery leafy gardens,
their few houses mostly hidden, the very chimney-
pots vailed under blossomy umbrage, flowed gloriously down hill; gloriously issuing in wide-
tufted undulating plain-country, rich in all charms
of field and town. Waving blooming country of
the brightest green; dotted all over with handsome villas, handsome groves; crossed by roads
and human traffic, here inaudible or heard only
as a musical hum: and behind all swam, under
olive-tinted haze, the illimitable limitary ocean
of London, with its domes and steeples definite
in the sun, big Paul's and the many memories

attached to it hanging high over all. Nowhere, of its kind, could you see a grander prospect on a bright summer day, with the set of the air going southward,—southward, and so draping with the city-smoke not *you*, but the city. Here for hours would Coleridge talk, concerning all conceivable or inconceivable things: and liked nothing better than to have an intelligent, or failing that, even a silent and patient human listener. He distinguished himself to all that ever heard him as at least the most surprising talker extant in this world,—and to some small minority, by no means to all, as the most excellent.

"The good man, he was now getting old, towards sixty, perhaps; and gave you the idea of a life that had been full of sufferings; a life heavy-laden, half-vanquished, still swimming painfully in seas of manifold physical and other bewilderment. Brow and head were round, and of massive weight, but the face was flabby and irresolute. The deep eyes, of a light hazel, were as full of sorrow as of inspiration; confused pain looked mildly from them, as in a kind of mild astonishment. The whole figure and air, good and amiable otherwise, might be called flabby and irresolute; expressive of weakness under possibility of strength. He hung loosely on his limbs, with knees bent, and stooping attitude; in walking, he rather shuffled than decisively stept; and a lady once remarked, he never could fix

which side of the garden-walk would suit him
best, but continually shifted, in corkscrew fashion,
and kept trying both.   A heavy-laden, high-
aspiring and surely much-suffering man.   His
voice, naturally soft and good, had contracted
itself into a plaintive snuffle and singsong; he
spoke as if preaching,—you would have said,
preaching earnestly and also hopelessly the
weightiest things.   I still recollect his 'object'
and 'subject,' terms of continual recurrence in
the Kantean province; and how he sung and
snuffled them into "om-m-mject" and "sum-m-
mject," with a kind of solemn shake or quaver,
as he rolled along.   No talk, in his century or in
any other, could be more surprising. . . . . . .
Nothing could be more copious than his talk;
and furthermore it was always virtually or literally, of the nature of a monologue; suffering no
interruption, however reverent; hastily putting
aside all foreign additions, annotations, or most
ingenuous desires for elucidation, as well-meant
superfluities which would never do.   Besides, it
was talk not flowing anywhither like a river, but
spreading everywhither in inextricable currents
and regurgitations like a lake or sea; terribly
deficient in definite goal or aim, nay often in
logical intelligibility; *what* you were to believe
or do, on any earthly or heavenly thing, obsti-
nately refusing to appear from it.   So that, most
times, you felt logically lost; swamped near to

drowning in this tide of ingenious vocables, spreading out boundless as if to submerge the world.

"To sit as a passive bucket and be pumped into, whether you consent or not, can in the long-run be exhilarating to no creature ; how eloquent soever the flood of utterance that is descending. But if it be withal a confused unintelligible flood of utterance, threatening to submerge all known landmarks of thought, and drown the world and you!—I have heard Coleridge talk, with eager musical energy, two stricken hours, his face radiant and moist, and communicate no meaning whatsoever to any individual of his hearers,—certain of whom, I for one, still kept eagerly listening in hope; the most had long before given up, and formed (if the room were large enough) secondary humming groups of their own." . . . . . " In close colloquy, flowing within narrower banks, I suppose he was more definite and apprehensible : Sterling in after times did not complain of his unintelligibility, or imputed it only to the abstruse high nature of the topics handled. Let us hope so, let us try to believe so! There is no doubt but Coleridge could speak plain words on things plain : his observations and responses on the trivial matters that occurred were as simple as the commonest man's, or were even distinguished by superior simplicity as well as pertinency. "Ah, your tea is too cold, Mr. Coleridge!"

mourned the good Mrs. Gillman once, in her kind, reverential and yet protective manner, handing him a very tolerable though belated cup. 'It's better than I deserve!' snuffled he, in a low hoarse murmur, partly courteous, chiefly pious, the tone of which still abides with me : 'It's better than I deserve!' . . . . . .

"The truth is, I now see, Coleridge's talk and speculation was the emblem of himself: in it as in him, a ray of heavenly inspiration struggled, in a tragically ineffectual degree, with the weakness of flesh and blood. He says once, he 'had skirted the howling deserts of Infidelity;' this was evident enough: but he had not had the courage, in defiance of pain and terror, to press resolutely across said deserts to the new firm lands of Faith beyond; he preferred to create logical fatamorganas for himself on this hither side, and laboriously solace himself with these.

"To the man himself Nature had given, in high measure, the seeds of a noble endowment; and to unfold it had been forbidden him. A subtle lynx-eyed intellect, tremulous pious sensibility to all good and all beautiful; truly a ray of empyrean light;—but imbedded in such weak laxity of character, in such indolences and esuriences as had made strange work with it. Once more, the tragic story of a high endowment with an insufficient will. An eye to discern the divineness of the Heaven's splendours and lightnings,

the insatiable wish to revel in their godlike radi-
ances and brilliances; but no heart to front the
scathing terrors of them, which is the first condition of your conquering an abiding-place there.
The courage necessary for him, above all things,
had been denied this man. His life, with such
ray of the empyrean in it, was great and terrible
to him; and he had not valiantly grappled with
it, he had fled from it; sought refuge in vague
daydreams, hollow compromises, in opium, in
theosophic metaphysics. Harsh pain, danger,
necessity, slavish harnessed toil, were of all things
abhorrent to him. And so the empyrean element, lying smothered under the terrene, and
yet inextinguishable there, made sad writhings.
For pain, danger, difficulty, steady slaving toil,
and other highly disagreeable behests of destiny,
shall in no wise be shirked by any brightest mortal that will approve himself loyal to his mission
in this world; nay precisely the higher he is, the
deeper will be the disagreeableness, and the de-
testability to flesh and blood, of the tasks laid on
him; and the heavier, too, and more tragic, his
penalties if he neglect them." *

Such is the picture of Coleridge in his later
years, as age was coming upon him. The sickness and infirmities of advanced life were ten-

* Carlyle's *Life of Sterling*, pp. 69–80.

derly ministered to, but their burden was not lightened by the pious offices of children or of wife.
From them he had separated himself, never to be
reunited with them in the same home on earth.
His daughter was married from Southey's house,
and her father was not present at her wedding.
But though not supported by the common ties,
the affection between them was not wholly broken,
and till the close of her own sad life Sara Coleridge devoted herself to the filial task of defending and illustrating her father's memory.

Of the last days of Coleridge little is known.
He died on the 25th of July, 1834.

The life of Coleridge is a melancholy record of
powers wasted, of resolves unaccomplished, through
weakness of will and moral infirmity. But his
genius was so great, that, in spite of his errors and
his failures, it has secured for him not only a high
place in the ranks of English poets, but also in
those of the philosophical thinkers of his time.
The Ancient Mariner, Christabel, and many of
his minor poems are works of such pure imagination and such poetic art, that they will always
retain their charm and be familiar to successive
generations of the lovers of poetry. No poet of
this century has possessed more genuine and original faculty, and in their special range his poems
have never been surpassed. They form a class

by themselves, and hold a place unshared by the works of any other poet. His permanent fame will depend more upon them than upon his other contributions to literature.

But though his prose works will not, it is probable, be widely read hereafter, they exerted an influence upon the generation of English thinkers that immediately succeeded him, which, in connection with the direct influence of his conversation, produced a remarkable effect, and one which has been distinctly visible in the progress and tendencies of philosophic and religious thought, not only in England, but also in America. He was the first to introduce to England, and to familiarize to English readers, the profound speculations of the German metaphysicians and critics of the last and of the early part of the present century.

His own criticisms of Shakespeare and other great English writers exhibit the depth and fulness of the methods of his German masters. And though his philosophy partook of German mysticism, and was never developed into a complete and consecutive system, but remained crude and fragmentary, his speculations were often profound, and served as a strong protest against the prevailing sensualism of the English school of metaphysics. His influence on thought has been transmitted through the lives and works of many men, who, though not to be classed as his disciples, yet received from him intellectual stimulus and fertilization. From Carlyle to Stuart Mill there is scarcely one of the English thinkers of the present day who does not owe much, directly or indirectly, to the teachings of Coleridge.

Ite hinc, Camenæ! vos quoque ite, suaves,
Dulces Camenæ! nam (fatebimur enim)
Dulces fuistis.   Et tamen meas chartas
Revisitote, sed pudenter et raro.—VIRG. *Catal.* vii.

       (*From the Preface to the Sibylline Leaves.*)

POEMS WRITTEN IN YOUTH.

Felix curarum, cui non Heliconia cordi
Serta, nec imbelles Parnassi e vertice laurus!
Sed viget ingenium, et magnos accinctus in usus
Fert animus quascunque vices.—Nos tristia vitæ
Solamur cantu.

Stat. Silv., lib. iv. 4.

POEMS WRITTEN IN YOUTH.

FIRST ADVENT OF LOVE.*

O FAIR is Love's first hope to gentle mind!
As Eve's first star thro' fleecy cloudlet peeping;
And sweeter than the gentle south-west wind,
O'er willowy meads and shadowed waters creeping,
And Ceres' golden fields;—the sultry hind
Meets it with brow uplift, and stays his reaping.

1788.

.

GENEVIEVE.

MAID of my love, sweet Genevieve!
In beauty's light you glide along:
Your eye is like the star of eve,
And sweet your voice, as seraph's song.
Yet not your heavenly beauty gives
This heart with passion soft to glow:

* See Note at the end of the volume.

Within your soul a voice there lives!
It bids you hear the tale of woe.
When sinking low the sufferer wan
Beholds no hand outstretched to save,
Fair as the bosom of the swan
That rises graceful o'er the wave,
I've seen your breast with pity heave,
And therefore love I you, sweet Genevieve!

THE RAVEN.

A CHRISTMAS TALE, TOLD BY A SCHOOL-BOY TO HIS LITTLE BROTHERS AND SISTERS.

UNDERNEATH an old oak tree
There was of swine a huge company,
That grunted as they crunched the mast:
For that was ripe, and fell full fast.
Then they trotted away, for the wind grew high:
One acorn they left, and no more might you spy.
Next came a Raven, that liked not such folly:
He belonged, they did say, to the witch Melan-
    choly!
Blacker was he than blackest jet,
Flew low in the rain, and his feathers not wet.
He picked up the acorn and buried it straight
By the side of a river both deep and great.

Where then did the Raven go?
He went high and low,
Over hill, over dale, did the black Raven go.
    Many autumns, many springs
    Travelled he with wandering wings:
    Many summers, many winters—
    I can't tell half his adventures.
At length he came back, and with him a She,
And the acorn was grown to a tall oak tree.
They built them a nest in the topmost bough,
And young ones they had, and were happy enow.
But soon came a woodman in leathern guise,
His brow, like a pent-house, hung over his eyes.
He'd an axe in his hand, not a word he spoke,
But with many a hem! and a sturdy stroke,
At length he brought down the poor Raven's own
    oak.
His young ones were killed; for they could not
    depart,
And their mother did die of a broken heart.
The boughs from the trunk the Woodman did
    sever;
And they floated it down on the course of the
    river.
They sawed it in planks, and its bark they did
    strip,   [ship.
And with this tree and others they made a good
The ship, it was launched; but in sight of the land
Such a storm there did rise as no ship could with-
    stand.

It bulged on a rock, and the waves rushed in fast:
Round and round flew the Raven, and cawed to
    the blast.
He heard the last shriek of the perishing souls—
See! see! o'er the topmast the mad water rolls!
    Right glad was the Raven, and off he went fleet,
And Death riding home on a cloud he did meet,
And he thank'd him again and again for this treat:
    They had taken his all, and revenge it was
    sweet!

TIME, REAL AND IMAGINARY.

AN ALLEGORY.

On the wide level of a mountain's head,
(I knew not where, but 'twas some faery place)
Their pinions, ostrich-like, for sails outspread,
Two lovely children run an endless race,
    A sister and a brother!
    That far outstripp'd the other;
  Yet ever runs she with reverted face,
And looks and listens for the boy behind:
    For he, alas! is blind!
O'er rough and smooth with even step he pass'd,
And knows not whether he be first or last.

ABSENCE.

A FAREWELL ODE ON QUITTING SCHOOL FOR JESUS COLLEGE, CAMBRIDGE.

WHERE graced with many a classic spoil
Cam rolls his reverend stream along,
I haste to urge the learned toil
That sternly chides my love-lorn song:
Ah me! too mindful of the days
Illumed by Passion's orient rays,
When Peace, and Cheerfulness, and Health
Enriched me with the best of wealth.
Ah fair delights! that o'er my soul
On Memory's wing, like shadows, fly!
Ah flowers! which Joy from Eden stole
While Innocence stood smiling by!—
But cease, fond Heart! this bootless moan:
Those Hours on rapid pinions flown
Shall yet return, by Absence crowned,
And scatter livelier roses round.
The sun, who ne'er remits his fires,
On heedless eyes may pour the day:
The Moon, that oft from Heaven retires,
Endears her renovated ray.

What though she leave the sky unblest
To mourn awhile in murky vest?
When she relumes her lovely Light,
We bless the Wanderer of the Night.

EPITAPH ON AN INFANT

ERE Sin could blight or Sorrow fade,
   Death came with friendly care;
The opening bud to Heaven conveyed,
   And bade it blossom there.

SONGS OF THE PIXIES.

The Pixies, in the superstition of Devonshire, are a race of beings invisibly small, and harmless or friendly to man. At a small distance from a village in that county, half way up a wood-covered hill, is an excavation called the Pixies' Parlour. The roots of old trees form its ceiling; and on its sides are innumerable ciphers, among which the Author discovered his own and those of his brothers, cut by the hand of their childhood. At the foot of the hill flows the river Otter.

To this place the Author, during the summer months of the year 1793, conducted a party of young ladies; one of whom, of stature elegantly small, and of complexion colourless yet clear, was proclaimed the Faery Queen. On which occasion the following Irregular Ode was written.

I.

Whom the untaught Shepherds call
   Pixies in their madrigal,
Fancy's children, here we dwell:
   Welcome, Ladies! to our cell.
Here the wren of softest note
   Builds its nest and warbles well;
Here the blackbird strains his throat;
   Welcome, Ladies! to our cell.

II.

When fades the moon to shadowy-pale,
And scuds the cloud before the gale,
Ere the Morn, all gem-bedight,
Hath streak'd the East with rosy light,
We sip the furze-flower's fragrant dews
Clad in robes of rainbow hues:
Or sport amid the shooting gleams
To the tune of distant-tinkling teams,
While lusty Labour, scouting sorrow,
Bids the dame a glad good-morrow,
Who jogs the accustomed road along,
And paces cheery to her cheering song.

III.

But not our filmy pinion
   We scorch amid the blaze of day,
When Noontide's fiery-tresséd minion
   Flashes the fervid ray.
   Aye from the sultry heat
   We to the cave retreat
O'ercanopied by huge roots intertwined
With wildest texture, blackened o'er with age:
Round them their mantle green the ivies bind,
   Beneath whose foliage pale
   Fanned by the unfrequent gale
We shield us from the Tyrant's mid-day rage.

IV.

Thither, while the murmuring throng
Of wild-bees hum their drowsy song,
By Indolence and Fancy brought,
A youthful Bard, " unknown to Fame,"
Wooes the Queen of solemn Thought,
And heaves the gentle misery of a sigh
     Gazing with tearful eye,
    As round our sandy grot appear
    Many a rudely sculptured name
     To pensive Memory dear!
Weaving gay dreams of sunny-tinctured hue
    We glance before his view ;
O'er his hush'd soul our soothing witcheries
    shed
And twine the future garland round his head.

V.

    When Evening's dusky car
    Crowned with her dewy star
Steals o'er the fading sky in shadowy flight;
    On leaves of aspen trees
    We tremble to the breeze
Veiled from the grosser ken of mortal sight.
    Or, haply, at the visionary hour,
Along our wildly-bowered sequestered walk,
We listen to the enamoured rustic's talk ;
Heave with the heavings of the maiden's breast,

Where young-eyed Loves have hid their turtle
    nest;
  Or guide of soul-subduing power
The glance, that from the half-confessing eye
Darts the fond question or the soft reply.

VI.

  Or through the mystic ringlets of the vale
  We flash our faery feet in gamesome prank:
  Or, silent-sandaled, pay our defter court,
  Circling the Spirit of the western gale,
  Where, wearied with his flower-caressing
    sport,
Supine he slumbers on a violet bank;
Then with quaint music hymn the parting gleam
By lonely Otter's sleep-persuading stream;
Or where his wave, with loud unquiet song,
Dashed o'er the rocky channel, froths along;
Or where, his silver waters smoothed to rest,
The tall tree's shadow sleeps upon his breast.

VII.

    Hence, thou lingerer, Light!
    Eve saddens into Night.
Mother of wildly-working dreams! we view
    The sombre hours, that round thee stand
    With downcast eyes (a duteous band!)
Their dark robes dripping with the heavy dew.
    Sorceress of the ebon throne!
    Thy power the Pixies own,

When round thy raven brow
Heaven's lucent roses glow,
And clouds in watery colours drest
Float in light drapery o'er thy sable vest:
What time the pale moon sheds a softer day,
Mellowing the woods beneath its pensive beam:
For 'mid the quivering light 'tis ours to play,
Aye dancing to the cadence of the stream.

VIII.

Welcome, Ladies! to the cell
Where the blameless Pixies dwell:
But thou, sweet Nymph! proclaimed our Faery
Queen,
With what obeisance meet
Thy presence shall we greet?
For lo! attendant on thy steps are seen
.   Graceful Ease in artless stole,
And white-robed Purity of soul,
With Honour's softer mien;
Mirth, of the loosely-flowing hair,
And meek-eyed Pity, eloquently fair,
Whose tearful cheeks are lovely to the view,
As snow-drop wet with dew.

IX.

Unboastful Maid! though now the Lily pale
Transparent grace thy beauties meek;
Yet ere again along the impurpling vale,
The purpling vale and elfin-haunted grove,

Young Zephyr his fresh flowers profusely throws,
  We'll tinge with livelier hues thy cheek;
And, haply, from the nectar-breathing Rose
    Extract a blush for Love!

1792

THE ROSE.

As late each flower that sweetest blows
I plucked, the Garden's pride!
Within the petals of a Rose
A sleeping Love I spied.

Around his brows a beamy wreath
Of many a lucent hue;
All purple glowed his cheek, beneath,
Inebriate with dew.

I softly seized the unguarded Power,
Nor scared his balmy rest:
And placed him, caged within the flower,
On spotless Sara's breast.

But when unweeting of the guile,
Awoke the prisoner sweet,
He struggled to escape awhile
And stamped his faery feet.

Ah! soon the soul-entrancing sight
Subdued the impatient boy!
He gazed! he thrilled with deep delight!
Then clapped his wings for joy.

"And O! he cried—"of magic kind
What charms this Throne endear!
Some other Love let Venus find—
I'll fix my empire here."

1798.

KISSES.*

Cupid, if storying legends tell aright,
Once framed a rich Elixir of Delight.
A chalice o'er love-kindled flames he fixed,
And in it Nectar and Ambrosia mixed:
With these the magic dews, which Evening brings,
Brushed from the Idalian star by faery wings:
Each tender pledge of sacred Faith he joined,
Each gentler Pleasure of the unspotted mind—
Day-dreams, whose tints with sportive brightness
     glow,
And Hope, the blameless parasite of Woe.

* See Note.

The eyeless chemist heard the process rise,
The steamy chalice bubbled up in sighs;
Sweet sounds transpired, as when the enamoured
    dove
Pours the soft murmuring of responsive love.
The finished work might Envy vainly blame,
And " Kisses" was the precious compound's name.
With half the God his Cyprian mother blest,
And breathed on Sara's lovelier lips the rest.

July, 1793.

TO SARA.

ONE kiss, dear maid! I said and sighed—
Your scorn the little boon denied.
Ah why refuse the blameless bliss?
Can danger lurk within a kiss?
Yon viewless wanderer of the vale,
The Spirit of the western gale,
At morning's break, at evening's close,
Inhales the sweetness of the Rose,
And hovers o'er the uninjured bloom
Sighing back the soft perfume.
Vigour to the Zephyr's wing
Her nectar-breathing kisses fling;

And he the glitter of the dew
Scatters on the Rose's hue.
Bashful lo! she bends her head,
And darts a blush of deeper red!
Too well those lovely lips disclose
The triumphs of the opening Rose;
O fair! O graceful! bid them prove
As passive to the breath of love.
In tender accents, faint and low,
Well-pleased I hear the whispered "No!"
The whispered "No"—how little meant!
Sweet falsehood that endears consent!
For on those lovely lips the while
Dawns the soft relenting smile,
And tempts with feigned dissuasion coy
The gentle violence of joy.

THE SIGH.

WHEN Youth his faery reign began
Ere sorrow had proclaimed me man;
While Peace the present hour beguiled,
And all the lovely prospect smiled;
Then Mary! 'mid my lightsome glee
I heav'd the painless Sigh for thee.

And when, along the waves of woe,
My harassed Heart was doomed to know
The frantic burst of Outrage keen,
And the slow Pang that gnaws unseen;
Then shipwrecked on Life's stormy sea
I heaved an anguished Sigh for thee!

But soon Reflection's power imprest
A stiller sadness on my breast;
And sickly Hope with waning eye
Was well content to droop and die:
I yielded to the stern decree,
Yet heaved a languid Sigh for thee!

And though in distant climes to roam,
A wanderer from my native home,
I fain would soothe the sense of care,
And lull to sleep the joys that were,
Thy image may not banished be—
Still, Mary! still I sigh for thee.

June, 1794.

LINES

ONCE more, sweet Stream! with slow foot wan-
    dering near,
I bless thy milky waters cold and clear.
Escaped the flashing of the noontide hours,
With one fresh garland of Pierian flowers,
(Ere from thy zephyr-haunted brink I turn,)
My languid hand shall wreathe thy mossy urn.
For not through pathless grove with murmur rude
Thou soothest the sad wood-nymph, Solitude ;
Nor thine unseen in cavern depths to well,
The hermit-fountain of some dripping cell!
Pride of the Vale! thy useful streams supply
The scattered cots and peaceful hamlet nigh.
The elfin tribe around thy friendly banks
With infant uproar and soul-soothing pranks,
Released from school, their little hearts at rest,
Launch paper navies on thy waveless breast.
The rustic here at eve with pensive look
Whistling lorn ditties leans upon his crook,
Or starting pauses with hope-mingled dread
To list the much-loved maid's accustomed tread :
She, vainly mindful of her dame's command,
Loiters, the long-filled pitcher in her hand.

Unboastful Stream! thy fount with pebbled falls
The faded form of past delight recalls,
What time the morning sun of Hope arose,
And all was joy; save when another's woes
A transient gloom upon my soul imprest,
Like passing clouds impictured on thy breast.
Life's current then ran sparkling to the noon,
Or silvery stole beneath the pensive Moon:
Ah! now it works rude brakes and thorns among,
Or o'er the rough rock bursts and foams along!

LINES ON AN AUTUMNAL EVENING.*

O THOU wild Fancy, check thy wing! No more
Those thin white flakes, those purple clouds ex-
    plore!
Nor there with happy spirits speed thy flight
Bathed in rich amber-glowing floods of light;
Nor in yon gleam, where slow descends the day,
With western peasants hail the morning ray!
Ah! rather bid the perished pleasures move,
A shadowy train, across the soul of Love!
O'er Disappointment's wintry desert fling
Each flower that wreathed the dewy locks of
    Spring,

* See Note.

When blushing, like a bride, from Hope's trim
    bower
She leapt, awakened by the pattering shower.
Now sheds the sinking Sun a deeper gleam,
Aid, lovely Sorceress! aid thy Poet's dream!
With faery wand O bid the Maid arise,
Chaste Joyance dancing in her bright-blue eyes:
As erst when from the Muses' calm abode
I came, with Learning's meed not unbestowed;
When as she twined a laurel round my brow,
And met my kiss, and half returned my vow,
O'er all my frame shot rapid my thrilled heart,
And every nerve confessed the electric dart.

  O dear deceit! I see the maiden rise,
Chaste Joyance dancing in her bright-blue eyes,
When first the lark high soaring swells his throat,
Mocks the tired eye, and scatters the loud note,
I trace her footsteps on the accustomed lawn,
I mark her glancing 'mid the gleams of dawn.
When the bent flower beneath the night dew
    weeps
And on the lake the silver lustre sleeps,
Amid the paly radiance soft and sad,
She meets my lonely path in moon-beams clad.
With her along the streamlet's brink I rove;
With her I list the warblings of the grove;
And seems in each low wind her voice to float,
Lone whispering pity in each soothing note!

Spirits of Love! ye heard her name!   Obey
The powerful spell, and to my haunt repair.
Whether on clustering pinions ye are there,
Where rich snows blossom on the myrtle trees,
Or with fond languishment around my fair
Sigh in loose luxuriance of her hair;
O heed the spell, and hither wing your way,
Like far-off music, voyaging the breeze!

Spirits! to you the infant Maid was given
Formed by the wondrous alchemy of Heaven!
No fairer Maid does Love's wide empire know,
No fairer Maid e'er heaved the bosom's snow.
A thousand Loves around her forehead fly;
A thousand Loves sit melting in her eye;
Love lights her smile—in Joy's red nectar dips
His myrtle flower, and plants it on her lips.
She speaks! and hark that passion-warbled song—
Still, Fancy! still that voice, those notes prolong.
As sweet as when that voice with rapturous falls
Shall wake the softened echoes of Heaven's halls!

O (have I sighed) were mine the wizard's rod,
Or mine the power of Proteus, changeful God!
A flower-entangled Arbour I would seem
To shield my Love from Noontide's sultry beam:
Or bloom a Myrtle, from whose odorous boughs
My Love might weave gay garlands for her brows.
When Twilight stole across the fading vale,
To fan my Love I'd be the Evening Gale;

Mourn in the soft folds of her swelling vest,
And flutter my faint pinions on her breast!
On Seraph wing I'd float a Dream by night,
To soothe my Love with shadows of delight:—
Or soar aloft to be the Spangled Skies,
And gaze upon her with a thousand eyes!

As when the savage, who his drowsy frame
Had basked beneath the Sun's unclouded flame,
Awakes amid the troubles of the air,
The skyey deluge, and white lightning's glare—
Aghast he scours before the tempest's sweep,
And sad recalls the sunny hour of sleep:—
So tossed by storms along Life's wildering way,
Mine eye reverted views that cloudless day,
When by my native brook I wont to rove,
While Hope with kisses nursed the infant Love.
Dear native brook! like Peace, so placidly
Smoothing through fertile fields thy current meek!
Dear native brook! where first young Poesy
Stared wildly-eager in her noontide dream!
Where blameless pleasures dimple Quiet's cheek,
As water-lilies ripple thy slow stream!
Dear native haunts! where Virtue still is gay,
Where Friendship's fixed star sheds a mellowed
        ray,
Where Love a crown of thornless roses wears,
Where softened Sorrow smiles within her tears;
And Memory, with a Vestal's chaste employ,
Unceasing feeds the lambent flame of joy!

No more your skylarks melting from the sight
Shall thrill the attuned heart-string with delight—
No more shall deck your pensive Pleasures sweet
With wreaths of sober hue my evening seat.
Yet dear to Fancy's eye your varied scene
Of wood, hill, dale, and sparkling brook between!
Yet sweet to Fancy's ear the warbled song,
That soars on Morning's wing your vales among!

Scenes of my Hope! the aching eye ye leave
Like yon bright hues that paint the clouds of eve!
Tearful and saddening with the saddened blaze
Mine eye the gleam pursues with wistful gaze:
Sees shades on shades with deeper tint impend,
Till chill and damp the moonless night descend.

TO A YOUNG LADY,

WITH A POEM ON THE FRENCH REVOLUTION.

MUCH on my early youth I love to dwell,
Ere yet I bade that friendly dome farewell,
Where first, beneath the echoing cloisters pale,
I heard of guilt and wondered at the tale!
Yet though the hours flew by on careless wing,
Full heavily of Sorrow would I sing.
Aye as the star of evening flung its beam
In broken radiance on the wavy stream,
My soul amid the pensive twilight gloom
Mourned with the breeze, O Lee Boo!* o'er thy
      tomb.
Where'er I wandered, Pity still was near,
Breathed from the heart and glistened in the tear:
No knell that tolled, but filled my anxious eye,
And suffering Nature wept that one should die!†

   Thus to sad sympathies I soothed my breast,
Calm, as the rainbow in the weeping West:

---

 * Lee Boo, the son of Abba Thule, Prince of the Pelew
Islands, came over to England with Captain Wilson, died of
the small-pox, and is buried in Rotherhithe churchyard. See
Keate's Account.
  † Southey's Retrospect.

When slumbering Freedom roused by high Disdain
With giant fury burst her triple chain!
Fierce on her front the blasting Dog-star glowed;
Her banners, like a midnight meteor, flowed;
Amid the yelling of the storm-rent skies
She came, and scattered battles from her eyes!
Then Exultation waked the patriot fire
And swept with wild hand the Tyrtæan lyre:
Red from the Tyrant's wound I shook the lance,
And strode in joy the reeking plains of France!

Fallen is the oppressor, friendless, ghastly, low,
And my heart aches, though Mercy struck the
        blow.
With wearied thought once more I seek the shade,
Where peaceful Virtue weaves the myrtle braid.
And O! if Eyes whose holy glances roll,
Swift messengers, and eloquent of soul;
If Smiles more winning, and a gentler Mien
Than the love-wildered Maniac's brain hath seen
Shaping celestial forms in vacant air,
If these demand the impassioned Poet's care—
If Mirth and softened Sense and Wit refined,
The blameless features of a lovely mind;
Then haply shall my trembling hand assign
No fading wreath to Beauty's saintly shrine.
Nor, Sara! thou these early flowers refuse—
Ne'er lurked the snake beneath their simple hues;
No purple bloom the Child of Nature brings
From Flattery's night-shade: as he feels he sings.

September, 1792.

IMITATED FROM OSSIAN.

The stream with languid murmur creeps,
  In Lumin's flowery vale:
Beneath the dew the Lily weeps
  Slow-waving to the gale.

" Cease, restless gale!" it seems to say,
  " Nor wake me with thy sighing!
The honours of my vernal day
  On rapid wing are flying.

"To-morrow shall the Traveller come
  Who late beheld me blooming:
His searching eye shall vainly roam
  The dreary vale of Lumin."

With eager gaze and wetted cheek
  My wonted haunts along,
Thus, faithful Maiden! thou shalt seek
  The Youth of simplest song.

But I along the breeze shall roll
  The voice of feeble power;
And dwell, the Moon-beam of thy soul,
  In slumber's nightly hour.

1794.

THE COMPLAINT OF NINATHOMA.

How long will ye round me be swelling,
  O ye blue-tumbling waves of the sea?
Not always in caves was my dwelling,
  Nor beneath the cold blast of the tree.

Through the high-sounding halls of Cathlóma
  In the steps of my beauty I strayed;
The warriors beheld Ninathóma,
  And they blessed the white-bosomed Maid!

A Ghost! by my cavern it darted!
  In moon-beams the Spirit was drest —
For lovely appear the departed
  When they visit the dreams of my rest!

But disturbed by the tempest's commotion
  Fleet the shadowy forms of delight—
Ah cease, thou shrill blast of the Ocean!
  To howl through my cavern by night.

TO A YOUNG ASS.

POOR little Foal of an oppressed Race !
I love the languid patience of thy face :
And oft with gentle hand I give thee bread,
And clap thy ragged coat, and pat thy head.
But what thy dulled Spirits hath dismayed,
That never thou dost sport along the glade ?
And (most unlike the nature of things young)
That earthward still thy moveless head is hung ?
Do thy prophetic Fears anticipate,
Meek child of Misery ! thy future fate ?
The starving meal, and all the thousand aches
" Which patient Merit of the unworthy takes ? "
Or is thy sad heart thrilled with filial pain
To see thy wretched Mother's shortened chain ?
And, truly very piteous is her lot—
Chained to a log within a narrow spot,
Where the close-eaten grass is scarcely seen,
While sweet around her waves the tempting
     green.
Poor Ass ! thy master should have learnt to show
Pity—best taught by fellowship of woe !

For much I fear me that he lives like thee,
Half famished in a land of luxury!
How askingly its footsteps hither bend,
It seems to say, "And have I then one Friend?"
Innocent Foal! thou poor despised Forlorn!
I hail thee Brother—spite of the fool's scorn!
And fain would take thee with me, in the dell
Of peace and mild Equality to dwell,
Where Toil shall call the charmer Health his bride,
And Laughter tickle Plenty's ribless side!
How thou wouldst toss thy heels in gamesome play,
And frisk about, as lamb or kitten gay!
Yea! and more musically sweet to me
Thy dissonant harsh bray of joy would be,
Than warbled melodies that soothe to rest
The aching of pale Fashion's vacant breast!

December, 1794.

TO AN INFANT.

AH! cease thy tears and sobs, my little Life!
I did but snatch away the unclasped knife:
Some safer toy will soon arrest thine eye,
And to quick laughter change this peevish cry
Poor stumbler on the rocky coast of woe,
Tutored by pain each source of pain to know!
Alike the foodful fruit and scorching fire
Awake thy eager grasp and young desire;
Alike the Good, the Ill offend thy sight,
And rouse the stormy sense of shrill affright!
Untaught, yet wise! 'mid all thy brief alarms
Thou closely clingest to thy Mother's arms,
Nestling thy little face in that fond breast
Whose anxious heavings lull thee to thy rest!
Man's breathing Miniature! thou mak'st me sigh—
A Babe art thou—and such a Thing am I!
To anger rapid and as soon appeased,
For trifles mourning and by trifles pleased,
Break Friendship's mirror with a tetchy blow,
    Yet snatch what coals of fire on Pleasure's altar
        glow!

O thou that rearest with celestial aim
The future Seraph in my mortal frame,
Thrice holy Faith! whatever thorns I meet,
As on I totter with unpractised feet,
Still let me stretch my arms and cling to thee,
Meek nurse of souls through their long infancy!

IMITATED FROM THE WELSH.

If, while my passion I impart,
  You deem my words untrue,
O place your hand upon my heart—
  Feel how it throbs for you.

Ah no! reject the thoughtless claim
  In pity to your Lover!
That thrilling touch would aid the flame,
  It wishes to discover.

DOMESTIC PEACE.

TELL me, on what holy ground
May Domestic Peace be found—
Halcyon Daughter of the skies !
Far on fearful wings she flies,
From the pomp of sceptered State,
From the rebel's noisy hate,
In a cottaged vale She dwells
Listening to the Sabbath bells !
Still around her steps are seen
Spotless Honour's meeker mien,
Love, the sire of pleasing fears,
Sorrow, smiling through her tears,
And, conscious of the past employ,
Memory, bosom-spring of joy.

1794

LINES

WRITTEN AT THE KING'S ARMS, ROSS, FORMERLY
THE HOUSE OF "THE MAN OF ROSS."

RICHER than Miser o'er his countless hoards,
Nobler than Kings, or king-polluted Lords,
Here dwelt the Man of Ross! O Traveller, hear!
Departed Merit claims a reverent tear.
Friend to the friendless, to the sick man health,
With generous joy he viewed his modest wealth;
He heard the widow's heaven-breathed prayer of
 praise,
He marked the sheltered orphan's tearful gaze,
Or where the sorrow-shrivelled captive lay,
Poured the bright blaze of Freedom's noontide
 ray.
Beneath this roof if thy cheered moments pass,
Fill to the good man's name one grateful glass:
To higher zest shall Memory wake thy soul,
And Virtue mingle in the ennobled bowl.
But if, like me, through life's distressful scene
Lonely and sad thy pilgrimage hath been;
And if thy breast with heart-sick anguish fraught,
Thou journeyest onward tempest-tossed in
 thought;
Here cheat thy cares! in generous visions melt,
And dream of Goodness, thou hast never felt!

TO A FRIEND,

TOGETHER WITH AN UNFINISHED POEM.

THUS far my scanty brain hath built the rhyme
Elaborate and swelling ; yet the heart
Not owns it.   From thy spirit-breathing powers
I ask not now, my Friend! the aiding verse,
Tedious to thee, and from thy anxious thought
Of dissonant mood.   In fancy (well I know)
From business wandering far and local cares,
Thou creepest round a dear-loved Sister's bed
With noiseless step, and watchest the faint look,
Soothing each pang with fond solicitude,
And tenderest tones medicinal of love.
I too a Sister had, an only Sister—
She loved me dearly, and I doted on her!
To her I poured forth all my puny sorrows
(As a sick Patient in his Nurse's arms)
And of the heart those hidden maladies
That shrink ashamed from even Friendship's eye.
O! I have woke at midnight, and have wept,
Because she was not!—Cheerily, dear Charles!
Thou thy best friend shalt cherish many a year;
Such warm presages feel I of high Hope.
For not uninterested the dear maid.

I've viewed—her soul affectionate yet wise,
Her polished wit as mild as lambent glories
That play around a sainted infant's head.
(He knows, the Spirit that in secret sees,
Of whose omniscient and all-spreading Love
Aught to implore were impotence of mind)*
That my mute thoughts are sad before His throne,
Prepared, when He his healing ray vouchsafes,
To pour forth thanksgiving with lifted heart,
And praise Him Gracious with a Brother's joy!

December, 1794.

* I utterly recant the sentiment contained in the lines—

> Of whose omniscient and all-spreading Love
> Aught to *implore* were impotence of mind,

it being written in Scripture, "*Ask*, and it shall be given you;" and my human reason being, moreover, convinced of the propriety of offering petitions as well as thanksgivings to Deity.—S. T. C., 1797.

TO THE NIGHTINGALE.

SISTER of love-lorn Poets, Philomel!
How many Bards in city garret pent,
While at their window they with downward eye
Mark the faint lamp-beam on the kennelled mud,
And listen to the drowsy cry of watchmen,
(Those hoarse unfeathered nightingales of time!)
How many wretched Bards address *thy* name,
And Hers, the full-orbed Queen, that shines above.
But I *do* hear thee, and the high bough mark,
Within whose mild moon-mellowed foliage hid
Thou warblest sad thy pity-pleading strains.
O! I have listened, till my working soul,
Waked by those strains to thousand phantasies,
Absorbed, hath ceased to listen! Therefore oft
I hymn thy name; and with a proud delight
Oft will I tell thee, Minstrel of the Moon!
" Most musical, most melancholy " Bird!
That all thy soft diversities of tone,
Tho' sweeter far than the delicious airs
That vibrate from a white-armed lady's harp,
What time the languishment of lonely love
Melts in her eye, and heaves her breast of snow,
Are not so sweet, as is the voice of her,
My Sara,—best beloved of human kind!
When, breathing the pure soul of tenderness,
She thrills me with the Husband's promised name!

1794.

LINES ON A FRIEND

WHO DIED OF A FRENZY FEVER INDUCED BY
CALUMNIOUS REPORTS.

EDMUND! thy grave with aching eye I scan,
And inly groan for Heaven's poor outcast—Man!
'Tis tempest all or gloom : in early youth,
If gifted with the Ithuriel lance of Truth,
We force to start amid her feigned caress
Vice, siren-hag! in native ugliness;
A Brother's fate will haply rouse the tear,
And on we go in heaviness and fear!
But if our fond hearts call to Pleasure's bower
Some pigmy Folly in a careless hour,   [ground,
The faithless guest shall stamp the enchanted
And mingled forms of Misery rise around:
Heart-fretting Fear, with pallid look aghast,
That courts the future woe to hide the past;
Remorse, the poisoned arrow in his side;
And loud lewd Mirth, to Anguish close allied;
Till Frenzy, fierce-eyed child of moping pain,
Darts her hot lightning-flash athwart the brain.
Rest, injured shade! Shall Slander squatting near
Spit her cold venom in a dead Man's ear?
'Twas thine to feel the sympathetic glow
In Merit's joy, and Poverty's meek woe;
Thine all, that cheer the moment as it flies,
The zoneless Cares, and smiling Courtesies.

Nursed in thy heart the firmer Virtues grew,
And in thy heart they withered ! Such chill dew
Wan indolence on each young blossom shed ;
And Vanity her filmy network spread
With eye that rolled around in asking gaze,
And tongue that trafficked in the trade of praise.
Thy follies such ! the hard world marked them well !
Were they more wise, the proud who never fell ?
Rest, injured Shade ! the poor man's grateful
          prayer,
On heavenward wing thy wounded soul shall bear.
As oft at twilight gloom thy grave I pass,
And sit me down upon its recent grass,
With introverted eye I contemplate
Similitude of soul, perhaps of—fate.
To me hath Heaven with bounteous hand assigned
Energic Reason and a shaping mind,
The daring ken of Truth, the Patriot's part,
And Pity's sigh, that breathes the gentle heart.
Sloth-jaundiced all ! and from my graspless hand
Drop Friendship's precious pearls, like hour-glass
          sand.
I weep, yet stoop not ! the faint anguish flows,
A dreamy pang in Morning's feverish doze.

    Is this piled earth our Being's passless mound ?
Tell me, cold grave ! is death with poppies crowned ?
Tired Sentinel ! 'Mid fitful starts I nod,
And fain would sleep, though pillowed on a clod !

November, 1794.

MONODY ON THE DEATH OF CHATTERTON.*

O WHAT a wonder seems the fear of death,
Seeing how gladly we all sink to sleep,
Babes, Children, Youths, and Men,
Night following night for threescore years and ten!
But doubly strange, where life is but a breath
To sigh and pant with, up Want's rugged steep.

Away, Grim Phantom! Scorpion King, away!
Reserve thy terrors and thy stings display
For coward Wealth and Guilt in robes of state!
Lo! by the grave I stand of one, for whom
A prodigal Nature and a niggard Doom
(That all bestowing, this withholding all,)
Made each chance knell from distant spire or dome
Sound like a seeking Mother's anxious call,
Return, poor Child! Home, weary Truant, home!

Thee, Chatterton! these unblest stones protect
From want, and the bleak freezings of neglect.
Too long before the vexing Storm-blast driven
Here hast thou found repose! beneath this sod!

* See Note.

Thou! O vain word! thou dwell'st not with the
    clod!
Amid the shining Host of the Forgiven
Thou at the throne of Mercy and thy God
The triumph of redeeming Love dost hymn
(Believe it, O my soul!) to harps of Seraphim.

Yet oft, perforce, ('tis suffering Nature's call)
I weep, that heaven-born Genius so should fall;
And oft, in Fancy's saddest hour, my soul
Averted shudders at the poisoned bowl.
Now groans my sickening heart, as still I view
    Thy corse of livid hue;
Now indignation checks the feeble sigh,   [eye!
Or flashes through the tear that glistens in mine

Is this the land of song-ennobled line?
Is this the land, where Genius ne'er in vain
    Poured forth his lofty strain?
Ah me! yet Spenser, gentlest bard divine,
Beneath chill Disappointment's shade,
His weary limbs in lonely anguish laid;
    And o'er her darling dead
    Pity hopeless hung her head,
While "mid the pelting of that merciless storm,"
Sunk to the cold earth Otway's famished form!

Sublime of thought, and confident of fame
From vales where Avon winds the Minstrel* came.

  * Avon, a river near Bristol, the birthplace of Chatterton.

Light-hearted youth! aye, as he hastes **along,**
He meditates the future song,
How dauntless Ælla fray'd the Dacyan foe;
　And while the numbers flowing strong
　In eddies whirl, in surges throng,
Exulting in the spirits' genial throe
In tides of power his life-blood seems to flow.

And now his cheeks with deeper ardours flame,
His eyes have glorious meanings, that declare
More than the light of outward day shines there,
A holier triumph and a sterner aim!
Wings grow within him, and he soars above
Or Bard's or Minstrel's lay of war or love.
Friend to the friendless, to the Sufferer health,
He hears the widow's prayer, the good man's
　　　praise;
To scenes of bliss transmutes his fancied wealth,
And young and old shall now see happy days.
On many a waste he bids trim Gardens rise,
Gives the blue sky to many a prisoner's eyes;
And now in wrath he grasps the patriot steel,
And her own iron rod he makes Oppression
　　　feel.

Sweet Flower of Hope! free Nature's genial
　　　child!
That didst so fair disclose thy early bloom,
Filling the wide air with a rich perfume!
For thee in vain all heavenly aspects smiled;

From the hard world brief respite could they win—
The frost nipped sharp without, the canker preyed
    within!
Ah! where are fled the charms of vernal Grace,
And Joy's wild gleams that lightened o'er thy face?
Youth of tumultuous soul, and haggard eye!
Thy wasted form, thy hurried steps I view,
On thy wan forehead starts the lethal dew,
And oh! the anguish of that shuddering sigh!

    Such were the struggles of the gloomy hour,
      When Care, of withered brow,
    Prepared the poison's death-cold power:
  Already to thy lips was raised the bowl,
      When near thee stood Affection meek,
    (Her bosom bare, and wildly pale her cheek.)
Thy sullen gaze she bade thee roll
On scenes that well might melt thy soul;
Thy native cot she flashed upon thy view,
Thy native cot, where still, at close of day,
Peace smiling sate, and listened to thy lay;
Thy Sister's shrieks she bade thee hear,
And mark thy Mother's thrilling tear;
      See, see her breast's convulsive throe,
      Her silent agony of woe!
Ah! dash the poisoned chalice from thy hand!

And thou had'st dashed it, at her soft command,
But that Despair and Indignation rose,
And told again the story of thy woes:

Told the keen insult of the unfeeling heart
The dread dependence on the low-born mind;
Told every pang, with which thy soul must smart,
Neglect, and grinning Scorn, and Want combined!
Recoiling quick, thou bad'st the friend of pain
Roll the black tide of Death through every freez-
    ing vein!

      O Spirit blest!
Whether the Eternal's throne around,
Amidst the blaze of Seraphim,
Thou pourest forth the grateful hymn;
Or soaring thro' the blest domain
Enrapturest Angels with thy strain,—
Grant me, like thee, the lyre to sound,
Like thee with fire divine to glow;—
But ah! when rage the waves of woe,
Grant me with firmer breast to meet their hate,
And soar beyond the storm with upright eye elate!

Ye woods! that wave o'er Avon's rocky steep,
To Fancy's ear sweet is your murmuring deep!
For here she loves the cypress wreath to weave
Watching, with wistful eye, the saddening tints of
    eve.
Here, far from men, amid this pathless grove,
In solemn thought the Minstrel wont to rove,
Like star-beam on the slow sequestered tide
Lone-glittering, thro' the high tree branching
    wide.

And here, in Inspiration's eager hour,
When most the big soul feels the mastering power,
   These wilds, these caverns roaming o'er,
   Round which the screaming sea-gulls soar,
With wild unequal steps he passed along,
Oft pouring on the winds a broken song :
Anon, upon some rough rock's fearful brow
Would pause abrupt—and gaze upon the waves
   below.

Poor Chatterton ! he sorrows for thy fate   [late.
Who would have praised and loved thee, ere too
Poor Chatterton ! farewell ! of darkest hues
This chaplet cast I on thy unshaped tomb ;
But dare no longer on the sad theme muse,
Lest kindred woes persuade a kindred doom :
For oh ! big gall-drops, shook from Folly's wing,
Have blackened the fair promise of my spring ;
And the stern Fate transpierced with viewless dart
The last pale Hope that shivered at my heart !

Hence, gloomy thoughts ! no more my soul shall
   dwell
On joys that were ! No more endure to weigh
The shame and anguish of the evil day,
Wisely forgetful ! O'er the ocean swell
Sublime of Hope I seek the cottaged dell
Where Virtue calm with careless step may stray ;
And, dancing to the moonlight roundelay,
The wizard Passions weave a holy spell !

O Chatterton! that thou wert yet alive!
Sure thou wouldst spread the canvas to the gale,
And love with us the tinkling team to drive
O'er peaceful Freedom's undivided dale;
And we, at sober eve, would round thee throng,
Would hang, enraptured, on thy stately song,
And greet with smiles the young-eyed Poesy
All deftly masked, as hoar Antiquity.

Alas, vain Phantasies! the fleeting brood
Of Woe self-solaced in her dreamy mood!
Yet will I love to follow the sweet dream,
Where Susquehanna pours his untamed stream,
And on some hill, whose forest-frowning side
Waves o'er the murmurs of his calmer tide,
Will raise a solemn Cenotaph to thee,
Sweet Harper of time-shrouded Minstrelsy!
And there soothed sadly by the dirgeful wind,
Muse on the sore ills I had left behind.

1790-96.

SONNET I.

"Content, as random Fancies might inspire,
If his weak harp at times or lonely lyre
He struck with desultory hand, and drew
Some softened tones to Nature not untrue."

BOWLES.

My heart has thanked thee, Bowles! for those
    soft strains
Whose sadness soothes me, like the murmuring
Of wild bees in the sunny showers of spring!
For hence not callous to the mourner's pains
Through Youth's gay prime and thornless paths I
    went:
And when the mightier throes of mind began,
And drove me forth, a thought-bewildered man,
Their mild and manliest melancholy lent
A mingled charm, such as the pang consigned
To slumber, though the big tear it renewed;
Bidding a strange mysterious Pleasure brood
Over the wavy and tumultuous mind,
As the great Spirit erst with plastic sweep
Moved on the darkness of the unformed deep.

SONNET II.

As late I lay in slumber's shadowy vale,
With wetted cheek and in a mourner's guise,
I saw the sainted form of Freedom rise:
She spake! not sadder moans the autumnal gale—
" Great Son of Genius! sweet to me thy name,
Ere in an evil hour with altered voice
Thou bad'st Oppression's hireling crew rejoice,
Blasting with wizard spell my laurelled fame.
Yet never, Burke! thou drank'st Corruption's
       bowl!
Thee stormy Pity and the cherished lure
Of Pomp, and proud Precipitance of soul
Wildered with meteor fires. Ah Spirit pure!
That error's mist had left thy purged eye:
So might I clasp thee with a Mother's joy! "

Not always should the tear's ambrosial dew
Roll its soft anguish down thy furrowed cheek!
Not always heaven-breathed tones of suppliance
    meek
Beseem thee, Mercy!   Yon dark Scowler view,
Who with proud words of dear-loved Freedom
    came—
More blasting than the mildew from the South!
And kissed his country with Iscariot mouth
(Ah! foul apostate from his Father's fame!)
Then fixed her on the cross of deep distress,
And at safe distance marks the thirsty lance
Pierce her big side!   But O! if some strange
    trance
The eyelids of thy stern-browed Sister press,
Seize, Mercy! thou more terrible the brand,
And hurl her thunderbolts with fiercer hand!

* See Note.

SONNET IV.

THOUGH, roused by that dark Vizir, Riot rude
Have driven our Priestley o'er the ocean swell;
Though Superstition and her wolfish brood
Bay his mild radiance, impotent and fell;
Calm in his halls of brightness he shall dwell!
For lo! Religion at his strong behest
Starts with mild anger from the Papal spell,
And flings to earth her tinsel-glittering vest,
Her mitred state and cumbrous pomp unholy;
And Justice wakes to bid the Oppressor wail
Insulting aye the wrongs of patient Folly:
And, from her dark retreat by Wisdom won,
Meek Nature slowly lifts her matron veil
To smile with fondness on her gazing son!

SONNET V.

WHEN British Freedom for a happier land
Spread her broad wings, that fluttered with
      affright,
Erskine! thy voice she heard, and paused her flight
Sublime of hope! For dreadless thou didst stand
(Thy censer glowing with the hallowed flame)
A hireless Priest before the insulted shrine,
And at her altar pour the stream divine
Of unmatched eloquence. Therefore thy name
Her sons shall venerate, and cheer thy breast
With blessings heavenward breathed. And when
      the doom
Of Nature bids thee die, beyond the tomb
Thy light shall shine: as sunk beneath the West
Though the great Summer Sun eludes our gaze,
Still burns wide Heaven with his distended blaze.

SONNET VI.

IT was some Spirit, Sheridan ! that breathed
O'er thy young mind such wildly various power !
My soul hath mark'd thee in her shaping hour,
Thy temples with Hymettian flow'rets wreathed :
And sweet thy voice, as when o'er Laura's bier
Sad music trembled through Vauclusa's glade ;
Sweet, as at dawn the love-lorn Serenade
That wafts soft dreams to Slumber's listening ear.
Now patriot Rage and Indignation high
Swell the full tones ! And now thine eye-beams
    dance
Meanings of Scorn and Wit's quaint revelry !
Writhes inly from the bosom-probing glance
The Apostate by the brainless rout adored,
As erst that elder Fiend beneath great Michael's
    sword.

SONNET VII.

O WHAT a loud and fearful shriek was there,
As though a thousand souls one death-groan
      poured!
Ah me! they saw beneath a hireling's sword
Their Kosciusko fall! Though the swart air
(As pauses the tired Cossac's barbarous yell
Of triumph) on the chill and midnight gale
Rises with frantic burst or sadder swell
The dirge of murdered Hope! while Freedom
      pale
Bends in such anguish o'er her destined bier,
As if from eldest time some Spirit meek
Had gathered in a mystic urn each tear
That ever on a patriot's furrowed cheek
Fit channel found, and she had drained the bowl
In the mere wilfulness, and sick despair of soul!

SONNET VIII.

As when far off the warbled strains are heard
That soar on Morning's wing the vales among,
Within his cage the imprisoned matin bird
Swells the full chorus with a generous song:
He bathes no pinion in the dewy light,
No Father's joy, no Lover's bliss he shares,
Yet still the rising radiance cheers his sight ;
His fellows' freedom soothes the captive's cares!
Thou, Fayette! who didst wake with startling
       voice
Life's better sun from that long wintry night,
Thus in thy Country's triumphs shalt rejoice,
And mock with raptures high the dungeon's might:
For lo! the morning struggles into day,
And Slavery's spectres shriek and vanish from
       the ray !

SONNET IX.

Not, Stanhope! with the Patriot's doubtful name
I mock thy worth—Friend of the Human Race!
Since, scorning Faction's low and partial aim,
Aloof thou wendest in thy stately pace,
Thyself redeeming from that leprous stain,
Nobility : and aye unterrify'd
Pourest thine Abdiel warnings on the train
That sit complotting with rebellious pride
'Gainst her,* who from the Almighty's bosom leapt
With whirlwind arm, fierce Minister of Love !
Wherefore, ere Virtue o'er thy tomb hath wept,
Angels shall lead thee to the throne above :
And thou from forth its clouds shalt hear the voice,
Champion of Freedom and her God! rejoice!

* Gallic Liberty.

SONNET X.

Thou gentle look, that didst my soul beguile,
Why hast thou left me ? Still in some fond dream
Revisit my sad heart, auspicious Smile!
As falls on closing flowers the lunar beam :
What time, in sickly mood, at parting day
I lay me down and think of happier years ;
Of Joys, that glimmered in Hope's twilight ray,
Then left me darkling in a vale of tears.
O pleasant days of Hope—for ever gone !—
Could I recall you !—But that thought is vain.
Availeth not Persuasion's sweetest tone
To lure the fleet-winged Travellers back again :
Yet fair, though faint, their images shall gleam
Like the bright Rainbow on a willowy stream.

SONNET XI.

PALE Roamer through the night! thou poor
    Forlorn!
Remorse that man on his death-bed possess,
Who in the credulous hour of tenderness
Betrayed, then cast thee forth to want and scorn!
The world is pitiless: the chaste one's pride
Mimic of Virtue, scowls on thy distress:
Thy Loves and they that envied thee, deride:
And Vice alone will shelter wretchedness!
O! I could weep to think, that there should be
Cold-bosomed lewd ones, who endure to place
Foul offerings on the shrine of misery,
And force from famine the caress of Love;
May He shed healing on thy sore disgrace,
He, the great Comforter that rules above!

SONNET XII.

SWEET Mercy! how my very heart has bled
To see thee, poor Old Man! and thy gray hairs
Hoar with the snowy blast: while no one cares
To clothe thy shrivelled limbs and palsied head.
My Father! throw away this tattered vest
That mocks thy shivering! take my garment—use
A young man's arm! I'll melt these frozen dews
That hang from thy white beard and numb thy
      breast.
My Sara too shall tend thee, like a child:
And thou shall talk, in our fire-side's recess,
Of purple pride, that scowls on wretchedness.
He did not so, the Galilean mild,
Who met the Lazars turned from rich men's doors,
And called them Friends, and healed their noisome
      sores!

SONNET XIII.

TO THE AUTUMNAL MOON.

MILD Splendour of the various-vested Night!
Mother of wildly-working visions! hail!
I watch thy gliding, while with watery light
Thy weak eye glimmers through a fleecy veil;
And when thou lovest thy pale orb to shroud
Behind the gathered blackness lost on high;
And when thou dartest from the wind-rent cloud
Thy placid lightning o'er the awakened sky.
Ah such is Hope! as changeful and as fair!
Now dimly peering on the wistful sight;
Now hid behind the dragon-winged Despair:
But soon emerging in her radiant might
She o'er the sorrow-clouded breast of Care
Sails, like a meteor kindling in its flight.

SONNET XIV.

THOU bleedest, my poor Heart! and thy distress
Reasoning I ponder with a scornful smile,
And probe thy sore wound sternly, though the
    while
Swoln be mine eye and dim with heaviness.
Why didst thou listen to Hope's whisper bland?
Or, listening, why forget the healing tale,
When Jealousy, with feverous fancies pale,
Jarred thy fine fibres with a maniac's hand?
Faint was that Hope, and rayless!—Yet 'twas fair,
And soothed with many a dream the hour of rest:
Thou shouldst have loved it most when most
    opprest,
And nursed it with an agony of care,
Even as a Mother her sweet infant heir
That wan and sickly droops upon her breast!

SONNET XV.

TO THE AUTHOR OF "THE ROBBERS."

SCHILLER! that hour I would have wished to die,
If through the shuddering midnight I had sent
From the dark dungeon of the tower time-rent
That fearful voice, a famished Father's cry—
Lest in some after moment aught more mean
Might stamp me mortal! A triumphant shout
Black Horror screamed, and all her goblin rout
Diminished shrunk from the more withering scene
Ah! Bard tremendous in sublimity!
Could I behold thee in thy loftier mood
Wandering at eve with finely frenzied eye
Beneath some vast old tempest-swinging wood!
Awhile with mute awe gazing I would brood:
Then weep aloud in a wild ecstasy!

LINES

COMPOSED WHILE CLIMBING THE LEFT ASCENT OF
BROCKLEY COOMB, SOMERSETSHIRE,
MAY, 1795.

WITH many a pause and oft reverted eye
I climb the Coomb's ascent: sweet songsters near
Warble in shade their wild-wood melody:
Far off the unvarying cuckoo soothes my ear.
Up scour the startling stragglers of the flock
That on green plots o'er precipices browse:
From the deep fissures of the naked rock
The yewtree bursts! Beneath its dark green
      boughs
('Mid which the May-thorn blends its blossoms
      white)
Where broad smooth stones jut out in mossy seats,
I rest:—and now have gained the topmost site.
Ah! what a luxury of landscape meets
My gaze! Proud towers, and cots more dear to me,
Elm-shadow'd fields, and prospect-bounding sea!
Deep sighs my lonely heart: I drop the tear:
Enchanting spot! O were my Sara here!

LINES

O PEACE, that on a lilied bank dost love
To rest thine head beneath an olive tree,
I would that from the pinions of thy dove
One quill withouten pain yplucked might be!
For O! I wish my Sara's frowns to flee,
And fain to her some soothing song would write,
Lest she resent my rude discourtesy,
Who vowed to meet her ere the morning light,
But broke my plighted word—ah! false and re-
    creant wight!

Last night as I my weary head did pillow
With thoughts of my dissevered Fair engrost,
Chill Fancy drooped wreathing herself with
    willow,
As though my breast entombed a pining ghost.
"From some blest couch, young Rapture's bridal
    boast,
Rejected Slumber! hither wing thy way;
But leave me with the matin hour, at most!
As night-closed floweret to the orient ray,
My sad heart will expand, when I the Maid
    survey."

But Love, who heard the silence of my thought,
Contrived a too successful wile, I ween:
And whispered to himself, with malice fraught—
"Too long our Slave the Damsel's smiles hath
     seen:
To-morrow shall he ken her altered mien!"
He spake, and ambushed lay, till on my bed
The morning shot her dewy glances keen,
When as I 'gan to lift my drowsy head—
"Now, Bard! I'll work thee woe!" the laughing
     Elfin said.

Sleep, softly-breathing God! his downy wing
Was fluttering now, as quickly to depart;
When twanged an arrow from Love's mystic
     string,
With pathless wound it pierced him to the heart.
Was there some magic in the Elfin's dart?
Or did he strike my couch with wizard lance?
For straight so fair a Form did upwards start
(No fairer decked the bowers of old Romance)
That Sleep enamoured grew, nor moved from his
     sweet trance!

My Sara came, with gentlest look divine;
Bright shone her eye, yet tender was its beam:
I felt the pressure of her lip to mine!
Whispering we went, and Love was all our
     theme—
Love pure and spotless, as at first, I deem,

He sprang from Heaven! Such joys with Sleep
    did 'bide, ,
That I the living image of my dream
Fondly forgot. Too late I woke, and sigh'd—
"O! how shall I behold my Love at even-tide!"

July, 1795.

TO THE AUTHOR OF POEMS

PUBLISHED ANONYMOUSLY AT BRISTOL, IN
SEPTEMBER, 1795.

UNBOASTFUL Bard! whose verse concise yet clear
Tunes to smooth melody unconquered sense,
May your fame fadeless live, as " never-sere "
The Ivy wreathes yon Oak, whose broad defence
Embowers me from Noon's sultry influence !
For like that nameless Rivulet stealing by,
Your modest verse to musing quiet dear,
Is rich with tints heaven-borrowed ; the charmed
    eye
Shall gaze undazzled there, and love the softened
    sky.

Circling the base of the Poetic mount
A stream there is, which rolls in lazy flow
Its coal-black waters from Oblivion's fount;

The vapour-poisoned Birds, that fly too low,
Fall with dead swoop, and to the bottom go.
Escaped that heavy stream on pinion fleet
Beneath the Mountain's lofty frowning brow,
Ere aught of perilous ascent you meet,
A mead of mildest charm delays the unlabouring
    feet.

Not there the cloud-climbed rock, sublime and
    vast,
That like some giant king o'erglooms the hill;
Nor there the Pine-grove to the midnight blast
Makes solemn music!   But the unceasing rill
To the soft Wren or Lark's descending trill
Murmurs sweet under-song mid jasmine bowers.
In this same pleasant medow, at your will
I ween, you wandered—there collecting flowers
Of sober tint, and herbs of med'cinable powers!

There for the monarch-murdered Soldier's tomb
You wove the unfinished wreath of saddest hues; *
And to that holier chaplet added bloom,
Besprinkling it with Jordan's cleansing dews.†
But lo! your Henderson awakes the Muse—‡
His Spirit beckoned from the Mountain's height!
You left the plain and soared 'mid richer views!

    * War, a Fragment.
    † John the Baptist, a Poem.
    ‡ Monody on John Henderson.

So Nature mourned, when sunk the First Day's
      light,
With stars, unseen before, spangling her robe of
      night.

Still soar, my Friend, those richer views among,
Strong, rapid, fervent, flashing Fancy's beam !
Virtue and Truth shall love your gentler song,
But Poesy demands the impassioned theme ;
Waked by Heaven's silent dews at Eve's mild
      gleam
What balmy sweets Pomona breathes around !
But if the vext air rush a stormy stream,
Or Autumn's shrill gust moan in plaintive sound,
With fruits and flowers she loads the tempest-
      honoured ground.

LINES

WRITTEN AT SHURTON BARS, NEAR BRIDGEWATER,
SEPTEMBER, 1795, IN ANSWER TO A LETTER
FROM BRISTOL.

" Good verse most good, and bad verse then seems better,
Received from absent friend, by way of Letter,
For what so sweet can laboured lays impart
As one rude rhyme warm from a friendly heart."

ANON.

NOR travels my meandering eye
The starry wilderness on high ;
  Nor now with curious sight
I mark the glow-worm, as I pass,
Move with " green radiance" through the grass,
  An emerald of light.

O ever present to my view !
My wafted spirit is with you,
  And soothes your boding fears :
I see you all oppressed with gloom
Sit lonely in that cheerless room—
  Ah me ! You are in tears !

Beloved Woman ! did you fly
Chilled Friendship's dark disliking eye,
  Or Mirth's untimely din ?

With cruel weight these trifles press
A temper sore with tenderness,
   When aches the Void within.

But why with sable wand unblest
Should Fancy rouse within my breast
   Dim-visaged shapes of dread?
Untenanting its beauteous clay,
My Sara's soul has winged its way,
   And hovers round my head!

I felt it prompt the tender dream,
When slowly sank the day's last gleam;
   You roused each gentler sense,
As, sighing o'er the blossom's bloom,
Meek Evening wakes its soft perfume
   With viewless influence.

And hark, my Love! The sea-breeze moans
Through yon reft house! O'er rolling stones
   In bold ambitious sweep,
The onward-surging tides supply
The silence of the cloudless sky
   With mimic thunders deep.

Dark reddening from the channelled Isle *
(Where stands one solitary pile
   Unslated by the blast)

     * The Holmes, in the Bristol Channel.

The watchfire, like a sullen star,
Twinkles to many a dozing tar
   Rude cradled on the mast.

Even there—beneath that light-house tower—
In the tumultuous evil hour,
   Ere Peace with Sara came,
Time was, I should have thought it sweet
To count the echoings of my feet,
   And watch the storm-vexed flame.

And there in black soul-jaundiced fit,
A sad gloom-pampered Man to sit,
   And listen to the roar:
When mountain surges bellowing deep
With an uncouth monster leap
   Plunged foaming on the shore.

Then by the lightning's blaze to mark
Some toiling tempest-shattered bark;
   Her vain distress-guns hear;
And when a second sheet of light
Flashed o'er the blackness of the night—
   To see no vessel there!

But Fancy now more gaily sings;
Or if awhile she droop her wings,
   As sky-larks 'mid the corn,
On summer fields she grounds her breast:
The oblivious poppy o'er her nest
   Nods, till returning morn.

O mark those smiling tears, that swell
The opened rose !   From heaven they fell,
   And with the sun-beam blend.
Blest visitations from above,
Such are the tender woes of Love,
   Fostering the heart they bend !

When stormy Midnight howling round
Beats on our roof with clattering sound,
   To me your arms you'll stretch :
Great God ! you'll say—To us so kind,
O shelter from this loud bleak wind
   The houseless, friendless wretch !

The tears that tremble down your cheek,
Shall bathe my kisses chaste and meek
   In Pity's dew divine ;
And from your heart the sighs that steal
Shall make your rising bosom feel
   The answering swell of mine !

How oft, my Love ! with shapings sweet
I paint the moment, we shall meet !
   With eager speed I dart—
I seize you in the vacant air,
And fancy, with a husband's care
   I press you to my heart !

'Tis said, in Summer's evening hour
Flashes the golden-colored flower

A fair electric flame :
And so shall flash my love-charged eye
When all the heart's big ecstasy
   Shoots rapid through the frame !

LINES

TO A FRIEND IN ANSWER TO A MELANCHOLY LETTER.

AWAY, those cloudy looks, that labouring sigh,
The peevish offspring of a sickly hour !
Nor meanly thus complain of Fortune's power,
When the blind gamester throws a luckless
   die.

Yon setting sun flashes a mournful gleam
Behind those broken clouds, his stormy train :
To-morrow shall the many-colored main
In brightness roll beneath his orient beam !

Wild, as the autumnal gust, the hand of Time
Flies o'er his mystic lyre : in shadowy dance
The alternate groups of Joy and Grief advance
Responsive to his varying strains sublime !

Bears on its wing each hour a load of Fate ;
The swain, who, lulled by Seine's mild murmurs,
    led
His weary oxen to their nightly shed,
To-day may rule a tempest-troubled State.

Nor shall not Fortune with a vengeful smile
Survey the sanguinary despot's might,
And haply hurl the pageant from his height
Unwept to wander in some savage isle.

There shiv'ring sad beneath the tempest's frown
Round his tired limbs to wrap the purple vest ;
And, mixed with nails and beads, an equal jest !
Barter for food the jewels of his crown.

RELIGIOUS MUSINGS;

A DESULTORY POEM, WRITTEN ON THE CHRISTMAS EVE OF 1794.

This is the time, when most divine to hear,
The voice of adoration rouses me,
As with a Cherub's trump : and high upborne,
Yea, mingling with the choir, I seem to view
The vision of the heavenly multitude,
Who hymned the song of peace o'er Bethlehem's
      fields !
Yet thou more bright than all the angel blaze,
That harbingered thy birth, Thou, Man of Woes!
Despised Galilean ! For the great
Invisible (by symbols only seen,)
With a peculiar and surpassing light
Shines from the visage of the oppressed good man,
When heedless of himself the scourged Saint
Mourns for the oppressor. Fair the vernal mead,
Fair the high grove, the sea, the sun, the stars ;
True impress each of their creating Sire !
Yet nor high grove, nor many-coloured mead,
Nor the green Ocean with his thousand isles,
Nor the starred azure, nor the sovran Sun,

E'er with such majesty of portraiture
Imaged the supreme beauty uncreate,
As thou, meek Saviour! at the fearful hour
When thy insulted anguish winged the prayer
Harped by Archangels, when they sing of mercy!
Which when the Almighty heard from forth his
   throne
Diviner light filled Heaven with ecstasy!
Heaven's hymnings paused: and Hell her yawn-
   ing mouth
Closed a brief moment.

       Lovely was the death
Of Him whose life was Love! Holy with power
He on the thought-benighted Sceptic beamed
Manifest Godhead, melting into day
What floating mists of dark idolatry
Broke and misshaped the omnipresent Sire:
And first by Fear uncharmed the drowsed Soul,
Till of its nobler nature it 'gan feel
Dim recollections; and thence soared to Hope,
Strong to believe whate'er of mystic good
The Eternal dooms for his immortal sons.
From Hope and firmer Faith to perfect Love
Attracted and absorbed: and centred there
God only to behold, and know, and feel,
Till by exclusive consciousness of God
All self-annihilated it shall make
God its identity: God all in all!   —
We and our Father one!

And blest are they,
Who in this fleshly World, the elect of Heaven,
Their strong eye darting through the deeds of men,
Adore with steadfast unpresuming gaze
Him, Nature's essence, mind, and energy!
And gazing, trembling, patiently ascend,
Treading beneath their feet all visible things
As steps, that upward to their Father's throne
Lead gradual—else nor glorified nor loved.
They nor contempt embosom nor revenge:
For they dare know of what may seem deform
The Supreme Fair sole operant: in whose sight
All things are pure, his strong controlling Love
Alike from all educing perfect good.
Theirs too celestial courage, inly armed—
Dwarfing Earth's giant brood, what time they muse
On their great Father, great beyond compare!
And marching onwards view high o'er their heads
His waving banners of Omnipotence.

Who the Creator love, created might
Dread not: within their tents no terrors walk.
For they are holy things before the Lord
Aye unprofaned, though Earth should league with
        Hell;
God's altar grasping with an eager hand,
Fear, the wild-visaged, pale, eye-starting wretch,
Sure-refuged hears his hot pursuing fiends
Yell at vain distance. Soon refreshed from Heaven
He calms the throb and tempest of his heart.

His countenance settles; a soft solemn bliss
Swims in his eye—his swimming eye upraised;
And Faith's whole armour glitters on his limbs!
And thus transfigured with a dreadless awe,
A solemn hush of soul, meek he beholds
All things of terrible seeming: yea, unmoved
Views e'en the inmitigable ministers
That shower down vengeance on these latter days.
' For kindling with intenser Deity
From the celestial Mercy-seat they come,
And at the renovating wells of Love
Have filled their vials with salutary wrath,
To sickly Nature more medicinal
Than what soft balm the weeping good man pours
Into the lone despoiled traveller's wounds!

Thus from the Elect, regenerate through faith,
Pass the dark Passions and what thirsty Cares
Drink up the Spirit, and the dim regards
Self-centre. Lo they vanish! or acquire
New names, new features—by supernal grace
Enrobed with Light, and naturalized in Heaven.
As when a shepherd on a vernal morn
Through some thick fog creeps timorous with slow
      foot,
Darkling he fixes on the immediate road
His downward eye: all else of fairest kind
Hid or deformed. But lo! the bursting Sun!
Touched by the enchantment of that sudden beam
Straight the black vapour melteth, and in globes

Of dewy glitter gems each plant and tree;
On every leaf, on every blade it hangs!
Dance glad the new-born intermingling rays,
And wide around the landscape streams with glory!

There is one Mind, one omnipresent Mind,
Omnific.   His most holy name is Love.
Truth of subliming import! with the which
Who feeds and saturates his constant soul,
He from his small particular orbit flies,
With blest outstarting! From himself he flies,
Stands in the sun, and with no partial gaze
Views all creation; and he loves it all,
And blesses it, and calls it very good!
This is indeed to dwell with the Most High!
Cherubs and rapture-trembling Seraphim
Can press no nearer to the Almighty's throne.
But that we roam unconscious, or with hearts
Unfeeling of our universal Sire,
And that in his vast family no Cain
Injures uninjured (in her best-aimed blow
Victorious murder a blind suicide)
Haply for this some younger Angel now
Looks down on human nature: and, behold!
A sea of blood bestrewed with wrecks, where mad
Embattling interests on each other rush
With unhelmed rage!

'Tis the sublime of man,
Our noontide majesty, to know ourselves

Parts and proportions of one wondrous whole!
This fraternizes man, this constitutes
Our charities and bearings. But 'tis God
Diffused through all, that doth make all one whole;
This the worst superstition, him except
Aught to desire, Supreme Reality!
The plenitude and permanence of bliss!
O Fiends of Superstition! not that oft
The erring priest hath stained with brother's blood
Your grisly idols, not for this may wrath
Thunder against you from the Holy One!
But o'er some plain that steameth to the sun,
Peopled with death; or where more hideous Trade
Loud-laughing packs his·bales of human anguish;
I will raise up a mourning, O ye Fiends!
And curse your spells, that film the eye of Faith,
Hiding the present God; whose presence lost,
The moral world's cohesion, we become
An anarchy of Spirits! Toy-bewitched,
Made blind by lusts, disherited of soul,
No common centre Man, no common sire
Knoweth! A sordid solitary thing,
'Mid countless brethren with a lonely heart
Through courts and cities the smooth savage roams
Feeling himself, his own low self the whole;
When he by sacred sympathy might make
The whole one self! self, that no alien knows!
Self, far diffused as Fancy's wing can travel!
Self, spreading still! Oblivious of its own,
Yet all of all possessing! This is Faith!

This the Messiah's destined victory !
But first offences needs must come ! Even now *
(Black Hell laughs horrible—to hear the scoff !)
Thee to defend, meek Galilean ! Thee
And thy mild laws of Love unutterable,
Mistrust and enmity have burst the bands
Of social peace ; and listening treachery lurks
With pious fraud to snare a brother's life ;
And childless widows o'er the groaning land
Wail numberless ; and orphans weep for bread
Thee to defend, dear Saviour of mankind !
Thee, Lamb of God ! Thee, blameless Prince of
     peace !
From all sides rush the thirsty brood of War,—
Austria, and that foul Woman of the North,
The lustful murderess of her wedded lord !
And he, connatural mind ! whom (in their songs

---

* January 21st, 1794, in the debate on the address to his
Majesty, on the speech from the Throne, the Earl of Guildford
moved an amendment to the following effect:—" That the
House hoped his Majesty would seize the earliest opportunity
to conclude a peace with France," &c. This motion was
opposed by the Duke of Portland, who " considered the war
to be merely grounded on one principle—the preservation of
the Christian Religion." May 30th, 1794, the Duke of Bedford moved a number of resolutions, with a view to the
establishment of a peace with France. He was opposed
(among others) by Lord Abingdon, in these remarkable
words: " The best road to Peace, my Lords, is War! and
War carried on in the same manner in which we are taught
to worship our Creator, namely, with all our souls, and with
all our minds, and with all our hearts, and with all our
strength."

So bards of elder time had haply feigned)
Some Fury fondled in her hate to man,
Bidding her serpent hair in mazy surge
Lick his young face, and at his mouth imbreathe
Horrible sympathy! And leagued with these
Each petty German princeling, nursed in gore!
Soul-hardened barterers of human blood!
Death's prime slave-merchants! Scorpion-whips
    of Fate!
Nor least in savagery of holy zeal,
Apt for the yoke, the race degenerate,
Whom Britain erst had blushed to call her sons!
Thee to defend the Moloch priest prefers
The prayer of hate, and bellows to the herd
That Deity, accomplice Deity,
In the fierce jealousy of wakened wrath,
Will go forth with our armies and our fleets
To scatter the red ruin on their foes!
O blasphemy! to mingle fiendish deeds
With blessedness!

         Lord of unsleeping Love,*
From everlasting Thou! We shall not die.
These, even these, in mercy didst thou form,
Teachers of Good through Evil, by brief wrong
Making Truth lovely, and her future might
Magnetic o'er the fixed untrembling heart.

* Art thou not from everlasting, O Lord, my God, mine
Holy One? We shall not die. O Lord, thou hast ordained
them for judgment. &c. *Habakkuk.*

In the primeval age a dateless while
The vacant Shepherd wandered with his flock,
Pitching his tent where'er the green grass waved.
But soon Imagination conjured up
A host of new desires : with busy aim,
Each for himself, Earth's eager children toiled.
So Property began, twy-streaming fount,
Whence Vice and Virtue flow, honey and gall.
Hence the soft couch, and many-coloured robe,
The timbrel, and arch'd dome and costly feast,
With all the inventive arts, that nursed the soul
To forms of beauty, and by sensual wants
Unsensualized the mind, which in the means
Learnt to forget the grossness of the end,
Best pleasured with its own activity.
And hence Disease that withers manhood's arm,
The daggered Envy, spirit-quenching Want,
Warriors, and Lords, and Priests—all the sore ills
That vex and desolate our mortal life.
Wide-wasting ills ! yet each the immediate source
Of mightier good.   Their keen necessities,
To ceaseless action goading human thought,
Have made Earth's reasoning animal her Lord ;
And the pale-featured Sage's trembling hand
Strong as a host of armed Deities,
Such as the blind Ionian fabled erst.

From avarice thus, from luxury and war,
Sprang heavenly Science ; and from science Freedom.
O'er wakened realms Philosophers and Bards

Spread in concentric circles : they whose souls,
Conscious of their high dignities from God,
Brook not wealth's rivalry ! and they who long
Enamoured with the charms of order hate
The unseemly disproportion : and whoe'er
Turn with mild sorrow from the victor's car
And the low puppetry of thrones, to muse
On that blest triumph, when the patriot Sage
Called the red lightnings from the o'er-rushing
    cloud
And dashed the beauteous terrors on the earth
Smiling majestic.   Such a phalanx ne'er
Measured firm paces to the calming sound
Of Spartan flute !   These on the fated day,
When, stung to rage by pity, eloquent men
Have roused with pealing voice the unnumbered
    tribes
That toil and groan and bleed, hungry and blind,—
These hushed awhile with patient eye serene
Shall watch the mad careering of the storm ;
Then o'er the wild and wavy chaos rush
And tame the outrageous mass, with plastic might
Moulding confusion to such perfect forms
As erst were wont,—bright visions of the day !—
To float before them, when, the summer noon,
Beneath some arch'd romantic rock reclined,
They felt the sea-breeze lift their youthful locks ;
Or in the month of blossoms, at mild eve,
Wandering with desultory feet, inhaled
The wafted perfumes, and the flocks and woods,

And many-tinted streams, and setting sun,
With all his gorgeous company of clouds,
Ecstatic gazed! then homeward as they **strayed**
Cast the sad eye to earth, and inly mused
Why there was misery in a world so fair.
Ah! far removed from all that glads the sense,
From all that softens or ennobles Man,
The wretched Many! Bent beneath their loads
They gape at pageant Power, nor recognize
Their cots' transmuted plunder! From the tree
Of Knowledge, ere the vernal sap had risen,
Rudely disbranched! Blest Society!
Fitliest depictured by some sun-scorched waste,
Where oft majestic through the tainted noon
The Simoom sails, before whose purple pomp
Who falls not prostrate dies! And where by night,
Fast by each precious fountain on green herbs
The lion couches; or hyæna dips
Deep in the lucid stream his bloody jaws;
Or serpent plants his vast moon-glittering bulk,
Caught in whose monstrous twine Behemoth* yells,
His bones loud-crashing!

                    O ye numberless,
Whom foul oppression's ruffian gluttony [wretch
Drives from life's plenteous feast! O thou poor

---

* Behemoth, in Hebrew, signifies wild beasts in general.
Some believe it is the elephant, some the hippopotamus; some
affirm it is the wild bull. Poetically, it designates any large
quadruped.

Who, nursed in darkness and made wild by want,
Roamest for prey, yea, thy unnatural hand
Dost lift to deeds of blood! O pale-eyed form,
The victim of seduction, doomed to know
Polluted nights and days of blasphemy;
Who in loathed orgies with lewd wassailers
Must gaily laugh, while thy remembered home
Gnaws like a viper at thy secret heart!
O aged women! ye who weekly catch
The morsel tossed by law-forced charity,
And die so slowly, that none call it murder!
O loathly suppliants! ye, that unreceived
Totter heart-broken from the closing gates
Of the full Lazar-house: or, gazing, stand
Sick with despair! O ye to glory's field
Forced or ensnared, who, as ye gasp in death,
Bleed with new wounds beneath the vulture's
      beak!
O thou poor widow, who in dreams dost view
Thy husband's mangled corse, and from short doze
Start'st with a shriek; or in thy half-thatched cot,
Waked by the wintry night-storm, wet and cold,
Cow'r'st o'er thy screaming baby! Rest awhile,
Children of wretchedness! More groans must
      rise,
More blood must stream, or ere your wrongs be
      full.
Yet is the day of retribution nigh:
The Lamb of God hath opened the fifth seal:
And upward rush on swiftest wing of fire

The innumerable multitude of Wrongs
By man on man inflicted! Rest awhile,
Children of wretchedness! The hour is nigh;
And lo! the great, the rich, the mighty Men,
The Kings and the chief Captains of the World,
With all that fixed on high like stars of Heaven
Shot baleful influence, shall be cast to earth,
Vile and down-trodden, as the untimely fruit
Shook from the fig-tree by a sudden storm.
Even now the storm begins :* each gentle name,
Faith and meek Piety, with fearful joy
Tremble far-off—for lo! the giant Frenzy,
Uprooting empires with his whirlwind arm,
Mocketh high Heaven; burst hideous from the
      cell
Where the old Hag, unconquerable, huge,
Creation's eyeless drudge, black Ruin, sits
Nursing the impatient earthquake.

                    O return!
Pure Faith! meek Piety! The abhorred Form
Whose scarlet robe was stiff with earthly pomp,
Who drank iniquity in cups of gold,
Whose names were many and all blasphemous,
Hath met the horrible judgment! Whence that
      cry?
The mighty army of foul Spirits shrieked
Disherited of earth! For she hath fallen

---

* Alluding to the French Revolution.

On whose black front was written Mystery;
She that reeled heavily, whose wine was blood;
She that worked whoredom with the Demon
   Power,
And from the dark embrace all evil things
Brought forth and nurtured: mitred Atheism!
And patient Folly who on bended knee [Fear,
Gives back the steel that stabbed him; and pale
Haunted by ghastlier shapings than surround
Moon-blasted Madness when he yells at midnight!
Return pure Faith! return meek Piety!
The kingdoms of the world are yours: each heart
Self-governed, the vast family of Love
Raised from the common earth by common toil
Enjoy the equal produce. Such delights
As float to earth, permitted visitants!
When in some hour of solemn jubilee
The massy gates of Paradise are thrown
Wide open, and forth come in fragments wild
Sweet echoes of unearthly melodies,
And odours snatched from beds of amaranth,
And they, that from the crystal river of life
Spring up on freshened wing, ambrosial gales!
The favoured good man in his lonely walk
Perceives them, and his silent spirit drinks
Strange bliss which he shall recognize in heaven.
And such delights, such strange beatitudes,
Seize on my young anticipating heart
When that blest future rushes on my view!
For in his own and in his Father's might

The Saviour comes! While, as the thousand
    Years
Lead up their mystic dance, the Desert shouts!
Old Ocean claps his hands! The mighty Dead
Rise to new life, whoe'er from earliest time
With conscious zeal had urged Love's wondrous
    plan,
Coadjutors of God. To Milton's trump
The high groves of the renovated Earth
Unbosom their glad echoes : inly hushed,
Adoring Newton his serener eye
Raises to Heaven : and he of mortal kind
Wisest, he * first who marked the ideal tribes
Up the fine fibres through the sentient brain.
Lo! Priestley there, patriot, and saint, and sage,
Him, full of years, from his loved native land
Statesmen blood-stained and priests idolatrous
By dark lies maddening the blind multitude
Drove with vain hate. Calm, pitying he retired,
And mused expectant on these promised years.

O Years! the blest preëminence of saints!
Ye sweep athwart my gaze, so heavenly bright,
The wings that veil the adoring Seraphs' eyes,
What time they bend before the Jasper Throne†

---

  * David Hartley.

  † Rev. chap. iv. verses 2 and 3.—And immediately I was
in the Spirit: and behold, a throne was set in Heaven and
one sat on the Throne. And he that sat was to look upon
like a jasper and a sardine stone, &c.

Reflect no lovelier hues! Yet ye depart,
And all beyond is darkness! Heights most
    strange,
Whence Fancy falls, fluttering her idle wing.
For who of woman born may paint the hour,
When, seized in his mid course, the Sun shall
    wane
Making noon ghastly! Who of woman born
May image in the workings of his thought,
How the black-visaged, red-eyed Fiend out-
    stretched *
Beneath the unsteady feet of Nature groans,
In feverous slumbers—destined then to wake,
When fiery whirlwinds thunder his dread name
And Angels shout, Destruction! How his arm
The last great Spirit lifting high in air
Shall swear by Him, the ever-living One,
Time is no more!

                Believe thou, O my soul,
Life is a vision shadowy of Truth;
And vice, and anguish, and the wormy grave,
Shapes of a dream! The veiling clouds retire,
And lo! the Throne of the redeeming God,
Forth flashing unimaginable day,
Wraps in one blaze earth, heaven, and deepest
    hell.

* The final destruction impersonated.

Contemplant Spirits! ye that hover o'er
With untired gaze the immeasurable fount
Ebullient with creative Deity!
And ye of plastic power, that interfused
Roll through the grosser and material mass
In organizing surge! Holies of God!
(And what if Monads of the infinite mind?)
I haply journeying my immortal course
Shall sometime join your mystic choir. Till then
I discipline my young and novice thought
In ministries of heart-stirring song,
And aye on Meditation's heaven-ward wing
Soaring aloft I breathe the empyreal air
Of Love, omnific, omnipresent Love,
Whose day-spring rises glorious in my soul,
As the great Sun, when he his influence
Sheds on the frost-bound waters—The glad stream
Flows to the ray and warbles as it flows.

THE DESTINY OF NATIONS.

A VISION.

AUSPICIOUS Reverence! Hush all meaner song,
Ere we the deep preluding strain have poured
To the Great Father, only Rightful King,
Eternal Father! King Omnipotent!
To the Will Absolute, the One, the Good!
The I AM, the Word, the Life, the Living God!

Such symphony requires best instrument.
Seize, then, my soul! from Freedom's trophied
    dome
The harp which hangeth high between the shields
Of Brutus and Leonidas! With that
Strong music, that soliciting spell, force back
Man's free and stirring spirit that lies entranced.

For what is freedom, but the unfettered use
Of all the powers which God for use had given?
But chiefly this, him first, him last to view
Through meaner powers and secondary things
Effulgent, as through clouds that veil his blaze.
For all that meets the bodily sense I deem
Symbolical, one mighty alphabet
For infant minds; and we in this low world

Placed with our backs to bright reality,
That we may learn with young unwounded ken
The substance from its shadow. Infinite Love,
Whose latence is the plenitude of all,
Thou with retracted beams, and self-eclipse
Veiling, revealest thine eternal Sun.

But some there are who deem themselves most
    free
When they within this gross and visible sphere
Chain down the winged thought, scoffing ascent,
Proud in their meanness: and themselves they
    cheat
With noisy emptiness of learned phrase,
Their subtle fluids, impacts, essences,
Self-working tools, uncaused effects, and all
Those blind omniscients, those almighty slaves,
Untenanting creation of its God.

But properties are God: the naked mass
(If mass there be, fantastic guess or ghost,)
Acts only by its inactivity.
Here we pause humbly. Others boldlier think
That as one body seems the aggregate
Of atoms numberless, each organized;
So by a strange and dim similitude
Infinite myriads of self-conscious minds
Are one all-conscious Spirit, which informs
With absolute ubiquity of thought
(His one eternal self-affirming act!)

All his involved Monads, that yet seem
With various province and apt agency
Each to pursue its own self-centring end.
Some nurse the infant diamond in the mine;
Some roll the genial juices through the oak;
Some drive the mutinous clouds to clash in air,
And, rushing on the storm with whirlwind speed,
Yoke the red lightnings to their volleying car.
Thus these pursue their never-varying course,
No eddy in their stream. Others, more wild,
With complex interests weaving human fates,
Duteous or proud, alike obedient all,
Evolve the process of eternal good.

And what if some rebellious o'er dark realms
Arrogate power? yet these train up to God,
And on the rude eye, unconfirmed for day,
Flash meteor-lights better than total gloom.
As ere from Lieule-Oaive's vapoury head
The Laplander beholds the far-off sun
Dart his slant beam on unobeying snows,
While yet the stern and solitary night
Brooks no alternate sway, the Boreal Morn
With mimic lustre substitutes its gleam,
Guiding his course or by Niemi lake
Or Balda Zhiok,* or the mossy stone
Of Solfar-kapper,† while the snowy blast

* Balda Zhiok; *i. e.* mons altitudinis, the highest mountain in Lapland.

† Solfar-kapper; capitium Solfar, hic locus omnium quot-

Drifts arrowy by, or eddies round his sledge,
Making the poor babe at its mother's back*
Scream in its scanty cradle : he the while
Wins gentle solace as with upward eye
He marks the streamy banners of the North,
Thinking himself those happy spirits shall join
Who there in floating robes of rosy light
Dance sportively.   For Fancy is the power
That first unsensualizes the dark mind,
Giving it new delights ; and bids it swell
With wild activity ; and peopling air,
By obscure fears of beings invisible,
Emancipates it from the grosser thrall
Of the present impulse, teaching self-control,
Till Superstition, with unconscious hand,

quot veterum Lapponum superstitio sacrificiis religiosoque
cultui dedicavit, celebratissimus erat, in parte sinus australis
situs semimilliaris spatio a mari distans. Ipse locus, quem
curiositatis gratia aliquando me invisisse memini, duabus
praealtis lapidibus, sibi invicem oppositis, quorum alter musco
circumdatus erat, constabat.—*Leemius de Lapponibus.*

* The Lapland women carry their infants at their back in
a piece of excavated wood, which serves them for a cradle.
Opposite to the infant's mouth there is a hole for it to breathe
through.—Mirandum prorsus est et vix credibile nisi cui
vidisse contigit. Lappones hyeme iter facientes per vastos
montes, perque horrida et invia tesqua, eo presertim tempore
quo omnia perpetuis nivibus obtecta sunt et nives ventis agi-
tantur et in gyros aguntur, viam ad destinata loca absque
errore invenire posse, lactantem autem infantem si quem
habeat, ipsa mater in dorso bajulat, in excavato ligno (Gieed'k
ipsi vocant) quod pro cunis utuntur: in hoc infans pannis et
pellibus convolutus colligatus jacet.—*Leemius de Lapponibus.*

Seat Reason on her throne. Wherefore not vain,
Nor yet without permitted power impressed,
I deem those legends terrible, with which
The polar ancient thrills his uncouth throng :
Whether of pitying Spirits that make their moan
O'er slaughtered infants, or that giant bird
Vuokho, of whose rushing wings the noise
Is tempest, when the unutterable* shape
Speeds from the mother of Death, and utters
  once
That shriek, which never murderer heard, and
  lived.

Or if the Greenland Wizard in strange trance
Pierces the untravelled realms of Ocean's bed
Over the abysm, even to that uttermost cave
By misshaped prodigies beleaguered, such
As earth ne'er bred, nor air, nor the upper sea :
Where dwells the Fury Form, whose unheard
  name
With eager eye, pale cheek, suspended breath,
And lips half-opening with the dread of sound,
Unsleeping Silence guards, worn out with fear
Lest haply 'scaping on some treacherous blast
The fateful word let slip the elements
And frenzy Nature. Yet the wizard her,
Armed with Torngarsuck's † power, the Spirit of
  Good,

---

* Jaibme Aibmo.

† They call the Good Spirit Torngarsuck. The other great

Forces to unchain the foodful progeny
Of the Ocean stream ;——thence thro' the realm
　　of Souls,
Where live the Innocent, as far from cares
As from the storms and overwhelming waves
That tumble on the surface of the Deep,
Returns with far-heard pant, hotly pursued
By the fierce Warders of the Sea, once more,
Ere by the frost foreclosed, to repossess
His fleshly mansion, that had staid the while
In the dark tent within a cow'ring group
Untenanted.—Wild phantasies! yet wise,
On the victorious goodness of high God
Teaching reliance, and medicinal hope,
Till from Bethabra northward, heavenly Truth
With gradual steps, winning her difficult way,
Transfer their rude Faith perfected and pure.

If there be beings of higher class than Man,
I deem no nobler province they possess,
Than by disposal of apt circumstance
To rear up kingdoms: and the deeds they prompt

but malignant spirit is a nameless female; she dwells under
the sea in a great house, where she can detain in captivity
all the animals of the ocean by her magic power. When a
dearth befalls the Greenlanders, an Angekok or magician
must undertake a journey thither. He passes through the
kingdom of souls, over a horrible abyss into the palace of
this phantom, and by his enchantments causes the captive
creatures to ascend directly to the surface of the ocean.—*See
Crantz's History of Greenland,* vol. i. 206.

Distinguishing from mortal agency,
They choose their human ministers from such
    states
As still the Epic song half fears to name,
Repelled from all the minstrelsies that strike
The palace-roof and soothe the monarch's pride.

And such, perhaps, the Spirit, who (if words
Witnessed by answering deeds may claim our
    faith,)
Held commune with that warrior-maid of France
Who scourged the invader. From her infant
    days,
With Wisdom, mother of retired thoughts,
Her soul had dwelt ; and she was quick to mark
The good and evil thing, in human lore
Undisciplined. For lowly was her birth,
And Heaven had doomed her early years to toil;
That pure from tyranny's least deed, herself
Unfeared by fellow-natures, she might wait
On the poor labouring man with kindly looks,
And minister refreshment to the tired
Way-wanderer, when along the rough-hewn bench
The sweltry man had stretched him, and aloft
Vacantly watched the rudely pictured board
Which on the mulberry-bough with welcome creak
Swung to the pleasant breeze. Here, too, the
    Maid
Learnt more than schools could teach: Man's
    shifting mind,

His vices and his sorrows!   And full oft
At tales of cruel wrong and strange distress
Had wept and shivered.   To the tottering eld
Still as a daughter would she run: she placed
His cold limbs at the sunny door, and loved
To hear him story, in his garrulous sort,
Of his eventful years, all come and gone.

So twenty seasons past.   The Virgin's form,
Active and tall, nor sloth nor luxury
Had shrunk or paled.   Her front sublime and
        broad,
Her flexile eye-brows wildly haired and low,
And her full eye, now bright, now unillumed,
Spake more than Woman's thought; and all her
        face
Was moulded to such features as declared
That pity there had oft and strongly worked,
And sometimes indignation.   Bold her mien,
And like a haughty huntress of the woods
She moved : yet sure she was a gentle maid !
And in each motion her most innocent soul
Beamed forth so brightly, that who saw would say
Guilt was a thing impossible in her !
Nor idly would have said—for she had lived
In this bad world as in a place of tombs,
And touched not the pollutions of the dead.

'Twas the cold season when the rustic's eye
From the drear desolate whiteness of his fields

Rolls for relief to watch the skyey tints
And clouds slow varying their huge imagery,
When now, as she was wont, the healthful Maid
Had left her pallet ere one beam of day
Slanted the fog-smoke. She went forth alone
Urged by the indwelling angel-guide, that oft,
With dim inexplicable sympathies
Disquieting the heart, shapes out Man's course
To the predoomed adventure. Now the ascent
She climbs of that steep upland, on whose top
The Pilgrim-man, who long since eve had watched
The alien shine of unconcerning stars,
Shouts to himself, there first the Abbey-lights
Seen in Neufchatel's vale; now slopes adown
The winding sheep-track valeward: when, behold
In the first entrance of the level road
An unattended team! The foremost horse
Lay with stretched limbs; the others, yet alive
But stiff and cold, stood motionless, their manes
Hoar with the frozen night dews. Dismally
The dark-red dawn now glimmered; but its gleams
Disclosed no face of man. The maiden paused,
Then hailed who might be near. No voice
          replied:
From the thwart wain at length there reached
          her ear
A sound so feeble that it almost seemed
Distant: and feebly, with slow effort pushed,
A miserable man crept forth: his limbs
The silent frost had eat, scathing like fire.

Faint on the shafts he rested.   She, meantime,
Saw crowded close beneath the coverture
A mother and her children—lifeless all,
Yet lovely ! not a lineament was marred—
Death had put on so slumber-like a form !
It was a piteous sight; and one, a babe,
The crisp milk frozen on its innocent lips,
Lay on the woman's arm, its little hand
Stretched on her bosom.

      Mutely questioning,
The maid gazed wildly at the living wretch.
He, his head feebly turning, on the group
Looked with a vacant stare, and his eye spoke
The drowsy calm that steals on worn-out anguish.
She shuddered; but, each vainer pang subdued,
Quick disentangling from the foremost horse
The rustic bands, with difficulty and toil
The stiff cramped team forced homeward.   There
  arrived,
Anxiously tends him she with healing herbs,
And weeps and prays—but the numb power of
  Death
Spreads o'er his limbs; and ere the noontide hour,
The hovering spirits of his wife and babes
Hail him immortal !   Yet amid his pangs,
With interruptions long from ghastly throes,
His voice had faltered out this simple tale.

The village, where he dwelt a husbandman,

By sudden inroad had been seized and fired
Late on the yester-evening. With his wife
And little ones he hurried his escape.
They saw the neighboring hamlets flame, they
    heard
Uproar and shrieks! and terror-struck drove on
Through unfrequented roads, a weary way!
But saw nor house nor cottage. All had quenched
Their evening hearth-fire: for the alarm had
    spread.
The air clipped keen, the night was fanged with
    frost,
And they provisionless! The weeping wife
Ill hushed her children's moans; and still they
    moaned,
Till fright and cold and hunger drank their life.
They closed their eyes in sleep, nor knew 'twas
    death.
He only, lashing his o'er wearied team,
Gained a sad respite, till beside the base
Of the high hill his foremost horse dropped dead.
Then hopeless, strengthless, sick for lack of food,
He crept beneath the coverture, entranced,
Till wakened by the Maiden.—Such his tale.

Ah! suffering to the height of what was suf-
    fered,
Stung with too keen a sympathy, the Maid
Brooded with moving lips, mute, startful, dark!
And now her flushed tumultuous features shot

Such strange vivacity as fires the eye
Of misery fancy-crazed! and now once more
Naked, and void, and fixed, and all within
The unquiet silence of confused thought
And shapeless feelings. For a mighty hand
Was strong upon her, till in the heat of soul
To the high hill-top tracing back her steps,
Aside the beacon, up whose smouldered stones
The tender ivy-trails crept thinly, there,
Unconscious of the driving element,
Yea, swallowed up in the ominous dream, she sate
Ghastly as broad-eyed Slumber! a dim anguish
Breathed from her look! and still with pant and
      sob,
Inly she toil'd to flee, and still subdued,
Felt an inevitable Presence near.

  Thus as she toiled in troublous ecstasy,
A horror of great darkness wrapt her round,
And a voice uttered forth unearthly tones,
Calming her soul,—"O Thou of the Most High
Chosen, whom all the perfected in Heaven
Behold expectant——

  [The following fragments were intended to form part of
the poem when finished.]

       "Maid beloved of Heaven!
(To her the tutelary Power exclaimed)
Of Chaos the adventurous progeny
Thou seest; foul missionaries of foul sire,

Fierce to regain the losses of that hour
When Love rose glittering, and his gorgeous
      wings
Over the abyss fluttered with such glad noise,
As what time after long and pestful calms,
With slimy shapes and miscreated life
Poisoning the vast Pacific, the fresh breeze
Wakens the merchant-sail uprising.   Night
A heavy unimaginable moan
Sent forth, when she the Protoplast beheld
Stand beauteous on confusion's charmed wave.
Moaning she fled, and entered the Profound
That leads with downward windings to the cave
Of darkness palpable, desert of Death
Sunk deep beneath Gehenna's massy roots.
There many a dateless age the beldam lurked
And trembled; till, engendered by fierce Hate,
Fierce Hate and gloomy Hope, a Dream arose,
Shaped like a black cloud marked with streaks of
      fire.
It roused the Hell-Hag: she the dew damp wiped
From off her brow, and through the uncouth maze
Retraced her steps; but ere she reached the
      mouth
Of that drear labyrinth, shuddering she paused,
Nor dared reënter the diminished Gulf.
As through the dark vaults of some mouldered
      tower,
(Which, fearful to approach, the evening hind
Circles at distance in his homeward way,)

The winds breathe hollow, deemed the plaining
    groan
Of prisoned spirits ; with such fearful voice
Night murmured, and the sound thro' Chaos went.
Leaped at her call her hideous-fronted brood!
A dark behest they heard, and rushed on earth ;
Since that sad hour, in camps and courts adored,
Rebels from God, and tyrants o'er Mankind!"

         From his obscure haunt
Shrieked Fear, of Cruelty the ghastly dam,
Feverous yet freezing, eager-paced yet slow,
As she that creeps from forth her swampy reeds,
Ague, the biform hag! when early Spring
Beams on the marsh-bred vapours.

    " Even so (the exulting Maiden said)
The sainted heralds of good tidings fell,
And thus they witnessed God! But now the clouds
Treading, and storms beneath their feet, they soar
Higher, and higher soar, and soaring sing
Loud songs of triumph!   O ye spirits of God,
Hover around my mortal agonies!"
She spake, and instantly faint melody
Melts on her ear, soothing and sad, and slow,
Such measures, as at calmest midnight heard
By aged hermit in his holy dream,
Foretell and solace death ; and now they rise

Louder, as when with harp and mingled voice
The white-robed* multitude of slaughtered saints
At Heaven's wide-opened·portals gratulant
Receive some martyr'd patriot. The harmony
Entranced the Maid, till each suspended sense
Brief slumber seized, and confused ecstasy.

At length awakening slow, she gazed around :
And through a mist, the relique of that trance
Still thinning as she gazed, an Isle appeared,
Its high, o'erhanging, white, broad-breasted cliffs,
Glassed on the subject ocean. A vast plain
Stretched opposite, where ever and anon
The ploughman, following sad his meagre team,
Turned up fresh sculls unstartled, and the bones
Of fierce hate-breathing combatants, who there
All mingled lay beneath the common earth,
Death's gloomy reconcilement ! O'er the fields
Stept a fair Form, repairing all she might,
Her temples olive-wreathed ; and where she trod,
Fresh flowerets rose, and many a foodful herb.
But wan her cheek, her footsteps insecure,
And anxious pleasure beamed in her faint eye,
As she had newly left a couch of pain,
Pale convalescent ! (yet some time to rule

* Revelations, vi. 9, 11. And when he had opened the fifth
seal, I saw under the altar the souls of them that were slain
for the word of God, and for the testimony which they held.
And white robes were given unto every one of them, and it
was said unto them, that they should rest yet for a little season, until their fellow servants also and their brethren, that
should be killed as they were, should be fulfilled.

With power exclusive o'er the willing world,
That blest prophetic mandate then fulfilled—
Peace be on Earth!) A happy while, but brief,
She seemed to wander with assiduous feet,
And healed the recent harm of chill and blight,
And nursed each plant that fair and virtuous grew.

But soon a deep precursive sound moaned
hollow :
Black rose the clouds, and now, (as in a dream,)
Their reddening shapes, transformed to warrior-
hosts,
Coursed o'er the sky, and battled in mid-air.
Nor did not the large blood-drops fall from heaven
Portentous! while aloft were seen to float,
Like hideous features booming on the mist,
Wan stains of ominous light! Resigned, yet sad,
The fair Form bowed her olive-crowned brow,
Then o'er the plain with oft reverted eye
Fled till a place of tombs she reached, and there
Within a ruined sepulchre obscure
Found hiding-place.

The delegated Maid
Gazed through her tears, then in sad tones ex-
claimed ;—
"Thou mild-eyed Form! wherefore, ah! where-
fore fled?
The power of Justice, like a name all light,
Shone from thy brow ; but all they, who unblamed

Dwelt in thy dwellings, call thee Happiness.
Ah! why, uninjured and unprofited,
Should multitudes against their brethren rush?
Why sow they guilt, still reaping misery?
Lenient of care, thy songs, O Peace! are sweet,
As after showers the perfumed gale of eve,
That flings the cool drops on a feverous cheek;
And gay thy grassy altar piled with fruits.
But boasts the shrine of demon War one charm,
Save that with many an orgie strange and foul,
Dancing around with interwoven arms,
The maniac Suicide and giant Murder
Exult in their fierce union! I am sad,
And know not why the simple peasants crowd
Beneath the Chieftains' standard!" Thus the
    Maid.

   To her the tutelary Spirit said:
" When luxury and lust's exhausted stores
No more can rouse the appetites of kings;
When the low flattery of their reptile lords
Falls flat and heavy on the accustomed ear;
When eunuchs sing, and fools buffoonery make,
And dancers writhe their harlot-limbs in vain;
Then War and all its dread vicissitudes
Pleasingly agitate their stagnant hearts;
Its hopes, its fears, its victories, its defeats,
Insipid royalty's keen condiment!
Therefore uninjured and unprofited,
(Victims at once and executioners)

The congregated husbandmen lay waste
The vineyard and the harvest. As along
The Bothnic coast, or southward of the Line,
Though hushed the winds and cloudless the high
       noon,
Yet if Leviathan, weary of ease,
In sports unwieldy toss his island-bulk,
Ocean behind him billows, and before
A storm of waves breaks foamy on the strand.
And hence, for times and seasons bloody and dark,
Short Peace shall skin the wounds of causeless
       War,
And War, his strained sinews knit anew,
Still violate the unfinished works of Peace.
But yonder look! for more demands thy view!"
He said: and straightway from the opposite Isle
A vapour sailed, as when a cloud, exhaled
From Egypt's fields that steam hot pestilence,
Travels the sky for many a trackless league,
Till o'er some death-doomed land, distant in vain,
It broods incumbent. Forthwith from the plain,
Facing the Isle, a brighter cloud arose,
And steered its course which way the vapour went.

     The Maiden paused, musing what this might
       mean.
But long time passed not, ere that brighter cloud
Returned more bright; along the plain it swept;
And soon from forth its bursting sides emerged
A dazzling form, broad-bosomed, bold of eye,

And wild her hair, save where with laurels bound.
Not more majestic stood the healing God,
When from his bow the arrow sped that slew
Huge Python. Shriek'd Ambition's giant throng,
And with them hissed the locust-fiends that crawled
And glittered in Corruption's slimy track.
Great was their wrath, for short they knew their
  reign ;
And such commotion made they, and uproar,
As when the mad tornado bellows through
The guilty islands of the western main,
What time departing from their native shores,
Eboe, or * Koromantyn's plain of palms,

* The Slaves in the West-Indies consider death as a
passport to their native country. This sentiment is thus
expressed in the introduction to a Greek Prize-Ode on the
Slave-Trade, of which the thoughts are better than the language in which they are conveyed.

'Ω σκότου πύλας, Θάνατε, προλείπων
'Ες γένος σπεύδοις ὑποζευχθὲν 'Ατᾳ·
Οὐ ξενισθήσῃ γενύων σπαργμοῖς,
   Οὐδ' ὀλολυγμῷ,

'Αλλὰ καὶ κύκλοισι χοροιτύποισι,
 Κἀσμάτων χαρᾷ· φοβερὸς μὲν ἐσσὶ,
'Αλλ' ὅμως 'Ελευθερίᾳ συνοικεῖς,
   Στυγνὲ τύραννε!

Δασκίοις ἐπὶ πτερύγεσσι σῇσι,
'Αἱ θαλάσσιον καθορῶντες οἶδμα,
Αἰθεροπλάγκτοις ὑπὸ πόσσ' ἄνεισι
   Πατρίδ' ἐπ' αἶαν

The infuriate spirits of the murdered make
Fierce merriment, and vengeance ask of Heaven.
Warmed with new influence, the unwholesome plain
Sent up its foulest fogs to meet the morn:
The Sun that rose on Freedom, rose in blood!

" Maiden beloved, and Delegate of Heaven!
(To her the tutelary Spirit said,)
Soon shall the morning struggle into day,
The stormy morning into cloudless noon.
Much hast thou seen, nor all canst understand—
But this be thy best omen—Save thy Country!"
Thus saying, from the answering Maid he passed,
And with him disappeared the heavenly Vision!

" Glory to Thee, Father of Earth and Heaven!
All conscious presence of the Universe!

'Ένθα μὰν ἐρασταὶ ἐρωμένῃσιν
'Αμφὶ πηγῇσιν κιτρίνων ὑπ' ἀλσῶν,
'Όσσ' ὑπὸ βροτοῖς ἐπαθον βροτοὶ, τὰ
    Δεινὰ λέγοντι.

LITERAL TRANSLATION.

Leaving the gates of darkness, O Death! hasten thou to a
race yoked with misery! Thou wilt not be received with
lacerations of cheeks, nor with funeral ululation—but with
circling dances and the joy of songs. Thou art terrible indeed, yet thou dwellest with Liberty, stern Genius! Borne
on thy dark pinions over the swelling of Ocean, they return
to their native country. There, by the side of fountains, beneath citron-groves, the lovers tell to their beloved what horrors, being men, they had endured from men.

Nature's vast ever-acting energy !
In will, in deed, impulse of All to All!
Whether thy Love with unrefracted ray
Beam on the Prophet's purged eye, or if
Diseasing realms the enthusiast, wild of thought,
Scatter new frenzies on the infected throng,
Thou both inspiring and predooming both,
Fit instruments and best, of perfect end :
Glory to Thee, Father of Earth and Heaven ! "

And first a landscape rose
More wild and waste and desolate than where
The white bear, drifting on a field of ice,
Howls to her sundered cubs with piteous rage
And savage agony.

1794.

POEMS

WRITTEN IN EARLY MANHOOD, AND MIDDLE LIFE.

VOL. I.   8

FACILE credo, plures esse Naturas invisibiles quam visibiles in rerum universitate. Sed horum omnium familiam quis nobis enarrabit, et gradus et cognationes et discrimina et singulorum munera? Quid agunt? quæ loca habitant? Harum rerum notitiam semper ambivit ingenium humanum, nunquam attigit. Juvat, interea, non diffiteor, quandoque in animo, tanquam in tabulâ, majoris et melioris mundi imaginem contemplari: ne mens assuefacta hodiernæ vitæ minutiis se contrahat nimis, et tota subsidat in pusillas cogitationes. Sed veritati interea invigilandum est, modusque servandus, ut certa ab incertis, diem a nocte, distinguamus.—T. BURNET. ARCHÆOL. PHIL. p. 68.

RIME OF THE ANCIENT MARINER.*

IN SEVEN PARTS.

PART I.

It is an ancient Mariner,
And he stoppeth one of three.
"By thy long gray beard and glittering
    eye,
Now wherefore stopp'st thou me?

An ancient Mariner meeteth three gallants bidden to a wedding-feast, and detaineth one.

The Bridegroom's doors are opened
    wide,
And I am next of kin;
The guests are met, the feast is set:
May'st hear the merry din."

He holds him with his skinny hand;
"There was a ship," quoth he.
"Hold off! unhand me, gray-beard
    loon!"
Eftsoons his hand dropt he.

* See Note.

The Wedding-Guest is spellbound by the eye of the old seafaring man, and constrained to hear his tale.

He holds him with his glittering eye—
The Wedding-Guest stood still,
And listens like a three years' child:
The Mariner hath his will.

The Wedding-Guest sat on a stone:
He cannot choose but hear;
And thus spake on that ancient man,
The bright-eyed Mariner.

" The ship was cheered, the harbour
        cleared,
Merrily did we drop
Below the kirk, below the hill,
Below the light-house top.

The Mariner tells how the ship sailed southward with a good wind and fair weather, till it reached the Line.

The sun came up upon the left,
Out of the sea came he;
And he shone bright, and on the right
Went down into the sea.

Higher and higher every day,
Till over the mast at noon—"
The Wedding-Guest here beat his
        breast,
For he heard the loud bassoon.

The Wedding-Guest heareth the bridal music; but the Mariner continueth his tale.

The bride hath paced into the hall,
Red as a rose is she;
Nodding their heads before her goes
The merry minstrelsy.

he Wedding-Guest he beat his breast,
et he cannot choose but hear;
and thus spake on that ancient man,
The bright-eyed Mariner.

" And now the storm-blast came, and he
Was tyrannous and strong:
He struck with his o'ertaking wings,
And chased us south along.

The ship drawn by a storm toward the south pole.

With sloping masts and dipping prow,
As who pursued with yell and blow
Still treads the shadow of his foe,
And forward bends his head,
The ship drove fast, loud roared the blast,
And southward aye we fled.

And now there came both mist and snow,
And it grew wondrous cold:
And ice, mast-high, came floating by,
As green as emerald.

And through the drifts the snowy clifts
Did send a dismal sheen:
Nor shapes of men nor beasts we ken—
The ice was all between.

The land of ice, and of fearful sounds where no living thing was to be seen.

The ice was here, the ice was there,
The ice was all around: [howled,
It cracked and growled, and roared and
Like noises in a swound!

Till a great sea-bird, called the Albatross, came through the snow-fog, and was received with great joy and hospitality.

At length did cross an Albatross,
  Thorough the fog it came;
As if it had been a Christian soul,
  We hailed it in God's name.

It ate the food it ne'er had eat,
  And round and round it flew.
The ice did split with a thunder-fit;
  The helmsman steered us through!

And lo! the Albatross proveth a bird of good omen, and followeth the ship as it returned northward through fog and floating ice.

And a good south wind sprung up
    behind;
The Albatross did follow,
And every day, for food or play,
Came to the mariners' hollo!

In mist or cloud, on mast or shroud,
  It perched for vespers nine;
Whiles all the night, through fog-smoke
    white,
  Glimmered the white moon-shine."

The ancient Mariner inhospitably killeth the pious bird of good omen.

" God save thee, ancient Mariner!
From the fiends, that plague thee
    thus!—
Why look'st thou so?"—"With my
    cross-bow
  I shot the Albatross!"

PART II.

THE Sun now rose upon the right :
Out of the sea came he,
Still hid in mist, and on the left
Went down into the sea.

And the good south wind still blew
    behind,
But no sweet bird did follow,
Nor any day for food or play
Came to the mariners' hollo !

And I had done a hellish thing,
And it would work 'em woe :
For all averred, I had killed the bird
That made the breeze to blow.
Ah wretch ! said they, the bird to slay,
That made the breeze to blow !

His shipmates cry out against the ancient Mariner, for killing the bird of good luck.

Nor dim nor red, like God's own head,
The glorious Sun uprist:
Then all averred, I had killed the bird
That brought the fog and mist.
'Twas right, said they, such birds to
    slay,
That bring the fog and mist.

But when the fog cleared off, they justify the same, and thus make themselves accomplices in the crime.

The fair
breeze con-
tinues; the
ship enters
the Pacific
Ocean, and
sails north-
ward, even
till it reach-
es the Line.

The fair breeze blew, the white foam
    flew,
The furrow followed* free ;
We were the first that ever burst
Into that silent sea.

The ship
hath been
suddenly
becalmed

Down dropt the breeze, the sails dropt
    down,
'Twas sad as sad could be ;
And we did speak only to break
The silence of the sea !

All in a hot and copper sky,
The bloody Sun, at noon,
Right up above the mast did stand,
No bigger than the Moon.

Day after day, day after day,
We stuck, nor breath nor motion ;
As idle as a painted ship
Upon a painted ocean.

And the
Albatross
begins to be
avenged.

Water, water, everywhere,
And all the boards did shrink ;
Water, water, everywhere,
Nor any drop to drink.

The very deep did rot: O Christ !
That ever this should be !
Yea, slimy things did crawl with legs
Upon the slimy sea.

[* See Note at the end of the volume.]

About, about, in reel and rout
The death-fires danced at night;
The water, like a witch's oils,
Burnt green, and blue and white.

.

And some in dreams assured were
Of the Spirit that plagued us so;
Nine fathom deep he had followed us
From the land of mist and snow.

A Spirit had followed them; one of the invisible inhabitants of this planet, neither departed souls nor angels; concerning whom the learned Jew, Josephus, and the Platonic Constantinopolitan, Michael Psellus, may be consulted. They are very numerous, and there is no climate or element without one or more.

And every tongue, through utter drought,
Was withered at the root;
We could not speak, no more than if
We had been choked with soot.

Ah! well a-day! what evil looks
Had I from old and young!
Instead of the cross, the Albatross
About my neck was hung.

The shipmates, in their sore distress, would fain throw the whole guilt on the ancient Mariner: in sign whereof they hang the dead sea-bird round his neck.

PART III.

THERE passed a weary time. Each
   throat
Was parched, and glazed each eye.
A weary time! a weary time!
How glazed each weary eye,

The ancient
Mariner be-
holdeth a
sign in the
element afar
off.
When looking westward, I beheld
A something in the sky.

At first it seemed a little speck,
And then it seemed a mist;
It moved and moved, and took at last
A certain shape, I wist.

A speck, a mist, a shape, I wist!
And still it neared and neared:
As if it dodged a water-sprite,
It plunged and tacked and veered.

At its nearer
approach,
it seemeth
him to be a
ship; and at
a dear ran-
som he
freeth his
speech from
the bonds of
thirst.
With throats unslaked, with black lips
   baked,
We could nor laugh nor wail;
Through utter drought all dumb we
   stood!
I bit my arm, I sucked the blood,
And cried, A sail! a sail!

With throats unslaked, with black lips
    baked,
Agape they heard me call:
Gramercy! they for joy did grin,
And all at once their breath drew in,   *A flash of joy;*
As they were drinking all.

See! see! (I cried) she tacks no more!   *And horror follows.*
Hither to work us weal,—   *For can it be a ship that comes onward without wind or tide?*
Without a breeze, without a tide,
She steadies with upright keel!

The western wave was all a-flame.
The day was well nigh done!
Almost upon the western wave
Rested the broad bright Sun;
When that strange shape drove suddenly
Betwixt us and the Sun.

And straight the Sun was flecked with   *It seemeth him but the skeleton of a ship.*
    bars,
(Heaven's Mother send us grace!)
As if through a dungeon-grate he peered
With broad and burning face.

Alas! (thought I, and my heart beat
    loud)
How fast she nears and nears!
Are those her sails that glance in the
    Sun,
Like restless gossameres?

And its ribs are seen as bars on the face of the setting Sun.
Are those her ribs through which the Sun
Did peer, as through a grate?

The Spectre-Woman and her Death-mate, and no other on board the skeleton-ship.
And is that Woman all her crew?
Is that a Death? and are there two?
Is Death that woman's mate?

Like vessel, like crew!
Her lips were red, her looks were free,
Her locks were yellow as gold:
Her skin was as white as leprosy,
The Night-mare Life-in-Death was she,
Who thicks man's blood with cold.

Death and Life-in-Death have diced for the ship's crew, and she (the latter) winneth the ancient Mariner.
The naked hulk alongside came,
And the twain were casting dice;
'The game is done! I've won! I've won!'
Quoth she, and whistles thrice.*

The Sun's rim dips; the stars rush out:

No twilight within the courts of the Sun.
At one stride comes the dark;
With far-heard whisper, o'er the sea,
Off shot the spectre-bark.

At the rising of the Moon.
We listened and looked sideways up!
Fear at my heart, as at a cup,
My life-blood seemed to sip!
The stars were dim, and thick the night,
The steersman's face by his lamp gleamed white;

[* See Note at the end of the volume.]

From the sails the dew did drip—
Till clomb above the eastern bar
The horned Moon, with one bright star
Within the nether tip.

One after one, by the star-dogged
    Moon,
Too quick for groan or sigh,
Each turned his face with a ghastly
    pang,
And cursed me with his eye.

One after another,

Four times fifty living men,
(And I heard nor sigh nor groan)
With heavy thump, a lifeless lump,
They dropped down one by one.

His shipmates drop down dead.

The souls did from their bodies fly,—
They fled to bliss or woe!
And every soul, it passed me by,
Like the whizz of my cross-bow!"

But Life-in-Death begins her work on the ancient Mariner

PART IV.

"I FEAR thee, ancient Mariner!
I fear thy skinny hand!
And thou art long, and lank, and brown,
As is the ribbed sea-sand.*

I fear thee and thy glittering eye,
And thy skinny hand, so brown."—

"Fear not, fear not, thou Wedding-
        Guest!
This body dropt not down.

Alone, alone, all, all alone,
Alone on a wide wide sea!
And never a saint took pity on
My soul in agony.

The many men, so beautiful!
And they all dead did lie:
And a thousand thousand slimy things
Lived on ; and so did I.

* For the last two lines of this stanza, I am
indebted to Mr. Wordsworth. It was on a delightful walk from Nether Stowey to Dulverton,
with him and his sister, in the autumn of 1797,
that this poem was planned, and in part composed.

I looked upon the rotting sea,
And drew my eyes away;
I looked upon the rotting deck,
And there the dead men lay.

And envieth
that they
should live,
and so many
lie dead.

I looked to heaven, and tried to pray;
But or ever a prayer had gusht,
A wicked whisper came, and made
My heart as dry as dust.

I closed my lids, and kept them close,
And the balls like pulses beat;
For the sky and the sea, and the sea and
     the sky
Lay like a load on my weary eye,
And the dead were at my feet.

The cold sweat melted from their
          limbs,
Nor rot nor reek did they:
The look with which they looked on
     me
Had never passed away.

But the
curse liveth
for him in
the eye of
the dead
men.

An orphan's curse would drag to hell
A spirit from on high;
But oh! more horrible than that
Is the curse in a dead man's eye!
Seven days, seven nights, I saw that
     curse,
And yet I could not die.

In his lone-
liness and
fixedness
he yearneth
towards the
journeying
Moon, and
the stars
that still
sojourn, yet still move onward; and everywhere the blue sky belongs to them, and is their appointed rest, and their native country
and their own natural homes, which they enter unannounced, as lords
that are certainly expected, and yet there is a silent joy at their
arrival.

The moving Moon went up the sky,
And nowhere did abide:
Softly she was going up,
And a star or two beside—

Her beams bemocked the sultry main,
Like April hoar-frost spread;
But where the ship's huge shadow lay,
The charmed water burnt alway
A still and awful red.

By the light
of the Moon
he behold-
eth God's
creatures of
the great
calm.

Beyond the shadow of the ship,
I watched the water-snakes:
They moved in tracks of shining white,
And when they reared, the elfish light
Fell off in hoary flakes.

Within the shadow of the ship
I watched their rich attire:
Blue, glossy green, and velvet black,
They coiled and swam; and every track
Was a flash of golden fire.

Their beau-
ty and their
happiness.

O happy living things! no tongue
Their beauty might declare:
A spring of love gushed from my heart,

He blesseth
them in his
heart.

And I blessed them unaware ·
Sure my kind saint took pity on me,
And I blessed them unaware.

The selfsame moment I could pray; *The spell begins to break.*
And from my neck so free
The Albatross fell off, and sank
Like lead into the sea.

PART V.

Oh sleep! it is a gentle thing,
Beloved from pole to pole!
To Mary Queen the praise be given!
She sent the gentle sleep from Heaven,
That slid into my soul.

The silly buckets on the deck, *By grace of the holy*
That had so long remained, *Mother, the ancient Ma-*
I dreamt that they were filled with dew; *riner is re-freshed*
And when I awoke, it rained. *with rain.*

My lips were wet, my throat was cold,
My garments all were dank;
Sure I had drunken in my dreams,
And still my body drank.

I moved, and could not feel my limbs:
I was so light—almost
I thought that I had died in sleep,
And was a blessed ghost.

He heareth
sounds and
seeth
strange
sights and
commotions
in the sky
and the ele-
ment.

And soon I heard a roaring wind :
It did not come anear ;
But with its sound it shook the sails,
That were so thin and sere.

The upper air burst into life !
And a hundred fire-flags sheen,
To and fro they were hurried about!
And to and fro, and in and out,
The wan stars danced between.

And the coming wind did roar more
    loud,
And the sails did sigh like sedge ;
And the rain poured down from one
    black cloud ;
The moon was at its edge.

The thick black cloud was cleft, and
    still
The moon was at its side :
Like waters shot from some high
    crag,
The lightning fell with never a jag,
A river steep and wide.

The bodies
of the ship's
crew are
inspired,
and the ship
moves on ;

The loud wind never reached the
    ship,
Yet now the ship moved on !
Beneath the lightning and the Moon
The dead men gave a groan.

They groaned, they stirred, they all
    uprose,
Nor spake, nor moved their eyes;
It had been strange, even in a dream,
To have seen those dead men rise.

The helmsman steered, the ship moved on;
Yet never a breeze up blew;
The mariners all 'gan work the ropes,
Where they were wont to do;
They raised their limbs like lifeless
    tools—
We were a ghastly crew.

The body of my brother's son
Stood by me, knee to knee:
The body and I pulled at one rope,
But he said nought to me."

" I fear thee, ancient Mariner!"
" Be calm, thou Wedding-Guest!
'Twas not those souls that fled in pain,
Which to their corses came again,
But a troop of spirits blest:

For when it dawned—they dropped their
    arms,
And clustered round the mast;
Sweet sounds rose slowly through their
    mouths,
And from their bodies passed.

But not by the souls of the men, nor by demons of earth or middle air, but by a blessed troop of angelic spirits, sent down by the invocation of the guardian saint.

Around, around, flew each sweet sound,
Then darted to the Sun ;
Slowly the sounds came back again,
Now mixed, now one by one.

Sometimes a-dropping from the sky
I heard the skylark sing ;
Sometimes all little birds that are,
How they seemed to fill the sea and air
With their sweet jargoning !

And now 'twas like all instruments,
Now like a lonely flute ;
And now it is an angel's song,
That makes the heavens be mute.

It ceased ; yet still the sails made on
A pleasant noise till noon,
A noise like of a hidden brook
In the leafy month of June,
That to the sleeping woods all night
Singeth a quiet tune.

Till noon we quietly sailed on,
Yet never a breeze did breathe :
Slowly and smoothly went the ship,
Moved onward from beneath.

The lonesome Spirit from the south-pole carries on

Under the keel nine fathom deep,
From the land of mist and snow,
The Spirit slid : and it was he

That made the ship to go.
The sails at noon left off their tune,
And the ship stood still also.

The Sun, right up above the mast,
Had fixed her to the ocean :
But in a minute she 'gan stir,
With a short uneasy motion—
Backwards and forwards half her length
With a short uneasy motion.   .

Then like a pawing horse let go,
She made a sudden bound :
It flung the blood into my head,
And I fell down in a swound.

How long in that same fit I lay,
I have not to declare ;
But ere my living life returned,
I heard, and in my soul discerned
Two voices in the air.

'Is it he?' quoth one, 'Is this the man?
By him who died on cross,
With his cruel bow he laid full low
The harmless Albatross.

The Spirit who bideth by himself
In the land of mist and snow,
He loved the bird that loved the man
Who shot him with his bow.'

the ship as far as the Line, in obedience to the angelic troop, but still requireth vengeance.

The Polar Spirit's fellow demons, the invisible inhabitants of the element, take part in his wrong; and two of them relate, one to the other, that penance long and heavy for the ancient Mariner hath been accorded to the Polar Spirit, who returneth southward.

The other was a softer voice,
As soft as honey-dew:
Quoth he, 'The man hath penance
      done,
And penance more will do.'

PART VI.

FIRST VOICE.

'But tell me, tell me! speak again,
Thy soft response renewing—
What makes that ship drive on so
      fast?
What is the ocean doing?'

SECOND VOICE.

'Still as a slave before his lord,
The ocean hath no blast;
His great bright eye most silently
Up to the Moon is cast—

If he may know which way to go;
For she guides him smooth or grim.
See, brother, see! how graciously
She looketh down on him.'

FIRST VOICE.

' But why drives on that ship so fast,
Without or wave or wind ? '

SECOND VOICE.

' The air is cut away before,
And closes from behind.

Fly, brother, fly ! more high, more high !
Or we shall be belated :
For slow and slow that ship will go,
When the Mariner's trance is abated.'

I woke, and we were sailing on
As in a gentle weather :
'Twas night, calm night, the moon was
    high ;
The dead men stood together.

All stood together on the deck,
For a charnel-dungeon fitter :
All fixed on me their stony eyes,
That in the Moon did glitter.

The pang, the curse, with which they
    died,
Had never passed away :
I could not draw my eyes from theirs,
Nor turn them up to pray.

[Marginal gloss, right column:]

The Mariner hath been cast into a trance ; for the angelic power causeth the vessel to drive northward faster than human life could endure.

The supernatural motion is retarded ; the Mariner awakes, and his penance begins anew.

The curse is finally expiated.

And now this spell was snapt: once more
I viewed the ocean green,
And looked far forth, yet little saw
Of what had else been seen—

Like one, that on a lonesome road
Doth walk in fear and dread,
And having once turned round, walks on,
And turns no more his head;
Because he knows, a frightful fiend
Doth close behind him tread.

But soon there breathed a wind on me,
Nor sound nor motion made:
Its path was not upon the sea,
In ripple or in shade.

It raised my hair, it fanned my cheek
Like a meadow-gale of spring—
It mingled strangely with my fears,
Yet it felt like a welcoming.

Swiftly, swiftly flew the ship,
Yet she sailed softly too:
Sweetly, sweetly blew the breeze—
On me alone it blew.

Oh! dream of joy! is this indeed

And the ancient Mariner beholdeth his native country.

The light-house top I see?
Is this the hill? is this the kirk?
Is this mine own countree?

We drifted o'er the harbour-bar,
And I with sobs did pray—
O let me be awake, my God!
Or let me sleep alway.

The harbour-bay was clear as glass,
So smoothly it was strewn!
And on the bay the moonlight lay,
And the shadow of the Moon.

The rock shone bright, the kirk no
    less,
That stands above the rock:
The moonlight steeped in silentness
The steady weathercock.

And the bay was white with silent
    light
Till, rising from the same,
Full many shapes, that shadows were, *The angelic spirits leave the dead bodies.*
In crimson colours came.

A little distance from the prow *And appear in their own forms of light.*
Those crimson shadows were:
I turned my eyes upon the deck—
Oh, Christ! what saw I there!

Each corse lay flat, lifeless and flat,
And, by the holy rood!
A man all light, a seraph-man,
On every corse there stood.

This seraph-band, each waved his hand:
It was a heavenly sight!
They stood as signals to the land,
Each one a lovely light;

This seraph-band, each waved his hand,
No voice did they impart—
No voice; but oh! the silence sank
Like music on my heart.

But soon I heard the dash of oars,
I heard the Pilot's cheer;
My head was turned perforce away,
And I saw a boat appear.

The Pilot and the Pilot's boy,
I heard them coming fast:
Dear Lord in Heaven! it was a joy
The dead men could not blast.

I saw a third—I heard his voice:
It is the Hermit good!
He singeth loud his godly hymns
That he makes in the wood.
He'll shrieve my soul, he'll wash away
The Albatross's blood.

PART VII.

Tнıs Hermit good lives in that wood
Which slopes down to the sea.
How loudly his sweet voice he rears!
He loves to talk with marineres
That come from a far countree.

He kneels at morn, and noon, and
    eve—
He hath a cushion plump:
It is the moss that wholly hides
The rotted old oak-stump.

The skiff-boat neared: I heard them
    talk,
' Why, this is strange, I trow!
Where are those lights so many and
    fair,
That signal made but now?'

' Strange, by my faith!' the Hermit
    said—
' And they answered not our cheer!

The Hermit of the wood,

Approacheth the ship with wonder.

The planks looked warped! and see
 those sails,
How thin they are and sere!
I never saw aught like to them,
Unless perchance it were

Brown skeletons of leaves that lag
My forest-brook along;
When the ivy-tod is heavy with snow,
And the owlet whoops to the wolf below,
That eats the she-wolf's young.'

'Dear Lord! it hath a fiendish look—
(The Pilot made reply)
I am a-feared'—'Push on, push on!'
Said the Hermit cheerily.

The boat came closer to the ship,
But I nor spake nor stirred;
The boat came close beneath the ship,
And straight a sound was heard.

The ship suddenly sinketh. Under the water it rumbled on,
Still louder and more dread:
It reached the ship, it split the bay;
The ship went down like lead.

The ancient Mariner is saved in the Pilot's boat. Stunned by that loud and dreadful
 sound,
Which sky and ocean smote,

Like one that hath been seven days
    drowned
My body lay afloat;
But swift as dreams, myself I found
Within the Pilot's boat.

Upon the whirl, where sank the ship,
The boat spun round and round;
And all was still, save that the hill
Was telling of the sound.

I moved my lips—the Pilot shrieked
And fell down in a fit;
The holy Hermit raised his eyes,
And prayed where he did sit.

I took the oars: the Pilot's boy,
Who now doth crazy go,
Laughed loud and long, and all the
    while
His eyes went to and fro.
'Ha! ha!' quoth he, 'full plain I
    see,
The Devil knows how to row.'

And now, all in my own countree,
I stood on the firm land!
The Hermit stepped forth from the
    boat,
And scarcely he could stand.

'O shrieve me, shrieve me, holy man!'
The Hermit crossed his brow.
'Say quick,' quoth he, 'I bid thee
        say—
What manner of man art thou?'

Forthwith this frame of mine was
        wrenched
With a woful agony,
Which forced me to begin my tale;
And then it left me free.

Since then, at an uncertain hour,
That agony returns :
And till my ghastly tale is told,
This heart within me burns.

I pass, like night, from land to land;
I have strange power of speech;
That moment that his face I see,
I know the man that must hear me :
To him my tale I teach.

What loud uproar bursts from that
        door !
The wedding-guests are there :
But in the garden-bower the bride
And bride-maids singing are :
And hark the little vesper bell,
Which biddeth me to prayer !

O Wedding-Guest! this soul hath been
Alone on a wide wide sea:
So lonely 'twas, that God himself
Scarce seemed there to be.

O sweeter than the marriage-feast,
'Tis sweeter far to me,
To walk together to the kirk
With a goodly company !—

To walk together to the kirk,
And all together pray,
While each to his great Father bends,
Old men, and babes, and loving friends
And youths and maidens gay !

Farewell! farewell! but this I tell
To thee, thou Wedding-Guest!
He prayeth well, who loveth well
Both man and bird and beast.

And to teach
by his own
example
love and re-
verence to
all things
that God
made and
loveth.

He prayeth best, who loveth best
All things both great and small ;
For the dear God who loveth us,
He made and loveth all."

The Mariner, whose eye is bright,
Whose beard with age is hoar,
Is gone : and now the Wedding-Guest
Turned from the bridegroom's door.

He went like one that hath been stunned,
And is of sense forlorn :
A sadder and a wiser man,
He rose the morrow morn.

1797.

CHRISTABEL.

PREFACE.*

THE first part of the following poem was written in the year 1797, at Stowey, in the county of Somerset. The second part, after my return from Germany, in the year 1800, at Keswick, Cumberland. It is probable, that if the poem had been finished at either of the former periods, or if even the first and second part had been published in the year 1800, the impression of its originality would have been much greater than I dare at present expect. But for this, I have only my own indolence to blame. The dates are mentioned for the exclusive purpose of precluding charges of plagiarism or servile imitation from myself. For there is amongst us a set of critics, who seem to hold, that every possible thought and image is traditional; who have no notion that there are such things as fountains in the world, small as well as great; and who would therefore charitably derive every rill they behold flowing, from a perforation made in some other man's tank. I am confident, however, that as far as the present poem is concerned, the celebrated poets whose writings I might be suspected of having imitated, either in particular passages, or in the tone and the spirit of the whole, would be among the first to vindicate me from the charge, and who, on any striking coincidence, would permit me to address them in this doggerel version of two monkish Latin hexameters.

'Tis mine and it is likewise yours;
But an if this will not do,
Let it be mine, good friend! for I
Am the poorer of the two.

* To the edition of 1816.

I have only to add, that the metre of the Christabel is not, properly speaking, irregular, though it may seem so from its being founded on a new principle; namely, that of counting in each line the accents, not the syllables. Though the latter may vary from seven to twelve, yet in each line the accents will be found to be only four. Nevertheless this occasional variation in number of syllables is not introduced wantonly, or for the mere ends of convenience, but in correspondence with some transition, in the nature of the imagery or passion.

PART I.

'Tis the middle of night by the castle clock,
And the owls have awakened the crowing cock;
Tu—whit!——Tu—whoo!
And hark, again! the crowing cock,
How drowsily it crew.

Sir Leoline, the Baron rich,
Hath a toothless mastiff bitch;
From her kennel beneath the rock
She maketh answer to the clock,
Four for the quarters, and twelve for the hour;
Ever and aye, by shine and shower,
Sixteen short howls, not over loud;
Some say, she sees my lady's shroud.

Is the night chilly and dark?
The night is chilly, but not dark.
The thin gray cloud is spread on high,
It covers but not hides the sky.

The moon is behind, and at the full;
And yet she looks both small and dull.
The night is chill, the cloud is gray:
'Tis a month before the month of May,
And the Spring comes slowly up this way.

The lovely lady, Christabel,
Whom her father loves so well,
What makes her in the wood so late,
A furlong from the castle gate?
She had dreams all yesternight
Of her own betrothed knight;
And she in the midnight wood will pray
For the weal of her lover that's far away.

She stole along, she nothing spoke,
The sighs she heaved were soft and low,
And naught was green upon the oak,
But moss and rarest mistletoe:
She kneels beneath the huge oak tree,
And in silence prayeth she.

The lady sprang up suddenly,
The lovely lady, Christabel!*
It moaned as near, as near can be,
But what it is, she cannot tell.—
On the other side it seems to be,
Of the huge, broad-breasted, old oak tree.

The night is chill; the forest bare;

Is it the wind that moaneth bleak?
There is not wind enough in the air
To move away the ringlet curl
From the lovely lady's cheek—
There is not wind enough to twirl
The one red leaf, the last of its clan,
That dances as often as dance it can,
Hanging so light, and hanging so high,
On the topmost twig that looks up at the sky.

Hush, beating heart of Christabel!
Jesu, Maria, shield her well!
She folded her arms beneath her cloak,
And stole to the other side of the oak.
　　What sees she there?

There she sees a damsel bright,
Drest in a silken robe of white,
That shadowy in the moonlight shone:
The neck that made that white robe wan,
Her stately neck, and arms were bare;
Her blue-veined feet unsandal'd were,
And wildly glittered here and there
The gems entangled in her hair.
I guess, 'twas frightful there to see
A lady so richly clad as she—
Beautiful exceedingly!

Mary mother, save me now!
(Said Christabel,) And who art thou?

The lady strange made answer meet,
And her voice was faint and sweet :—
Have pity on my sore distress,
I scarce can speak for weariness :
Stretch forth thy hand, and have no fear !
Said Christabel, How camest thou here ?
And the lady, whose voice was faint and sweet,
Did thus pursue her answer meet :—

My sire is of a noble line,
And my name is Geraldine :
Five warriors seized me yestermorn,
Me, even me, a maid forlorn :   .
They choked my cries with force and fright
And tied me on a palfrey white.
The palfrey was as fleet as wind,
And they rode furiously behind.
They spurred amain, their steeds were white ,
And once we crossed the shade of night.
As sure as heaven shall rescue me,
I have no thought what men they be ;
Nor do I know how long it is
(For I have lain entranced I wis)
Since one, the tallest of the five,
Took me from the palfrey's back,
A weary woman, scarce alive.
Some muttered words his comrades spoke :
He placed me underneath this oak ;
He swore they would return with haste ;
Whither they went I cannot tell—

I thought I heard, some minutes past,
Sounds as of a castle bell.
Stretch forth thy hand (thus ended she,)
And help a wretched maid to flee.

Then Christabel stretched forth her hand
And comforted fair Geraldine:
O well, bright dame ! may you command
The service of Sir Leoline ;
And gladly our stout chivalry
Will he send forth, and friends withal,
To guide and guard you safe and free
Home to your noble father's hall.

She rose : and forth with steps they passed
That strove to be, and were not, fast.
Her gracious stars the lady blest,
And thus spake on sweet Christabel :
All our household are at rest,
The hall as silent as the cell :
Sir Leoline is weak in health,
And may not well awakened be,
But we will move as if in stealth,
And I beseech your courtesy,
This night, to share your couch with me.

They crossed the moat, and Christabel
Took the key that fitted well ;
A little door she opened straight,
All in the middle of the gate ;

The gate that was ironed within and without,
Where an army in battle array had marched
    out.
The lady sank, belike through pain,
And Christabel with might and main
Lifted her up, a weary weight,
Over the threshold of the gate :
Then the lady rose again,
And moved, as she were not in pain.

So free from danger, free from fear,
They crossed the court: right glad they were.
And Christabel devoutly cried
To the Lady by her side ;
Praise we the Virgin all divine
Who hath rescued thee from thy distress !
Alas, alas ! said Geraldine,
I cannot speak for weariness.
So free from danger, free from fear,
They crossed the court ; right glad they were.

Outside her kennel the mastiff old
Lay fast asleep, in moonshine cold.
The mastiff old did not awake,
Yet she an angry moan did make !
And what can ail the mastiff bitch ?
Never till now she uttered yell
Beneath the eye of Christabel.
Perhaps it is the owlet's scritch :
For what can ail the mastiff bitch ?

They passed the hall, that echoes still,
Pass as lightly as you will!
The brands were flat, the brands were dying,
Amid their own white ashes lying;
But when the lady passed, there came
A tongue of light, a fit of flame;
And Christabel saw the lady's eye,
And nothing else saw she thereby,
Save the boss of the shield of Sir Leoline tall,
Which hung in a murky old niche in the wall.
O softly tread, said Christabel,
My father seldom sleepeth well.

Sweet Christabel her feet doth bare,
And, jealous of the listening air,
They steal their way from stair to stair,
Now in glimmer, and now in gloom,
And now they pass the Baron's room,
As still as death with stifled breath!
And now have reached her chamber door;
And now doth Geraldine press down
The rushes of the chamber floor.

The moon shines dim in the open air,
And not a moonbeam enters here.
But they without its light can see
The chamber carved so curiously,
Carved with figures strange and sweet,
All made out of the carver's brain,
For a lady's chamber meet:

The lamp with twofold silver chain
Is fastened to an angel's feet.
The silver lamp burns dead and dim;
• But Christabel the lamp will trim.
She trimmed the lamp, and made it bright,
And left it swinging to and fro,
While Geraldine, in wretched plight,
Sank down upon the floor below.

O weary lady, Geraldine,
I pray you, drink this cordial wine!
It is a wine of virtuous powers;
My mother made it of wild flowers.

And will your mother pity me,
Who am a maiden most forlorn?
Christabel answered—Woe is me!
She died the hour that I was born.
I have heard the gray-haired friar tell,
How on her death-bed she did say,
That she should hear the castle-bell
Strike twelve upon my wedding-day.
O mother dear! that thou wert here!
I would, said Geraldine, she were!
But soon with altered voice, said she—
"Off, wandering mother! Peak and pine!
I have power to bid thee flee."
Alas! what ails poor Geraldine?
Why stares she with unsettled eye?
Can she the bodiless dead espy?

And why with hollow voice cries she,
" Off, woman, off! this hour is mine—
Though thou her guardian spirit be,
Off, woman, off! 'tis given to me."

    Then Christabel knelt by the lady's side,
And raised to heaven her eyes so blue—
Alas! said she, this ghastly ride—
Dear lady! it hath wildered you!
The lady wiped her moist cold brow,
And faintly said, " 'tis over now!"

    Again the wild-flower wine she drank:
Her fair large eyes 'gan glitter bright,
And from the floor whereon she sank,
The lofty lady stood upright;
She was most beautiful to see,
Like a lady of a far countrée.

    And thus the lofty lady spake—
All they, who live in the upper sky,
Do love you, holy Christabel!
And you love them, and for their sake
And for the good which me befell,
Even I in my degree will try,
Fair maiden, to requite you well.
But now unrobe yourself; for I
Must pray, ere yet in bed I lie.

    Quoth Christabel, so let it be!

And as the lady bade, did she.
Her gentle limbs did she undress,
And lay down in her loveliness.

But through her brain of weal and woe
So many thoughts moved to and fro,
That vain it were her lids to close :
So half-way from the bed she rose,
And on her elbow did recline
To look at the lady Geraldine.

Beneath the lamp the lady bowed,
And slowly rolled her eyes around ;
Then drawing in her breath aloud,
Like one that shuddered, she unbound
The cincture from beneath her breast :
Her silken robe, and inner vest,
Dropt to her feet, and full in view,
Behold ! her bosom and half her side——
A sight to dream of, not to tell !
O shield her ! shield sweet Christabel !

Yet Geraldine nor speaks nor stirs ;
Ah ! what a stricken look was hers !
Deep from within she seems half-way
To lift some weight with sick assay,
And eyes the maid and seeks delay ;
Then suddenly as one defied
Collects herself in scorn and pride
And lay down by the maiden's side !—

And in her arms the maid she took,
     Ah well-a-day !
And with low voice and doleful look
     These words did say :
In the touch of this bosom there worketh a spell,
Which is lord of thy utterance, Christabel !
Thou knowest to-night, and wilt know to-morrow
This mark of my shame, this seal of my sorrow ;
     But vainly thou warrest,
     For this is alone in
     Thy power to declare,
     That in the dim forest
     Thou heard'st a low moaning,
And found'st a bright lady, surpassingly fair :
And didst bring her home with thee in love and
     in charity,
To shield her and shelter her from the damp air.

THE CONCLUSION TO PART I.

It was a lovely sight to see
The lady Christabel, when she
Was praying at the old oak tree.
     Amid the jagged shadows
     Of mossy leafless boughs,
     Kneeling in the moonlight,
     To make her gentle vows ;

Her slender palms together prest,
Heaving sometimes on her breast;
Her face resigned to bliss or bale—
Her face, oh call it fair not pale,
And both blue eyes more bright than clear,
Each about to have a tear.

With open eyes (ah woe is me!)
Asleep, and dreaming fearfully,
Fearfully dreaming, yet I wis,
Dreaming that alone, which is—
O sorrow and shame! Can this be she,
The lady, who knelt at the old oak tree?
And lo! the worker of these harms,
That holds the maiden in her arms,
Seems to slumber still and mild,
As a mother with her child.

A star hath set, a star hath risen,
O Geraldine! since arms of thine
Have been the lovely lady's prison.
O Geraldine! one hour was thine—
Thou'st had thy will! By tairn and rill,
The night-birds all that hour were still.
But now they are jubilant anew,
From cliff and tower, tu—whoo! tu—whoo!
Tu—whoo! tu—whoo! from wood and fell!
And see! the lady Christabel
Gathers herself from out her trance;
Her limbs relax, her countenance

Grows sad and soft; the smooth thin lids
Close o'er her eyes; and tears she sheds—
Large tears that leave the lashes bright!
And oft the while she seems to smile
As infants at a sudden light!
Yea, she doth smile, and she doth weep,
Like a youthful hermitess,
Beauteous in a wilderness,
Who, praying always, prays in sleep.
And, if she move unquietly,
Perchance, 'tis but the blood so free,
Comes back and tingles in her feet.
No doubt she hath a vision sweet.
What if her guardian spirit 'twere?
What if she knew her mother near?
But this she knows, in joys and woes,
That saints will aid if men will call:
For the blue sky bends over all!

PART II.

EACH matin bell, the Baron saith,
Knells us back to a world of death.
These words Sir Leoline first said,
When he rose and found his lady dead:
These words Sir Leoline will say,
Many a morn to his dying day!

And hence the custom and law began,
That still at dawn the sacristan,
Who duly pulls the heavy bell,
Five and forty beads must tell
Between each stroke—a warning knell,
Which not a soul can choose but hear
From Bratha Head to Wyndermere.

Saith Bracy the bard, So let it knell!
And let the drowsy sacristan
Still count as slowly as he can!
There is no lack of such, I ween,
As well fill up the space between.
In Langdale Pike and Witch's Lair,
And Dungeon-ghyll so foully rent,
With ropes of rock and bells of air
Three sinful sextons' ghosts are pent,

Who all give back, one after t'other,
The death-note to their living brother;
And oft too, by the knell offended,
Just as their one! two! three! is ended,
The devil mocks the doleful tale
With a merry peal from Borodale.

The air is still! through mist and cloud
That merry peal comes ringing loud;
And Geraldine shakes off her dread,
And rises lightly from the bed;
Puts on her silken vestments white,
And tricks her hair in lovely plight,
And nothing doubting of her spell
Awakens the lady Christabel.
" Sleep you, sweet lady Christabel?
I trust that you have rested well."

And Christabel awoke and spied
The same who lay down by her side—
O rather say, the same whom she
Raised up beneath the old oak tree!
Nay, fairer yet! and yet more fair!
For she belike hath drunken deep
Of all the blessedness of sleep!
And while she spake, her look, her air
Such gentle thankfulness declare,
That (so it seemed) her girded vests
Grew tight beneath her heaving breasts.
" Sure I have sinned!" said Christabel,

"Now heaven be praised if all be well!"
And in low faltering tones, yet sweet,
Did she the lofty lady greet,
With such perplexity of mind
As dreams too lively leave behind.

So quickly she rose, and quickly arrayed
Her maiden limbs, and having prayed
That He, who on the cross did groan,
Might wash away her sins unknown,
She forthwith led fair Geraldine
To meet her sire, Sir Leoline.

The lovely maid and the lady tall
Are pacing both into the hall,
And pacing on through page and groom,
Enter the Baron's presence room.

The Baron rose, and while he prest
His gentle daughter to his breast,
With cheerful wonder in his eyes
The lady Geraldine espies,
And gave such welcome to the same,
As might beseem so bright a dame!

But when he heard the lady's tale,
And when she told her father's name,
Why waxed Sir Leoline so pale,
Murmuring o'er the name again,
Lord Roland de Vaux of Tryermaine?

Alas! they had been friends in youth;
But whispering tongues can poison truth;
And constancy lives in realms above;
And life is thorny; and youth is vain;
And to be wroth with one we love
Doth work like madness in the brain.
And thus it chanced, as I divine,
With Roland and Sir Leoline.
Each spake words of high disdain
And insult to his heart's best brother:
They parted—ne'er to meet again!
But never either found another
To free the hollow heart from paining—
They stood aloof, the scars remaining,
Like cliffs which had been rent asunder;
A dreary sea now flows between;—
But neither heat, nor frost, nor thunder,
Shall wholly do away, I ween,
The marks of that which once hath been.

Sir Leoline, a moment's space,
Stood gazing on the damsel's face:
And the youthful Lord of Tryermaine
Came back upon his heart again.

O then the Baron forgot his age,
His noble heart swelled high with rage;
He swore by the wounds in Jesu's side,
He would proclaim it far and wide
With trump and solemn heraldry,

That they who thus had wronged the dame,
Were base as spotted infamy !
" And if they dare deny the same,
My herald shall appoint a week,
And let the recreant traitors seek
My tourney court—that there and then
I may dislodge their reptile souls
From the bodies and forms of men ! "
He spake : his eye in lightning rolls !
For the lady was ruthlessly seized; and he
      kenned
In the beautiful lady the child of his friend !

And now the tears were on his face,
And fondly in his arms he took
Fair Geraldine, who met the embrace,
Prolonging it with joyous look.
Which when she viewed, a vision fell
Upon the soul of Christabel,
The vision of fear, the touch and pain !
She shrunk and shuddered, and saw again—
(Ah, woe is me ! Was it for thee,
Thou gentle maid ! such sights to see ?)
Again she saw that bosom old,
Again she felt that bosom cold,
And drew in her breath with a hissing sound :
Whereat the Knight turned wildly round,
And nothing saw but his own sweet maid
With eyes upraised, as one that prayed.

The touch, the sight, had passed away,
And in its stead that vision blest,
Which comforted her after-rest
While in the lady's arms she lay,
Had put a rapture in her breast,
And on her lips and o'er her eyes
Spread smiles like light!
                              With new surprise,
" What ails then my beloved child?"
The Baron said—His daughter mild
Made answer, "All will yet be well!"
I ween, she had no power to tell
Aught else: so mighty was the spell.

    Yet he, who saw this Geraldine,
Had deemed her sure a thing divine.
Such sorrow with such grace she blended,
As if she feared she had offended
Sweet Christabel, that gentle maid!
And with such lowly tones she prayed,
She might be sent without delay
Home to her father's mansion.
                              " Nay!
Nay, by my soul!" said Leoline.
" Ho! Bracy, the bard, the charge be thine!
Go thou, with music sweet and loud,
And take two steeds with trappings proud,
And take the youth whom thou lov'st best
To bear thy harp, and learn thy song,
And clothe you both in solemn vest,

And over the mountains haste along,
Lest wandering folk, that are abroad,
Detain you on the valley road.
And when he has crossed the Irthing flood,
My merry bard! he hastes, he hastes
Up Knorren Moor, through Halegarth Wood,
And reaches soon that castle good
Which stands and threatens Scotland's wastes.

"Bard Bracy! bard Bracy! your horses are fleet,
Ye must ride up the hall, your music so sweet,
More loud than your horses' echoing feet!
And loud and loud to Lord Roland call,
Thy daughter is safe in Langdale hall!
Thy beautiful daughter is safe and free—
Sir Leoline greets thee thus through me.
He bids thee come without delay
With all thy numerous array;
And take thy lovely daughter home:
And he will meet thee on the way
With all his numerous array
White with their panting palfreys' foam:
And by mine honor! I will say,
That I repent me of the day
When I spake words of fierce disdain
To Roland de Vaux of Tryermaine!—
—For since that evil hour hath flown,
Many a summer's sun hath shone;
Yet ne'er found I a friend again
Like Roland de Vaux of Tryermaine."

The lady fell, and clasped his knees,
Her face upraised, her eyes o'erflowing;
And Bracy replied, with faltering voice,
His gracious hail on all bestowing!—
"Thy words, thou sire of Christabel,
Are sweeter than my harp can tell;
Yet might I gain a boon of thee,
This day my journey should not be,
So strange a dream hath come to me;
That I had vowed with music loud
To clear yon wood from thing unblest,
Warned by a vision in my rest!
For in my sleep I saw that dove,
That gentle bird, whom thou dost love,
And call'st by thy own daughter's name—
Sir Leoline! I saw the same
Fluttering, and uttering fearful moan,
Among the green herbs in the forest alone.
Which when I saw and when I heard,
I wonder'd what might ail the bird;
For nothing near it could I see,   [old tree.
Save the grass and green herbs underneath the

"And in my dream methought I went
To search out what might there be found;
And what the sweet bird's trouble meant,
That thus lay fluttering on the ground.
I went and peered, and could descry
No cause for her distressful cry;
But yet for her dear lady's sake

I stooped, methought, the dove to take,
When lo! I saw a bright green snake
Coiled around its wings and neck,
Green as the herbs on which it couched,
Close by the dove's its head it crouched;
And with the dove it heaves and stirs,
Swelling its neck as she swelled hers!
I woke; it was the midnight hour,
The clock was echoing in the tower;
But though my slumber was gone by,
This dream it would not pass away—
It seems to live upon my eye!
And thence I vowed this self-same day,
With music strong and saintly song
To wander through the forest bare,
Lest aught unholy loiter there."

Thus Bracy said: the Baron, the while,
Half-listening heard him with a smile;
Then turned to Lady Geraldine,
His eyes made up of wonder and love;
And said in courtly accents fine,
"Sweet maid, Lord Roland's beauteous dove
With arms more strong than harp or song,
Thy sire and I will crush the snake!"
He kissed her forehead as he spake,
And Geraldine, in maiden wise,
Casting down her large bright eyes,
With blushing cheek and courtesy fine
She turned her from Sir Leoline;

Softly gathering up her train,
That o'er her right arm fell again;
And folded her arms across her chest.
And couched her head upon her breast,
And looked askance at Christabel——
Jesu Maria, shield her well!

A snake's small eye blinks dull and shy,
And the lady's eyes they shrunk in her head,
Each shrunk up to a serpent's eye,
And with somewhat of malice, and more of dread,
At Christabel she looked askance!—
One moment—and the sight was fled!
But Christabel in dizzy trance
Stumbling on the unsteady ground
Shuddered aloud, with a hissing sound;
And Geraldine again turned round,
And like a thing, that sought relief,
Full of wonder and full of grief,
She rolled her large bright eyes divine
Wildly on Sir Leoline.

The maid, alas! her thoughts are gone,
She nothing sees—no sight but one!
The maid, devoid of guile and sin,
I know not how, in fearful wise
So deeply had she drunken in
That look, those shrunken serpent eyes,
That all her features were resigned
To this sole image in her mind;

And passively did imitate
That look of dull and treacherous hate !
And thus she stood in dizzy trance,
Still picturing that look askance
With forced unconscious sympathy
Full before her father's view——
As far as such a look could be,
In eyes so innocent and blue !
And when the trance was o'er, the maid
Paused awhile, and inly prayed :
Then falling at the Baron's feet,
" By my mother's soul do I entreat
That thou this woman send away ! "
She said : and more she could not say :
For what she knew she could not tell,
O'ermastered by the mighty spell.

   Why is thy cheek so wan and wild,
Sir Leoline ?   Thy only child
Lies at thy feet, thy joy, thy pride,
So fair, so innocent, so mild ;
The same, for whom thy lady died !
O by the pangs of her dear mother
Think thou no evil of thy child !
For her, and thee, and for no other,
She prayed the moment ere she died :
Prayed that the babe for whom she died,
Might prove her dear lord's joy and pride !
That prayer her deadly pangs beguiled,
      Sir Leoline !

And wouldst thou wrong thy only child,
    Her child and thine?

Within the Baron's heart and brain
If thoughts, like these, had any share,
They only swelled his rage and pain,
And did but work confusion there.
His heart was cleft with pain and rage,
His cheeks they quivered, his eyes were wild.
Dishonoured thus in his old age;
Dishonoured by his only child,
And all his hospitality
To the wronged daughter of his friend
By more than woman's jealousy
Brought thus to a disgraceful end—
He rolled his eye with stern regard
Upon the gentle minstrel bard,
And said in tones abrupt, austere—
" Why, Bracy! dost thou loiter here?
I bade thee hence!"   The bard obeyed;
And turning from his own sweet maid,
The aged knight, Sir Leoline,
Led forth the lady Geraldine!

THE CONCLUSION TO PART II.

A LITTLE child, a limber elf,
Singing, dancing to itself,

A fairy thing with red round cheeks,
That always finds, and never seeks,
Makes such a vision to the sight
As fills a father's eyes with light;
And pleasures flow in so thick and fast
Upon his heart, that he at last
Must needs express his love's excess
With words of unmeant bitterness.
Perhaps 'tis pretty to force together
Thoughts so all unlike each other;
To mutter and mock a broken charm,
To dally with wrong that does no harm.
Perhaps 'tis tender too and pretty
At each wild word to feel within
A sweet recoil of love and pity.
And what, if in a world of sin
(O sorrow and shame should this be true!)
Such giddiness of heart and brain
Comes seldom save from rage and pain,
So talks as it's most used to do.

PART I., 1797.—PART II., 1800.

KUBLA KHAN; OR, A VISION IN A DREAM

A FRAGMENT.

In the summer of the year 1797, the Author, then in ill health, had retired to a lonely farm-house between Porlock and Linton, on the Exmoor confines of Somerset and Devonshire. In consequence of a slight indisposition, an anodyne had been prescribed, from the effect of which he fell asleep in his chair at the moment he was reading the following sentence, or words of the same substance, in "Purchas's Pilgrimage:"—"Here the Khan Kubla commanded a palace to be built, and a stately garden thereunto: and thus ten miles of fertile ground were inclosed with a wall." The author continued for about three hours in a profound sleep, at least of the external senses, during which time he has the most vivid confidence that he could not have composed less than from two to three hundred lines; if that indeed can be called composition in which all the images rose up before him as things, with a parallel production of the correspondent expressions, without any sensation or consciousness of effort. On awaking he appeared to himself to have a distinct recollection of the whole, and taking his pen, ink, and paper, instantly and eagerly wrote down the lines that are here preserved. At this moment he was unfortunately called out by a person on business from Porlock, and detained by him above an hour, and on his return to his room, found, to his no small surprise and mortification, that though he still retained some vague and dim recollection of the general purport of the vision, yet, with the exception of some eight or ten scattered lines and images, all the rest had passed away like the images on the surface of a stream into which a stone had been cast, but, alas! without the after restoration of the latter.

Then all the charm
Is broken — all that phantom-world so fair
Vanishes, and a thousand circlets spread,
And each mis-shape the other. Stay awhile,
Poor youth! who scarcely dar'st lift up thine eyes—
The stream will soon renew its smoothness, soon
The visions will return! And lo! he stays,
And soon the fragments dim of lovely forms
Come trembling back, unite, and now once more
The pool becomes a mirror.

Yet from the still surviving recollections in his mind, the Author has frequently purposed to finish for himself what had been originally, as it were, given to him. Αὔριον ἄδιον ᾄσω· but the to-morrow is yet to come.

1816.

In Xanadu did Kubla Khan
A stately pleasure-dome decree:
Where Alph, the sacred river, ran
Through caverns measureless to man
    Down to a sunless sea.
So twice five miles of fertile ground
With walls and towers were girdled round:
And there were gardens bright with sinuous rills
Where blossomed many an incense-bearing tree;
And here were forests ancient as the hills,
Enfolding sunny spots of greenery.

But oh! that deep romantic chasm which slanted
Down the green hill athwart a cedarn cover!
A savage place! as holy and enchanted
As e'er beneath a waning moon was haunted
By woman wailing for her demon-lover!

And from this chasm, with ceaseless turmoil
    seething,
As if this earth in fast thick pants were breathing,
A mighty fountain momently was forced;
Amid whose swift half-intermitted burst
Huge fragments vaulted like rebounding hail,
Or chaffy grain beneath the thresher's flail:
And 'mid these dancing rocks at once and ever
It flung up momently the sacred river.
Five miles meandering with a mazy motion
Through wood and dale the sacred river ran,
Then reached the caverns measureless to man,
And sank in tumult to a lifeless ocean:
And 'mid this tumult Kubla heard from far
Ancestral voices prophesying war!

    The shadow of the dome of pleasure
    Floated midway on the waves;
    Where was heard the mingled measure
    From the fountain and the caves.
  It was a miracle of rare device,
  A sunny pleasure-dome with caves of ice!
    A damsel with a dulcimer
    In a vision once I saw:
    It was an Abyssinian maid,
    And on her dulcimer she played,
    Singing of Mount Abora.
    Could I revive within me
    Her symphony and song,
    To such a deep delight 'twould win me

That with music loud and long,
I would build that dome in air,
That sunny dome ! those caves of ice !
And all who heard should see them there,
And all should cry, Beware ! Beware !
His flashing eyes, his floating hair !
Weave a circle round him thrice,
And close your eyes with holy dread,
For he on honey-dew hath fed,
And drunk the milk of Paradise.

1797.

THE WANDERINGS OF CAIN.

PREFATORY NOTE.

A PROSE composition, one not in metre at least, seems *primâ facie* to require explanation or apology. It was written in the year 1798, near Nether Stowey, in Somersetshire, at which place (*sanctum et amabile nomen!* rich by so many associations and recollections) the author had taken up his residence in order to enjoy the society and close neighbourhood of a dear and honoured friend, T. Poole, Esq. The work was to have been written in concert with another, whose name is too venerable within the precincts of genius to be unnecessarily brought into connection with such a trifle, and who was then residing at a small distance from Nether Stowey. The title and subject were suggested by myself, who likewise drew out the scheme and the contents for each of the three books or cantos, of which the work was to consist, and which, the reader is to be informed, was to have been finished in one night! My partner undertook the first canto: I the second: and which ever had done first, was to set about the third. Almost thirty years have passed by; yet at this moment I cannot, without something more than a smile, moot the question which of the two things was the more impracticable, for a mind so eminently original to compose another man's thoughts and fancies, or for a taste so austerely pure and simple to imitate the Death of Abel? Methinks I see his grand and noble countenance as at the moment when having despatched my own portion of the task at full finger-speed, I hastened to him with my manuscript—that look of humourous despondency fixed on his almost blank sheet of paper, and then its silent mock-piteous admission of failure struggling with the sense of the exceeding ridiculousness of the whole scheme—which broke up in a laugh: and the Ancient Mariner was written instead.

Years afterward, however, the draft of the plan and proposed incidents, and the portion executed, obtained favour in the eyes of more than one person, whose judgment on a poetic work could not but have weighed with me, even though no parental partiality had been thrown into the same scale, as a makeweight: and I determined on commencing anew, and composing the whole in stanzas, and made some progress in realizing this intention, when adverse gales drove my bark off the " Fortunate Isles " of the Muses: and then other and more momentous interests prompted a different voyage, to firmer anchorage and a securer port. I have in vain tried to recover the lines from the palimpsest tablet of my memory: and I can only offer the introductory stanza, which had been committed to writing for the purpose of procuring a friend's judgment on the metre, as a specimen.

Encinctured with a twine of leaves,
That leafy twine his only dress!
A lovely Boy was plucking fruits,
By moonlight, in a wilderness.
The moon was bright, the air was free,
And fruits and flowers together grew
On many a shrub and many a tree:
And all put on a gentle hue
Hanging in the shadowy air
Like a picture rich and rare.
It was a climate where, they say,
The night is more belov'd than day.
But who that beauteous Boy beguil'd,
That beauteous Boy to linger here?
Alone, by night, a little child,
In place so silent and so wild—
Has he no friend, no loving mother near?

CANTO II.

"A LITTLE further, O my father, yet a little further, and we shall come into the open moonlight." Their road was through a forest of fir-trees; at its entrance the trees stood at distances from each other, and the path was broad, and the moonlight and the moonlight shadows reposed upon it, and appeared quietly to inhabit that solitude. But soon the path winded and became narrow; the sun at high noon sometimes speckled, but never illumined it, and now it was dark as a cavern.

"It is dark, O my father!" said Enos, "but the path under our feet is smooth and soft, and we shall soon come out into the open moonlight."

"Lead on, my child!" said Cain: "guide me, little child!" And the innocent little child clasped a finger of the hand which had murdered the righteous Abel, and he guided his father. "The fir branches drip upon thee, my son." "Yea, pleasantly, father, for I ran fast and eagerly to bring thee the pitcher and the cake, and my body is not yet cool. How happy the squirrels are that feed on these fir-trees! they leap from bough to bough, and the old squirrels play round their young ones in the nest. I clomb a tree yesterday at noon, O my father, that I might play with them, but they leaped away from the branches, even to the slender twigs did they leap, and in a moment I beheld them on another tree. Why, O my father, would they not play with me? I would be good to them as thou art good to me : and I groaned to them even as thou groanest when thou givest me to eat, and when thou coverest me at evening, and as often as I stand at thy knee and thine eyes look at me." Then Cain stopped, and stifling his groans he sank to the earth, and the child Enos stood in the darkness beside him.

And Cain lifted up his voice and cried bitterly, and said, " The Mighty One that persecuteth me is on this side and on that ; he pursueth my soul like the wind, like the sand-blast he passeth through me ; he is around me even as the air ! O that I might be utterly no more ! I desire to die—yea, the things that never had life, neither move they upon the earth—behold ! they seem precious to mine eyes. O that a man might live without the breath of his nostrils. So I might abide in darkness, and blackness, and an empty space ! Yea, I would lie down, I would not rise, neither would I stir my limbs till I became as the rock in the den of the lion, on which the young lion resteth his head whilst he sleepeth. For the torrent that roareth far off hath a voice : and the clouds in heaven look terribly on me ; the

Mighty One who is against me speaketh in the wind of the cedar grove; and in silence am I dried up." Then Enos spake to his father, "Arise, my father, arise, we are but a little way from the place where I found the cake and the pitcher." And Cain said, "How knowest thou?" and the child answered—"Behold the bare rocks are a few of thy strides distant from the forest; and while even now thou wert lifting up thy voice, I heard the echo." Then the child took hold of his father, as if he would raise him: and Cain being faint and feeble rose slowly on his knees and pressed himself against the trunk of a fir, and stood upright and followed the child.

The path was dark till within three strides' length of its termination, when it turned suddenly; the thick black trees formed a low arch, and the moonlight appeared for a moment like a dazzling portal. Enos ran before and stood in the open air; and when Cain, his father, emerged from the darkness, the child was affrighted. For the mighty limbs of Cain were wasted as by fire; his hair was as the matted curls on the bison's forehead, and so glared his fierce and sullen eye beneath: and the black abundant locks on either side, a rank and tangled mass, were stained and scorched, as though the grasp of a burning iron hand had striven to rend them; and his countenance told in a strange and terrible language of agonies that had been, and were, and were still to continue to be.

The scene around was desolate; as far as the
eye could reach it was desolate: the bare rocks
faced each other, and left a long and wide interval of thin white sand.   You might wander on and
look round and round, and peep into the crevices
of the rocks, and discover nothing that acknow-
ledged the influence of the seasons.   There was
no spring, no summer, no autumn: and the winter's snow, that would have been lovely, fell not
on these hot rocks and scorching sands.   Never
morning lark had poised himself over this desert;
but the huge serpent often hissed there beneath
the talons of the vulture, and the vulture screamed,
his wings imprisoned within the coils of the serpent.   The pointed and shattered summits of the
ridges of the rocks made a rude mimicry of human concerns, and seemed to prophesy mutely of
things that then were not; steeples, and battle-
ments, and ships with naked masts.   As far from
the wood as a boy might sling a pebble of the
brook, there was one rock by itself at a small distance from the main ridge.   It had been precipitated there perhaps by the groan which the Earth
uttered when our first father fell.   Before you
approached, it appeared to lie flat on the ground,
but its base slanted from its point, and between
its point and the sands a tall man might stand upright.   It was here that Enos had found the pitcher
and cake, and to this place he led his father.   But
ere they had reached the rock they beheld a hu-

man shape: his back was towards them, and they were advancing unperceived, when they heard him smite his breast and cry aloud, " Woe is me ! woe is me ! I must never die again, and yet I am perishing with thirst and hunger."

Pallid, as the reflection of the sheeted lightning on the heavy-sailing night-cloud, became the face of Cain ; but the child Enos took hold of the shaggy skin, his father's robe, and raised his eyes to his father, and listening whispered, " Ere yet I could speak, I am sure, O my father, that I heard that voice. Have not I often said that I remembered a sweet voice ? O my father ! this is it :" and Cain trembled exceedingly. The voice was sweet indeed, but it was thin and querulous, like that of a feeble slave in misery, who despairs altogether, yet cannot refrain himself from weeping and lamentation. And, behold ! Enos glided forward, and creeping softly round the base of the rock, stood before the stranger, and looked up into his face. And the Shape shrieked, and turned round, and Cain beheld him, that his limbs and his face were those of his brother Abel whom he had killed ! And Cain stood like one who struggles in his sleep because of the exceeding terribleness of a dream.

Thus as he stood in silence and darkness of soul, the Shape fell at his feet, and embraced his knees, and cried out with a bitter outcry, " Thou eldest born of Adam, whom Eve, my mother, brought

forth, cease to torment me! I was feeding my
flocks in green pastures by the side of quiet rivers,
and thou killedst me; and now I am in misery."
Then Cain closed his eyes, and hid them with his
hands; and again he opened his eyes, and looked
around him, and said to Enos, "What beholdest
thou? Didst thou hear a voice, my son?" "Yes, my
father, I beheld a man in unclean garments, and he
uttered a sweet voice, full of lamentation." Then
Cain raised up the Shape that was like Abel, and
said: "The Creator of our father, who had respect
unto thee, and unto thy offering, wherefore hath he
forsaken thee?" Then the Shape shrieked a second time, and rent his garment, and his naked skin
was like the white sands beneath their feet; and
he shrieked yet a third time, and threw himself on
his face upon the sand that was black with the
shadow of the rock, and Cain and Enos sate beside
him; the child by his right hand, and Cain by his
left. They were all three under the rock, and
within the shadow. The Shape that was like Abel
raised himself up, and spake to the child: "I
know where the cold waters are, but I may not
drink, wherefore didst thou then take away my
pitcher?" But Cain said, "Didst thou not find
favour in the sight of the Lord thy God?" The
Shape answered, "The Lord is God of the living
only, the dead have another God." Then the
child Enos lifted up his eyes and prayed; but
Cain rejoiced secretly in his heart. "Wretched shall

they be all the days of their mortal life," exclaimed
the Shape, " who sacrifice worthy and acceptable
sacrifices to the God of the dead ; but after death
their toil ceaseth.   Woe is me, for I was well beloved by the God of the living, and cruel wert
thou, O my brother, who didst snatch me away
from his power and his dominion."   Having uttered these words, he rose suddenly and fled over
the sands: and Cain said in his heart, " The curse
of the Lord is on me ; but who is the God of the
dead ? " and he ran after the Shape, and the Shape
fled shrieking over the sands, and the sands rose
like white mists behind the steps of Cain, but the
feet of him that was like Abel disturbed not the
sands.   He greatly outrun Cain, and turning short,
he wheeled round, and came again to the rock
where they had been sitting, and where Enos still
stood ; and the child caught hold of his garment
as he passed by, and he fell upon the ground.
And Cain stopped, and beholding him not, said,
" he has passed into the dark woods," and he
walked slowly back to the rocks ; and when he
reached it the child told him that he had caught
hold of his garment as he passed by, and that the
man had fallen upon the ground : and Cain once
more sate beside him, and said, "Abel, my brother,
I would lament for thee, but that the spirit within
me is withered, and burnt up with extreme agony.
Now, I pray thee, by thy flocks, and by thy pastures, and by the quiet rivers which thou lovedst,

that thou tell me all that thou knowest. Who is the God of the dead? where doth he make his dwelling? what sacrifices are acceptable unto him? for I have offered, but have not been received; I have prayed, and have not been heard; and how can I be afflicted more than I already am?" The Shape arose and answered, "O that thou hadst had pity on me as I will have pity on thee. Follow me, Son of Adam! and bring thy child with thee!"

And they three passed over the white sands between the rocks, silent as the shadows.

SIBYLLINE LEAVES.

I.—POEMS OCCASIONED BY POLITICAL EVENTS OR
FEELINGS CONNECTED WITH THEM.

WHEN I have borne in memory what has tamed
Great nations, how ennobling thoughts depart
When men change swords for ledgers, and desert
The student's bower for gold, some fears unnamed
I had, my country! Am I to be blamed?
Now, when I think of thee, and what thou art,
Verily, in the bottom of my heart,
Of those unfilial fears I am ashamed.
For dearly must we prize thee; we who find
In thee a bulwark for the cause of men;
And I by my affection was beguiled.
What wonder if a poet now and then,
Among the many movements of his mind,
Felt for thee as a Lover or a Child!

WORDSWORTH

ODE TO THE DEPARTING YEAR.[*]

'Ιοὺ, ἰοὺ, ὦ ὦ κακά.
'Υπ' αὖ με δεινὸς ὀρθομαντείας πόνος
Στροβεῖ, ταράσσων φροιμίοις ἐφημίοις.

*   *   *   *   *

Τὸ μέλλον ἥξει. Καὶ σύ μ' ἐν τάχει παρὼν
'Αγαν γ' ἀληθόμαντιν οἰκτείρας ἐρεῖς.

Æschyl. Agam. 1225.

ARGUMENT.

THE Ode commences with an address to the Divine Providence, that regulates into one vast harmony all the events of time, however calamitous some of them may appear to mortals. The second Strophe calls on men to suspend their private joys and sorrows, and devote them for a while to the cause of human nature in general. The first Epode speaks of the Empress of Russia, who died of an apoplexy on the 17th of November, 1796; having just concluded a subsidiary treaty with the Kings combined against France. The first and second Antistrophe describe the image of the Departing Year, &c. as in a vision. The second Epode prophesies, in anguish of spirit, the downfall of this country.

I.

SPIRIT who sweepest the wild harp of Time !
  It is most hard, with an untroubled ear
  Thy dark inwoven harmonies to hear !

---

[*] This Ode was composed on the 24th, 25th, and 26th days of December, 1796; and was first published on the last day of that year.

Yet, mine eye fixed on Heaven's unchanging
    clime,
Long had I listened, free from mortal fear,
  With inward stillness, and submitted mind;
  When lo! its folds far waving on the wind,
I saw the train of the Departing Year!
  Starting from my silent sadness
  Then with no unholy madness
Ere yet the entered cloud foreclosed my sight,
I raised the impetuous song, and solemnized his
    flight.

II.

  Hither, from the recent tomb,
  From the prison's direr gloom,
  From Distemper's midnight anguish;
And thence, where Poverty doth waste and
    languish!
  Or where, his two bright torches blending,
  Love illumines manhood's maze;
  Or where o'er cradled infants bending
  Hope has fixed her wistful gaze;
  Hither, in perplexed dance,
Ye Woes! ye young-eyed Joys! advance!
By Time's wild harp, and by the hand
  Whose indefatigable sweep
  Raises its fateful strings from sleep,
I bid you haste, a mixed tumultuous band!
  From every private bower,
  And each domestic hearth,

Haste for one solemn hour ;
And with a loud and yet a louder voice,
O'er Nature struggling in portentous birth,
Weep and rejoice !
Still echoes the dread name that o'er the earth
Let slip the storm, and woke the brood of hell :
And now advance in saintly jubilee
Justice and Truth ! They too have heard thy
spell !
They too obey thy name, divinest Liberty !

III.

I marked Ambition in his war-array !
I heard the mailed Monarch's troublous cry—
" Ah ! wherefore does the Northern Conqueress
stay !
Groans not her chariot on its onward way ? "
Fly, mailed Monarch, fly !
Stunned by Death's twice mortal mace,
No more on Murder's lurid face
The insatiate hag shall gloat with drunken eye !
Manes of the unnumbered slain !
Ye that gasped on Warsaw's plain !
Ye that erst at Ismail's tower,
When human ruin choked the streams,
Fell in conquest's glutted hour,
'Mid women's shrieks and infants' screams !
Spirits of the uncoffined slain !
Sudden blasts of triumph swelling,
Oft, at night, in misty train,

Rush around her narrow dwelling!
The exterminating fiend is fled—
  (Foul her life, and dark her doom;)
Mighty armies of the dead
  Dance, like death-fires, round her tomb!
Then with prophetic song relate,
Each some tyrant-murderer's fate!

IV.

Departing Year! 'twas on no earthly shore
  My soul beheld thy vision! Where alone,
  Voiceless and stern, before the cloudy throne,
Aye Memory sits: thy robe inscribed with gore,
With many an unimaginable groan
  Thou storied'st thy sad hours! Silence ensued,
  Deep silence o'er the ethereal multitude,
Whose locks with wreaths, whose wreaths with
    glories shone.
  Then, his eye wild ardours glancing,
  From the choired Gods advancing,
The Spirit of the Earth made reverence meet,
And stood up, beautiful, before the cloudy seat.

V.

  Throughout the blissful throng,
  Hushed were harp and song:
Till wheeling round the throne the Lampads
    seven,
  (The mystic Words of Heaven)
  Permissive signal make:

The fervent Spirit bowed, then spread his wings
    and spake !
  " Thou in stormy blackness throning
    Love and uncreated Light,
By the Earth's unsolaced groaning,
    Seize thy terrors, Arm of might !
By peace with proffered insult scared,
    Masked hate and envying scorn !
  By years of havoc yet unborn !
And hunger's bosom to the frost winds bared !
    But chief by Afric's wrongs,
      Strange, horrible, and foul !
    By what deep guilt belongs
To the deaf Synod, ' full of gifts and lies !'
By wealth's insensate laugh ! by torture's howl !
    Avenger, rise !
For ever shall the thankless Island scowl,
Her quiver full, and with unbroken bow ?
Speak ! from thy storm-black Heaven O speak
    aloud !
    And on the darkling foe
Open thine eye of fire from some uncertain cloud !
  O dart the flash !   O rise and deal the blow !
The Past to thee, to thee the Future cries !
  Hark ! how wide Nature joins her groans below !
    Rise, God of Nature ! rise."

VI.

The voice had ceased, the vision fled ;
Yet still I gasped and reeled with dread.

And ever, when the dream of night
Renews the phantom to my sight,
Cold sweat-drops gather on my limbs;
  My ears throb hot; my eye-balls start;
My brain with horrid tumult swims;
  Wild is the tempest of my heart;
And my thick and struggling breath
Imitates the toil of death!
No stranger agony confounds
  The soldier on the war-field spread,
When all foredone with toil and wounds,
  Death-like he dozes among heaps of dead!
(The strife is o'er, the day-light fled,
  And the night-wind clamours hoarse!
See! the starting wretch's head
  Lies pillowed on a brother's corse!)

VII.

Not yet enslaved, not wholly vile,
O Albion!   O my mother Isle!
Thy valleys, fair as Eden's bowers,
Glitter green with sunny showers;
Thy grassy uplands' gentle swells
  Echo to the bleat of flocks;
(Those grassy hills, those glittering dells
  Proudly ramparted with rocks)
And Ocean mid his uproar wild
Speaks safety to his island-child.
  Hence for many a fearless age
  Has social Quiet loved thy shore;

Nor ever proud invader's rage
Or sacked thy towers, or stained thy fields with
  gore.

VIII.

Abandoned of Heaven! mad avarice thy guide,
At cowardly distance, yet kindling with pride—
Mid thy herds and thy corn-fields secure thou hast
  stood,
And joined the wild yelling of famine and blood!
The nations curse thee! They with eager won-
  dering
  Shall hear Destruction, like a vulture, scream!
  Strange-eyed Destruction! who with many a
  dream
Of central fires through nether seas upthundering
  Soothes her fierce solitude; yet as she lies
  By livid fount, or red volcanic stream,
  If ever to her lidless dragon-eyes,
  O Albion! thy predestined ruins rise,
The fiend-hag on her perilous couch doth leap,
Muttering distempered triumph in her charmed
  sleep.

IX.

Away, my soul, away!
In vain, in vain the birds of warning sing—
And hark! I hear the famished brood of prey
Flap their lank pennons on the groaning wind!
Away, my soul, away!
I unpartaking of the evil thing,

With daily prayer and daily toil
   Soliciting for food my scanty soil,
    Have wailed my country with a loud Lament.
Now I recentre my immortal mind
    In the deep sabbath of meek self-content;
Cleansed from the vaporous passions that bedim
God's Image, sister of the Seraphim.

FRANCE. AN ODE.

I.

Ye Clouds! that far above me float and pause,
   Whose pathless march no mortal may control!
   Ye Ocean-Waves! that, wheresoe'er ye roll,
Yield homage only to eternal laws!
Ye Woods! that listen to the night-birds singing,
   Midway the smooth and perilous slope reclined,
Save when your own imperious branches swinging,
   Have made a solemn music of the wind!
Where, like a man beloved of God,
Through glooms, which never woodman trod,
    How oft, pursuing fancies holy,
My moonlight way o'er flowering weeds I wound,
    Inspired, beyond the guess of folly,
By each rude shape and wild unconquerable
    sound!

O ye loud Waves! and O ye Forests high!
And O ye clouds that far above me soared!
Thou rising Sun! thou blue rejoicing Sky!
  Yea, every thing that is and will be free!
  Bear witness for me, wheresoe'er ye be,
  With what deep worship I have still adored
    The spirit of divinest Liberty.

II.

When France in wrath her giant-limbs upreared,
  And with that oath, which smote air, earth, and
    sea,
  Stamped her strong foot and said she would be
    free,
Bear witness for me, how I hoped and feared!
With what a joy my lofty gratulation
Unawed I sang, amid a slavish band:
And when to whelm the disenchanted nation,
  Like fiends embattled by a wizard's wand,
    The Monarchs marched in evil day,
    And Britain joined the dire array;
  Though dear her shores and circling ocean,
Though many friendships, many youthful loves
  Had swol'n the patriot emotion
And flung a magic light o'er all her hills and
    groves;
Yet still my voice, unaltered, sang defeat
  To all that braved the tyrant-quelling lance,
And shame too long delayed and vain retreat!
For ne'er, O Liberty! with partial aim

I dimmed thy light or damped thy holy flame;
   But blessed the pœans of delivered France,
And hung my head and wept at Britain's name.

III.

" And what," I said, " though Blasphemy's loud
      scream
   With that sweet music of deliverance strove!
   Though all the fierce and drunken passions wove
A dance more wild than e'er was maniac's dream!
   Ye storms, that round the dawning east as-
      sembled,
The Sun was rising, though ye hid his light!"
   And when, to soothe my soul, that hoped and
      trembled,
The dissonance ceased, and all seemed calm and
      bright;
   When France her front deep-scarr'd and gory
   Concealed with clustering wreaths of glory;
    When, insupportably advancing,
   Her arm made mockery of the warrior's tramp;
    While timid looks of fury glancing,
Domestic treason, crushed beneath her fatal
      stamp,
Writhed like a wounded dragon in his gore;
   Then I reproached my fears that would not
      flee;
"And soon," I said, " shall Wisdom teach her lore
In the low huts of them that toil and groan!
And, conquering by her happiness alone,

Shall France compel the nations to be free,
Till Love and Joy look round, and call the Earth
  their own."

IV.

Forgive me, Freedom! O forgive those dreams!
 I hear thy voice, I hear thy loud lament,
 From bleak Helvetia's icy cavern sent —
I hear thy groans upon her blood-stained streams!
 Heroes, that for your peaceful country perished,
And ye that, fleeing, spot your mountain-snows
 With bleeding wounds; forgive me, that I che-
  rished
One thought that ever blessed your cruel foes!
 To scatter rage, and traitorous guilt,
 Where Peace her jealous home had built;
  A patriot-race to disinherit
Of all that made their stormy wilds so dear;
  And with inexpiable spirit
To taint the bloodless freedom of the moun-
  taineer —
O France, that mockest Heaven, adulterous,
  blind,
 And patriot only in pernicious toils,
Are these thy boasts, Champion of human kind?
 To mix with Kings in the low lust of sway,
 Yell in the hunt, and share the murderous
  prey;
 To insult the shrine of Liberty with spoils
 From freemen torn; to tempt and to betray?

V.

The Sensual and the Dark rebel in vain,
Slaves by their own compulsion! In mad game
They burst their manacles and wear the name
   Of Freedom, graven on a heavier chain!
O Liberty! with profitless endeavour
Have I pursued thee, many a weary hour;
   But thou nor swell'st the victor's strain, nor ever
Didst breathe thy soul in forms of human power.
   Alike from all, howe'er they praise thee,
   (Nor prayer, nor boastful name delays thee)
    Alike from Priestcraft's harpy minions,
   And factious Blasphemy's obscener slaves,
    Thou speedest on thy subtle pinions,
The guide of homeless winds, and playmate of
    the waves!
And there I felt thee!—on that sea-cliff's verge
   Whose pines, scarce travelled by the breeze
    above,
Had made one murmur with the distant surge!
Yes, while I stood and gazed, my temples bare,
And shot my being through earth, sea, and air,
   Possessing all things with intensest love,
    O Liberty! my spirit felt thee there.

February, 1797.

FEARS IN SOLITUDE,

WRITTEN IN APRIL, 1798, DURING THE ALARM OF
AN INVASION.

A GREEN and silent spot, amid the hills,
A small and silent dell!   O'er stiller place
No singing skylark ever poised himself.
The hills are heathy, save that swelling slope,
Which hath a gay and gorgeous covering on,
All golden with the never-bloomless furze,
Which now blooms most profusely: but the dell,
Bathed by the mist, is fresh and delicate
As vernal corn-field, or the unripe flax,
When, through its half-transparent stalks, at eve,
The level sunshine glimmers with green light.
Oh! 'tis a quiet spirit-healing nook!
Which all, methinks, would love; but chiefly he,
The humble man, who, in his youthful years,
Knew just so much of folly, as had made
His early manhood more securely wise!
Here he might lie on fern or withered heath,
While from the singing-lark, (that sings unseen
The minstrelsy that solitude loves best,)
And from the sun, and from the breezy air,

Sweet influences trembled o'er his frame;
And he, with many feelings, many thoughts,
Made up a meditative joy, and found
Religious meanings in the forms of nature!
And so, his senses gradually wrapt
In a half sleep, he dreams of better worlds,
And dreaming hears thee still, O singing-lark;
That singest like an angel in the clouds!

My God! it is a melancholy thing
For such a man, who would full fain preserve
His soul in calmness, yet perforce must feel
For all his human brethren—O my God!
It weighs upon the heart, that he must think
What uproar and what strife may now be stirring
This way or that way o'er these silent hills—
Invasion, and the thunder and the shout,
And all the crash of onset; fear and rage,
And undetermined conflict—even now,
Even now, perchance, and in his native isle:
Carnage and groans beneath this blessed sun!
We have offended, Oh! my countrymen!
We have offended very grievously,
And been most tyrannous.   From east to west
A groan of accusation pierces Heaven!
The wretched plead against us; multitudes
Countless and vehement, the sons of God,
Our brethren!   Like a cloud that travels on,
Steamed up from Cairo's swamps of pestilence,
Even so, my countrymen! have we gone forth

And borne to distant tribes slavery and pangs,
And, deadlier far, our vices, whose deep taint
With slow perdition murders the whole man,
IIis body and his soul!   Meanwhile, at home,
All individual dignity and power,
Engulfed in courts, committees, institutions,
Associations and societies,
A vain, speech-mouthing, speech-reporting guild,
One benefit-club for mutual flattery,
We have drunk up, demure as at a grace,
Pollutions from the brimming cup of wealth ;
Contemptuous of all honourable rule,
Yet bartering freedom and the poor man's life
For gold, as at a market!   The sweet words
Of Christian promise, words that even yet
Might stem destruction, were they wisely preached,
Are muttered o'er by men, whose tones proclaim
IIow flat and wearisome they feel their trade :
Rank scoffers some, but most too indolent
To deem them falsehoods or to know their truth.
Oh! blasphemous! the book of life is made
A superstitious instrument, on which
We gabble o'er the oaths we mean to break ;
For all must swear—all and in every place,
College and wharf, council and justice-court ;
All, all must swear, the briber and the bribed,
Merchant and lawyer, senator and priest,
The rich, the poor, the old man and the young ;
All, all make up one scheme of perjury,
That faith doth reel ; the very name of God

Sounds like a juggler's charm; and, bold with joy,
Forth from his dark and lonely hiding-place,
(Portentous sight!) the owlet Atheism,
Sailing on obscene wings athwart the noon,
Drops his blue-fringed lids, and holds them close,
And hooting at the glorious sun in Heaven,
Cries out, " Where is it?"

      Thankless too for peace,
(Peace long preserved by fleets and perilous seas)
Secure from actual warfare, we have loved
To swell the warwhoop, passionate for war!
Alas! for ages ignorant of all
Its ghastlier workings, (famine or blue plague,
Battle, or siege, or flight through wintry snows,)
We, this whole people, have been clamorous
For war and bloodshed; animating sports,
The which we pay for as a thing to talk of,
Spectators and not combatants! No guess
Anticipative of a wrong unfelt,
No speculation or contingency,
However dim and vague, too vague and dim
To yield a justifying cause; and forth,
(Stuffed out with big preamble, holy names,
And adjurations of the God in Heaven,)
We send our mandates for the certain death
Of thousands, and ten thousands! Boys and girls,
And women, that would groan to see a child
Pull off an insect's leg, all read of war,
The best amusement for our morning-meal!

The poor wretch, who has learnt his only prayers
From curses, who knows scarcely words enough
To ask a blessing from his Heavenly Father,
Becomes a fluent phraseman, absolute
And technical in victories and defeats,
And all our dainty terms for fratricide;
Terms which we trundle smoothly o'er our tongues
Like mere abstractions, empty sounds to which
We join no feeling and attach no form!
As if the soldier died without a wound;
As if the fibres of this godlike frame
Were gored without a pang; as if the wretch,
Who fell in battle, doing bloody deeds,
Passed off to Heaven, translated and not killed;
As though he had no wife to pine for him,
No God to judge him! Therefore, evil days
Are coming on us, O my countrymen!
And what if all-avenging Providence,
Strong and retributive, should make us know
The meaning of our words, force us to feel
The desolation and the agony
Of our fierce doings.

              Spare us yet awhile,
Father and God! O! spare us yet awhile!
Oh! let not English women drag their flight
Fainting beneath the burthen of their babes,
Of the sweet infants, that but yesterday
Laughed at the breast! Sons, brothers, husbands, all

Who ever gazed with fondness on the forms
Which grew up with you round the same fireside,
And all who ever heard the sabbath-bells
Without the infidel's scorn, make yourselves pure!
Stand forth! be men! repel an impious foe,
Impious and false, a light yet cruel race,
Who laugh away all virtue, mingling mirth
With deeds of murder; and still promising
Freedom, themselves too sensual to be free,
Poison life's amities, and cheat the heart
Of faith and quiet hope, and all that soothes
And all that lifts the spirit!   Stand we forth;
Render them back upon the insulted ocean,
And let them toss as idly on its waves
As the vile sea-weed, which some mountain-blast
Swept from our shores! And oh! may we return
Not with a drunken triumph, but with fear,
Repenting of the wrongs with which we stung
So fierce a foe to frenzy!

                              I have told,
O Britons! O my brethren! I have told
Most bitter truth, but without bitterness.
Nor deem my zeal or factious or mistimed;
For never can true courage dwell with them,
Who, playing tricks with conscience, dare not look
At their own vices.   We have been too long
Dupes of a deep delusion! Some, belike,
Groaning with restless enmity, expect
All change from change of constituted power;

As if a Government had been a robe,
On which our vice and wretchedness were tagged
Like fancy-points and fringes, with the robe
Pulled off at pleasure.   Fondly these attach
A radical causation to a few
Poor drudges of chastising Providence,
Who borrow all their hues and qualities
From our own folly and rank wickedness,
Which gave them birth and nursed them. Others,
      meanwhile,
Dote with a mad idolatry ; and all
Who will not fall before their images,
And yield them worship, they are enemies
Even of their country !

             Such have I been deemed—
But, O dear Britain ! O my Mother Isle !
Needs must thou prove a name most dear and
      holy
To me, a son, a brother, and a friend,
A husband, and a father ! who revere
All bonds of natural love, and find them all
Within the limits of thy rocky shores.
O native Britain ! O my Mother Isle !
How shouldst thou prove aught else but dear and
      holy
To me, who from thy lakes and mountain-hills,
Thy clouds, thy quiet dales, thy rocks and seas,
Have drunk in all my intellectual life,
All sweet sensations, all ennobling thoughts,

All adoration of the God in nature,
All lovely and all honourable things,
Whatever makes this mortal spirit feel
The joy and greatness of its future being?
There lives nor form nor feeling in my soul
Unborrowed from my country.   O divine
And beauteous island! thou hast been my sole
And most magnificent temple, in the which
I walk with awe, and sing my stately songs,
Loving the God that made me!

                   May my fears,
My filial fears, be vain! and may the vaunts
And menace of the vengeful enemy
Pass like the gust, that roared and died away
In the distant tree : which heard, and only heard
In this low dell, bowed not the delicate grass.

   But now the gentle dew-fall sends abroad
The fruit-like perfume of the golden furze :
The light has left the summit of the hill,
Though still a sunny gleam lies beautiful,
Aslant the ivied beacon.   Now farewell,
Farewell, awhile, O soft and silent spot!
On the green sheep-track, up the heathy hill,
Homeward I wind my way; and lo! recalled
From bodings that have well nigh wearied me
I find myself upon the brow, and pause
Startled!   And after lonely sojourning
In such a quiet and surrounded nook,

This burst of prospect, here the shadowy main,
Dim tinted, there the mighty majesty
Of that huge amphitheatre of rich
And elmy fields, seems like society —
Conversing with the mind, and giving it
A livelier impulse and a dance of thought!
And now, beloved Stowey! I behold
Thy church-tower, and, methinks, the four huge
    elms
Clustering, which mark the mansion of my friend;
And close behind them, hidden from my view,
Is my own lowly cottage, where my babe
And my babe's mother dwell in peace! With
    light
And quickened footsteps thitherward I tend,
Remembering thee, O green and silent dell!
And grateful, that by nature's quietness
And solitary musings, all my heart
Is softened, and made worthy to indulge
Love, and the thoughts that yearn for human
    kind.

   NETHER STOWEY,
     April 28th, 1798.

FIRE, FAMINE, AND SLAUGHTER.

APOLOGETIC PREFACE.

At the house of a gentleman, who, by the principles and corresponding virtues of a sincere Christian, consecrates a cultivated genius and the favourable accidents of birth, opulence, and splendid connections, it was my good fortune to meet, in a dinner-party, with more men of celebrity in science or polite literature, than are commonly found collected round the same table. In the course of conversation, one of the party reminded an illustrious poet, then present, of some verses which he had recited that morning, and which had appeared in a newspaper under the name of a War-Eclogue, in which Fire, Famine, and Slaughter were introduced as the speakers. The gentleman so addressed replied, that he was rather surprised that none of us should have noticed or heard of the poem, as it had been, at the time, a good deal talked of in Scotland. It may be easily supposed, that my feelings were at this moment not of the most comfortable kind. Of all present, one only knew, or suspected me to be the author; a man who would have established himself in the first rank of England's living poets, if the Genius of our country had not decreed that he should rather be the first in the first rank of its philosophers and scientific benefactors. It appeared the general wish to hear the lines. As my friend chose to remain silent, I chose to follow his example, and Mr. ***** recited the poem. This he could do with the better grace, being known to have ever been not only a firm and active Anti-Jacobin and Anti-Gallican, but likewise a zealous admirer of Mr. Pitt, both as a good man and a great statesman. As a poet exclusively, he had been amused with the Eclogue;

as a poet he recited it; and in a spirit, which made it evident, that he would have read and repeated it with the same pleasure, had his own name been attached to the imaginary object or agent.

After the recitation, our amiable host observed, that in his opinion Mr. ***** had overrated the merits of the poetry; but had they been tenfold greater, they could not have compensated for that malignity of heart, which could alone have prompted sentiments so atrocious.   I perceived that my illustrious friend became greatly distressed on my account; but fortunately I was able to preserve fortitude and presence of mind enough to take up the subject without exciting even a suspicion how nearly and painfully it interested me.

What follows, is the substance of what I then replied, but dilated and in language less colloquial. It was not my intention, I said, to justify the publication, whatever its author's feelings might have been at the time of composing it.   That they are calculated to call forth so severe a reprobation from a good man, is not the worst feature of such poems. Their moral deformity is aggravated in proportion to the pleasure which they are capable of affording to vindictive, turbulent, and unprincipled readers.   Could it be supposed, though for a moment, that the author seriously wished what he had thus wildly imagined, even the attempt to palliate an inhumanity so monstrous would be an insult to the hearers. But it seemed to me worthy of consideration, whether the mood of mind, and the general state of sensations, in which a poet produces such vivid and fantastic images, is likely to coexist, or is even compatible with, that gloomy and deliberate ferocity which a serious wish to realize them would presuppose. It had been often observed, and all my experience tended to confirm the observation, that prospects of pain and evil to others, and in general, all deep feelings of revenge, are commonly expressed in a few words, ironically tame, and mild. The mind under so direful and fiend-like an influence seems to take a morbid pleasure in contrasting the intensity of its wishes and feelings with the slightness or levity of the expressions by which they are hinted; and indeed feelings so intense and solitary, if they were not precluded (as in almost all cases they would be) by a constitutional activity of fancy and association, and by the specific joyousness combined with it, would assuredly themselves preclude such activity. Passion, in its own quality, is the antagonist of action; though in an ordinary and natural degree the former alternates with the latter, and thereby revives and strengthens it. But the more intense and insane the passion is, the fewer and the more fixed are the correspondent forms and notions. A rooted hatred, an inveterate thirst of revenge, is a sort of madness, and still eddies round its favourite object, and exercises as it were a perpetual tautology of mind in thoughts and words, which admit of no adequate substitutes. Like a fish in a globe of glass, it moves restlessly round and round the scanty circumference, which it cannot leave without losing its vital element.

There is a second character of such imaginary representations as spring from a real and earnest desire of evil to another, which we often see in real life, and might even anticipate from the nature of the mind. The images, I mean, that a vindictive man places before his imagination, will most often be taken from the realities of life: they will be images of pain and suffering which he has himself seen inflicted on other men, and which he can fancy himself as inflicting on the object of his hatred. I will suppose that we had heard at different times two common sailors, each speaking of some one who had wronged or offended him; that the first with apparent violence had devoted every part of his adversary's body and soul to all the horrid phantoms and fantastic places that ever Quevedo dreamt of, and this in a rapid flow of those outrageous and wildly combined execrations, which too often with our lower classes serve for escape-valves to carry off the excess of their passions, as so much superfluous steam that would endanger the vessel if it were retained. The other, on the contrary, with that sort of calmness of tone which is to the ear what the paleness of anger is to the eye, shall simply say, "If I chance to be made boatswain, as I hope I soon shall, and can but once get that fellow under my hand, (and I shall be upon the watch for him,) I'll tickle his pretty skin! I wont hurt him! oh no! I 'll only cut the —— to the liver!" I dare appeal to all present, which of the two they would regard as the least deceptive symptom of deliberate malignity? nay, whether it would surprise them to see the first fellow, an hour or two afterwards, cordially shaking hands with the very man, the fractional parts of whose body and soul he had been so charitably disposing of; or even perhaps risking his life for him.   What language Shakespeare considered characteristic of malignant disposition, we see in the speech of the good-natured Gratiano, who spoke " an infinite deal of nothing, more than any man in all Venice;"

———" Too wild, too rude and bold of voice!"

the skipping spirit, whose thoughts and words reciprocally ran away with each other;

———" O be thou damn'd, inexorable dog!
And for thy life let justice be accused!"

and the wild fancies that follow, contrasted with Shylock's tranquil "I stand here for Law."

Or, to take a case more analogous to the present subject, should we hold it either fair or charitable to believe it to have been Dante's serious wish, that all the persons mentioned by him, (many recently departed, and some even alive at the time.)should actually suffer the fantastic and horrible punishments to which he has sentenced them in his Hell and Purgatory? Or what shall we say of the passages in which Bishop Jeremy Taylor anticipates the state of those who, vicious themselves, have been the cause of vice and misery to their fellow-creatures. Could we endure for a moment to think that a spirit, like Bishop Taylor's, burning with Christian love; that a man constitutionally overflowing with pleasurable kindliness; who scarcely even in a casual illustration introduces the image of woman, child, or bird, but he embalms the thought with so rich a tenderness, as makes the very words seem beauties and fragments of poetry from Euripides or Simonides; — can we endure to think, that a man so natured and so disciplined, did at the time of composing this horrible picture, attach a sober feeling of reality to the phrases? or that he would have described in the same tone of justification, in the same luxuriant flow of phrases, the tortures about to be inflicted on a living individual by a verdict of the Star-Chamber? or the still more atrocious sentences executed on the Scotch anti-prelatists and schismatics, at the command, and in some instances under the very eye of the Duke of Lauderdale, and of that wretched bigot who afterwards dishonoured and forfeited the throne of Great Britain? Or do we not rather feel and understand, that these violent words were mere bubbles, flashes and electrical apparitions, from the magic caldron of a fervid and ebullient fancy, constantly fuelled by an unexampled opulence of language.

Were I now to have read by myself for the first time the poem in question, my conclusion, I fully believe, would be, that the writer must have been some man of warm feelings and active fancy; that he had painted to himself the circumstances that accompany war in so many vivid and yet fantastic forms, as proved that neither the images nor the feelings were the result of observation, or in any way derived from realities. I should judge, that they were the product of his own seething imagination, and therefore impregnated with that pleasurable exultation which is experienced in all energetic exertion of intellectual power; that in the same mood he had generalized the causes of the war, and then personified the abstract and christened it by the name which he had been accustomed to hear most often associated with its management and measures. I should guess that the minister was in the author's mind at the moment of composition, as completely ἀπαθῆς, ἀναιμόσαρκος, as Anacreon's grasshopper, and that he had as little notion of a real person of flesh and blood,

" Distinguishable in member, joint, or limb,"

as Milton had in the grim and terrible phantoms (half person, half allegory) which he has placed at the gates of Hell. I concluded by observing, that the poem was not calculated to excite passion in any mind, or to make any impression except on poetic readers; and that from the culpable levity betrayed at the close of the eclogue by the grotesque union of epigrammatic wit with allegoric personification, in the allusion to the most fearful of thoughts, I should conjecture that the "rantin' Bardie," instead of really believing, much less wishing, the fate spoken of in the last line, in application to any human individual, would shrink from passing the verdict even on the Devil himself, and exclaim with poor Burns,

> But fare ye weel, auld Nickie-ben!
> Oh! wad ye tak a thought and men'!
> Ye aiblins might—I dinna ken—
>   Still hae a stake—
> I'm wae to think upo' yon den,
>   Ev'n for your sake.

I need not say that these thoughts, which are here dilated, were in such a company only rapidly suggested. Our kind host smiled, and with a courteous compliment observed, that the defence was too good for the cause. My voice faltered a little, for I was somewhat agitated; though not so much on my own account as for the uneasiness that so kind and friendly a man would feel from the thought that he had been the occasion of distressing me. At length I brought out these words: "I must now confess, Sir! that I am author of that poem. It was written some years ago. I do not attempt to justify my past self, young as I then was; but as little as I would now write a similar poem, so far was I even then from imagining, that the lines would be taken as more or less than a sport of fancy. At all events, if I know my own heart, there was never a moment in my existence in which I should have been more ready, had Mr. Pitt's person been in hazard, to interpose my own body, and defend his life at the risk of my own."

I have prefaced the poem with this anecdote, because to have printed it without any remark might well have been understood as implying an unconditional approbation on my part, and this after many years' consideration. But if it be asked why I republished it at all, I answer, that the poem had been attributed at different times to different other **persons**; and what I had dared beget, I thought it neither **manly** nor honourable not to dare father. From the same motives I should have published perfect copies of two poems, the one entitled The Devil's Thoughts, and the other, The Two round Spaces on the Tomb-Stone, * but that the first three stanzas of the former, which were worth all the rest of the poem, and the best stanza of the remainder, were written by a friend of deserved celebrity; and because there are passages in both, which might have given offence to the religious feelings of certain readers. I myself indeed see no reason why vulgar superstitions, and absurd conceptions that deform the pure faith of a Christian, should possess a greater immunity from ridicule than stories of witches, or the fables of Greece and Rome. But there are those who deem it profaneness and irreverence to call an ape an ape, if it but wear a monk's cowl on its head; and I would rather reason with this weakness than offend it.

The passage from Jeremy Taylor to which I referred, is found in his second Sermon on Christ's Advent to Judgment; which is likewise the second in his year's course of sermons. Among many remarkable passages of the same character in those discourses, I have selected this as the most so. " But

---

* Both these poems were subsequently admitted by the author into the general collection of his poetical works; " The Devil's Thoughts," in 1828, with the omission of several stanzas, afterwards restored; the " Two Round Spaces on a Tomb-stone," in 1834, with a statement prefixed, in which he expressed a regret that this sportive production of his youth, then for the first time published by himself, had not been allowed to perish. In the present edition the former piece is retained, the latter omitted, as the course which appears to the Editors most agreeable to the implied wish and judgment of the author. " The Devil's Thoughts," under the name of " The Devil's Walk," has also been published with large additions by Mr. Southey, *Poetical Works*, vol. iii. p. 83.— Edd.

when this Lion of the tribe of Judah shall appear, then Justice shall strike, and Mercy shall not hold her hands; she shall strike sore strokes, and Pity shall not break the blow. As there are treasures of good things, so hath God a treasure of wrath and fury, and scourges and scorpions; and then shall be produced the shame of lust and the malice of envy, and the groans of the oppressed and the persecutions of the saints, and the cares of covetousness and the troubles of ambition, and the insolences of traitors and the violences of rebels, and the rage of anger, and the uneasiness of impatience, and the restlessness of unlawful desires; and by this time the monsters and diseases will be numerous and intolerable, when God's heavy hand shall press the sanies and the intolerableness, the obliquity and the unreasonableness, the amazement and the disorder, the smart and the sorrow, the guilt and the punishment, out from all our sins, and pour them into one chalice, and mingle them with an infinite wrath, and make the wicked drink off all the vengeance, and force it down their unwilling throats with the violence of devils and accursed spirits."

That this Tartarean drench displays the imagination rather than the discretion of the compounder; that, in short, this passage and others of the same kind are in a bad taste, few will deny at the present day. It would, doubtless, have more behoved the good bishop not to be wise beyond what is written on a subject in which Eternity is opposed to Time, and a death threatened, not the negative, but the positive Opposite of Life; a subject, therefore, which must of necessity be indescribable to the human understanding in our present state. But I can neither find nor believe, that it ever occurred to any reader to ground on such passages a charge against Bishop Taylor's humanity, or goodness of heart. I was not a little surprised therefore to find, in the Pursuits of Literature and other works, so horrible a sentence passed on Milton's moral character, for a passage in his prose writings, as nearly parallel to this of Taylor's as two passages can well be conceived to be. All his merits, as a poet, forsooth—all the glory of having written the Paradise Lost, are light in the scale, nay, kick the beam, compared with the atrocious malignity of heart,

expressed in the offensive paragraph. I remembered, in general, that Milton had concluded one of his works on Reformation, written in the fervor of his youthful imagination, in a
high poetic strain, that wanted metre only to become a lyrical
poem. I remembered that in the former part he had formed
to himself a perfect ideal of human virtue, a character of heroic, disinterested zeal and devotion for Truth, Religion, and
public Liberty, in act and in suffering, in the day of triumph
and in the hour of martyrdom. Such spirits, as more excellent than others, he describes as having a more excellent reward, and as distinguished by a transcendent glory: and this
reward and this glory he displays and particularizes with an
energy and brilliance that announced the Paradise Lost as
plainly, as ever the bright purple clouds in the east announced
the coming of the Sun. Milton then passes to the gloomy
contrast, to such men as from motives of selfish ambition and
the lust of personal aggrandizement should, against their
own light, persecute truth and the true religion, and wilfully
abuse the powers and gifts intrusted to them, to bring vice,
blindness, misery and slavery, on their native country, on
the very country that had trusted, enriched and honored
them. Such beings, after that speedy and appropriate removal from their sphere of mischief which all good and hu-
mane men must of course desire, will, he takes for granted,
by parity of reason, meet with a punishment, an ignominy,
and a retaliation, as much severer than other wicked men, as
their guilt and its consequences were more enormous. His
description of this imaginary punishment presents more distinct pictures to the fancy than the extract from Jeremy
Taylor; but the thoughts in the latter are incomparably more
exaggerated and horrific. All this I knew; but I neither remembered, nor by reference and careful reperusal could discover, any other meaning, either in Milton or Taylor, but that
good men will be rewarded, and the impenitent wicked pun-
ished, in proportion to their dispositions and intentional acts
in this life; and that if the punishment of the least wicked
be fearful beyond conception, all words and descriptions must
be so far true, that they must fall short of the punishment
that awaits the transcendently wicked. Had Milton stated

either his ideal of virtue, or of depravity, as an individual or
individuals actually existing? Certainly not. Is this representation worded historically, or only hypothetically? Assuredly the latter. Does he express it as his own wish, that
after death they should suffer these tortures? or as a general
consequence, deduced from reason and revelation, that such
will be their fate? Again, the latter only. His wish is ex-
pressly confined to a speedy stop being put by Providence
to their power of inflicting misery on others. But did he
name or refer to any persons living or dead? No But the
calumniators of Milton dare say, (for what will calumny not
dare say?) that he had Laud and Strafford in his mind, while
writing of remorseless persecution, and the enslavement of
a free country, from motives of selfish ambition. Now, what
if a stern anti-prelatist should dare say, that in speaking of
the insolences of traitors and the violences of rebels, Bishop
Taylor must have individualized in his mind, Hampden, Hol-
lis, Pym, Fairfax, Ireton, and Milton? And what if he should
take the liberty of concluding, that, in the after description,
the Bishop was feeding and feasting his party-hatred, and
with those individuals before the eyes of his imagination
enjoying, trait by trait, horror after horror, the picture of
their intolerable agonies? Yet this bigot would have an
equal right thus to criminate the one good and great man,
as these men have to criminate the other. Milton has said,
and I doubt not but that Taylor with equal truth could have
said it, "that in his whole life he never spake against a man
even that his skin should be grazed." He asserted this when
one of his opponents (either Bishop Hall or his nephew) had
called upon the women and children in the streets to take
up stones and stone him (Milton.) It is known that Milton
repeatedly used his interest to protect the royalists; but even
at a time when all lies would have been meritorious against
him, no charge was made, no story pretended, that he had
ever directly or indirectly engaged or assisted in their persecution. Oh! methinks there are other and far better feelings,
which should be acquired by the perusal of our great elder
writers. When I have before me on the same table, the works
of Hammond and Baxter: when I reflect with what joy and

dearness their blessed spirits are now loving each other; it seems a mournful thing that their names should be perverted to an occasion of bitterness among us, who are enjoying that happy mean which the human too-much on both sides was perhaps necessary to produce. "The tangle of delusions which stifled and distorted the growing tree of our well-being has been torn away; the parasite-weeds that fed on its very roots have been plucked up with a salutary violence. To us there remain only quiet duties, the constant care, the gradual improvement, the cautious unhazardous labours of the indus trious though contented gardener—to prune, to strengthen, to engraft, and one by one to remove from its leaves and fresh shoots the slug and the caterpillar. But far be it from us to undervalue with light and senseless detraction the con-scientious hardihood of our predecessors, or even to condemn in them that vehemence, to which the blessings it won for us leave us now neither temptation nor pretext. We ante-date the feelings, in order to criminate the authors, of our present liberty, light and toleration." *

If ever two great men might seem, during their whole lives, to have moved in direct opposition, though neither of them has at any time introduced the name of the other, Milton and Jeremy Taylor were they. The former commenced his career by attacking the Church-Liturgy and all set forms of prayer. The latter, but far more successfully, by defending both. Milton's next work was then against the Prelacy and the then existing Church-Government—Taylor's in vindica-tion and support of them. Milton became more and more a stern republican, or rather an advocate for that religious and moral aristocracy which, in his day, was called repub-licanism, and which, even more than royalism itself, is the direct antipode of modern jacobinism. Taylor, as more and more sceptical concerning the fitness of men in general for power, became more and more attached to the prerogatives of monarchy. From Calvinism, with a still decreasing respect for Fathers, Councils, and for Church-antiquity in general, Milton seems to have ended in an indifference, if not a dis-

---

* The Friend, vol. i. p. 82.

like, to all forms of ecclesiastic government, and to have
retreated wholly into the inward and spiritual church communion of his own spirit with the Light that lighteth every
man that cometh into the world. Taylor, with a growing
reverence for authority, an increasing sense of the insuffi-
ciency of the Scriptures without the aids of tradition and the
consent of authorized interpreters, advanced as far in his ap-
proaches (not indeed·to Popery, but) to Roman-Catholicism,
as a conscientious minister of the English Church could well
venture.   Milton would be, and would utter the same, to all,
on all occasions: he would tell the truth, the whole truth, and
nothing but the truth. Taylor would become all things to
all men, if by any means he might benefit any; hence he
availed himself, in his popular writings, of opinions and representations which stand often in striking contrast with the
doubts and convictions expressed in his more philosophical
works.   He appears, indeed, not too severely to have blamed
that management of truth (istam falsitatem dispensativam)
authorized and exemplified by almost all the Fathers: Inte-
grum omnino doctoribus et cœtus Christiani antistitibus esse,
ut dolos versent, falsa veris intermisceant, et imprimis reli-
gionis hostes fallant, dummodo veritatis commodis et utilitati
inserviant.*

The same antithesis might be carried on with the elements
of their several intellectual powers. Milton, austere, condens-
ed, imaginative, supporting his truth by direct enunciation of
lofty moral sentiment and by distinct visual representations,
and in the same spirit overwhelming what he deemed falsehood by moral denunciation and a succession of pictures ap-
palling or repulsive. In his prose, so many metaphors, so many
allegorical miniatures. Taylor, eminently discursive, accumu-
lative, and (to use one of his own words) agglomerative; still
more rich in images than Milton himself, but images of fancy,
and presented to the common and passive eye, rather than to
the eye of the imagination. Whether supporting or assailing, he

---

* Such is the unwilling confession of Ribof (*Program. de
Œconomia Patrum,*) quoted in The Friend, vol. i. p. 42.

makes his way either by argument or by appeals to the affec-
tions, unsurpassed even by the schoolmen in subtlety, agility,
and logic wit, and unrivalled by the most rhetorical of the
fathers in the copiousness and vividness of his expressions and
illustrations.   Here words that convey feelings, and words
that flash images, and words of abstract notion, flow together,
and whirl and rush onward like a stream, at once rapid and
full of eddies; and yet still interfused here and there, we see
a tongue or islet of smooth water, with some picture in it of
earth or sky, landscape or living group of quiet beauty.

Differing, then, so widely, and almost contrariantly, wherein
did these great men agree? wherein did they resemble each
other?   In genius, in learning, in unfeigned piety, in blameless purity of life, and in benevolent aspirations and purposes
for the moral and temporal improvement of their fellow-creatures!   Both of them wrote a Latin Accidence, to render education less painful to children; both of them composed hymns
and psalms proportioned to the capacity of common congre-
gations; both, nearly at the same time, set the glorious example of publicly recommending and supporting general toleration, and the liberty both of the pulpit and the press!   In the
writings of neither shall we find a single sentence, like those
meek deliverances to God's mercy, with which Laud accompanied his votes for the mutilations and loathsome dungeon-
ing of Leighton and others!—nowhere such a pious prayer as
we find in Bishop Hall's memoranda of his own life, concerning the subtle and witty atheist that so grievously perplexed
and gravelled him at Sir Robert Drury's till he prayed to the
Lord to remove him, and behold! his prayers were heard: for
shortly afterward this Philistine-combatant went to London,
and there perished of the plague in great misery!   In short, nowhere shall we find the least approach, in the lives and writings of John Milton or Jeremy Taylor, to that guarded gentle-
ness, to that sighing reluctance, with which the holy brethren
of the Inquisition deliver over a condemned heretic to the
civil magistrate, recommending him to mercy, and hoping that
the magistrate will treat the erring brother with all possible
mildness!—the magistrate, who too well knows what would
be his own fate, if he dared offend them by acting on their re-
commendation.

The opportunity of diverting the reader from myself to characters more worthy of his attention, has led me far beyond my first intention; but it is not unimportant to expose the false zeal which has occasioned these attacks on our elder patriots. It has been too much the fashion, first to personify the Church of England, and then to speak of different individuals, who in different ages have been rulers in that Church, as if in some strange way they constituted its personal identity. Why should a clergyman of the present day feel interested in the defence of Laud or Sheldon? Surely it is sufficient for the warmest partisan of our establishment, that he can assert with truth,—when our Church persecuted, it was on mis taken principles held in common by all Christendom; and at all events, far less culpable was this intolerance in the Bishops, who were maintaining the existing laws, than the persecuting spirit afterwards shown by their successful opponents, who had no such excuse, and who should have been taught mercy by their own sufferings, and wisdom by the utter failure of the experiment in their own case. We can say, that our Church, apostolical in its faith, primitive in its ceremonies, unequalled in its liturgical forms; that our Church, which has kindled and displayed more bright and burning lights of genius and learning, than all other protestant churches since the reformation, was (with the single exception of the times of Laud and Sheldon) least intolerant, when all Christians unhappily deemed a species of intolerance their religious duty; that Bishops of our Church were among the first that contended against this error; and finally, that since the reformation, when tolerance became a fashion, the Church of England in a tolerating age, has shown herself eminently tolerant, and far more so, both in spirit and in fact, than many of her most bitter opponents, who profess to deem toleration itself an insult on the rights of mankind! As to myself, who not only know the Church-Establishment to be tolerant, but who see in it the greatest, if not the sole safe bulwark of toleration, I feel no necessity of defending or palliating oppressions under the two Charleses, in order to exclaim with a full and fervent heart, *Esto perpetua!*

FIRE, FAMINE, AND SLAUGHTER.

A WAR ECLOGUE.

The Scene a desolated Tract in La Vendée. FAMINE
is discovered lying on the ground; to her enter FIRE
and SLAUGHTER.

FAMINE.

SISTERS! sisters! who sent you here?

SLAUGHTER. [*to* FIRE.]

I will whisper it in her ear.

FIRE.

No! no! no!
Spirits hear what spirits tell:
'Twill make a holiday in Hell.
No! no! no!
Myself, I named him once below,
And all the souls, that damned be,
Leaped up at once in anarchy,
Clapped their hands and danced for glee.
They no longer heeded me;
But laughed to hear Hell's burning rafters
Unwillingly re-echo laughters!

No! no! no!
Spirits hear what spirits tell:
'Twill make a holiday in Hell!

FAMINE.

Whisper it, sister! so and so!
In a dark hint, soft and slow.

SLAUGHTER.

Letters four do form his name—
And who sent you?

BOTH.

The same! the same!

SLAUGHTER.

He came by stealth, and unlocked my den,
And I have drunk the blood since then
Of thrice three hundred thousand men.

BOTH.

Who bade you do it?

SLAUGHTER.

The same! the same!
Letters four do form his name.
He let me loose and cried Halloo!
To him alone the praise is due.

FAMINE.

Thanks, sister, thanks! the men have bled,
Their wives and their children faint for bread.

I stood in a swampy field of battle ;
With bones and skulls I made a rattle,
To frighten the wolf and carrion-crow
And the homeless dog—but they would not go.
So off I flew : for how could I bear
To see them gorge their dainty fare ?
I heard a groan and a peevish squall,
And through the chink of a cottage-wall—
Can you guess what I saw there ?

BOTH.

Whisper it, sister ! in our ear.

FAMINE.

A baby beat its dying mother:
I had starved the one and was starving the other:

BOTH.

Who bade you do't ?

FAMINE.

The same ! the same !
Letters four do form his name.
He let me loose, and cried, Halloo !
To him alone the praise is due.

FIRE.

Sisters ! I from Ireland came !
Hedge and corn-fields all on flame,
I triumphed o'er the setting sun !
And all the while the work was done,

On as I strode with my huge strides,
I flung back my head and I held my sides,
It was so rare a piece of fun
To see the sweltered cattle run
With uncouth gallop through the night,
Scared by the red and noisy light!
By the light of his own blazing cot
Was many a naked rebel shot:
The house-stream met the flame and hissed,
While crash! fell in the roof, I wist,
On some of those old bed-rid nurses,
That deal in discontent and curses.

BOTH.

Who bade you do't?

FIRE.

The same! the same!
Letters four do form his name.
He let me loose, and cried Halloo!
To him alone the praise is due.

ALL.

He let us loose, and cried Halloo!
How shall we yield him honour due?

FAMINE.

Wisdom comes with lack of food.
I'll gnaw, I'll gnaw the multitude,
Till the cup of rage o'erbrim:
They shall seize him and his brood—

SLAUGHTER.

They shall tear him limb from limb!

FIRE.

O thankless beldames and untrue!
And is this all that you can do
For him, who did so much for you?
Ninety months he, by my troth!
Hath richly catered for you both;
And in an hour would you repay
An eight years' work?—Away! away!
I alone am faithful! I
Cling to him everlastingly.

1798.

THE DEVIL'S THOUGHTS.

I.

FROM his brimstone bed at break of day
  A walking the Devil is gone,
To visit his snug little farm the Earth,
  And see how his stock goes on.

II.

Over the hill and over the dale,
  And he went over the plain,
And backward and forward he switched his long
    tail
  As a gentleman switches his cane.

III.

And how then was the Devil drest?
Oh ! he was in his Sunday's best:
His jacket was red and his breeches were blue,
And there was a hole where the tail came through

IV.

He saw a Lawyer killing a viper
  On a dunghill hard by his own stable ;
And the Devil smiled, for it put him in mind
  Of Cain and his brother Abel.

V.

He saw an Apothecary on a white horse
   Ride by on his vocations;
And the Devil thought of his old friend
   Death in the Revelations.

VI.

He saw a cottage with a double coach-house,
   A cottage of gentility;
And the Devil did grin, for his darling sin
   Is pride that apes humility.

VII.

He peeped into a rich bookseller's shop,
   Quoth he, " We are both of one college!
For I sate myself, like a cormorant, once
   Hard by the tree of knowledge." *

---

* And all amid them stood the tree of life
  High eminent, blooming ambrosial fruit
  Of vegetable gold (query paper money:) and next to Life
  Our Death, the tree of knowledge, grew fast by.—

    *   *   *   *   *

  So clomb this first grand thief———
  Thence up he flew, and on the tree of life
  Sat like a cormorant.   *Par. Lost,* iv.

  The allegory here is so apt, that in a catalogue of various
readings obtained from collating the MSS. one might expect
to find it noted, that for "life" Cod. quid. habent, "trade."
Though indeed the trade, *i. e.* the bibliopolic, called κατ'
ἐξοχήν, may be regarded as Life sensu eminentiori; a sug-

VIII.

Down the river did glide, with wind and with tide,
  A pig with vast celerity ;
And the Devil look'd wise as he saw how tho
    while,
It cut its own throat. "There !" quoth he with a
    smile,
  " Goes England's commercial prosperity."

IX.

As he went through Cold-Bath Fields he saw
  A solitary cell ;
And the Devil was pleased, for it gave him a hint
  For improving his prisons in Hell.

---

gestion, which I owe to a young retailer in the hosiery line, who on hearing a description of the net profits, dinner parties, country houses, &c. of the trade, exclaimed, "Ay! that's what I call Life now!"—This "Life, our Death," is thus happily contrasted with the fruits of authorship—Sic nos non nobis mellificamus apes.

Of this poem, which with the Fire, Famine, and Slaughter, first appeared in the Morning Post, the 1st, 2d, 3d, 9th, and 16th stanzas were dictated by Mr. Southey. See Apologetic Preface.

If any one should ask who General —— meant, the Author begs leave to inform him, that he did once see a red-faced person in a dream whom by the dress he took for a General; but he might have been mistaken, and most certainly he did not hear any names mentioned. In simple verity, the author never meant any one, or indeed any thing but to put a concluding stanza to his doggerel.

X.

He saw a Turnkey in a trice
    Fetter a troublesome blade;
"Nimbly," quoth he, "do the fingers move
    If a man be but used to his trade."

XI.

He saw the same Turnkey unfetter a man
    With but little expedition,
Which put him in mind of the long debate
    On the Slave-trade abolition.

XII.

He saw an old acquaintance
    As he passed by a Methodist meeting;—
She holds a consecrated key,
    And the Devil nods her a greeting.

XIII.

She turned up her nose, and said,
    "Avaunt! my name's Religion,"
And she looked to Mr. ——
    And leered like a love-sick pigeon.

XIV.

He saw a certain minister
    (A minister to his mind)
Go up into a certain House,
    With a majority behind.

XV.

The Devil quoted Genesis,
  Like a very learned clerk,
How " Noah and his creeping things
  Went up into the Ark."

XVI.

He took from the poor,
  And he gave to the rich,
And he shook hands with a Scotchman,
  For he was not afraid of the ——
        *   *   *   *

XVII.

General ———— burning face
  He saw with consternation,
And back to hell his way did he take,
For the Devil thought by a slight mistake
  It was general conflagration.

Sept. 6, 1799.

II.—LOVE POEMS.

Quas humilis tenero stylus olim effudit in ævo,
Perlegis hic lacrymas, et quod pharetratus acuta
Ille puer puero fecit mihi cuspide vulnus.
Omnia paulatim consumit longior ætas,
Vivendoque simul morimur, rapimurque manendo.
Ipse mihi collatus enim non ille videbor:
Frons alia est, moresque alii, nova mentis imago,
Voxque aliud sonat—
Pectore nunc gelido calidos miseremur amantes,
Jamque arsisse pudet.   Veteres tranquilla tumultus
Mens horret, relegensque alium putat ista locutum.

PETRARCH.

LEWTI,

OR THE CIRCASSIAN LOVE-CHAUNT.

AT midnight by the stream I roved,
To forget the form I loved.
Image of Lewti! from my mind
Depart; for Lewti is not kind.

The moon was high, the moonlight gleam
 And the shadow of a star
Heaved upon Tamaha's stream;
 But the rock shone brighter far,

The rock half sheltered from my view
By pendent boughs of tressy yew—
So shines my Lewti's forehead fair,
Gleaming through her sable hair.
Image of Lewti! from my mind
Depart; for Lewti is not kind.

I saw a cloud of palest hue,
    Onward to the moon it passed;
Still brighter and more bright it grew,
With floating colours not a few,
    Till it reached the moon at last:
Then the cloud was wholly bright,
With a rich and amber light!
And so with many a hope I seek,
    And with such joy I find my Lewti;
And even so my pale wan cheek
    Drinks in as deep a flush of beauty!
Nay, treacherous image! leave my mind,
If Lewti never will be kind.

The little cloud—it floats away,
    Away it goes; away so soon?
Alas! it has no power to stay:
Its hues are dim, its hues are gray—
    Away it passes from the moon!
How mournfully it seems to fly,
    Ever fading more and more,
To joyless regions of the sky—
    And now 'tis whiter than before!.

As white as my poor cheek will be,
　　When, Lewti! on my couch I lie,
A dying man for love of thee.
Nay, treacherous image! leave my mind—
And yet, thou didst not look unkind.

　　I saw a vapour in the sky,
　　Thin, and white, and very high;
I ne'er beheld so thin a cloud:
　　Perhaps the breezes that can fly
　　Now below and now above,
Have snatched aloft the lawny shroud
　　Of Lady fair—that died for love.
For maids, as well as youths, have perished
From fruitless love too fondly cherished.
Nay, treacherous image! leave my mind—
For Lewti never will be kind.

Hush! my heedless feet from under
　　Slip the crumbling banks for ever:
Like echoes to a distant thunder,
　　They plunge into the gentle river.
The river-swans have heard my tread,
And startle from their reedy bed.
O beauteous birds! methinks ye measure
　　Your movements to some heavenly tune!
O beauteous birds! 'tis such a pleasure
　　To see you move beneath the moon,
I would it were your true delight
To sleep by day and wake all night.

I know the place where Lewti lies,
When silent night has closed her eyes:
　It is a breezy jasmine-bower,
The nightingale sings o'er her head:
　Voice of the night! had I the power
That leafy labyrinth to thread,
And creep, like thee, with soundless tread,
I then might view her bosom white
Heaving lovely to my sight,
As these two swans together heave
On the gently swelling wave.

Oh! that she saw me in a dream,
　And dreamt that I had died for care;
All pale and wasted I would seem,
　Yet fair withal, as spirits are!
I'd die indeed, if I might see
Her bosom heave, and heave for me!
Soothe, gentle image! soothe my mind!
To-morrow Lewti may be kind.

                                    1795.

LOVE.

ALL thoughts, all passions, all delights,
Whatever stirs this mortal frame,
All are but ministers of Love,
    And feed his sacred flame.

Oft in my waking dreams do I
Live o'er again that happy hour,
When midway on the mount I lay,
    Beside the ruined tower.

The moonshine, stealing o'er the scene,
Had blended with the lights of eve;
And she was there, my hope, my joy,
    My own dear Genevieve!

She lean'd against the armed man,
The statue of the armed knight;
She stood and listened to my lay,
    Amid the lingering light.

Few sorrows hath she of her own.
My hope! my joy! my Genevieve!
She loves me best, whene'er I sing
    The songs that make her grieve.

I played a soft and doleful air,
I sang an old and moving story—
An old rude song, that suited well
 That ruin wild and hoary.

She listened with a flitting blush,
With downcast eyes and modest grace;
For well she knew, I could not choose
 But gaze upon her face.

I told her of the knight that wore
Upon his shield a burning brand;
And that for ten long years he wooed
 The Lady of the Land.

I told her how he pined: and ah!
The deep, the low, the pleading tone
With which I sang another's love,
 Interpreted my own.

She listened with a flitting blush,
With downcast eyes, and modest grace;
And she forgave me, that I gazed
 Too fondly on her face!

But when I told the cruel scorn
That crazed that bold and lovely Knight,
And that he crossed the mountain-woods,
 Nor rested day nor night;

That sometimes from the savage den,
And sometimes from the darksome shade,
And sometimes starting up at once
    In green and sunny glade,—

There came and looked him in the face
An angel beautiful and bright;
And that he knew it was a Fiend,
    This miserable Knight!

And that, unknowing what he did,
He leaped amid a murderous band,
And saved from outrage worse than death
    The Lady of the Land;—

And how she wept, and clasped his knees;
And how she tended him in vain—
And ever strove to expiate
    The scorn that crazed his brain;—

And that she nursed him in a cave;
And how his madness went away,
When on the yellow forest-leaves
    A dying man he lay;—

His dying words—but when I reached
That tenderest strain of all the ditty,
My faltering voice and pausing harp
    Disturbed her soul with pity!

All impulses of soul and sense
Had thrilled my guileless Genevieve;
The music and the doleful tale,
 The rich and balmy eve;

And hopes, and fears that kindle hope,
An undistinguishable throng,
And gentle wishes long subdued,
 Subdued and cherished long!

She wept with pity and delight,
She blushed with love, and virgin shame;
And like the murmur of a dream,
 I heard her breathe my name.

Her bosom heaved—she stepped aside,
As conscious of my look she stept—
Then suddenly, with timorous eye
 She fled to me and wept.

She half inclosed me with her arms,
She pressed me with a meek embrace;
And bending back her head, looked up,
 And gazed upon my face.

'Twas partly love, and partly fear,
And partly 'twas a bashful art,
That I might rather feel, than see,
 The swelling of her heart.

I calmed her fears, and she was calm,
And told her love with virgin pride;
And so I won my Genevieve,
 My bright and beauteous Bride.

LINES SUGGESTED AT —— THEATRE.

MAIDEN, that with sullen brow
 Sitt'st behind those virgins gay,
Like a scorched and mildewed bough,
 Leafless 'mid the blooms of May!

Him who lured thee and forsook,
 Oft I watched with angry gaze,
Fearful saw his pleading look,
 Anxious heard his fervid phrase.

Soft the glances of the youth,
 Soft his speech, and soft his sigh;
But no sound like simple truth,
 But no true love in his eye.

Loathing thy polluted lot,
 Hie thee, Maiden, hie thee hence!
Seek thy weeping Mother's cot,
 With a wiser innocence.

Thou hast known deceit and folly,
　　Thou hast felt that vice is woe:
With a musing melancholy
　　Inly armed, go, Maiden! go.

Mother sage of self-dominion,
　　Firm thy steps, O Melancholy!
The strongest plume in wisdom's pinion
　　Is the memory of past folly.

Mute the skylark and forlorn,
　　While she moults the firstling plumes,
That had skimmed the tender corn,
　　Or the bean-field's odorous blooms.

Soon with renovated wing
　　Shall she dare a loftier flight,
Upward to the day-star spring,
　　And embathe in heavenly light.

TO ——.

MYRTLE-LEAF that, ill besped,
  Pinest in the gladsome ray,
Soiled beneath the common tread,
  Far from thy protecting spray!

When the partridge o'er the sheaf
  Whirred along the yellow vale,
Sad I saw thee, heedless leaf!
  Love the dalliance of the gale.

Lightly didst thou, foolish thing!
  Heave and flutter to his sighs,
While the flatterer, on his wing,
  Wooed and whispered thee to rise.

Gayly from thy mother-stalk
  Wert thou danced and wafted high—
Soon on this unsheltered walk
  Flung to fade, to rot and die.

THE PICTURE,

OR THE LOVER'S RESOLUTION.

THROUGH weeds and thorns, and matted under-
    wood
I force my way; now climb, and now descend
O'er rocks, or bare or mossy, with wild foot
Crushing the purple whorts; while oft unseen,
Hurrying along the drifted forest-leaves,
The scared snake rustles. Onward still I toil
I know not, ask not whither! A new joy,
Lovely as light, sudden as summer gust,
And gladsome as the first-born of the spring,
Beckons me on, or follows from behind,
Playmate, or guide! The master-passion quelled,
I feel that I am free. With dun-red bark
The fir-trees, and the unfrequent slender oak,
Forth from this tangle wild of bush and brake
Soar up, and form a melancholy vault
High o'er me, murmuring like a distant sea.

Here Wisdom might resort, and here Remorse;
Here too the love-lorn man, who, sick in soul,
And of this busy human heart aweary,

Worships the spirit of unconscious life
In tree or wild-flower.—Gentle lunatic!
If so he might not wholly cease to be,
He would far rather not be that he is ;
But would be something that he knows not of,
In winds or waters, or among the rocks !

But hence, fond wretch ! breathe not contagion
     here !
No myrtle-walks are these : these are no groves
Where Love dare loiter !   If in sullen mood
He should stray hither, the low stumps shall gore
His dainty feet, the brier and the thorn
Make his plumes haggard.   Like a wounded bird
Easily caught, ensnare him, O ye Nymphs,
Ye Oreads chaste, ye dusky Dryades !
And you, ye Earth-winds ! you that make at
     morn
The dew-drops quiver on the spiders' webs !
You, O ye wingless Airs ! that creep between
The rigid stems of heath and bitten furze,
Within whose scanty shade, at summer-noon,
The mother-sheep hath worn a hollow bed—
Ye, that now cool her fleece with dropless damp
Now pant and murmur with her feeding lamb.
Chase, chase him, all ye Fays, and elfin Gnomes !
With prickles sharper than his darts bemock
His little Godship, making him perforce
Creep through a thorn-bush on yon hedgehog's
     back.

This is my hour of triumph! I can now
With my own fancies play the merry fool,
And laugh away worse folly, being free.
Here will I seat myself, beside this old,
Hollow, and weedy oak, which ivy-twine
Clothes as with net-work: here will I couch my
    limbs,
Close by this river, in this silent shade,
As safe and sacred from the step of man
As an invisible world—unheard, unseen,
And listening only to the pebbly brook
That murmurs with a dead, yet tinkling sound;
Or to the bees, that in the neighboring trunk
Make honey-hoards. The breeze, that visits me
Was never Love's accomplice, never raised
The tendril ringlets from the maiden's brow,
And the blue, delicate veins above her cheek;
Ne'er played the wanton—never half disclosed
The maiden's snowy bosom, scattering thence
Eye-poisons for some love-distempered youth,
Who ne'er henceforth may see an aspen-grove
Shiver in sunshine, but his feeble heart
Shall flow away like a dissolving thing.

Sweet breeze! thou only, if I guess aright,
Liftest the feathers of the robin's breast,
That swells its little breast, so full of song,
Singing above me, on the mountain-ash.
And thou too, desert stream! no pool of thine,
Though clear as lake in latest summer-eve,

Did e'er reflect the stately virgin's robe,
The face, the form divine, the downcast look
Contemplative! Behold! her open palm
Presses her cheek and brow! her elbow rests
On the bare branch of half-uprooted tree,
That leans towards its mirror! Who erewhile
Had from her countenance turned, or looked by
    stealth,
(For fear is true love's cruel nurse,) he now
With steadfast gaze and unoffending eye,
Worships the watery idol, dreaming hopes
Delicious to the soul, but fleeting, vain,
E'en as that phantom-world on which he gazed,
But not unheeded gazed: for see, ah! see,
The sportive tyrant with her left hand plucks
The heads of tall flowers that behind her grow,
Lychnis, and willow-herb, and foxglove bells:
And suddenly, as one that toys with time,
Scatters them on the pool! Then all the charm
Is broken—all that phantom-world so fair
Vanishes, and a thousand circlets spread,
And each misshape the other. Stay awhile,
Poor youth, who scarcely dar'st lift up thine eyes!
The stream will soon renew its smoothness, soon
The visions will return! And lo! he stays:
And soon the fragments dim of lovely forms
Come trembling back, unite, and now once more
The pool becomes a mirror; and behold
Each wild-flower on the marge inverted there,
And there the half-uprooted tree—but where,

O where the virgin's snowy arm, that leaned
On its bare branch?   He turns, and she is gone!
Homeward she steals through many a woodland
  maze
Which he shall seek in vain.   Ill-fated youth!
Go, day by day, and waste thy manly prime
In mad love-yearning by the vacant brook,
Till sickly thoughts bewitch thine eyes, and thou
Behold'st her shadow still abiding there,
The Naiad of the mirror!

       Not to thee,
O wild and desert stream! belongs this tale:
Gloomy and dark art thou—the crowded firs
Spire from thy shores, and stretch across thy bed,
Making thee doleful as a cavern well;
Save when the shy kingfishers build their nest
On thy steep banks, no loves hast thou, wild stream!

 This be my chosen haunt—emancipate
From passion's dreams, a freeman and alone,
I rise and trace its devious course.   O lead,
Lead me to deeper shades and lonelier glooms.
Lo! stealing through the canopy of firs,
How fair the sunshine spots that mossy rock,
Isle of the river, whose disparted waves
Dart off asunder with an angry sound,
How soon to reunite!   And see! they meet,
Each in the other lost and found: and see
Placeless, as spirits, one soft water sun

Throbbing within them, heart at once and eye!
With its soft neighbourhood of filmy clouds,
The stains and shadings of forgotten tears,
Dimness o'erswum with lustre!   Such the hour
Of deep enjoyment, following love's brief feuds;
And hark, the noise of a near waterfall!
I pass forth into light—I find myself
Beneath a weeping birch, (most beautiful
Of forest-trees, the lady of the woods,)
Hard by the brink of a tall weedy rock
That overbrows the cataract.   How bursts
The landscape on my sight!   Two crescent hills
Fold in behind each other, and so make
A circular vale, and land-locked, as might seem,
With brook and bridge, and gray stone cottages,
Half hid by rocks and fruit-trees.   At my feet,
The whortleberries are bedewed with spray,
Dashed upwards by the furious waterfall.
How solemnly the pendant ivy-mass
Swings in its winnow; all the air is calm.
The smoke from cottage chimneys, tinged with light,
Rises in columns; from this house alone,
Close by the waterfall, the column slants,
And feels its ceaseless breeze.   But what is this?
That cottage, with its slanting chimney-smoke,
And close beside its porch a sleeping child,
His dear head pillowed on a sleeping dog—
One arm between its fore-legs, and the hand
Holds loosely its small handful of wild flowers,
Unfilleted, and of unequal lengths.

A curious picture, with a master's haste
Sketched on a strip of pinky-silver skin,
Peeled from the birchen bark!   Divinest maid!
Yon bark her canvas, and those purple berries
Her pencil!   See, the juice is scarcely dried
On the fine skin!   She has been newly here;
And lo! yon patch of heath has been her couch—
The pressure still remains!   O blessed couch!
For this mayst thou flower early, and the sun,
Slanting at eve, rest bright, and linger long
Upon thy purple bells!   O Isabel!
Daughter of genius!   stateliest of our maids!
More beautiful than whom Alcæus wooed
The Lesbian woman of immortal song!
O child of genius!   stately, beautiful,
And full of love to all, save only me,
And not ungentle e'en to me!   My heart,
Why beats is thus?   Through yonder coppice-
    wood
Needs must the pathway turn, that leads straight-
    way
On to her father's house.   She is alone!
The night draws on—such ways are hard to hit—
And fit it is I should restore this sketch,
Dropt unawares no doubt.   Why should I yearn
To keep the relique? 'twill but idly feed
The passion that consumes me.   Let me haste!
The picture in my hand which she has left,
She cannot blame me that I followed her:
And I may be her guide the long wood through.

THE NIGHT-SCENE.

A DRAMATIC FRAGMENT.

Sandoval. You loved the daughter of Don Manrique?

Earl Henry.   Loved?

Sandoval. Did you not say you wooed her?

Earl Henry.   Once I loved
Her whom I dared not woo!

Sandoval.   And wooed, perchance,
One whom you loved not!

Earl Henry.   Oh! I were most base,
Not loving Oropeza. True, I wooed her,
Hoping to heal a deeper wound; but she
Met my advances with impassioned pride,
That kindled love with love. And when her sire,
Who in his dream of hope already grasped
The golden circlet in his hand, rejected
My suit with insult, and in memory
Of ancient feuds poured curses on my head,
Her blessings overtook and baffled them!
But thou art stern, and with unkindly countenance
Art inly reasoning whilst thou listenest to me.

Sandoval. Anxiously, Henry! reasoning anxiously.
But Oropeza —

Earl Henry. Blessings gather round her!
Within this wood there winds a secret passage,
Beneath the walls, which opens out at length
Into the gloomiest covert of the garden.—
The night ere my departure to the army,
She, nothing trembling, led me through that gloom,
And to that covert by a silent stream,
Which, with one star reflected near its marge,
Was the sole object visible around me.
No leaflet stirred; the air was almost sultry;
So deep, so dark, so close, the umbrage o'er us!
No leaflet stirred;—yet pleasure hung upon
The gloom and stillness of the balmy night-air.
A little further on an arbour stood,
Fragrant with flowering trees—I well remember
What an uncertain glimmer in the darkness
Their snow-white blossoms made—thither she led
    me,
To that sweet bower! Then Oropeza trembled—
I heard her heart beat—if 'twere not my own.
    Sandoval. A rude and scaring note, my friend.
    Earl Henry.   Oh! no!
I have small memory of aught but pleasure.
The inquietudes of fear, like lesser streams
Still flowing, still were lost in those of love:
So love grew mightier from the fear, and Nature,
Fleeing from pain, sheltered herself in joy.
The stars above our heads were dim and steady,
Like eyes suffused with rapture.—Life was in us:
We were all life, each atom of our frames

A living soul—I vowed to die for her:
With the faint voice of one who, having spoken,
Relapses into blessedness, I vowed it:
That solemn vow, a whisper scarcely heard,
A murmur breathed against a lady's ear.
Oh! there is joy above the name of pleasure,
Deep self-possession, an intense repose.

    Sandoval (with a sarcastic smile.) No other
        than as eastern sages paint,
The God, who floats upon a lotos leaf,
Dreams for a thousand ages; then awaking,
Creates a world, and smiling at the bubble,
Relapses into bliss.

    Earl Henry.   Ah! was that bliss
Feared as an alien, and too vast for man?
For suddenly, impatient of its silence,
Did Oropeza, starting, grasp my forehead.
I caught her arms; the veins were swelling on
      them.
Through the dark bower she sent a hollow
      voice ;—
" Oh! what if all betray me? what if thou? "
I swore, and with an inward thought that seemed
The purpose and the substance of my being,
I swore to her, that were she red with guilt,
I would exchange my unblenched state with
      hers.—
Friend! by that winding passage, to that bower
I now will go—all objects there will teach me
Unwavering love, and singleness of heart.

Go, Sandoval! I am prepared to meet her—
Say nothing of me—I myself will seek her—
Nay, leave me, friend! I cannot bear the torment
And keen inquiry of that scanning eye.—

[EARL HENRY *retires into the wood.*

Sandoval (alone.)   O Henry! always striv'st
  thou to be great
By thine own act—yet art thou never great
But by the inspiration of great passion.
The whirl-blast comes, the desert-sands rise up
And shape themselves: from earth to heaven
  they stand,
As though they were the pillars of a temple,
Built by Omnipotence in its own honour!
But the blast pauses, and their shaping spirit
Is fled: the mighty columns were but sand,
And lazy snakes trail o'er the level ruins!

LINES COMPOSED IN A CONCERT-ROOM.

NOR cold, nor stern, my soul! yet I detest
   These scented rooms, where, to a gaudy throng,
Heaves the proud harlot her distended breast
   In intricacies of laborious song.

These feel not Music's genuine power, nor deign
   To melt at Nature's passion-warbled plaint;
But when the long-breathed singer's uptrilled
      strain
   Bursts in a squall—they gape for wonderment.

Hark! the deep buzz of vanity and hate!
   Scornful, yet envious, with self-torturing sneer
My lady eyes some maid of humbler state,
   While the pert captain, or the primmer priest,
Prattles accordant scandal in her ear.

O give me, from this heartless scene released,
   To hear our old musician, blind and gray,
(Whom stretching from my nurse's arms I kissed,)
   His Scottish tunes and warlike marches play,
By moonshine, on the balmy summer-night,
   The while I dance amid the tedded hay
With merry maids, whose ringlets toss in light.

Or lies the purple evening on the bay
Of the calm glossy lake, O let me hide
    Unheard, unseen, behind the alder-trees,
For round their roots the fisher's boat is tied,
    On whose trim seat doth Edmund stretch at
        ease,
And while the lazy boat sways to and fro,
    Breathes in his flute sad airs, so wild and slow,
That his own cheek is wet with quiet tears.

But O, dear Anne! when midnight wind careers,
And the gust pelting on the out-house shed
    Makes the cock shrilly on the rain storm crow,
    To hear thee sing some ballad full of woe,
Ballad of shipwrecked sailor floating dead,
    Whom his own true-love buried in the sands !
Thee, gentle woman, for thy voice remeasures
Whatever tones and melancholy pleasures
    The things of Nature utter ; birds or trees,
Or moan of ocean-gale in weedy caves,
Or where the stiff grass 'mid the heath-plant
        waves,
    Murmur and music thin of sudden breeze.

1799.

ANSWER TO A CHILD'S QUESTION.

Do you ask what the birds say? The sparrow,
    the dove,
The linnet and thrush say, " I love and I love ! "
In the winter they're silent—the wind is so
    strong ;
What it says, I don't know, but it sings a loud
    song.
But green leaves, and blossoms, and sunny warm
    weather,
And singing, and loving—all come back together.
But the lark is so brimful of gladness and love,
The green fields below him, the blue sky above,
That he sings, and he sings ; and for ever sings
    he—
" I love my Love, and my Love loves me ! "

1798-9.

TO A LADY,

WITH FALCONER'S "SHIPWRECK."

Aɪɪ! not by Cam or Isis, famous streams,
   In arched groves, the youthful poet's choice;
Nor while half-listening, 'mid delicious dreams,
   To harp and song from lady's hand and voice;

Nor yet while gazing in sublimer mood
   On cliff, or cataract, in Alpine dell;
Nor in dim cave with bladdery sea-weed strewed,
   Framing wild fancies to the ocean's swell;

Our sea-bard sang this song! which still he sings,
   And sings for thee, sweet friend! Hark, Pity,
      hark!
Now mounts, now totters on the tempest's wings,
   Now groans, and shivers, the replunging bark!

" Cling to the shrouds!" In vain! The breakers
   roar—
   Death shrieks! With two alone of all his clan
Forlorn the poet paced the Grecian shore,
   No classic roamer, but a shipwrecked man!

Say then, what muse inspired these genial strains
   And lit his spirit to so bright a flame?
The elevating thought of suffered pains,
    Which gentle hearts shall mourn; but chief, the
      name

Of gratitude! remembrances of friend,
   Or absent or no more! shades of the Past,
Which Love makes substance!   Hence to thee I
    send,
   O dear as long as life and memory last!

I send with deep regards of heart and head,
   Sweet maid, for friendship formed! this work to
    thee:
And thou, the while thou canst not choose but shed
   A tear for Falconer, wilt remember me.

TO A YOUNG LADY,

ON HER RECOVERY FROM A FEVER.

WHY need I say, Louisa dear!
How glad I am to see you here,
   A lovely convalescent;
Risen from the bed of pain and fear,
   And feverish heat incessant.

The sunny showers, the dappled sky,
The little birds that warble high,
   Their vernal loves commencing,
Will better welcome you than I
   With their sweet influencing.

Believe me, while in bed you lay,
Your danger taught us all to pray:
   You made us grow devouter!
Each eye looked up and seemed to say,
   How can we do without her?

Besides, what vexed us worse, we knew,
They have no need of such as you
   In the place where you were going:
This world has angels all too few,
   And Heaven is overflowing!

1799.

INTRODUCTION TO THE TALE OF THE DARK LADIE.

O LEAVE the lily on its stem;
O leave the rose upon the spray;
O leave the elder bloom, fair maids!
    And listen to my lay.

A cypress and a myrtle bough
This morn around my harp you twined,
Because it fashioned mournfully
    Its murmurs in the wind.

And now a tale of love and woe,
A woful tale of love I sing;
Hark, gentle maidens! hark, it sighs
    And trembles on the string.

But most, my own dear Genevieve,
It sighs and trembles most for thee!
O come and hear the cruel wrongs,
    Befell the Dark Ladie! *

    *   *   *   *   *   *

' Here followed the Stanzas, afterwards published separately under the title "Love," (see p. 238,) and after them came the other three stanzas printed above; the whole forming an introduction to the intended Dark Ladie, of which all that exists is subjoined.

And now, once more a tale of woe,
A woful tale of love I sing ;
For thee, my Genevieve, it sighs,
    And trembles on the string.

When last I sang the cruel scorn,
That crazed this bold and lovely knight,
And how he roamed the mountain woods,
    Nor rested day nor night ;

I promised thee a sister tale,
Of man's perfidious cruelty ;
Come then, and hear what cruel wrong
    Befell the Dark Ladie.

THE BALLAD OF THE DARK LADIE.

A FRAGMENT.

BENEATH yon birch with silver bark,
And boughs so pendulous and fair,
The brook falls scatter'd down the rock :
    And all is mossy there !

And there upon the moss she sits,
The Dark Ladie in silent pain ;
The heavy tear is in her eye,
    And drops and swells again.

Three times she sends her little page
Up the castled mountain's breast,
If he might find the Knight that wears
    The Griffin for his crest.

The sun was sloping down the sky,
And she had lingered there all day,
Counting moments, dreaming fears—
    O wherefore can he stay?

She hears a rustling o'er the brook,
She sees far off a swinging bough!
" 'Tis He! 'Tis my betrothed Knight!
    Lord Falkland, is it Thou!"

She springs, she clasps him round the neck,
She sobs a thousand hopes and fears,
Her kisses glowing on his cheeks
    She quenches with her tears.

    *   *   *   *   *   *

" My friends with rude ungentle words
They scoff and bid me fly to thee!
O give me shelter in thy breast!
    O shield and shelter me!

" My Henry, I have given thee much,
I gave what I can ne'er recall,
I gave my heart, I gave my peace,
    O Heaven! I gave thee all."

The Knight made answer to the Maid,
While to his heart he held her hand,
" Nine castles hath my noble sire,
    None statelier in the land.

" The fairest one shall be my love's,
The fairest castle of the nine!
Wait only till the stars peep out,
    The fairest shall be thine:

" Wait only till the hand of eve
Hath wholly closed yon western bars,
And through the dark we two will steal
    Beneath the twinkling stars ! "

" The dark? the dark? No! not the dark?
The twinkling stars? How, Henry? How?
O God! 'twas in the eye of noon
    He pledged his sacred vow !

"And in the eye of noon, my love,
Shall lead me from my mother's door,
Sweet boys and girls all clothed in white
    Strewing flow'rs before:

" But first the nodding minstrels go
With music meet for lordly bow'rs,
The children next in snow-white vests,
    Strewing buds and flow'rs !

"And then my love and I shall pace,
My jet black hair in pearly braids,
Between our comely bachelors
    And blushing bridal maids."

*   *   *   *   *   *

1799.

THE DAY-DREAM.

FROM AN EMIGRANT TO HIS ABSENT WIFE.

If thou wert here, these tears were tears of
        light!
But from as sweet a vision did I start
As ever made these eyes grow idly bright!
    And though I weep, yet still around my heart
A sweet and playful tenderness doth linger,
Touching my heart as with an infant's finger.

My mouth half open, like a witless man,
    I saw our couch, I saw our quiet room,
    Its shadows heaving by the fire-light gloom;
And o'er my lips a subtle feeling ran,
All o'er my lips a soft and breeze-like feeling—
I know not what—but had the same been
        stealing

Upon a sleeping mother's lips, I guess,
  It would have made the loving mother dream
That she was softly bending down to kiss
  Her babe, that something more than babe did
    seem,
A floating presence of its darling father,
And yet its own dear baby self far rather!

Across my chest there lay a weight so warm!
  As if some bird had taken shelter there;
And lo! I seemed to see a woman's form—
  Thine, Sara, thine? O joy, if thine it were!
I gazed with stifled breath and feared to stir it,
No deeper trance e'er wrapt a yearning spirit!

And now, when I seemed sure thy face to see,
  Thy own dear self in our own quiet home;
There came an elfish laugh, and wakened me:
  'Twas Frederic, who behind my chair had clomb,
And with his bright eyes at my face was peeping.
I blessed him, tried to laugh, and fell a weeping! *

1798 Ø.

* See Note.

SOMETHING CHILDISH, BUT VERY NATURAL.

WRITTEN IN GERMANY.

If I had but two little wings,
  And were a little feathery bird,
    To you I'd fly, my dear!
But thoughts like these are idle things,
    And I stay here.

But in my sleep to you I fly:
  I'm always with you in my sleep!
    The world is all one's own.
But then one wakes, and where am I?
    All, all alone.

Sleep stays not, though a monarch bids:
  So I love to wake ere break of day:
    For though my sleep be gone,
Yet while 'tis dark, one shuts one's lids,
    And still dreams on.

1798-9.

ON REVISITING THE SEA-SHORE,

AFTER LONG ABSENCE, UNDER STRONG MEDICAL RECOMMENDATION NOT TO BATHE.

GOD be with thee, gladsome Ocean !
  How gladly greet I thee once more !
Ships and waves and ceaseless motion,
  And men rejoicing on thy shore.

Dissuading spake the mild physician,
  " Those briny waves for thee are death ! "
But my soul fulfilled her mission,
  And lo ! I breathe untroubled breath !

Fashion's pining sons and daughters,
  That seek the crowd they seem to fly,
Trembling they approach thy waters ;
  And what cares Nature if they die ?

Me a thousand hopes and pleasures,
  A thousand recollections bland,
Thoughts sublime, and stately measures,
  Revisit on thy echoing strand :

Dreams, (the soul herself forsaking,)
   Tearful raptures, boyish mirth ;
Silent adorations, making
   A blessed shadow of this Earth !

O ye hopes, that stir within me,
   Health comes with you from above !
God is with me, God is in me !
   I cannot die, if Life be Love.

1801.

THE KEEPSAKE.

THE tedded hay, the first fruits of the soil,
The tedded hay and corn-sheaves in one field,
Show summer gone, ere come.' The foxglove
     tall
Sheds its loose purple bells, or in the gust,
Or when it bends beneath the up-springing
     lark,
Or mountain-finch alighting. And the rose
(In vain the darling of successful love)
Stands like some boasted beauty of past years,
The thorns remaining, and the flowers all gone.
Nor can I find, amid my lonely walk
By rivulet, or spring, or wet road-side,
That blue and bright-eyed floweret of the brook,

Hope's gentle gem, the sweet Forget-me-not! *
So will not fade the flowers which Emmeline
With delicate fingers on the snow white silk
Has worked, (the flowers which most she knew I
    loved,)
And, more beloved than they, her auburn hair.

In the cool morning twilight, early waked
By her full bosom's joyous restlessness,
Softly she rose, and lightly stole along,
Down the slope coppice to the woodbine bower,
Whose rich flowers, swinging in the morning
    breeze,
Over their dim fast-moving shadows hung,
Making a quiet image of disquiet
In the smooth, scarcely moving river-pool.
There, in that bower where first she owned her
    love,
And let me kiss my own warm tear of joy
From off her glowing cheek, she sate and
    stretched
The silk upon the frame, and worked her name
Between the Moss-Rose and Forget-me-not—
Her own dear name, with her own auburn hair!
That forced to wander till sweet spring return,

---

* One of the names (and meriting to be the only one) of
the *Myosotis Scorpivides Palustris*, a flower from six to twelve
inches high, with blue blossom and bright yellow eye. It
has the same name over the whole Empire of Germany (*Ver-
gissmeinnicht*) and, I believe, in Denmark and Sweden.

I yet might ne'er forget her smile, her look,
Her voice, (that even in her mirthful mood
Has made me wish to steal away and weep,)
Nor yet the entrancement of that maiden kiss
With which she promised, that when spring
  returned,
She would resign one half of that dear name,
And own thenceforth no other name but mine!

         1801.

THE VISIONARY HOPE.

Sad lot, to have no hope! Though lowly
  kneeling
He fain would frame a prayer within his breast,
Would fain entreat for some sweet breath of
  healing,
That his sick body might have ease and rest;
He strove in vain! the dull sighs from his chest
Against his will the stifling load revealing,
Though Nature forced; though like some captive
  guest,
Some royal prisoner at his conqueror's feast,
An alien's restless mood but half concealing,
The sternness on his gentle brow confessed,
Sickness within and miserable feeling:

Though obscure pangs made curses of his dreams,
And dreaded sleep, each night repelled in vain,
Each night was scattered by its own loud screams:
Yet never could his heart command, though fain,
One deep full wish to be no more in pain.

That Hope, which was his inward bliss and
    boast,
Which waned and died, yet ever near him stood,
Though changed in nature, wander where he
    would—
For Love's despair is but Hope's pining ghost!
For this one hope he makes his hourly moan,
He wishes and can wish for this alone!
Pierced, as with light from Heaven, before its
    gleams
(So the love-stricken visionary deems)
Disease would vanish, like a summer shower,
Whose dews fling sunshine from the noontide
    bower!
Or let it stay! yet this one Hope should give
Such strength that he would bless his pains and
    live.

HOME-SICK.

WRITTEN IN GERMANY.

'TIS sweet to him, who all the week
  Through city-crowds must push his way,
To stroll alone through fields and woods,
  And hallow thus the Sabbath-day.

And sweet it is, in summer bower,
  Sincere, affectionate and gay,
One's own dear children feasting round,
  To celebrate one's marriage-day.

But what is all, to his delight,
  Who having long been doomed to roam,
Throws off the bundle from his back,
  Before the door of his own home?

Home-sickness is a wasting pang;
  This feel I hourly more and more:
There's healing only in thy wings,
  Thou Breeze that play'st on Albion's shore!

1798-9.

THE HAPPY HUSBAND.

Oft, oft methinks, the while with Thee
  I breathe, as from the heart, thy dear
  And dedicated name, I hear
A promise and a mystery,
  A pledge of more than passing life,
  Yea, in that very name of Wife!

A pulse of love, that ne'er can sleep!
  A feeling that upbraids the heart
  With happiness beyond desert,
That gladness half requests to weep!
  Nor bless I not the keener sense
  And unalarming turbulence

Of transient joys, that ask no sting
  From jealous fears, or coy denying;
  But born beneath Love's brooding wing,
And into tenderness soon dying,
  Wheel out their giddy moment, then
  Resign the soul to love again;—

A more precipitated vein
  Of notes, that eddy in the flow
  Of smoothest song, they come, they go,
And leave their sweeter understrain
  Its own sweet self—a love of Thee
  That seems, yet cannot greater be!   1806.

RECOLLECTIONS OF LOVE.

I.

How warm this woodland wild Recess!
　Love surely hath been breathing here;
　And this sweet bed of heath, my dear!
Swells up, then sinks with faint caress,
　As if to have you yet more near.

II.

Eight springs have flown, since last I lay
　On seaward Quantock's heathy hills,
　Where quiet sounds from hidden rills
Float here and there, like things astray,
　And high o'er head the skylark shrills.

III.

No voice as yet had made the air
　Be music with your name; yet why
　That asking look? that yearning sigh?
That sense of promise everywhere?
　Beloved! flew your spirit by?

IV.

As when a mother doth explore
　The rose-mark on her long lost child,
　I met, I loved you, maiden mild!
As whom I long had loved before—
　So deeply had I been beguiled.

V.

You stood before me like a thought,
  A dream remembered in a dream.
  But when those meek eyes first did seem
To tell me, Love within you wrought—
  O Greta, dear domestic stream!

VI.

Has not, since then, Love's prompture deep,
  Has not Love's whisper evermore
  Been ceaseless, as thy gentle roar?
Sole voice, when other voices sleep,
  Dear under-song in clamor's hour.

                   1806.

THE PANG MORE SHARP THAN ALL.

AN ALLEGORY.

I.

He too has flitted from his secret nest,
Hope's last and dearest Child without a name!—
Has flitted from me, like the warmthless flame,
That makes false promise of a place of rest
To the tir'd Pilgrim's still believing mind;—
Or like some Elfin Knight in kingly court,
Who having won all guerdons in his sport,
Glides out of view, and whither none can find!

II.

Yes! He hath flitted from me—with what aim,
Or why, I know not! 'Twas a home of bliss,
And He was innocent, as the pretty shame
Of babe, that tempts and shuns the menaced kiss,
From its twy-cluster'd hiding place of snow!
Pure as the babe, I ween,. and all aglow
As the dear hopes, that swell the mother's
   breast—
Her eyes down gazing o'er her clasped charge;—
Yet gay as that twice happy father's kiss,
That well might glance aside, yet never miss,
Where the sweet mark emboss'd so sweet a targe—
Twice wretched he who hath been doubly blest!

III.

Like a loose blossom on a gusty night
He flitted from me—and has left behind
(As if to them his faith he ne'er did plight)
Of either sex and answerable mind
Two playmates, twin-births of his foster-dame:—
The one a steady lad (Esteem he hight)
And Kindness is the gentler sister's name.
Dim likeness now, tho' fair she be and good
Of that bright Boy who hath us all forsook;—
But in his full-eyed aspect when she stood,
And while her face reflected every look,
And in reflection kindled—she became
So like Him, that almost she seem'd the same!

IV.

Ah! He is gone, and yet will not depart!—
Is with me still, yet I from Him exil'd!
For still there lives within my secret heart
The magic image of the magic Child,
Which there He made up-grow by his strong art
As in that crystal * orb—wise Merlin's feat,—
The wondrous " World of Glass," wherein inisl'd
All long'd for things their beings did repeat ;—
And there He left it, like a Sylph beguiled,
To live and yearn and languish incomplete!

V.

Can wit of man a heavier grief reveal?
Can sharper pang from hate or scorn arise ?—
Yes! one more sharp there is that deeper lies,
Which fond Esteem but mocks when he would heal.
Yet neither scorn nor hate did it devise,
But sad compassion and atoning zeal!
One pang more blighting-keen than hope betray'd!
And this it is my woful hap to feel,
When at her Brother's hest, the twin-born Maid
With face averted and unsteady eyes,
Her truant playmate's faded robe puts on ;
And inly shrinking from her own disguise
Enacts the faery Boy that's lost and gone.
O worse than all! O pang all pangs above
Is Kindness counterfeiting absent Love!

* Faerie Queere, b. iii. c. 2, s. 19.

III.—MEDITATIVE POEMS.

IN BLANK VERSE.

YEA, he deserves to find himself deceived,
Who seeks a heart in the unthinking man.
Like shadows on a stream, the forms of life
Impress their characters on the smooth forehead:
Nought sinks into the bosom's silent depth.
Quick sensibility of pain and pleasure
Moves the light fluids lightly; but no soul
Warmeth the inner frame.   SCHILLER.

REFLECTIONS

ON HAVING LEFT A PLACE OF RETIREMENT.

Sermoni propriora.—HOR.

Low was our pretty Cot: our tallest rose
Peeped at the chamber-window. We could hear
At silent noon, and eve, and early morn,
The sea's faint murmur. In the open air
Our myrtles blossomed; and across the porch
Thick jasmins twined: the little landscape round
Was green and woody, and refreshed the eye.
It was a spot which you might aptly call
The Valley of Seclusion! Once I saw

(Hallowing his Sabbath-day by quietness)
A wealthy son of commerce saunter by,
Bristowa's citizen : methought, it calmed
His thirst of idle gold, and made him muse
With wiser feelings : for he paused, and looked
With a pleased sadness, and gazed all around,
Then eyed our Cottage, and gazed round again,
And sighed, and said, it was a Blessed Place.
And we were blessed.   Oft with patient ear
Long-listening to the viewless skylark's note
(Viewless, or haply for a moment seen
Gleaming on sunny wings) in whispered tones
I've said to my beloved, " Such, sweet girl !
The inobtrusive song of happiness,
Unearthly minstrelsy ! then only heard
When the soul seeks to hear; when all is hushed,
And the heart listens ! "

        But the time, when first
From that low dell, steep up the stony mount
I climbed with perilous toil and reached the top,
Oh ! what a goodly scene !   Here the bleak
       mount,
The bare bleak mountain speckled thin with
       sheep ;
Gray clouds, that shadowing spot the sunny
       fields ;
And river, now with bushy rocks o'erbrowed,
Now winding bright and full, with naked banks ;
And seats, and lawns, the Abbey and the wood,

And cots, and hamlets, and faint city-spire;
The Channel there, the Islands and white sails,
Dim coasts, and cloud-like hills, and shoreless
      Ocean—
It seemed like Omnipresence! God, methought,
Had built him there a temple : the whole World
Seemed imaged in its vast circumference,
No wish profaned my overwhelmed heart.
Blest hour! It was a luxury —to be!

   Ah! quiet dell! dear Cot, and mount sublime!
I was constrained to quit you. Was it right,
While my unnumbered brethren toiled and bled,
That I should dream away the entrusted hours
On rose-leaf beds, pampering the coward heart
With feelings all too delicate for use?
Sweet is the tear that from some Howard's eye
Drops on the cheek of one he lifts from earth:
And he that works me good with unmoved face,
Does it but half : he chills me while he aids,
My benefactor, not my brother man!
Yet even this, this cold beneficence,
Praise, praise it, O my soul! oft as thou scann'st
The sluggard Pity's vision-weaving tribe!
Who sigh for wretchedness, yet shun the wretched,
Nursing in some delicious solitude
Their slothful loves and dainty sympathies!
I therefore go, and join head, heart, and hand,
Active and firm, to fight the bloodless fight
Of science, freedom, and the truth in Christ.

Yet oft when after honourable toil
Rests the tired mind, and waking loves to
    dream,
My spirit shall revisit thee, dear Cot!
Thy jasmin and thy window-peeping rose,
And myrtles fearless of the mild sea-air.
And I shall sigh fond wishes—sweet abode!
Ah!—had none greater! And that all had
    such!
It might be so—but the time is not yet.
Speed it, O Father! Let thy kingdom come!

1796.

ON OBSERVING A BLOSSOM ON THE
FIRST OF FEBRUARY, 1796.

SWEET Flower! that peeping from thy russet
    stem
Unfoldest timidly, (for in strange sort
This dark, frieze-coated, hoarse, teeth-chattering
    Month
Hath borrowed Zephyr's voice, and gazed upon
    thee
With blue voluptuous eye,) alas, poor Flower!
These are but flatteries of the faithless year.
Perchance, escaped its unknown polar cave,

E'en now the keen North-East is on its way.
Flower that must perish! shall I liken thee
To some sweet girl of too too rapid growth
Nipped by consumption 'mid untimely charms?
Or to Bristowa's bard,* the wondrous boy!
An amaranth, which Earth scarce seemed to own,
Till disappointment came, and pelting wrong
Beat it to Earth? or with indignant grief
Shall I compare thee to poor Poland's hope,
Bright flower of Hope killed in the opening bud?
Farewell, sweet blossom! better fate be thine
And mock my boding! Dim similitudes
Weaving in moral strains, I've stolen one hour
From anxious self, Life's cruel task-master!
And the warm wooings of this sunny day
Tremble along my frame, and harmonize
The attempered organ, that even saddest thoughts
Mix with some sweet sensations, like harsh tunes
Played deftly on a soft-toned instrument.

* Chatterton.

THE EOLIAN HARP.

COMPOSED AT CLEVEDON, SOMERSETSHIRE.

My pensive Sara! thy soft cheek reclined
Thus on mine arm, most soothing sweet it is
To sit beside our cot, our cot o'ergrown
With white-flowered jasmin, and the broad-leaved
    myrtle,
(Meet emblems they of Innocence and Love!)
And watch the clouds, that late were rich with
    light,
Slow saddening round, and mark the star of eve
Serenely brilliant, (such should wisdom be,)
Shine opposite! How exquisite the scents
Snatched from yon bean-field! and the world so
    hushed!
The stilly murmur of the distant sea
Tells us of silence.

            And that simplest lute
Placed lengthways in the clasping casement,
    hark!
How by the desultory breeze caressed,
Like some coy maid half yielding to her lover,
It pours such sweet upbraiding, as must needs

Tempt to repeat the wrong! And now, its strings
Boldlier swept, the long sequacious notes
Over delicious surges sink and rise ;
Such a soft floating witchery of sound
As twilight Elfins make, when they at eve
Voyage on gentle gales from Fairy-Land,
Where Melodies round honey-dropping flowers,
Footless and wild, like birds of Paradise,
Nor pause, nor perch, hovering on untamed wing!
O the one life within us and abroad,
Which meets all motion and becomes its soul,
A light in sound, a sound-like power in light,
Rhythm in all thought, and joyance everywhere—
Methinks, it should have been impossible
Not to love all things in a world so filled ;
Where the breeze warbles, and the mute still air
Is Music slumbering on her instrument.

And thus, my love! as on the midway slope
Of yonder hill I stretch my limbs at noon,
Whilst through my half-closed eyelids I behold
The sunbeams dance, like diamonds, on the main,
And tranquil muse upon tranquillity ;
Full many a thought uncalled and undetained,
And many idle flitting phantasies,
Traverse my indolent and passive brain,
As wild and various as the random gales
That swell and flutter on this subject lute!

And what if all of animated nature

Be but organic harps diversely framed,
That tremble into thought, as o'er them sweeps
Plastic and vast, one intellectual breeze,
At once the Soul of each, and God of All?

    But thy more serious eye a mild reproof
Darts, O beloved woman! nor such thoughts
Dim and unhallowed dost thou not reject,
And biddest me walk humbly with my God.
Meek daughter in the family of Christ!
Well hast thou said and holily dispraised
These shapings of the unregenerate mind;
Bubbles that glitter as they rise and break
On vain Philosophy's aye-babbling spring.
For never guiltless may I speak of Him,
The Incomprehensible! save when with awe
I praise him, and with Faith that inly feels;
Who with his saving mercies healed me,
A sinful and most miserable man,
Wildered and dark, and gave me to possess
Peace, and this cot, and thee, heart-honoured
      Maid!

1796-1828

TO THE REV. GEORGE COLERIDGE

OF OTTERY ST. MARY, DEVON. WITH SOME POEMS.

Notus in fratres animi paterni.
Hor. Carm. lib. ii. 2.

A BLESSED lot hath he, who having passed
His youth and early manhood in the stir
And turmoil of the world, retreats at length,
With cares that move, not agitate the heart,
To the same dwelling where his father dwelt;
And haply views his tottering little ones
Embrace those aged knees and climb that lap,
On which first kneeling his own infancy
Lisped its brief prayer. Such, O my earliest
    Friend !
Thy lot, and such thy brothers too enjoy.
At distance did ye climb life's upland road,
Yet cheered and cheering: now fraternal love
Hath drawn you to one centre. Be your days
Holy, and blest and blessing may ye live.

To me the Eternal Wisdom hath dispensed
A different fortune and more different mind—
Me from the spot where first I sprang to light

Too soon transplanted, ere my soul had fixed
Its first domestic loves; and hence through life
Chasing chance-started friendships. A brief while
Some have preserved me from life's pelting ills;
But, like a tree with leaves of feeble stem,
If the clouds lasted, and a sudden breeze
Ruffled the boughs, they on my head at once
Dropped the collected shower; and some most
     false,
False and fair foliaged as the Manchineel,
Have tempted me to slumber in their shade
E'en 'mid the storm; then breathing subtlest
     damps,
Mixed their own venom with the rain from Heaven,
That I woke poisoned! But, all praise to Him
Who gives us all things, more have yielded me
Permanent shelter; and beside one friend,
Beneath the impervious covert of one oak,
I've raised a lowly shed, and know the names
Of husband and of father; not unhearing
Of that divine and nightly-whispering voice,
Which from my childhood to maturer years
Spake to me of predestinated wreaths,
Bright with no fading colours!

                Yet at times
My soul is sad, that I have roamed through life
Still most a stranger, most with naked heart
At mine own home and birthplace: chiefly then,
When I remember thee, my earliest friend!

Thee, who didst watch my boyhood and my youth;
Didst trace my wanderings with a father's eye;
And boding evil yet still hoping good,
Rebuked each fault, and over all my woes
Sorrowed in silence! He who counts alone
The beatings of the solitary heart,
That Being knows, how I have loved thee ever,
Loved as a brother, as a son revered thee!
Oh! 'tis to me an ever new delight,
To talk of thee and thine: or when the blast
Of the shrill winter, rattling our rude sash,
Endears the cleanly hearth and social bowl;
Or when as now, on some delicious eve,
We in our sweet sequestered orchard-plot
Sit on the tree crooked earth-ward; whose old
      boughs,
That hang above us in an arborous roof,
Stirred by the faint gale of departing May,
Send their loose blossoms slanting o'er our heads!

    Nor dost not thou sometimes recall those hours,
When with the joy of hope thou gav'st thine ear
To my wild firstling-lays. Since then my song
Hath sounded deeper notes, such as beseem
Or that sad wisdom folly leaves behind,
Or such as, tuned to these tumultuous times,
Cope with the tempest's swell!

             These various strains,
Which I have framed in many a various mood,

Accept, my brother! and, (for some perchance
Will strike discordant on thy milder mind,)
If aught of error or intemperate truth
Should meet thine ear, think thou that riper age
Will calm it down, and let thy love forgive it!

1797.

TO A FRIEND

WHO HAD DECLARED HIS INTENTION OF WRITING NO MORE POETRY.

DEAR Charles! whilst yet thou wert a babe, I
    ween
That Genius plunged thee in that wizard fount
Hight Castalie: and (sureties of thy faith)
That Pity and Simplicity stood by,
And promised for thee, that thou shouldst re-
    nounce
The world's low cares and lying vanities,
Steadfast and rooted in the heavenly Muse,
And washed and sanctified to Poesy.
Yes—thou wert plunged, but with forgetful hand
Held, as by Thetis erst her warrior son:
And with those recreant unbaptized heels
Thou'rt flying from thy bounden ministries—
So sore it seems and burthensome a task
To weave unwithering flowers! But take thou heed:

For thou art vulnerable, wild-eyed boy,
And I have arrows* mystically dipt,
Such as may stop thy speed. Is thy Burns dead?
And shall he die unwept, and sink to earth
" Without the meed of one melodious tear?"
Thy Burns, and Nature's own beloved bard,
Who to the " Illustrious † of his native Land
So properly did look for patronage."
Ghost of Mæcenas ! hide thy blushing face !
They snatched him from the sickle and the
      plough—
To gauge ale-firkins.

             Oh ! for shame return !
On a bleak rock, midway the Aonian mount,
There stands a lone and melancholy tree,
Whose aged branches to the midnight blast
Make solemn music : pluck its darkest bough,
Ere yet the unwholesome night-dew be exhaled,
And weeping wreathe it round thy Poet's tomb.
Then in the outskirts, where pollutions grow,
Pick the rank henbane and the dusky flowers
Of nightshade, or its red and tempting fruit,
These with stopped nostril and glove-guarded hand
Knit in nice intertexture, so to twine,
The illustrious brow of Scotch Nobility.

                    1796.

  * Pind. Olymp. ii. 1, 150.
  † Verbatim from Burns's dedication of his Poem to the
Nobility and Gentry of the Caledonian Hunt.

THIS LIME-TREE BOWER MY PRISON.

In the June of 1797, some long-expected Friends paid a visit to the author's cottage; and on the morning of their arrival, he met with an accident, which disabled him from walking during the whole time of their stay. One evening when they had left him for a few hours, he composed the following lines in the garden-bower.

WELL, they are gone, and here must I remain,
This lime-tree bower my prison! I have lost
Beauties and feelings, such as would have been
Most sweet to my remembrance even when age
Had dimmed mine eyes to blindness! They,
   meanwhile,
Friends, whom I never more may meet again,
On springy heath, along the hill-top edge,
Wander in gladness, and wind down, perchance,
To that still roaring dell, of which I told ;
The roaring dell, o'erwooded, narrow, deep,
And only speckled by the mid-day sun ;
Where its slim trunk the ash from rock to rock
Flings arching like a bridge ;—that branchless
   ash,
Unsunned and damp, whose few poor yellow
   leaves
Ne'er tremble in the gale, yet tremble still,

Fanned by the water-fall! and there my friends
Behold the dark green file of long lank weeds,*
That all at once (a most fantastic sight!)
Still nod and drip beneath the dripping edge
Of the blue clay-stone.

          Now, my friends emerge
Beneath the wide wide Heaven—and view again
The many-steepled tract magnificent
Of hilly fields and meadows, and the sea,
With some fair bark, perhaps, whose sails light up
The slip of smooth clear blue betwixt two Isles
Of purple shadow! Yes! they wander on
In gladness all; but thou, methinks, most glad,
My gentle-hearted Charles! for thou hast pined
And hungered after Nature, many a year,
In the great City pent, winning thy way
With sad yet patient soul, through evil and pain
And strange calamity! Ah! slowly sink
Behind the western ridge, thou glorious sun!
Shine in the slant beams of the sinking orb,
Ye purple heath-flowers! richlier burn, ye clouds!
Live in the yellow light, ye distant groves!
And kindle, thou blue ocean! So my Friend
Struck with deep joy may stand, as I have stood,
Silent with swimming sense; yea, gazing round

---

    * *Of long lank weeds.*] The asplenium scolopendrium,
called in some countries the Adder's Tongue, in others the
Hart's Tongue: but Withering gives the Adder's Tongue as
the trivial name of the ophioglossum only.

On the wide landscape, gaze till all doth seem
Less gross than bodily ; and of such hues
As veil the Almighty Spirit, when yet he makes
Spirits perceive his presence.

                         A delight
Comes sudden on my heart, and I am glad
As I myself were there ! Nor in this bower,
This little lime-tree bower, have I not marked
Much that has soothed me. Pale beneath the
        blaze
Hung the transparent foliage ; and I watched
Some broad and sunny leaf, and loved to see
The shadow of the leaf and stem above
Dappling its sunshine ! And that walnut-tree
Was richly tinged, and a deep radiance lay
Full on the ancient ivy, which usurps
Those fronting elms, and now, with blackest mass
Makes their dark branches gleam a lighter hue
Through the late twilight : and though now the
        bat
Wheels silent by, and not a swallow twitters,
Yet still the solitary humble bee
Sings in the bean-flower ! Henceforth I shall
        know
That Nature ne'er deserts the wise and pure;
No plot so narrow, be but Nature there,
No waste so vacant, but may well employ
Each faculty of sense, and keep the heart
Awake to Love and Beauty ! and sometimes

'Tis well to be bereft of promised good,
That we may lift the Soul, and contemplate
With lively joy the joys we cannot share.
My gentle-hearted Charles! when the last rook
Beat its straight path along the dusky air
Homewards, I blest it! deeming its black wing
(Now a dim speck, now vanishing in light)
Had crossed the mighty orb's dilated glory,
While thou stood'st gazing; or when all was still,
* Flew creeking o'er thy head, and had a charm
For thee, my gentle-hearted Charles, to whom
No sound is dissonant which tells of Life.

1797.

---

* *Flew creeking.*] Some months after I had written this line, it gave me pleasure to find that Bartram had observed the same circumstance of the Savanna Crane. " When these Birds move their wings in flight, their strokes are slow, moderate and regular; and even when at a considerable distance or high above us, we plainly hear the quill-feathers; their shafts and webs upon one another creek as the joints or working of a vessel in a tempestuous sea."

FROST AT MIDNIGHT.

THE frost performs its secret ministry,
Unhelped by any wind. The owlet's cry
Came loud—and hark again! loud as before.
The inmates of my cottage, all at rest,
Have left me to that solitude, which suits
Abstruser musings: save that at my side
My cradled infant slumbers peacefully.
'Tis calm indeed! so calm, that it disturbs
And vexes meditation with its strange
And extreme silentness. Sea, hill, and wood,
This populous village! Sea, and hill, and wood,
With all the numberless goings on of life
Inaudible as dreams! the thin blue flame
Lies on my low burnt fire, and quivers not;
Only that film, which fluttered on the grate,
Still flutters there, the sole unquiet thing.
Methinks, its motion in this hush of nature
Gives it dim sympathies with me who live,
Making it a companionable form,
Whose puny flaps and freaks the idling Spirit
By its own moods interprets, everywhere
Echo or mirror seeking of itself,
And makes a toy of Thought.

But O! how oft,
How oft, at school, with most believing mind,
Presageful, have I gazed upon the bars,
To watch that fluttering stranger! and as oft
With unclosed lids, already had I dreamt
Of my sweet birthplace, and the old church-tower,
Whose bells, the poor man's only music, rang
From morn to evening, all the hot Fair-day,
So sweetly, that they stirred and haunted me
With a wild pleasure, falling on mine ear
Most like articulate sounds of things to come!
So gazed I, till the soothing things I dreamt
Lulled me to sleep, and sleep prolonged my
    dreams!
And so I brooded all the following morn,
Awed by the stern preceptor's face, mine eye
Fixed with mock study on my swimming book:
Save if the door half opened, and I snatched
A hasty glance, and still my heart leaped up,
For still I hoped to see the stranger's face,
Townsman, or aunt, or sister more beloved,
My playmate when we both were clothed alike!

Dear babe, that sleepest cradled by my side,
Whose gentle breathings, heard in this deep calm,
Fill up the interspersed vacancies
And momentary pauses of the thought!
My babe so beautiful! it thrills my heart
With tender gladness, thus to look at thee,
And think that thou shalt learn far other lore

And in far other scenes! For I was reared
In the great city, pent 'mid cloisters dim,
And saw nought lovely but the sky and stars.
But thou, my babe! shalt wander like a breeze
By lakes and sandy shores, beneath the crags
Of ancient mountain, and beneath the clouds,
Which image in their bulk both lakes and shores
And mountain crags: so shalt thou see and hear
The lovely shapes and sounds intelligible
Of that eternal language, which thy God
Utters, who from eternity doth teach
Himself in all, and all things in himself.
Great universal Teacher! he shall mould
Thy spirit, and by giving make it ask.

Therefore all seasons shall be sweet to thee,
Whether the summer clothe the general earth
With greenness, or the redbreast sit and sing
Betwixt the tufts of snow on the bare branch
Of mossy apple-tree, while the nigh thatch
Smokes in the sunthaw; whether the eve-drops
  fall
Heard only in the trances of the blast,
Or if the secret ministry of frost
Shall hang them up in silent icicles,
Quietly shining to the quiet Moon.

       1798.

THE NIGHTINGALE.

A CONVERSATION POEM. APRIL, 1798.

No cloud, no relique of the sunken day
Distinguishes the West, no long thin slip
Of sullen light, no obscure trembling hues.
Come, we will rest on this old mossy bridge!
You see the glimmer of the stream beneath,
But hear no murmuring: it flows silently,
O'er its soft bed of verdure. All is still,
A balmy night! and though the stars be dim,
Yet let us think upon the vernal showers
That gladden the green earth, and we shall find
A pleasure in the dimness of the stars.
And hark! the Nightingale begins its song,
"Most musical, most melancholy" bird!*
A melancholy bird! Oh! idle thought!
In nature there is nothing melancholy.
But some night-wandering man whose heart was
      pierced

* "*Most musical, most melancholy.*"] This passage in Milton
possesses an excellence far superior to that of mere description. It is spoken in the character of the melancholy man,
and has therefore a dramatic propriety. The author makes
this remark, to rescue himself from the charge of having
alluded with levity to a line in Milton.

With the remembrance of a grievous wrong,
Or slow distemper, or neglected love,
(And so, poor wretch! filled all things with him-
self,
And made all gentle sounds tell back the tale
Of his own sorrow,) he, and such as he,
First named these notes a melancholy strain.
And many a poet echoes the conceit;
Poet who hath been building up the rhyme
When he had better far have stretched his limbs
Beside a brook in mossy forest-dell,
By sun or moonlight, to the influxes
Of shapes and sounds and shifting elements
Surrendering his whole spirit, of his song
And of his fame forgetful! so his fame
Should share in Nature's immortality,
A venerable thing! and so his song
Should make all Nature lovelier, and itself
Be loved like Nature!   But 'twill not be so;
And youths and maidens most poetical,
Who lose the deepening twilights of the spring
In ballrooms and hot theatres, they still
Full of meek sympathy must heave their sighs
O'er Philomela's pity-pleading strains.

My Friend, and thou, our Sister! we have
learnt
A different lore: we may not thus profane
Nature's sweet voices, always full of love
And joyance! 'Tis the merry Nightingale

That crowds, and hurries, and precipitates
With fast thick warble his delicious notes,
As he were fearful that an April night
Would be too short for him to utter forth
His love-chant, and disburthen his full soul
Of all its music !

   And I know a grove
Of large extent, hard by a castle huge,
Which the great lord inhabits not; and so
This grove is wild with tangling underwood,
And the trim walks are broken up, and grass,
Thin grass and kingcups grow within the paths.
But never elsewhere in one place I knew
So many nightingales ; and far and near,
In wood and thicket, over the wide grove,
They answer and provoke each other's song,
With skirmish and capricious passagings,
And murmurs musical and swift jug jug,
And one low piping sound more sweet than all—
Stirring the air with such a harmony,
That should you close your eyes, you might almost
Forget it was not day ! On moon-lit bushes,
Whose dewy leaflets are but half disclosed,
You may perchance behold them on the twigs,
Their bright, bright eyes, their eyes both bright and full
Glistening, while many a glowworm in the shade
Lights up her love-torch.

A most gentle Maid,
Who dwelleth in her hospitable home
Hard by the castle, and at latest eve,
(Even like a Lady vowed and dedicate
To something more than Nature in the grove,)
Glides through the pathways; she knows all their
    notes,
That gentle Maid ! and oft a moment's space,
What time the moon was lost behind a cloud,
Hath heard a pause of silence; till the moon
Emerging, hath awakened earth and sky
With one sensation, and these wakeful birds
Have all burst forth in choral minstrelsy,
As if some sudden gale had swept at once
A hundred airy harps!   And she hath watched
Many a nightingale perched giddily
On blossomy twig still swinging from the breeze,
And to that motion tune his wanton song
Like tipsy joy that reels with tossing head.

Farewell, O Warbler ! till to-morrow eve,
And you, my friends ! farewell, a short farewell !
We have been loitering long and pleasantly,
And now for our dear homes.—That strain again !
Full fain it would delay me !   My dear babe,
Who, capable of no articulate sound,
Mars all things with his imitative lisp,
How he would place his hand beside his ear,
His little hand, the small forefinger up,
And bid us listen !   And I deem it wise

To make him Nature's playmate. He knows well
The evening-star; and once when he awoke
In most distressful mood, (some inward pain
Had made up that strange thing, an infant's dream,)
I hurried with him to our orchard-plot,
And he beheld the moon, and, hushed at once,
Suspends his sobs, and laughs most silently,
While his fair eyes, that swam with undropped
        tears,
Did glitter in the yellow moon-beam! Well!—
It is a father's tale : But if that Heaven
Should give me life, his childhood shall grow up
Familiar with these songs, that with the night
He may associate joy. — Once more, farewell,
Sweet Nightingale ! Once more, my friends !
        farewell.

LINES

WRITTEN IN THE ALBUM AT ELBINGERODE, IN
THE HARTZ FOREST.

I STOOD on Brocken's* sovran height, and saw
Woods crowding upon woods, hills over hills,
A surging scene, and only limited
By the blue distance. Heavily my way
Downward I dragged through fir groves evermore,
Where bright green moss heaves in sepulchral forms
Speckled with sunshine ; and, but seldom heard,
The sweet bird's song became a hollow sound ;
And the breeze, murmuring indivisibly,
Preserved its solemn murmur most distinct
From many a note of many a waterfall,
And the brook's chatter ; 'mid whose islet stones
The dingy kidling with its tinkling bell
Leaped frolicsome, or old romantic goat
Sat, his white beard slow waving. I moved on
In low and languid mood :† for I had found

* The highest mountain in the Hartz, and indeed in North
Germany.

† ———————— When I have gazed
From some high eminence on goodly vales,
And cots and villages embowered below,
The thought would rise that all to me was strange
Amid the scenes so fair, nor one small spot
Where my tired mind might rest, and call it home.
Southey's Hymn to the Penates.

That outward forms, the loftiest, still **receive**
Their finer influence from the Life within; —
Fair ciphers else : fair, but of import vague
Or unconcerning, where the heart not finds
History or prophecy of friend, or child,
Or gentle maid, our first and early love,
Or father, or the venerable name
Of our adored country! O thou Queen,
Thou delegated Deity of Earth,
O dear, dear England! how my longing eye
Turned westward, shaping in the steady clouds
Thy sands and high white cliffs!

              My native Land!
Filled with the thought of thee this heart was
      proud,
Yea, mine eye swam with tears: that all the view
From sovran Brocken, woods and woody hills,
Floated away, like a departing dream,
Feeble and dim! Stranger, these impulses
Blame thou not lightly; nor will I profane,
With hasty judgment or injurious doubt,
That man's sublimer spirit, who can feel
That God is everywhere! the God who framed
Mankind to be one mighty family,
Himself our Father, and the World our Home.

1798-9.

HYMN

BEFORE SUNRISE, IN THE VALE OF CHAMOUNI.

BESIDES the Rivers, Arve and Arveiron, which have their sources in the foot of Mont Blanc, five conspicuous torrents rush down its sides; and within a few paces of the Glaciers, the Gentiana Major grows in immense numbers with its "flowers of loveliest blue."

HAST thou a charm to stay the morning-star
In his steep course? So long he seems to pause
On thy bald awful head, O sovran Blanc!
The Arve and Arveiron at thy base
Rave ceaselessly; but thou, most awful Form!
Risest from forth thy silent sea of pines,
How silently! Around thee and above
Deep is the air and dark, substantial, black,
An ebon mass: methinks thou piercest it,
As with a wedge! But when I look again,
It is thine own calm home, thy crystal shrine,
Thy habitation from eternity!
O dread and silent Mount! I gazed upon thee,
Till thou, still present to the bodily sense,
Didst vanish from my thought: entranced in
      prayer
I worshipped the Invisible alone.

Yet, like some sweet beguiling melody,
So sweet, we know not we are listening to it,
Thou, the meanwhile, wast blending with my
        thought,
Yea, with my life and life's own secret joy:
Till the dilating Soul, enrapt, transfused,
Into the mighty vision passing—there
As in her natural form, swelled vast to Heaven!

Awake, my soul! not only passive praise
Thou owest! not alone these swelling tears,
Mute thanks and secret ecstasy! Awake,
Voice of sweet song! Awake, my Heart, awake!
Green vales and icy cliffs, all join my Hymn.

Thou first and chief, sole sovran of the Vale!
O struggling with the darkness all the night,
And visited all night by troops of stars,
Or when they climb the sky or when they sink:
Companion of the morning-star at dawn,
Thyself Earth's rosy star, and of the dawn
Co-herald: wake, O wake, and utter praise!
Who sank thy sunless pillars deep in Earth?
Who filled thy countenance with rosy light?
Who made thee parent of perpetual streams?

And you, ye five wild torrents fiercely glad!
Who called you forth from night and utter death,
From dark and icy caverns called you forth,
Down those precipitous, black, jagged Rocks,

For ever shattered and the same for ever?
Who gave you your invulnerable life,
Your strength, your speed, your fury, and your
      joy,
Unceasing thunder and eternal foam ?
And who commanded, (and the silence came,)
Here let the billows stiffen, and have rest?

Ye ice-falls! ye that from the mountain's brow
Adown enormous ravines slope amain—
Torrents, methinks, that heard a mighty voice,
And stopped at once amid their maddest plunge !
Motionless torrents ! silent cataracts !
Who made you glorious as the gates of Heaven
Beneath the keen full moon ? Who bade the sun
Clothe you with rainbows ? Who, with living
      flowers
Of loveliest blue, spread garlands at your feet?—
God! let the torrents, like a shout of nations,
Answer! and let the ice-plains echo, God!
God! sing ye meadow-streams with gladsome
      voice !
Ye pine-groves, with your soft and soul-like
      sounds !
And they too have a voice, yon piles of snow,
And in their perilous fall shall thunder, God !

Ye living flowers that skirt the eternal frost !
Ye wild goats sporting round the eagle's nest !
Ye eagles, playmates of the mountain-storm !

Ye lightnings, the dread arrows of the clouds!
Ye signs and wonders of the element!
Utter forth God, and fill the hills with praise!

    Thou too, hoar Mount! with thy sky-pointing
        peaks,
Oft from whose feet the avalanche, unheard,
Shoots downward, glittering through the pure
    serene
Into the depth of clouds, that veil thy breast—
Thou too again, stupendous Mountain! thou
That as I raise my head, awhile bowed low
In adoration, upward from thy base
Slow travelling with dim eyes suffused with tears,
Solemnly seemest, like a vapoury cloud,
To rise before me—Rise, O ever rise,
Rise like a cloud of incense, from the Earth!
Thou kingly Spirit throned among the hills,
Thou dread ambassador from Earth to Heaven,
Great hierarch! tell thou the silent sky,
And tell the stars, and tell yon rising sun,
Earth, with her thousand voices, praises God.

TO WILLIAM WORDSWORTH.

COMPOSED ON THE NIGHT AFTER HIS RECITATION OF A POEM ON THE GROWTH OF AN INDIVIDUAL MIND.

FRIEND of the wise! and teacher of the good!
Into my heart have I received that lay
More than historic, that prophetic lay
Wherein (high theme, by thee first sung aright!)
Of the foundations and the building up
Of a Human Spirit thou hast dared to tell
What may be told, to the understanding mind
Revealable; and what within the mind,
By vital breathings secret as the soul
Of vernal growth, oft quickens in the heart
Thoughts all too deep for words! —

                    Theme hard as high,
Of smiles spontaneous, and mysterious fears,
(The first-born they of Reason and twin-birth,)
Of tides obedient to external force,
And currents self-determined, as might seem,
Or by some inner power; of moments awful,
Now in thy inner life, and now abroad,

When power streamed from thee, and thy soul
    received
The light reflected, as a light bestowed—
Of fancies fair, and milder hours of youth,
Hyblean murmurs of poetic thought
Industrious in its joy, in vales and glens
Native or outland, lakes and famous hills !
Or on the lonely high-road, when the stars
Were rising ; or by secret mountain-streams,
The guides and the companions of thy way !

Of more than Fancy, of the Social Sense
Distending wide, and man beloved as man,
Where France in all her towns lay vibrating
Like some becalmed bark beneath the burst
Of Heaven's immediate thunder, when no cloud
Is visible, or shadow on the main.
For thou wert there, thine own brows garlanded
Amid the tremor of a realm aglow,
Amid a mighty nation jubilant,
When from the general heart of human kind
Hope sprang forth like a full-born Deity !
——Of that dear Hope afflicted and struck down,
So summoned homeward, thenceforth calm and
    sure
From the dread watch-tower of man's absolute
    self,
With light unwaning on her eyes, to look
Far on—herself a glory to behold,
The Angel of the vision ! Then (last strain)

Of Duty, chosen laws controlling choice,
Action and joy !—An Orphic song indeed,
A song divine of high and passionate thoughts
To their own music chanted !

                O great Bard !
Ere yet that last strain dying awed the air,
With steadfast eye I viewed thee in the choir
Of ever-enduring men.   The truly great
Have all one age, and from one visible space
Shed influence ! They, both in power and act,
Are permanent, and Time is not with them,
Save as it worketh for them, they in it.
Nor less a sacred roll, than those of old,
And to be placed, as they, with gradual fame
Among the archives of mankind, thy work
Makes audible a linked lay of Truth,
Of Truth profound a sweet continuous lay,
Not learnt, but native, her own natural notes !
Ah ! as I listened with a heart forlorn,
The pulses of my being beat anew :
And even as life returns upon the drowned,
Life's joy rekindling roused a throng of pains—
Keen pangs of Love, awakening as a babe
Turbulent, with an outcry in the heart ;
And fears self-willed, that shunned the eye of
        hope ;
And hope that scarce would know itself from fear;
Sense of past youth, and manhood come in vain,
And genius given, and knowledge won in vain ;

And all which I had culled in wood-walks wild,
And all which patient toil had reared, and all,
Commune with thee had opened out—but flowers
Strewed on my corse, and borne upon my bier,
In the same coffin, for the self-same grave!

That way no more! and ill beseems it me,
Who came a welcomer in herald's guise,
Singing of glory, and futurity,
To wander back on such unhealthful road,
Plucking the poisons of self-harm! And ill
Such intertwine beseems triumphal wreaths
Strewed before thy advancing!

       Nor do thou,
Sage Bard! impair the memory of that hour
Of thy communion with my nobler mind
By pity or grief, already felt too long!
Nor let my words import more blame than needs.
The tumult rose and ceased: for peace is nigh
Where wisdom's voice has found a listening heart.
Amid the howl of more than wintry storms,
The halcyon hears the voice of vernal hours
Already on the wing.
     Eve following eve,
Dear tranquil time, when the sweet sense of Home
Is sweetest! moments for their own sake hailed
And more desired, more precious for thy song,
In silence listening, like a devout child,
My soul lay passive, by thy various strain

Driven as in surges now beneath the stars,
With momentary stars of my own birth,
Fair constellated foam,* still darting off
Into the darkness ; now a tranquil sea,
Outspread and bright, yet swelling to the moon.

And when — O Friend! my comforter and
        guide !
Strong in thyself, and powerful to give strength!—
Thy long sustained Song finally closed,
And thy deep voice had ceased—yet thou thyself
Wert still before my eyes, and round us both
That happy vision of beloved faces—
Scarce conscious, and yet conscious of its close
I sate, my being blended in one thought
(Thought was it ? or aspiration ? or resolve ?)
Absorbed, yet hanging still upon the sound —
And when I rose, I found myself in prayer.

* "A beautiful white cloud of foam at momentary intervals
coursed by the side of the vessel with a roar, and little stars
of flame danced and sparkled and went out in it: and every
now and then light detachments of this white cloud-like foam
darted off from the vessel's side, each with its own small
constellation, over the sea, and scoured out of sight like a
Tartar troop over a wilderness."—*The Friend*, p. 220.

INSCRIPTION

FOR A FOUNTAIN ON A HEATH.

This Sycamore, oft musical with bees,—
Such tents the Patriarchs loved! O long un-
    harmed
May all its aged boughs o'er-canopy
The small round basin, which this jutting stone
Keeps pure from falling leaves! Long may the
    Spring,
Quietly as a sleeping infant's breath,
Send up cold waters to the traveller
With soft and even pulse! Nor ever cease
Yon tiny cone of sand its soundless dance,
Which at the bottom, like a Fairy's page,
As merry and no taller, dances still,
Nor wrinkles the smooth surface of the Fount.
Here twilight is and coolness : here is moss,
A soft seat, and a deep and ample shade.
Thou may'st toil far and find no second tree.
Drink, Pilgrim, here ; Here rest! and if thy heart
Be innocent, here too shalt thou refresh
Thy Spirit, listening to some gentle sound,
Or passing gale or hum of murmuring bees!

A TOMBLESS EPITAPH.

'TIs true, Idoloclastes Satyrane !
(So call him, for so mingling blame with praise,
And smiles with anxious looks, his earliest friends,
Masking his birth-name, wont to character
His wild-wood fancy and impetuous zeal,)
'Tis true that, passionate for ancient truths,
And honouring with religious love the great
Of elder times, he hated to excess,
With an unquiet and intolerant scorn,
The hollow puppets of a hollow age,
Ever idolatrous, and changing ever
Its worthless idols ! learning, power, and time,
('Too much of all) thus wasting in vain war
Of fervid colloquy.   Sickness, 'tis true,
Whole years of weary days, besieged him close,
Even to the gates and inlets of his life !
But it is true, no less, that strenuous, firm,
And with a natural gladness, he maintained
The citadel unconquered, and in joy
Was strong to follow the delightful Muse :
For not a hidden path, that to the shades
Of the beloved Parnassian forest leads,
Lurked undiscovered by him ; not a rill
There issues from the fount of Hippocrene,

But he had traced it upward to its source,
Through open glade, dark glen, and secret dell,
Knew the gay wild flowers on its banks, and
      culled
Its med'cinable herbs.   Yea, oft alone,
Piercing the long-neglected holy cave,
The haunt obscure of old Philosophy,
He bade with lifted torch its starry walls
Sparkle, as erst they sparkled to the flame
Of odorous lamps tended by saint and sage.
O framed for calmer times and nobler hearts!
O studious Poet, eloquent for truth!
Philosopher! contemning wealth and death,
Yet docile, childlike, full of Life and Love!
Here, rather than on monumental stone,
This record of thy worth thy Friend inscribes,
Thoughtful, with quiet tears upon his cheek.

1809.

NOTES.

Page 3.—FIRST ADVENT OF LOVE.

The early date assigned to these exquisite lines is derived from a memorandum of the author. "Relics of my School-boy Muse; i. e. fragments of poems composed before my fifteenth year.

LOVE'S FIRST HOPE—

       'O fair is Love's first hope,' &c.

The concluding stanza of an Elegy on a Lady, who died in early youth :—

    O'er the raised earth the gales of evening sigh;
      And see, a Daisy peeps upon its slope!
    I wipe the dimming waters from mine eye;
      Even on the cold Grave lights the Cherub Hope!

AGE.—A stanza written forty years later than the preceding :—

    Dew-drops are the Gems of Morning,
      But the Tears of dewy Eve!
    Where no Hope is, Life's a warning,
      That only serves to make us grieve,
        When we are old.

                S. T. C. *Sept.* 1827."

GENEVIEVE.

"This little poem was written when the author was a boy." Note to the edition of 1796.

THE RAVEN and TIME, REAL AND IMAGINARY, are mentioned as "School-boy Poems" in the Preface to the "Sibylline Leaves," published in 1817.

PAGE 15.—KISSES.

This "Effusion" and "The Rose" were originally addressed to a Miss F. Nesbitt, at Plymouth, whither the author accompanied his eldest brother, to whom he was paying a visit, when he was twenty-one years of age. Both poems are written in pencil on the blank pages of a copy of Langhorne's Collins. "Kisses" is entitled "Cupid turned Chymist;" is signed S. T. Coleridge, and dated Friday evening, 1793.

" THE ROSE " has this heading:—" On presenting a Moss Rose to Miss F. Nesbitt." In both poems the name of Nesbitt appears instead of Sara, afterwards substituted.

" KISSES " has this note in the edition of 1796:—

" Effinxit quondam blandum meditata laborem,
　　Basia lascivâ Cypria Diva manu.
Ambrosiæ succos occultâ temperat arte,
　　Fragransque infuso nectare tingit opus.
Sufficit et partem mellis, quod subdolus olim
　　Non impune favis surripuisset Amor.
Decussos violæ foliis admiscet odores,
　　Et spolia æstivis plurima rapta rosis:
Addit et illecebras, et mille et mille lepores,
　　Et quot Acidalius gaudia cestus habet.
Ex his composuit Dea basia; et omnia libans
　　Invenias nitidæ sparsa per ora Cloes."
　　　　　　　　　　　　　　Carm. Quad. vol. ii.

PAGE 20.—LINES ON AN AUTUMNAL EVENING.

In the edition of 1796 this poem is stated to have been written in *early* youth; and in a note to the line " O (have I sighed) were mine the wizard's rod," the author " entreats the Public's pardon for having carelessly suffered to be printed such intolerable stuff as this and the thirteen following lines;" adding, "that they have not even the merit of originality, as every thought is to be found in the Greek epigrams." In the edition brought out the following year, the whole poem was first omitted, but eventually "reprieved," and printed in an Appendix, at the request of some intelligent friends, who observed, that "what most delighted the author when he was young in *writing* would probably best please those who are young in *reading* poetry," and that "a man must learn to be *pleased* with a subject before he can yield that attention to it which is necessary in order to acquire a just taste." In the edition of 1803 the poem appears in its proper place, without any remark. Few readers will have regretted that this bright and popular strain was thus rescued from the hasty condemnation of its youthful author. In the note, the author repels an imputation of plagiarism from Mr. Rogers's "Pleasures of Memory," and brings a similar charge against his distinguished contemporary. He finds the original of the tale of "Florio," "in 'Lochleven,' a poem of great merit by Michael Bruce." This assertion he afterwards withdrew, apologizing (in the Appendix above referred to) for his rashness, in very handsome terms. This occurred fifty-six years ago. Mr. Rogers still lives to wear his unwithering laurels. He has seen two generations of his poetic brethren pass away,—μετὰ δὲ τριτάτοισιν ἀνύσσει.

The following note, in the edition of 1796, may be cited as a proof how early, and how decidedly, the genius of Wordsworth was detected and proclaimed by Coleridge:—"The expression, 'green radiance,'" he says, (referring to the "Lines Written at Shurton Bars," p. 68 of the present edition,) "is borrowed from Mr. Wordsworth, a poet whose versification is occasionally harsh, and his diction too frequently obscure," (the "Descriptive Sketches," and "Evening Walk," published 1793, since republished, with numerous corrections, as juvenile pieces, were the poems thus characterized;) "but whom I deem unrivalled among the writers of the present day in manly sentiment, novel imagery, and vivid colouring."

D. C.

PAGE 40.—MONODY ON THE DEATH OF CHATTERTON.

This monody was sketched at Christ's Hospital; but meagre indeed is the boyish *schema*, with scarce any of the fire and felicity of the finished composition. October, 1794, is the date affixed by the author. It appears, from a passage in one of Mr. Southey's letters, that seven lines and a half, toward the end of the poem, were borrowed from a young friend and fellow-poet.

"Every thing is in the fairest trim. Favell and Le Grice" (a younger brother of Charles Lamb's Valentine Le Grice,) 'two young Pantisocrats of nineteen, join us. They possess great genius. You may perhaps like the sonnet on the subject of our emigration, by Favell:—

> " *No more my visionary soul shall dwell*
> *On joys that were: no more endure to weigh*
> *The shame and anguish of the evil day,*
> *Wisely forgetful! O'er the ocean swell,*
> *Sublime of Hope, I seek the cottaged dell,*
> *Where Virtue calm with careless step may stray,*
> *And dancing to the moonlight roundelay,*
> *The wizard Passion wears* (sic) *a holy spell.*
> Eyes that have ached with anguish! ye shall weep
> Tears of doubt-mingled joy, as those who start
> From precipices of distempered sleep,
> On which the fierce-eyed fiends their revels keep,
> And see the rising sun, and find it dart
> New rays of pleasure trembling to the heart."
> *Southey's Life and Correspondence,* vol. i. p. 224.

At the end of the Preface to the edition of 1796, Mr. Coleridge acknowledges himself indebted to Mr. Favell for the "rough sketch" of Effusion XVI. [Sonnet XII.]—

"Sweet Mercy! how my weary heart has bled;"

and to the author of "Joan of Arc" for the first half of Effusion XV. [Sonnet XI.]—

"Pale Roamer through the night," &c.

It is remarkable that when these obligations were particu
larized, the passage borrowed from the Monody should not
have been referred to its author. But this is but one of a
thousand instances that could be given of Mr. Coleridge's
partial and uncertain (though in some respects powerful)
memory. In 1803 he published, without signature, among
his own productions, Mr. Lamb's Sonnet to Mrs. Siddons,
which had appeared in the edition of 1796, signed C. L., and
in 1797 in Lamb's portion of the joint volume.

Page 49.—SONNET IIL

This Sonnet, and the ninth, to " Stanhope," were among
the pieces withdrawn from the second edition of 1797. They
reappeared in the edition of 1803, and were again withdrawn
in 1828, solely, it may be presumed, on account of their political vehemence. They will excite no angry feelings, and
lead to no misapprehensions now; and as they are fully equal
to their companions in poetical merit, the Editors have not
scrupled to reproduce them. These Sonnets were originally
entitled "Effusions."

Page 115.—THE RIME OF THE ANCIENT MARINER.

The following interesting notices concerning " The Ancient
Mariner" are contained in a letter of the Rev. Alexander
Dyce, the well-known admirable Editor of old Plays, to the
late H. N. Coleridge:—

" When my truly honoured friend Mr. Wordsworth was last
in London, soon after the appearance of De Quincey's papers
in ' Tait's Magazine,' he dined with me in Gray's Inn, and
made the following statement, which, I am quite sure, I give
you correctly: '" The Ancient Mariner" was founded on a
strange dream, which a friend of Coleridge had, who fancied
he saw a skeleton ship, with figures in it. We had both
determined to write some poetry for a monthly magazine,
the profits of which were to defray the expenses of a little
excursion we were to make together. "The Ancient Mariner" was intended for this periodical, but was too long. I

had very little share in the composition of it, for I soon found that the style of Coleridge and myself would not assimilate. Besides the lines (in the fourth part),

> " And thou art long, and lank, and brown,
>   As is the ribbed sea-sand,"

I wrote the stanza (in the first),

> " He holds him with his glittering eye—
>   The Wedding-Guest stood still,
>   And listens like a three-years' child:
>   The Mariner hath his will,"

and four or five lines more in different parts of the poem, which I could not now point out. The idea of "*shooting an albatross*" *was mine; for I had been reading Shelvocke's Voyages, which probably Coleridge never saw.* I also suggested the reanimation of the dead bodies, to work the ship.' " See also "Memoirs of William Wordsworth," by Dr. Christopher Wordsworth, vol. i. chap. xi. p. 107—8.

Page 266.—THE DAY-DREAM.

This little poem first appeared in the "Morning Post," in 1802, but was doubtless composed in Germany. It seems to have been forgotten by its author, for this was the only occasion on which it saw the light through him. The Editors think that it will plead against parental neglect in the mind of most readers.

ι

ADDITIONAL NOTES

BY THE AMERICAN EDITOR.

PAGE 120.

In the edition of 1817 this line is printed,

" The furrow streamed off free; "

and the following note is added: —

" In the former edition the line was, ' The furrow streamed off free,' but I had not been long on board a ship, before I perceived that this was the image as seen by a spectator from the shore, or from another vessel. From the ship itself the *wake* appears like a brook flowing off from the stern."

PAGE 124.

The following verse is inserted here, in earlier editions:

" A gust of wind sterte up behind
And whistled through his bones ;
Through the holes of his eyes and the hole of his mouth
Half whistles and half groans."

END OF VOL. L.